KILLER

KEEPSAKES

OTHER JOSIE PRESCOTT ANTIQUES MYSTERIES
BY JANE K. CLELAND

Antiques to Die For
Deadly Appraisal
Consigned to Death

KILLER

KEEPSAKES

JANE K. CLELAND

MINOTAUR BOOKS

NEW YORK

KILLER KEEPSAKES. Copyright © 2009 by Jane K. Cleland. All rights reserved. Printed in the United States of America. For information, address St. Martin's Press, 175 Fifth Avenue, New York, N.Y. 10010.

www.minotaurbooks.com

Library of Congress Cataloging-in-Publication Data

Cleland, Jane K.
    Killer keepsakes / Jane K. Cleland.—1st ed.
        p. cm.
    ISBN-13: 978-0-312-36944-6
    ISBN-10: 0-312-36944-1
    1. Prescott, Josie (Fictitious character)—Fiction.   2. Appraisers—Fiction.
3. Antiques—Fiction.   4. Murder—Investigation—Fiction.   5. NewHampshire—
Fiction.   I. Title.
    PS3603.L4555K56 2009
    813'.6—dc22

                                                                      2008041736

First Edition: April 2009

10 9 8 7 6 5 4 3 2 1

THIS IS FOR KATIE LONGHURST,

AND, OF COURSE, FOR JOE.

AUTHOR'S NOTE

While there is a Seacoast Region in New Hampshire, there is no town called Rocky Point, and many other geographic liberties have been taken.

KILLER

KEEPSAKES

CHAPTER ONE

I glanced at the Mickey Mouse clock on Gretchen's desk. It was nine thirty in the morning, a half hour after Prescott's: Antiques and Auctions' regular start time, and my assistant wasn't there. Gretchen, who was supposed to be back to work yesterday after a two-week Hawaiian vacation, and who, in four years, had never once been tardy, hadn't shown up or even called. I was worried sick.

I thought again of the man, the stranger, who'd been trying to reach her. He'd called frequently while she was out of town, wouldn't leave a message, and had seemed increasingly frustrated that we wouldn't reveal details of her schedule. It was company policy that we never gave out specific information about anyone on staff, but he took it as a personal affront.

"Has anyone spoken to that guy lately?" I asked. "You know, the one calling for Gretchen?"

"I did. Tuesday," Fred said, pushing up his square, black-framed glasses. Fred was an antiques appraiser who'd joined my firm a couple of years back, moving from New York City to New Hampshire. He was a terrific find—he had a keen eye and an educated sensibility.

"How did he sound?" I asked.

"Pissed off. He got sarcastic when I told him she wasn't available and offered to take a message. He asked if we kept her chained in the back."

"Wow. That's pretty intense."

Yesterday, I'd managed to contain my anxiety enough to limit myself to one cheerfully worded, "Welcome home, are you okay?"

voice mail message. Today, I needed to do something else, something more, but I didn't know what, and then I thought of
Gretchen's friend Mandy Tollerson.

I'd first met Mandy about four months ago when Gretchen had
solicited my help on her behalf. According to Gretchen, Mandy's
boyfriend, Vince Collins, was a complete creep, and she was en-
couraging Mandy to break away. When Mandy had confided to
Gretchen that she dreamed of starting her own business, an art
gallery, Gretchen had brought her to me, hoping that I'd fire her
up to act, and that somehow being independent in business would
make her independent in her romantic relationship, too. Since
then, Mandy had stopped by every few weeks with some business
questions. Last week, she'd asked about tracking sales and ex-
penses, and I'd taught her how to calculate break-even.

I dialed her home phone number. A machine picked up after
four rings. "Hi, Mandy. It's Josie. Josie Prescott. Would you give me
a call, please?" I asked, adding my phone number. It was too early
to call her at her job—she was an assistant manager at the Bow
Street Emporium, a high-end gift shop in Portsmouth—and I didn't
have her cell phone number. A dead end.

I turned to Sasha, my chief appraiser. "If you wanted to call someone who knows Gretchen, to see if they've heard from her, who
would it be?"

She tilted her head as she considered my question, her intelligence
apparent in her thoughtful expression. Her fine, shoulder-length
brown hair hung straight to her shoulders. "She mentioned that a
friend was watering her plants while she was gone, but I don't know
who."

I asked the same question of Fred and Eric, my back room supervisor, and got the same answer. I wasn't surprised. None of us
knew much about Gretchen. From the day she'd showed up on
my doorstep, promising to work hard and help my business grow,
until the day she'd left for vacation, she'd shared almost nothing
about herself. Not long after she started, Sasha had asked her if
she was traveling over the holidays to visit family, and she'd given

a vague, peppy response. "Home is where the heart is," she'd said.

I didn't even know if Gretchen had family. She was inexorably cheerful, physically beautiful, and quick to learn and adapt. She loved celebrity gossip, but about herself she was relentlessly private. I had no idea where she came from or what she did in her free time.

Trying to figure out what to do, I unlocked the file cabinet where I stored employee personnel files. On Gretchen's, the line for an emergency contact was blank. I'd never noticed that before. I located her condo contact information and called the property manager. Meryl, an associate in the office, listened to my explanation, then put me on hold while she asked for and received permission from her boss to allow me to enter Gretchen's unit. She agreed to meet me there right away with the key.

I told Sasha where I was going.

"Please call as soon as you know something," she requested.

I said I would, and as I spoke, I saw my apprehension reflected in her eyes. We shared the unspoken fear that something was very, very wrong.

I beat Meryl to the Pond View condo complex, where Gretchen owned unit eight, and while I waited for her to arrive, I knocked on Gretchen's door. Nothing. From my perch on the second-floor balcony, I noticed three cars in the lot, not counting mine, and Gretchen's wasn't one of them. An old Chevy with Tennessee plates was parked closest to Gretchen's front door. A Ford SUV and a Toyota sat on the other side of the lot.

A steady stream of traffic noise rose from the street. I heard a complaining *caw, caw* from the pond barely visible through a passageway between two buildings. A red minivan turned into the parking lot, parking near the Chevy.

A stocky woman of about forty stepped out of the van. She brushed unruly auburn hair out of her eyes as she scanned the area.

"Meryl?" I called.

"Josie?" she asked, squinting into the sun.

She saw me waving. "Have you knocked?" she asked when she joined me.

"Yeah. A couple of times."

"Just in case," she said. She banged the clapper, stared at the ground for a count of fifteen, then clapped again. After another ten seconds' wait, she looked up.

I met her anxious gaze and shrugged. "Let's do it," I said.

Meryl opened the door and shouted Gretchen's name before crossing the threshold. There was no reply. We walked inside. The apartment felt very still. Something smelled bad, like rotten eggs, except worse. I heard a hum—a low-pitched, soft, machine sound. The refrigerator, I thought, glancing into the empty kitchen. Shoulder to shoulder, Meryl and I edged down a short carpeted hall. Meryl stepped into the living area, stopped short, and screamed.

At the sound, my heart began to race, and my mouth went arid.

She turned to me, her eyes wide open, shocked, and then she crossed herself.

My stomach leapt into my throat, then plummeted. I stepped around her to gain a better view. Sprawled on the sofa was a man—dead—shot.

CHAPTER TWO

T he dead man was a stranger. He was in his early thirties and lean; picturing what his lifeless features might look like if he were alive, I imagined that he would have been handsome. Except for the angry slash of red on his forehead, just over his right eye. I covered my nose with my hand and breathed through my mouth. The stench was foul.

He was wearing jeans and a flannel shirt, the uniform of a working New Hampshire man. His skin was parchment white. There was a hole in the right side of his chest the size of an egg. Black singeing suggested that he'd been shot from close range, and the disgusting odor and black-purple stain of dried blood made me guess that his murder wasn't recent. His belt buckle was intricately designed. It showed an old Native American man in profile wearing a feathered headdress. There was no blood splatter, no disarray, no bullet holes in the walls or ceiling, nothing to suggest that there'd been a struggle. I didn't see a gun.

"Do you know him?" I asked.

"No," Meryl managed, and then she began to cry, covering her face with her hands.

Cope first, Josie—fall apart later, I told myself. I patted Meryl's shoulder. "We need to call the police," I said softly, finding my phone in my oversized tote bag and dialing 911.

As I talked to the emergency operator, Meryl began to back away. Rivulets of mascara-stained tears striped her cheeks.

I hung up and clutched my phone to my chest.

Gretchen, I thought, *where are you?* I glanced toward a door off to the left—to her bedroom, I guessed. *Was she in there, hurt—or worse?* I looked back at the corpse. "I want to see if Gretchen is here," I told Meryl.

"I can't," she whispered.

I could see in her eyes that she wanted to stay to help almost as much as she wanted to be gone. She was trembling, and her skin was too pale. I thought she might get sick.

"It's okay," I assured her. "Go and wait in your car. The police will be here in a sec."

She nodded, her lips quivering, and fled.

As soon as she left, I walked slowly through the rest of the apartment. I wasn't afraid, not really, but whatever small concern I felt faded to nothing in the face of my serious worry about Gretchen's well-being. I gingerly opened closet doors, held my breath as I slid open the shower curtain to peer into the tub, and knelt on the gray carpet to look under the bed. Gretchen wasn't anywhere.

The apartment was spotless, the bed neatly made, the fireplace swept, the counters bare. A flashing red "5" on the answering machine told me that I wasn't the only one to have called during her absence. Back in the entryway, I saw something I'd missed before—a crumpled checked baggage tag bearing the letters BOS lay against the baseboard. Gretchen had arrived home from her vacation.

Did Gretchen find the body? Or, I wondered, swallowing hard, did she kill him? I shook my head. Impossible!

As I stood in the carpeted hallway looking at nothing, other questions came to me. Had Gretchen known the man and welcomed him into her home? Or was he a stranger she had surprised in the middle of a break-in? I went to the front door and examined it; there was no sign of forced entry.

"Where are you, Gretchen?" I said aloud, adding in a whisper, "Are you okay?"

I'd never been to Gretchen's apartment before, and, looking around, I was impressed. Half a dozen fruit plates hung over the dining area table. An unusual light fixture in the hall, probably an antique, certainly hand-painted, showed a field lush with yellow and red tulips and a windmill in the background. An architectural pedestal stood in the corner. I approached it and noted that a faint circle in the center was less dusty than the rest of the top. *What had stood there? A sculpture mounted on a round base? A vase? A ewer?*

I heard a thump, and my heart stopped, then began to pound. Heavy footsteps were approaching the front door. It was Officer Griffin. He stepped into the apartment. I'd known Griff for years, from back when Ty, my boyfriend, had been the Rocky Point police chief.

"You okay?" he asked.

"Yeah. Sort of."

"You don't live here, do you?"

"No. It's Gretchen's apartment. Gretchen Brock, my assistant."

He nodded. "Where's the body?"

I pointed, and as he started toward the living room, he told me, "Wait by the door."

Moments later I heard him speaking to someone, confirming my report of the murder.

"You know him?" he asked as he rejoined me in the hall.

"No. I've never seen him before."

"Did you touch anything?"

I thought back. "Yes. Some things—the shower curtain, some door handles . . . I don't know what else."

He nodded and told me to wait again while he returned to the living room. I stood without moving until the recently promoted Detective Claire Brownley arrived about ten minutes later. She opened the door, and Griff stepped into view to greet her.

Detective Brownley had creamy white skin, celadon blue eyes, and thick black hair that fell in soft waves to her shoulders. She wore a burgundy pantsuit with a white blouse and low-heeled pumps. "What do you know about the situation?" she asked.

"Gretchen didn't come to work after her vacation. She's organized and thoughtful—she'd never get the dates wrong, and she'd never just not show up. I've been calling since yesterday. I left a message.

I knew something was wrong. I just knew it." I took a deep breath and looked at her straight on. "I didn't know what else to do, so I called the property manager." I glanced around the apartment, then looked at her again. "What in God's name happened here?"

CHAPTER THREE

G riff escorted me to the parking lot and handed me over to a young woman in uniform. She was tall and thin, with Scandinavian-pale skin and hair. She wore no makeup. Her badge said she was Officer F. Meade. Meryl sat on the backseat of the patrol car, her feet on the asphalt. Two men in plainclothes arrived carrying large black cases. I guessed they were crime scene technicians.

No one spoke. The sun was bright and warm, and I felt myself relax, just a little.

A gray Volvo station wagon pulled into the lot, slowing to a stop as the driver, an older woman with salt-and-pepper hair and pink glasses, gazed in our direction. She parked and hurried over.

"That's Gretchen's apartment," she said, pointing to the door the technicians had just entered. "Is she all right?"

"Could I get your name and contact information, please?" Officer Meade asked, ignoring her question.

I recalled what a local reporter, Wes Smith, once told me. The best way to avoid answering an unwanted question, he said, was to pose one of your own. Without hesitation, the woman told Officer Meade that her name was Fern Adams.

I listened in as Mrs. Adams gave the officer her home and office phone numbers, then pointed to the Chevy. "Is that car involved somehow?"

"Why would you ask that?"

"When I came home for lunch yesterday, that car was here. With a man in it. The engine was running." She shrugged. "I'd never seen it before."

"Can you describe him?" Officer Meade asked, flipping to a new page in her notebook.

"Thirty, maybe. Not much older than that. He had a deep tan, like he worked outdoors. Dark brown hair cut very short." She paused, concentrating, then shrugged. "I just saw him for a few seconds as I drove past."

Mrs. Adams was describing the dead man. Meryl, still seated in the police car, met my eyes. She looked frightened.

"When you left after lunch, was he still here?" Officer Meade asked.

"The car was here, but the man was gone."

"What time was that?"

"Just before one."

"Thank you. If you'd wait just a minute," Officer Meade said, "I'd appreciate it."

She walked around the car and spoke into a microphone pinned to her collar. I couldn't hear what she said.

"Can you tell me what happened?" Mrs. Adams asked me in a near-whisper.

"A man is dead." I fought a sudden, unexpected urge to cry and paused to regain some measure of composure. "In Gretchen's apartment."

"Oh, my," she murmured. "Was it him? The man in the Chevy?"

I shrugged. "From your description, it sounds like it."

Detective Brownley clambered down the steps. Officer Meade joined her, and they talked, their heads together, for several minutes.

A small gray bird with blue-tipped feathers circled the pond, its wings on high, then glided out of sight below the roofline. "How well did you know Gretchen?" I asked.

"Enough to chat with her about the weather and the fox I saw on the property, that sort of thing," Mrs. Adams said. "Gretchen's always got a smile and a kind word. Once when I had the flu, she brought me a bag of groceries. She didn't ask, she just did it. So sweet."

Detective Brownley joined us. She glanced down at Meryl, still sitting hunched over, then turned back to Fern Adams. "I'm Detective

Brownley, in charge of the investigation," she said. "Thanks for coming forward. You said that when you arrived home for lunch you saw the Chevy with the man sitting in it. Did you recognize him?"

"No." She shook her head. "I'd never seen him before."

"How about his car? Was it familiar?"

"No."

"How about Gretchen's car? Was it here, too?"

"No. I looked for it, but then I remembered it's in the shop for a tune-up."

"What? It's in the shop?" Detective Brownley asked.

She nodded. "I followed her to the garage myself, then dropped her at Portsmouth Circle—she took the bus to Logan Airport from there. She told me she'd arranged for someone else to pick her up when she got back, and when I saw the man in the car, I figured he was the person who got her and that Gretchen had run inside to get something, maybe her checkbook. Afterward, when I saw that his car was empty and that Gretchen's wasn't here, I thought he drove her to get her car, then brought his car back and parked it here, and that they'd gone out to lunch or something." She wrinkled her nose with distaste as she added, "I assumed they took Gretchen's car instead of his because hers is nicer. Her Heron is well maintained, and his Chevy, well, let's just say it's got more than a few miles on it." She paused and, with an awkward laugh, added, "You must think I'm just an old busybody!"

"We appreciate observant people," Detective Brownley said politely. "Which garage?"

"The Heron dealership on Main Street in Rocky Point, Archie's Herons."

I noticed Officer Meade taking notes.

"When you were leaving, besides noticing that his Chevy was here and her Heron wasn't, did you see or hear anything unusual?" Detective Brownley asked.

"Like what?"

"Like anything. Like someone running. Like a car barreling out of here. Like a stranger hiding under a bush. Like a gunshot. Anything."

Mrs. Adams shook her head. "No."

Detective Brownley nodded and handed her a business card. "If you remember anything else, anything at all, please call me."

Mrs. Adams promised that she would and began a slow walk across the parking lot.

Detective Brownley watched a still-tearful Meryl for several seconds, then turned to me and said, "Can you think of anything that might be helpful to us?"

"I don't know if it's related to whatever is going on—but a man's been calling Gretchen at work. Someone we don't know. He really wants to talk to her, but he won't leave a message, and he's getting increasingly angry about it."

"What's his name?" she asked.

"He hasn't given it."

"How about phone ID?"

"I never noticed," I admitted. "I should have, but I just didn't."

"We might be able to retrieve the number," she said, then asked, "Who else might have spoken to him?"

"Sasha, Fred, and the temp who covered for Gretchen. No one else."

Detective Brownley wrote down the temp's name and agency contact information. I doubted the lead would prove useful—she'd simply taken messages like the rest of us.

"When was the last time he called?"

"Fred spoke to him Tuesday, I think."

"I'll ask him about it," Detective Brownley said, looking thoughtful. "What else can you tell me?"

"I know one of her friends. A young woman named Mandy Tollerson." I explained what I knew about Mandy.

"Thank you. Anything else?" When I said no, she added, "I'll see you at your office in about an hour. Okay?"

I nodded somberly.

I felt her eyes on me as I walked to my car. Part of me wanted to talk to her some more, to ask the questions pinballing through my brain, but I didn't go back. I glanced over my shoulder one last time, and she was still watching me. I was glad to get away.

CHAPTER FOUR

Minutes later, I pulled off to the side of the road by some high dunes and scampered to the top. Frothy waves rolled into shore, tossing dark seaweed onto the sand. Sun-sparked sequins twinkled on the black-green ocean.

I called Ty. Solid and strong, confident and calm, Ty appealed to me in every way. I respected him and I liked him and I thought he was drop-dead gorgeous. Since taking the job as Homeland Security's head of first responders for northern New England, Ty traveled throughout Vermont, Maine, and New Hampshire. Today he was in Vermont.

Meeting Ty was an unexpected benefit of relocating from New York City to New Hampshire. I'd moved for rational, business reasons; the emotional rewards were unanticipated and joyous. I loved the hard-work ethic that permeated the coastal region and the circle of friends I'd started to build—and I loved Ty Alverez.

A sudden gust of wind, more winter cold than spring mild, hit me full in the face. Ty answered, and the sound of his voice warmed me. He listened with the quiet focus I'd come to expect as I recounted what I'd seen and thought.

"I'm so scared for Gretchen," I confessed. "I'm scared she's hurt—or worse." I looked out over the endless blue ocean. Whitecaps dotted the undulating surface. The wind was picking up, blowing from the east. "I know Gretchen couldn't have killed anyone—but still, if they find a body in your living room, I mean, you've got to be involved somehow."

"Detective Brownley is very thorough. She'll figure things out," Ty said, and I was comforted, just a little.

Wes Smith, a feature reporter for the *Seacoast Star,* was waiting by Prescott's front door as I pulled into the lot.

I wasn't happy about the prospect of being quoted in yet another of his articles on murder. Still, after years of getting upset at Wes's style, I'd come, in some small measure, to value his substance. What Wes lacked in bedside manner, he more than made up for in determination; when he picked up a scent, he was unstoppable.

In his midtwenties, Wes was pudgy with an indoor pallor. No one looking at Wes would ever mistake him for an outdoorsman.

"Josie," he called, heading toward my car. "I came as soon as I heard."

"Hi, Wes," I said.

"Fill me in," he demanded, sounding depressingly eager to hear the latest dirt.

"What do you know?" I asked.

"Nothing. I picked up the murder report on my police scanner, but when I got there, they chased me away." His eyes were blazing with excitement. "As soon as I heard there was a dead guy in your assistant's apartment, I came straight here. So tell me—do you think she killed him?"

"No! Of course not!" I said loyally.

"Who is he, anyway?"

"I have no idea. Do you?"

"No," Wes replied, sounding aggrieved. Wes hated not knowing things. "Who do you think he is?" he asked.

"Maybe a friend. Maybe a thief. I don't know." I paused, then asked, "Can you find out?"

Wes smiled. "Yup."

Gretchen's wind chimes jingled as I pushed open our front door. When she'd first hung them, I'd asked her why, and she'd looked at me as if she'd thought that I might be joking.

"Because they sound good," she'd replied.

Every time I heard them I was reminded not to overlook the obvious.

Fred was absorbed in reading something at his computer.

Sasha sat at Gretchen's desk. The phone rang as she was greeting me, and I listened while she gave directions to someone interested in attending Saturday's tag sale.

It was inefficient and inappropriate that my chief appraiser was spending the bulk of her time fielding administrative or logistical questions. Not for the first time, I toyed with the idea of installing an interactive phone system, but as always, I dismissed it. Prescott's business strategy relied on personal service, not canned messages. I needed to deal with the reality that Gretchen was missing and get someone in to cover her duties.

"Did you find out anything?" Sasha asked as she replaced the receiver.

"Not about Gretchen, but about something else." I paused, choosing my words carefully. "There's a dead man in her living room."

Fred looked up.

"What?" Sasha asked, disbelieving.

"I know it sounds incredible—and it is—it's horrible!" I told them what little I knew, then added, "I'll be in my office. If I hear anything, I'll let you—" I broke off as the front door opened and Gretchen's friend Mandy stepped inside.

Mandy's big brown eyes went to the framed *Antiques Insights* magazine cover that we'd finally got around to hanging by the door to the warehouse yesterday. In the magazine's December roundup of the year's "best of," Prescott's was featured as the top small antiques auction house.

"Wow! Look at that! Congratulations, Josie!" Mandy said, tucking her curly brown hair behind her ear.

In the photo, I was smiling broadly, my arms stretched wide to showcase an intriguing array of antiques. My entire full-time staff was visible in the background. Eric looked embarrassed, almost edging out of the shot; Sasha smiled shyly; Fred, his Brat Pack–cool tie loosened, appeared confident and relaxed; and Gretchen beamed proudly, her emerald eyes luminous.

It was, I knew, a great honor, but I always felt awkward being the center of attention, and I blushed a little at Mandy's praise. "Thanks," I said, then, eager to take the focus off myself, I asked, "How are you doing?"

"I'm late as usual. Lucky me, I get to work the late shift. I start at one today, and even so, I can't get to work on time." She smiled. "I just had to pop in and say hi to Gretchen. She didn't call last night. Did she have a good time in Hawaii? As if you could do anything but have a good time in Hawaii!" Her eyes took in Gretchen's empty desk. "Is she at lunch?"

"You haven't heard," I said.

"Heard what?"

I paused, then glanced at Sasha and Fred, both openly observing our interaction. Sasha twirled a strand of hair, a sign of stress. Fred was leaning back, his eyes fixed on Mandy. I took a deep breath and reported what I knew.

"What?" she gasped, gaping. "A dead man in Gretchen's apartment? *Murdered?*"

"You haven't heard from her?" I asked.

"No. Not since before she left. I can't believe it. I just can't believe it. When was he killed?"

"I don't know." Reacting to the tension in her voice and the fright evident in her eyes, I asked, "What is it, Mandy? Do you know something?"

She shook her head. "Me? I don't know anything. Listen, I've got to go. I'm going to be late. I'll be in touch."

Before I could think of another question to ask, Mandy was out the door, jogging to a waiting black Jeep. A sharp-featured man was behind the wheel. *Vince.* I thought, *the creepy boyfriend.* His entire demeanor was 1950s hip. He wore a black leather bomber jacket, and he had thick dark hair brushed straight back, Elvis style.

As I climbed the spiral steps that led to my private office, I realized how odd it was that the first question Mandy asked me was *when* the man died.

CHAPTER FIVE

pstairs, I called the temp agency. When they said the woman who'd filled in for Gretchen during her vacation wasn't available, and they'd have to call around, I thought of Cara.

Cara had been working part-time at the tag sale for just over a year. As she was a retiree, I thought there was a chance she'd be available to help out in a pinch. She was; she told me she could be at the office in a half hour.

I swiveled to face my old maple tree and looked past the white spire of the church down the street, into the conifer forest beyond. When Eric, an uneasy leader and inexperienced supervisor, had reluctantly agreed that we needed another part-time helper, he'd selected Cara. It had been a wise choice: Not only was she delightful to be around, easygoing, and a quick learner, she'd shown herself to be comfortable working for Eric. He was young enough to be her grandson, and her uncritical acceptance of him in his role as a manager boosted his confidence.

The intercom buzzed, startling me. It was Sasha.

"The police are here," she said, sounding worried.

Detective Brownley stood next to Officer Meade and a young man wearing a long-sleeved, collared T-shirt and khakis. She introduced him as Mitch, an IT expert who worked for the Rocky Point police.

"If it's all right with you," Detective Brownley requested, "I'd like him to look at your phone and Ms. Brock's computer."

"Sure," I agreed.

Mitch punched something into the phone unit, looked at the display, then shook his head. "The unit only stores twenty-five numbers."

Officer Brownley nodded. "So there's no way to recover a number from Tuesday?"

"No," Mitch said. "They've had twenty-five calls already today."

"That guy hasn't called today, has he? The one trying to reach Gretchen?"

She shook her head. "No."

Detective Brownley nodded. "We'll check the phone log. Where's Ms. Brock's computer?"

"It's this one," I said, pointing.

"Officer Meade will go through her desk."

"All right," I said, hating the thought of a stranger pawing through Gretchen's possessions and my company's papers.

"Any other computer or desk she could have used?" she asked.

"No, we each have our own workstation, and all our computers are password protected."

Detective Brownley nodded and looked around. "I'd like to talk with you all one-on-one." She gestured toward the guest chairs ranged around a small circular table near the windows. "We can talk here, if that's all right."

"Would you prefer to go upstairs? You can use my office," I offered.

"Great. Thank you." She looked at each of us. "This is just a preliminary conversation," she said, and as she spoke, a dreadful image of the hours I'd spent in Rocky Point police interrogation rooms came to me.

"We can't leave temps alone in the tag sale room, so when you're ready for Eric, I'll go in there. They're setting up for Saturday's sale," I explained to Detective Brownley.

She nodded. "Sounds fine. If it's all right, I'll start with you, Josie."

"Let's go," I said with forced cheerfulness.

As we headed out, Mitch asked for Gretchen's password, and I typed in the administrator codes to access the information.

My heart was in my throat as I led the way across the concrete floor to the spiral staircase that led to my private office. Preliminary conversations might be called interviews, not interrogations, but they were unsettling regardless.

I gestured that Detective Brownley should sit in one of the yellow Queen Anne wing chairs. I sat across from her on the love seat.

"Thank you for your cooperation, Josie. We appreciate it."

"Of course."

She eased a Poloraid photo out of her jacket pocket, glanced at it, and slid it across the butler's table that served as my coffee table. "You said you didn't know the victim. Take another look, will you? Are you sure you don't recognize him?"

I leaned forward to see the shot. It was the dead man. His lifeless eyes stared into the far distance. It was eerie. I shivered and looked away. "Yes," I told her. "I'm certain."

"What can you tell me about men in Ms. Brock's life?"

"None that I know of."

"She never mentioned she was dating someone?"

I shook my head. "No. In fact, she talked a lot about how tough it was to meet guys."

A memory came to me. About a year ago, Gretchen had gone on a first date with a fellow she'd met while house-hunting, and the next morning I'd been in the front office when Sasha asked how it had gone. Gretchen had rolled her eyes and said, "NGB." I'd asked for a translation and learned that "NGB" stood for "nice guy, but . . ."

Detective Brownley regained my attention with her next question. "Are you aware of any financial trouble? Is she late on her bills? Does she gamble? Is she struggling to support a family somewhere?"

"No. I've never heard any intimation of anything like that."

"Does she have any financial issues? For instance, do you have any idea how she could afford the apartment at Pond View? Those condos are pretty expensive for someone on an assistant's salary."

"Well, she's more than just an assistant—she's really more of an office manager—and last year was a good one for the firm. All full-timers got a bonus equivalent to three months' salary. I think she used the bonus as part of her down payment."

She nodded and made a note. "You seem to care about her a lot, and yet you aren't friends. Help me understand that."

I paused for a moment to think how to express it. "We don't have much in common, but that doesn't mean that I don't think the world of her—I do. We never hang out as girlfriends, but I really like her. She's a lot of fun, and she's an incredibly valuable employee."

"Where is she from?"

"I don't know. She never said."

"How about family?"

I shook my head. "I have no information."

"Did she ever mention going home for the holidays, attending a niece's school play, anything like that?"

"Nope."

"This Mandy Tollerson is the only friend you know about?"

"Yes."

"Can you think of anything else about the man who's been calling?"

"No. Just that the calls began shortly after Gretchen left on vacation."

"Okay, that's enough basic information for now. Who, besides you, knows her best?"

"I don't know that anyone knows her very well. Maybe Sasha."

"Send her up, would you?"

When I announced that Detective Brownley wanted to see Sasha next, she started at hearing her name and momentarily froze, like a small animal who senses that a predator is about to attack.

"Sure," Sasha said, her voice barely audible. She walked around the two police investigators working at Gretchen's desk.

"How did it go?" I asked when she returned.

"Okay, I guess." She twirled a strand of her lank brown hair. "Fred, you can go now."

Fred stood, pushed his glasses up, and headed out.

"Were you able to tell her anything useful?" I asked.

She shrugged. "I don't think so. I realized that I don't know very much about Gretchen." She sounded a little surprised.

"Did you recognize the photo?"

"No," she answered, her voice shaking a bit.

After Fred, Eric went upstairs, then the part-timers, one at a time. From all reports, Detective Brownley asked the same questions of each of us, and everyone's answers mimicked mine and Sasha's. No one, it seemed, knew anything personal about Gretchen. Only Fred was able to add anything salient about the mysterious caller—the time of the last call. He'd spoken to him at three, so if it was the dead man who'd been calling, he was alive then.

Downstairs again, Detective Brownley asked me, "What about Ms. Brock's job application?"

I glanced at Sasha and Fred, who were, no surprise, listening in. I was embarrassed at having to explain my spur-of-the-moment decision to hire Gretchen within minutes of meeting her.

"She didn't fill one out," I said, giving an awkward laugh. I raised a hand to stop her from asking the obvious follow-up question. "It's very unlike me, but she was so earnest." I shrugged. "I trusted my gut, and I was right. She's terrific."

At Detective Brownley's request, I photocopied Gretchen's tax forms, insurance security clearance report, annual performance appraisals, and health insurance opt-in card from her personnel file. I also provided a list of all employees who'd worked at the company over the last year and a printout of Gretchen's online calendar. Glancing at it as I handed it over, I saw an entry for next week reading "trk ltg."

Track lighting, I thought. Gretchen had scheduled an appointment with Tony, our electrician. It had been Gretchen's idea to add an additional row of movable spotlights in the auction venue. As soon as she mentioned it, Fred had jumped on it as a great idea, brainstorming with Gretchen and Sasha about the possibilities. It was Fred who'd explained why he thought it was worth the money: The additional tracks would allow us to add dramatic lighting to certain objects while highlighting others. I smiled as I recalled congratulating Gretchen on her idea. She'd grinned and said, "Now you know the truth! I'll do anything to add drama to life!"

Mitch broke into my reverie when he told Detective Brownley that he was done with Gretchen's computer. He reported that there weren't any hidden or encrypted files, all business folders were organized and accounted for, the only Web sites she'd bookmarked were magazine gossip sites, and the only personal information Gretchen had stored on her computer related to her Hawaiian vacation.

Detective Brownley looked at Officer Meade. "How about you? Have you found anything?"

She hadn't. I watched as Detective Brownley ran her finger down the inventory Officer Meade had written.

"Okay then," Detective Brownley said, returning the officer's notebook. "You two can go on ahead. I'll see you back at the station." To me, she added, "We're done for now, which means that you can use her workstation."

Gretchen's chimes tinkled, and Cara walked in. I introduced her to Detective Brownley, who handed her the photograph of the dead man.

"Have you ever seen him before?" she asked.

Cara stared at the photo for several seconds, then said, "Yes."

CHAPTER SIX

T ell me," Detective Brownley said.

Cara looked up at the detective, then back at the snapshot. "Is he dead?"

"Yes. Please. It's important. Please tell me how you know him."

"He was here last Saturday. At the tag sale. He asked to see Gretchen."

Rippling anxiety surged up my spine—a man had wanted to see Gretchen, and days later, he was dead, murdered. Was it cause and effect?

"Did he give his name?" Detective Brownley asked.

"No," Cara said, her face lined with concern.

"Start at the beginning. When did he arrive and what—exactly— did he do and say?"

Cara thought for a moment. "He came in around two in the afternoon. As soon as he stepped inside, he paused, looking around. A lot of customers do that. I was the greeter. We're trained to approach each person and ask if we can help them find anything special or if they just want to poke around. He didn't reply; he just kept looking. I greeted a couple who came in right behind him, then a single woman, then a woman I know from church. I remember, because he was sort of blocking the door, and they had to edge around him. Finally he told me that he wanted to talk to Gretchen."

"Can you remember his exact words?" Detective Brownley asked.

Cara looked down, clasping and unclasping her hands, then spoke, her tone soft. "He asked, 'Where's Gretchen?' I told him she was on vacation. Then he asked when she was due back. I said that

I wasn't sure but that I thought it was sometime this week. *Oh!* . . . I'm so sorry. I didn't realize it at the time, but I gave out schedule information, and I know we're never supposed to do that. I didn't think . . . I mean, it never occurred to me. I'm so sorry, Josie."

"It's okay, Cara," I reassured her. "You'll know better next time."

"What happened then?" Detective Brownley asked.

"Nothing." She opened her palms, and I took the gesture to express helplessness—Cara wanted to provide useful information but had none to give. "He left. He wasn't inside for more than a minute or two."

"What was he wearing?"

Cara closed her eyes for a few seconds. "Jeans and a flannel shirt. I don't remember the shirt color or his shoes. Nothing that stood out, or I would have noticed."

"Okay. Thanks." Detective Brownley handed her a card. She turned to include Sasha and Fred in her comment, placing a card in front of each of them. "If you remember anything else, call me, okay?"

Sasha nodded.

Cara said, "I will."

Fred murmured, "Sure."

Detective Brownley turned to me. "I'd like another word with Eric and the part-time staff."

"Cara, go ahead and get situated at this desk," I told her, pointing to Gretchen's workstation. "Sasha, Fred, one of you show her how to work the phone, okay?" To Detective Brownley, I said, "This way."

We entered the warehouse, and I led the way across the echoing expanse, past stacks of packing crates, rolls of bubble wrap, shelves of carefully arranged inventory, roped-off areas of consignment goods, and worktables where objects were graded, cleaned, and readied for sale or storage.

When we reached the tag sale room, I waved Eric over. He was in his early twenties, but he looked younger. He was tall and lanky and thin like a still-growing teen.

"Please call the part-timers over," Detective Brownley said. "I have something important to tell you all." When everyone had gathered around, she said, "I wanted to hand each of you a business card in case you remember anything else about Ms. Brock." She paused and took the time to meet each person's eyes. "Maybe one of you knows something that you don't want to mention in public. Even if you think it's silly or insignificant, call me and tell me privately, okay?"

Everyone nodded or said something affirmative, and after she was done, I walked her to the door. Once she was in her car and on her way, I took a deep breath, turned to scan the displays, and assessed the setup. I approached Eric, who was working with a part-timer to hang nineteenth-century samplers on a silk rope stretched against the back wall.

"Things look good in here," I told him.

"There's still a lot to do."

Out of the corner of my eye, I saw that Detective Brownley had returned. She waved me over, and my pulse began to throb. I nodded and held up a finger, indicating that I'd be with her in a minute.

"Are you worried about anything in particular?" I asked Eric.

"I'm not sure we have enough good stuff."

I nodded. Each week we seeded the tag sale with a few objects priced to move to encourage repeat business and bargain hunters. "I'll check it out," I told him.

Detective Brownley held the door open, jerking her head toward the outdoors, indicating that I was to follow her. The temperature had dropped, and a cold breeze stabbed at me.

"I have a question," she said. "With all respect, why would you, a successful, experienced businesswoman, hire Ms. Brock on the spot, without checking her references? You deal in valuable antiques. How could you give a stranger who just showed up at your door the run of the place? There's got to be more to the story."

"It's really not as outrageous as it sounds. My insurance company does in-depth background checks that go back three years. You have a copy of their report from her personnel file."

"What does it say?"

"She's clean as a whistle."

Detective Brownley nodded and looked over my shoulder into a stand of birch trees near the front of the property. "What do you think happened? Do you think she killed him?" she asked, turning back to me.

I met her unwavering gaze, then lowered my eyes. "I can't imagine Gretchen killing anyone." I looked up. "She won't kill a spider. I mean it. If she sees one inside, she won't step on it, and she won't let anyone else kill it, either. She'll trap it in a plastic container and release it outside."

"It doesn't have to be murder. Maybe it was self-defense."

I nodded, rubbing my upper arms for warmth, hugging myself. "I can see that."

"Would she have panicked?"

I shrugged and shivered as a blustery gust struck my face. "I don't think so."

"You know her. Would she? Would she panic?"

I thought about her question. Once, when a valuable Chinese tureen had been stolen from the auction venue, Gretchen had called the police and followed their instructions to the letter, maintaining her composure throughout. Another time, when we'd underestimated the popularity of an auction and scores of potential buyers had pressed to get in without waiting in long registration lines, she'd spoken kindly to people without giving in to their demands or losing control. *No,* I concluded, Gretchen wouldn't panic.

"I don't think she would," I said, citing the examples. "But I understand that business stuff isn't the same." I cleared my throat, hating the thought but wanting to know. "Have you considered whether . . . I mean . . . do you think that maybe she's been kidnapped by whoever killed that man?"

"It's a possibility."

Returning to the main office, I overheard Cara taking a message from someone who apparently sold telecommunication services.

Cara did a good job of politely revealing nothing. As I listened, my eyes lit on the Mickey Mouse clock sitting on Gretchen's desk.

It was a modern-era trinket sold in every Disney store. Unlike the victim's belt buckle, I realized with a thud of awareness—and what about the missing object, the round item that had stood on the pedestal in her living room?

Fred and Sasha were both reading on their monitors. Cara was hanging up the phone.

"Did Gretchen ever mention something she owned that might have been positioned on a pedestal?" I asked.

"Like what?" Fred responded, looking up.

"Something round like a bowl or a circular base for a sculpture—about this big." I used my hands to approximate its size. "The object isn't there. Did she mention taking something in for repair or cleaning? Even if she never mentioned it, could she have talked about the pedestal, maybe when she was buying it? Does anything about it ring a bell?"

Sasha and Cara shook their heads. "No idea," Fred said.

Upstairs in my office, I called Detective Brownley's cell phone. It went straight to voice mail.

"There's a chance that we can trace the dead man's belt buckle," I said in my message. "I won't know until I examine it, but if you want, I can take a look."

After I hung up, I tried to focus on work but was too worried about Gretchen. I spun my chair to look out my window, took a deep breath and, with a sigh, swiveled back to face the piles of papers on my desk. After a while, I walked downstairs again.

The warehouse and tag sale room were deserted. It was growing darker, not quite dusk, but close. The security cameras stood at the ready, a red pinprick of light indicating the power was on. Faint circles of white light marked the panic buttons my insurance company had had me install throughout the building. I wondered what time it was. I never wore a watch, since it always seemed to get in the way as I crawled under furniture and packed awkwardly shaped objects. As I walked toward the front office, I played a guessing game with myself—I bet it was just after five.

It was five twelve. Cara was gone. Fred was standing, stretching. Sasha was straightening papers on her desk.

A night owl, Fred often came in close to noon and worked late into the evening, but with Gretchen on vacation, he'd been keeping more standard hours to help provide office coverage. I spotted a color printout of a pink-faced doll on his desk and wondered what he'd learned about it. We were planning a major auction of antique and collectible dolls next fall. "Anything?" I asked him, pointing to the printout.

"I confirmed that it's a twenty-inch Madame Alexander Cissy doll from 1957," he said. "I was worried that it might be a Binnie/Winnie with the Cissy face, but it's not."

"How could you tell?" I asked.

"Binnie/Winnie is flatfooted."

"Great!" I responded, knowing that Cissy was more valuable than Binnie/Winnie.

"This one seems to be in really good shape—it comes with a stocked wardrobe of mostly tagged clothing, all of it in excellent condition. I still need to assess the doll itself—wig, joints, arm movement, eyes, eyelashes, cracks, and splits. The regular drill."

I glanced at the printout again. "The eyes do look cloudy, don't they?"

"Can't tell from the photo. It might only be dust."

The phone rang.

"I'll get it," I told them. "You guys go on home."

It was Detective Brownley returning my call, and as soon as I heard her voice, I exhaled. It felt as if I'd been holding my breath since I left her the message.

"Terrific idea about the belt buckle," she said. "It's at the lab. I'll get it to you as soon as they finish with it. I'd like your opinion on the artwork and other things in Ms. Brook's apartment. Can you meet me there?"

"Of course," I replied, and we settled on a time midmorning. I took a deep breath. "Do you have any news? Anything?"

She paused, then said, "Our investigation is progressing."

I didn't push. There was no point.

CHAPTER SEVEN

I was on my way to the gourmet shop for black truffle oil when I decided to stop by the nearby Bow Street Emporium and ask Mandy if she was the friend who'd been watering Gretchen's plants.

The Bow Street Emporium was stocked with aromatic soaps and candles, hand-painted glassware, delicately embroidered linen, elegant silk flowers, and one-of-a-kind baubles and knickknacks. Sleigh bells attached to the heavy oak door jangled as I entered the shop. A pretty woman with delicate features smiled as she approached me. In a tone rich with innuendo, she told me Mandy had left early.

"Is she all right?" I asked.

"The police came and took her away," the woman said, lowering her voice to enhance the dramatic effect.

I nodded.

"You've heard the news, then?" she asked. "It's all over the radio— a man was murdered in her friend's apartment. Can you imagine?"

I agreed that it was terrible and left. Once outside, I stepped around the corner, out of sight of the store, and called Mandy. I got her. She told me that the police had just dropped her off. She sounded fragile and on edge.

After we commiserated about the situation, I asked, "Did they show you the photo of the dead man?"

"Yes. I'd never seen him before. Had you?"

"No." I took a deep breath. "May I ask you something, Mandy?"

"Okay," she replied warily.

"Have you been to Gretchen's to water her plants while she's been gone?" I asked, keeping my tone neutral as if I were just making conversation. Mandy seemed like a skittish kitten. I didn't want to frighten her into darting away.

"A couple of times," she said, after a two-beat delay. "Why?"

"Just wondering," I replied lightly. "When was the last time?"

"Oh! Did you hear that? My oven timer is going off—I have to run."

I didn't hear anything. "How about friends—were you able to give the police some names?" I asked in a rush, wanting to get more information before she ended the call.

"A few. I suggested they talk to Lina."

"Who's Lina?"

"Gretchen's best friend, Lina. Don't you know her? We work together at the store." I heard a faint click in the background, maybe the sound of a door shutting. Before I could ask for more details about Lina, Mandy whispered, "I've got to go," and hung up.

I closed my phone slowly, my mind a whirlwind of half-stories and information gaps. *What,* I wondered, *had spooked Mandy just now? How had Gretchen gotten home from Boston? Where was Gretchen's car? And for God's sake, where was Gretchen?*

I walked back into the store and asked the young woman I'd spoken to earlier if Lina was around. She said it was Lina's day off.

"What's her last name?" I asked, smiling in an effort to rob the question of impertinence.

"Why?" she asked, on guard.

"Never mind. I'll stop by tomorrow," I said, smiling again and leaving quickly, before she could challenge me any further.

Walking to my car, I tried to figure out what to do next. Then I remembered something I'd read in college. Samuel Johnson wrote, "Knowledge is of two kinds. We know a subject ourselves, or we know where we can find information upon it."

I scooped up the phone to call Wes.

"Whatcha got?" Wes asked.

"I wanted to know what you've found out."

"We should meet."

I glanced at the clock again. It was almost six thirty. Ty was driving in from Vermont and wouldn't be home until eight or even later. My next-door neighbor, landlady, and friend, Zoë, and her kids were scheduled to come to dinner. I'd told her to come over around seven, but I could call and change it to seven thirty. The kids would already have eaten anyway, and Zoë, I knew, was completely flexible. I could get what I needed at the gourmet shop in five minutes flat.

"Can you meet me at Shaw's in Rocky Point?" I asked, naming the super-sized grocery store near my house. "In ten minutes?"

He agreed, and I tore through the gourmet store en route.

Wes was leaning up against his car when I pulled into a space next to him at the far end of the parking lot. His eyes were as intent and watchful as usual.

"So about the dead guy—nothing yet," he said, jumping in without saying hello. "ID'ing him is a tough one. According to my police source, his pockets were empty and his fingerprints aren't in the New Hampshire or federal system."

"How can he be identified, then?"

He shrugged. "Lots of ways. Mug shots, collection agencies, missing persons reports—but it takes time. I'm approaching it from the other way. I want to know how he came to be in Gretchen's apartment. Do you have any idea?"

"Me? I don't know anything."

"Maybe he was her boyfriend," Wes speculated.

I made a gesture of helplessness. "He could be, I guess. Although no one seems to recognize him, and you'd think that someone would if they were a couple. Have you learned anything about the car?"

Wes took a folded-up piece of lined paper from his inside pocket, turned it over, and read from his notes. "Chevy, Tennessee plates. Registered to a Sal Briscoe. His address is an SRO—single room occupancy—in Memphis. No one down there seems to know him. He arrived about four years ago, always pays in cash. The car was bought used last week, also for cash."

"It sounds so peculiar."

"Yeah. So what's your take on the situation?"

"I don't know."

"You keep saying that! Come on, Josie."

Knowing Wes, I understood that unless I gave him something, I wouldn't get anything. I swallowed my disinclination to gossip and told him about Gretchen's friend Mandy and the belt buckle we'd be appraising.

"Thanks, Josie. This is great stuff. Love the buckle. Shows the three-dimensional nature of an investigation. Can I get a photo?"

"No! Of course not!"

"It doesn't have to be top quality. You can use your cell."

I shook my head, but he wasn't looking at me; he was reviewing his notes.

He looked up. "Please? I won't say I got it from you."

"Maybe later," I said, holding out the possibility as a carrot. "Not now."

He sighed, Wesian for acquiescence.

Before I started shopping, I called Zoë.

"Seven thirty's fine," she said. "I'll feed the kids now. I'm making apple martinis."

"I'm not sure apple martinis go with what I've planned for dinner."

"What's that?"

"Linguine with Black Truffles."

"Sounds delish, very chichi—but I'm surprised that you didn't know that apple martinis go with everything. I'll feed the kids and bring dessert. See ya soon!"

Driving home, I speculated on Gretchen's whereabouts and Mandy's unexpected reticence. I was beyond eager, I was desperate, to know that Gretchen was safe and to understand why she'd disappeared. I couldn't picture Gretchen as a killer. I just couldn't.

Of course, if she'd been threatened or attacked, maybe she'd struck back the way anyone would. If that was the case, though, she would have come forward—unless she'd been kidnapped. It was the only alternative I could think of. My heart pounded so hard at the thought, I felt dizzy.

Who'd kidnap her? I asked myself. As far as I knew, she wasn't rich—she lived on her salary. If she came from money, she surely hid it well. Her apartment was attractive, but the mortgage payment was within her budget. She could afford to buy a previously owned, well-maintained Heron every few years, but she couldn't have swung a new one. I carried key man insurance to protect my company in case something happened to me, but Gretchen wasn't on the policy, and surely no one would think she would be. Plus, there'd been no ransom note. *Unless someone took her for a reason other than money.* My blood froze at the horrific images of depraved fetishes that flooded my brain. I needed to do more to find her, but I couldn't think of what that might be.

CHAPTER EIGHT

Y ou should have warned me to sell the family jewels," Ty said when he called.

It wasn't until I was home that I realized that I'd forgotten to buy the truffle oil. I'd called Ty and asked him to pick it up on his way home.

"Truffle oil is a bit pricey? Is that what you're saying?" I asked, giggling a little. I wedged the phone between my shoulder and ear so I could continue chopping vegetables while carrying on our conversation.

As usual, I was charmed by Ty's sense of humor, and tonight I was especially grateful for its effect. Despite my nonstop, frenzied worrying about Gretchen, he made me laugh.

"A little pricey?" he responded. "Are you insane, woman? One eight-ounce bottle costs more than a steak dinner!"

"Ah! But wait until you taste my linguine."

"You're right! Put that way—it's a bargain! See you soon!"

I slid the portable phone into its cradle and smiled again as I touched my mother's handwritten cookbook, stroking the soft leather. Ty's appreciation of my cooking was flattering to me, but it was also a compliment to my much loved mother, who'd died when I was thirteen. Back then, I'd missed her so much it hurt to breathe. Now, while the pain was still there, it was an ache, not a stab.

I stared out my window into the darkness, unable to see the meadow or the trees that marked the faraway property line, and thought again of Gretchen.

About six months ago, she'd brought in a miniature sandbox for her desk. Periodically, she'd drag a small wooden rake through the sand to create swirling patterns, then laughingly announce she could feel her blood pressure dropping.

One day, a consignment deal I hoped we would land fell through. Not wanting to let the staff see my disappointment, I took myself out to a coffee shop that played mournful jazz and drowned my sorrows in a double mocha extra cream cappuccino. When I got back to work, Gretchen's sandbox was on my desk. She'd tacked a Post-it Note on it reading "Stress Management 101. Rake away!" I had, and whether it was my act of raking or Gretchen's act of kindness, I'd felt a little better. Gretchen was one of the most sensitive and thoughtful people I'd ever met.

Before I had time to fret myself to tears, I heard laughter and chatter, then a knock, and called, "Come in!"

Zoë, Jake, and Emma entered through the back door. Zoë flashed a quick smile. Her eyes were striking—brown, and big enough to see everything. Her hair was thick, near-black, and long. She was tall, maybe half a head taller than me, and thin, like a model. Zoë wore jeans and a mustard yellow sweater and carried a huge red tote bag. The kids were dressed in pajamas, jackets, and boots. Jake's pj's had airplanes, spaceships, and shooting stars; Emma's were pink with white clouds.

"Hi, Josie!" Jake said, hugging my knees before tearing into the living room.

"Hi, Jake!" I called after him. "Your blocks are behind the sofa." I turned to Emma. "Hi, Emma."

"Look at Mary-Rose," she replied, thrusting a slightly battered stuffed monkey in my direction. "She's from the attic. I picked the name myself."

"She looks very well loved!" I responded.

Emma hugged the monkey and nodded. "She's a teddy monkey. Like a teddy bear, but a monkey."

"What a find!" I exclaimed, awed by Emma's vocabulary and comprehension.

Zoë unpacked apple juice, sippy cups, a container of fudge swirl ice cream, and a thermos of apple martinis. "Hell," she said, "it's only been two years since I moved in! *Of course* I'm still going through the stuff in the attic."

Her uncle, Mr. Winterelli, had been my landlord and next-door neighbor until he died a little more than two years ago. Apparently my house, a smaller version of his, had been built as an in-law unit in the early 1900s. When Zoë had inherited his entire estate, she'd left a bad marriage on the West Coast and moved back to New Hampshire. From her politely worded comments, I gathered that while Mr. Winterelli had been her favorite uncle and she'd loved him to death, she was having a hard time creating order out of the chaos he'd left behind because he'd been both a pack rat and a bad housekeeper.

"It's a pretty name," I told Emma. "How did you pick it?"

"I liked it," she said.

Emma's reply reminded me that decisions are often straightforward, based on personal preference or impulse, without any hidden agenda—like Gretchen's wind chimes.

"Do you want some apple juice?" Zoë asked Emma, standing nearby, smoothing the monkey's fur.

Emma nodded, and Zoë filled two sippy cups about half full. "Go give one to Jake, okay?"

"Okay," she said, gently tucking Mary-Rose under her arm and clutching the two sippy cups in her chubby hands.

"What a great kid," I said, smiling as I watched her.

"She really is. They both are." She double-tapped the wooden cutting board, then teasingly shook the thermos. "Martini, anyone?"

"You bet," I replied.

I watched Zoë pour the pale green, frothy liquid into martini glasses she took from the freezer, and without even being aware I was doing it, I tilted my head back and rolled it side to side, unconsciously trying to ease the ropelike tension gripping my shoulders and neck.

Zoë handed me a drink. "Okay, what's wrong?"

I took a sip. "It's Gretchen. Did you hear what happened?"

"Of course not. I'm a stay-at-home mom. The only news I hear is from my kids."

I reported the facts, and when I finished speaking, she exclaimed, "Josie, this is horrible! You must be beside yourself with worry!"

"I am," I acknowledged, my voice quivering. I swallowed to keep from crying and concentrated on the red pepper I was chopping. "I can't believe she killed him. If she had, no matter why, she would have called the police, don't you think?"

Zoë shrugged. "I don't know her. Maybe she flipped out—I know I would—and ran to a friend."

"Yeah, I've wondered about that, too."

"You don't know her friends, right?"

"Not really. Just a girl named Mandy. She said Gretchen's best friend is named Lina." I shrugged and swallowed hard as I used my knife to sweep the pepper bits into a bowl. I began chopping chives. "I'll tell you my worst nightmare—that Gretchen's been kidnapped. You hear such horrible . . . such *wicked* . . . things, you know?"

Zoë nodded soberly.

"Maybe she did run," I said, pausing with my knife in midair, turning to Zoë. "If, when she entered her apartment, she recognized the dead man, and knew that someone had a motive to kill him, she would have called the police. Unless she knew that the killer also had a motive to kill her. The killer arrives, intent on murdering Gretchen, and finds him there instead. A fight ensues, and the murderer kills him. Gretchen comes home and sees her friend—dead. Maybe she knows who wants to kill her. Or maybe she recognizes the killer from something he left behind—like his gun. Under those circumstances, she might flee. That's plausible, isn't it?"

"Sure, but there's another possibility, too," Zoë said. "Whenever you talk about Gretchen, there's one attribute that you always mention—her caretaking nature. Maybe she didn't kill that man and no one is out to kill her. Rather, what if she loves the person who did kill him? What would she do then?"

"She'd do everything she could to protect him," I acknowledged, following Zoë's logic. "*If* there is someone she cares about that much." I thought about it for a moment, then shook my head.

"Since she's worked for me for four years without mentioning anyone who qualifies, I think it's a stretch. Just because something is conceivable doesn't mean it's credible."

Gretchen was a kind, generous, and loving person by nature, but I didn't delude myself that she was a saint—and she certainly wouldn't be the first woman to do something foolish, even illegal, to help a murderer. I'd just read an article about women who love men who murder. One woman the author interviewed had chartered a helicopter to hover over the prison yard at a time when her boyfriend, a three-time convicted killer, was outside exercising. She'd lowered a rope, he'd quick-climbed high enough to clear the wall, and off they'd flown. The police caught up with them five days later, thirty miles away, in a motel room. In a jailhouse interview after she'd been convicted of multiple felonies and sentenced to fifteen years in prison, the woman claimed to feel no regrets, explaining that after years of mind-numbing boredom as a clerk in an insurance company, she'd had five days of bliss—and that was five more than anyone she knew had ever had.

Which is it? I asked myself as I resumed chopping chives. Had Gretchen been kidnapped for reasons too horrendous to mention? Was she a killer on the run? Was she shielding a lover in a misguided effort to help? Or was she herself running from a killer?

I turned to Zoë. "I just pray she's safe."

Ty walked in amid a blast of cold air. There was no longer any hint of spring warmth.

"Hey," he said, smiling and handing me a grocery bag. "Hey, Zoë."

Ty was just over six feet tall, broad, and fit. His dark brown hair was cut short, and his eyes were deep-set and almost black. His skin was weathered, not tanned, and his features were irregular. Just seeing him took my breath away.

"Hey," I replied. I pulled the bottle of truffle oil from the bag and held it high over my head like a trophy. "Good news. With this magic potion, I will create food fit for a king and," I said, turning to Zoë, "a queen."

While I finished cooking, Ty and Zoë dragged the twin-sized futons I kept rolled up in the front hall closet into the living room and settled the kids in front of a Disney movie. Between stirrings, I watched them snuggling under afghans.

After dinner, with an old Gerry Mulligan CD playing softly in the background, I sipped my second apple martini and kept Ty company as he loaded the dishwasher.

"I think they're down for the count," Zoë said, joining me at the table. She poured herself a refill and turned to me. "So, my friend, how are you holding up?"

Ty didn't speak, but I could sense his intense attention as he listened in.

"Not so well, actually," I replied. "I hate not knowing where Gretchen is, and I hate worrying. It's exhausting." I raised my glass. "As my father often said, 'Here's to silver light in the dark of night.'"

"Hear, hear!" Zoë toasted. "To no dark nights."

Ty started the dishwasher and joined us at the table with a mug of coffee. "Nothing dark about a night when Josie cooks."

"Aw, shucks," I said, pleased with the compliment. "Thanks."

Later, after Ty had carried both kids home and I'd rolled the futons back into the closet, and after I'd taken a hot shower and was warm in bed, I had a thought: *Maybe I should knock on Mandy's door and see if Gretchen is there, hiding in her friend's apartment. And Lina's. I should ask Mandy where she lives.*

I didn't really believe that either woman was hiding Gretchen, but checking could do no harm. Just as I was fading from wakefulness to sleep, I had another thought: *Maybe I can find out whether Gretchen's car is still in the shop, and if not, who drove her to pick it up.*

CHAPTER NINE

ith my morning cup of coffee in hand, I sat at my home computer and Googled Mandy's name and "New Hampshire." Ty was long gone, heading back to Vermont.

Her address popped up. She lived in a town house near the Fox Run Mall in Newington, about two miles from Prescott's in Portsmouth and about five miles from my house in Rocky Point.

Rocky Point was a small, affluent beach community a few miles south of Portsmouth. It claimed three of New Hampshire's eighteen miles of shoreline, the fewest of any state. A few blocks inland, main street boasted charming boutiques, gourmet restaurants, and an expensive hair salon and day spa. At one end of the park there was a central green with a gazebo where a band played on summer evenings. On the other end there was a small pond surrounded by forsythia bushes just in bloom. On the west side of the village, Main Street narrowed and became residential. At the edge of town, just before the dividing line between Rocky Point and Turnow Falls, Main Street widened again and turned rural. The Heron dealership sat on newly developed acreage at the far end of the street.

Wispy clouds streaked across a baby blue sky. It was warmer than yesterday.

I decided to visit the Heron dealership first.

I turned into the pennant-draped lot and drove slowly down the rows of vehicles. Gretchen's car wasn't there. I drove around the back to the service bays. The doors were down, but the lights were on and I could see workers through the windows. I parked off to the side and entered through the door marked CUSTOMERS.

A man at the window said, "And change the oil, okay?" He signed the form, thanked the clerk, and left.

I approached the round cutout in the acrylic divider and smiled at the young man. He was short. There were two earrings in his left ear. He had a tattoo on his neck that read MOM, and he wore a too-large pale green uniform with MAC embroidered on the pocket. He looked bored. His uninterested attitude changed my approach. I'd intended to tell the truth but decided to take some creative license. I was willing to bet that he wouldn't care about the details and didn't watch the news.

"Hi," I said, smiling broadly. "Gretchen Brock. Picking up."

"Girl reporter, huh? Sorry, babe, you're too late," he said. "The cops have already been here."

"Darn!" I exclaimed, letting his assumption stand. "Did they tow it away?"

"Nah," he said, grinning. "She already got it herself. Wednesday, 'bout noon."

"Just my luck, right?" I nodded, turned to leave, then spun back. "Did you see who drove her here?"

He shook his head. "Nope. She came in alone."

"Mac, is there anything else I should ask you?"

He thought about my question for a second, then leaned back in his chair, clasped his hands behind his head, and said, "Can't show you the paperwork. Cops got it."

I thanked him and left, thrilled to have learned that Gretchen had picked up her car on the day she returned. I felt one step closer to finding her.

At eight, I idled under a willow tree in Mandy's apartment complex and scanned the doors looking for her unit, number six. I spotted it halfway down on the left. A black Jeep was in the slot directly in front of her entryway. *Vince is here,* I thought. Gretchen's car was nowhere to be seen.

After I'd been there several minutes, trying to decide if it was too early to knock on the door, Vince walked out, and I dropped my eyes as if I were changing the radio station. He was wearing the leather bomber jacket and jeans. Out of the corner of my eye, I saw him unlock the vehicle and swing into the front seat, moving with an athlete's grace. He adjusted his rearview mirror. I felt his eyes on me. I kept my head turned away and still. As the Jeep pulled into traffic, I jotted down its plate number.

I circled the complex slowly but didn't see Gretchen's car anywhere.

A good way to hide in plain sight, I thought, might be to leave her car in a mall parking lot, so I drove the few blocks to Fox Run Mall and pulled into the lot through the entrance closest to JCPenney. There were only a half dozen cars in the entire place. Security, I figured, and I realized that hiding a car in a mall parking lot might work on a busy Saturday afternoon, but not on an early morning weekday.

I returned to Mandy's apartment. As I approached the front door, I noticed that all of the ground-floor blinds were drawn. I pressed the doorbell. Mandy smiled as she answered the door and said hello. She wasn't wearing any makeup and looked very young.

"I was a little worried," I said. "You sounded pretty upset yesterday."

Her eyes lost some of their luster. "I was. I am. Come on in." She led the way into her yellow and violet kitchen. "I just got the message you left last night—I've been staying at Vince's place."

One step into the kitchen, and I stopped short. Boldly painted irises, daffodils, crocuses, and forsythia covered every inch of walls and cupboard doors, transforming the room into a springtime garden.

"It's fantastic!" I exclaimed. "Did you do it yourself?"

"Yeah. It's kind of a hobby."

"You're really talented, Mandy. No wonder you're thinking of opening an art gallery."

"Vince says it's a pretty stupid way to spend time," she said with a self-conscious laugh, "but I have fun with it."

I didn't know how to respond. To express outrage at his absurd and mean-spirited edict was to jump into the middle of their disagreement, a place I didn't want to be. I stayed quiet.

After a long moment of awkward silence, she said, "I just made coffee. Want a cup?"

"Thanks. I'd love one."

"Do you have any news about Gretchen?" she asked, turning to face the coffeepot.

I shook my head. "No news, but I do have a couple of questions, if that's all right. Gretchen's best friend is named Lina, you said. What can you tell me about her?"

"She's great. I met her when I started working at the store—she's an assistant manager, too. She introduced me to Gretchen."

"How long have they known each other, do you know?"

"I'm not sure. Years, I think."

"Do you have any idea where Gretchen could be?" I asked, thinking, *Like upstairs?*

"No," she answered. "I have no idea, and Vince said I should be careful about speculating."

"I want to go look for her," I said, "to reassure her that no matter what happened, I'll help her."

She looked thoughtful. My gut told me not to believe that she had no idea where Gretchen might be, but my head warned me not to disbelieve her out of hand. From what I had observed myself and what Gretchen had reported, I knew that Mandy spent a lot of time braced for criticism, concerned that she might be disappointing someone. The bottom line was that I had no empirical evidence that Mandy was hiding or otherwise helping Gretchen.

"It's not speculating so much as guessing," I added. "Where would you tell me to look?"

"I don't know," she replied softly, shaking her head.

I nodded. "Maybe Lina would know. Can you tell me where she lives?"

She gave me Lina's phone number and address. I glanced at the paper. I knew the street. It was a middle-class neighborhood near the Piscataqua River.

"She's in the ground floor unit."

"Thanks," I said, slipping the paper into my bag. "Mandy, there's an architectural pedestal in Gretchen's living room, in the corner by the fireplace. Do you remember it?"

She scrunched her eyes a bit, thinking. "Yeah. Sure. That's where she keeps her vase."

I exhaled. Someone who had seen it! I felt a thrill of excitement shoot through me. "Can you describe it?"

"How come?"

"It's missing."

Her eyes opened wider. "Really? Did someone steal it?"

"I don't know. What can you remember about it?"

She shrugged and flipped her palms up. "It's Asian, I guess," she said.

"Kind of fat and squat? Or tall and elegant?"

She shook her head, the picture not clear in her mind. "Medium, I guess."

"How tall?" I asked, moving my hands up and down, approximating a height range of six inches up to more than two feet. She watched, then nodded and touched my hand at about eighteen inches.

"There, I guess. It's about that high."

"Did Gretchen keep flowers in it?"

"No." She considered, then added, "It has a top. I don't know how to describe it. It has a cover on it, so I guess it's not really a vase."

I nodded. "I know the kind of object you're describing—it's still called a vase. Can you remember anything about the design? Did it show flowers? Birds? People?"

She bit a corner of her lip, concentrating. "Not really."

"No problem—how about its color? Do you remember that? Was it mostly pinks? Blues? Oranges?"

"Blue, I think. I don't know—it looks Asian."

I nodded. Some people could recall every detail of an object; others couldn't remember the most obvious attributes—proving nothing except that people are different. Even artists like Mandy. I'd bet that if I showed her a Renoir, she could later detail the composition, color palette, and subject matter. But a vase? She barely noticed.

I drove straight to Lina's.

Parking in front of the well-maintained three-story house, I climbed a few steps and stood on a small, unadorned porch in front of a heavy, windowless oak door and stared at three unmarked buzzers. Shrugging, I pressed the buzzer on the far left and heard a tinny buzz echoing from somewhere inside. I looked around. There was a detached three-stall garage and a fenced backyard. A crackly voice asked, "Who is it?"

"Josie Prescott for Lina."

There was a flicker of static, then silence, and then the oak door opened about three inches. A petite woman peeked out, then stepped onto the porch, shutting the door behind her. I could hear a dog barking inside. She was of average height but small-framed. She wore a blue sweater and gray slacks, cool colors for a sunny spring day.

"Lina?"

"Yes, I'm Lina."

"I'm Josie Prescott."

"Oh, hi! That stupid intercom. I couldn't really hear what you said. You're Gretchen's boss. She's told me so much about you."

"Oh, no!" I joked.

She smiled a little. "All good, I promise."

"Have you heard from her?"

She shook her head. "Nothing. You?"

"No." I saw only worry in her eyes. "I spoke to Mandy. She told me you're Gretchen's best friend, so I was really hoping you'd know something—anything."

She shook her head. "That's very sweet, but I don't know why Mandy would say that. Maybe because I've known Gretchen for a long time."

"If you're not her best friend, who is?"

She shrugged. "I don't know. Gretchen's pretty private."

A recurring theme. "Have you talked to the police?" I asked.

"Yesterday. Why?"

"I was wondering if you had any news."

She shook her head again. "Nothing. It's all so strange and frightening."

I couldn't think of anything else to ask. I wished she'd invite me in. "If she contacts you, please ask her to call me, okay? I want her to know that no matter what happened, I'll help."

"Sure. Except I doubt I'll hear from her."

I gave her my business card and left, feeling that on some level I knew less than when I'd arrived.

Back at Prescott's, I entered the building through the tag sale shack. Eric and the part-timers were already at work. He stood by the inside door, huddling with his team. I waved hello to everyone, gestured that he should continue, and leaned against the back wall, listening in.

"We have a lot of glassware this week. As we bring it out, we'll line everything up on this table, and then, once we can see it all, we'll decide how to arrange it. Keep an eye out for some yellow bowls," Eric told them, referring to the small collection of Depression glass we'd acquired when an older couple, preparing to downsize, decided to sell off most of their collection. "We don't want to just mix them in with the regular stuff. We'll do something to make them stand out."

"Like what?" a new part-timer asked.

"Usually we create levels by covering plastic milk crates with tablecloths. Sometimes we put glasses on a tray. Once we even set a table with napkins and plates and everything." He shrugged. "Any other ideas to make the inventory look good, we're open!"

I caught his eye and mouthed, "Great job!" and waved, confident that when I returned, the Depression glass would be cleverly displayed.

As I stepped into the front office, Cara was dusting her desk—

Gretchen's desk. Sasha looked up from a catalogue she was reading. Fred was typing something.

"Any news about Gretchen?" Sasha asked.

I shook my head. "Not yet."

The phone rang. Cara answered, then put the caller on hold and told me it was Phil. Phil's Exeter-based auction company was known as a reliable source for architectural items, stocking everything from hinges and molding to fences and gates. He wouldn't have called if he didn't have something he knew I'd want. I had Cara tell him I'd be right with him and dashed upstairs.

"Josie," he said, "how ya doing?"

We were planning an auction of architectural remnants called Architectural Antiques in August. For two years, we'd worked to amass and catalogue an impressive collection of objects, both those that are generally available, like early nineteenth-century flooring and windows, and those that are harder to find, like built-in bookcases. I'd put the word out among local dealers that I was in the market for any high-end architectural antiques that came their way. Given the trend to rip down old structures to build new ones, there was no shortage of inventory, but as in all aspects of the business, most of the available objects were run-of-the-mill, not distinctive. From dolls to porcelain and from furniture to paintings, it was routine and easy to acquire objects but labor-intensive and difficult to acquire *good* objects.

All antiques dealers depend on pickers—itinerant sellers of antiques and collectibles. Pickers have favorite dealers for various items, giving the first look to those dealers known to pay a premium, which most dealers can do only when they specialize in a certain category. I didn't know who Phil's pickers were, but he sure had an in with someone.

His voice sounded husky, as if he had a bad cold.

"You okay, Phil? You sound a little rough around the edges."

"Got one of those damn colds going around. I'm okay. Listen, are you still interested in architectural antiques?"

"Definitely," I replied. I crossed my fingers. "What do you have?"

"I just got in a few nineteenth-century locks. I know for sure there's no gems, but they're pretty ornate."

My excitement waned. Because houses have so many doors, locks are fairly commonplace and sell for less than custom pieces like hand-carved mantels or decorative painted boards. *Supply and demand,* I thought. In an unregulated marketplace, it was one of the chief determinants of value. Still, there was a strong market for ornate antique hardware.

Phil named the price range he had in mind. "You can tell me what you think when you see them."

"That's fine, Phil," I agreed. Phil and I had a history of fair dealing. "I'll send Sasha or Fred over to look at them and settle up with you."

"I'll be heading out for lunch soon. If I'm not here, one of my guys can handle it."

I left it to Sasha to decide who should go to Phil's place to examine the locks and make the offer, then followed company protocol and signed out a video camera. I lugged the carry case to my car along with the supplies I'd need to pack up Gretchen's objects.

CHAPTER TEN

T he Chevy with the Tennessee plates was still there, increasing the probability, I thought, that it was, in fact, the murder victim's car. I wondered what it would take for the police to be able to impound it.

I climbed the steps to Gretchen's unit and discovered Detective Brownley standing at the rail, looking out over the pond. The sun was lost behind thickening clouds. It looked like rain. She greeted me, slit the police tape that sealed the door, and let us in.

"Thanks for telling me about Mandy," she said as we entered.

"You're welcome. You know about Lina, too, right?"

"Gretchen has lots of friends," she said.

"Any news about her?" I asked, aware that she hadn't answered my question.

"Nothing firm. Lots of avenues to look at."

Her answer seemed purposefully vague, and her watchful eyes didn't invite follow-up questions.

I turned to face the six small plates Gretchen had hung in her dining area.

"When we leave here, I'll go with you so you can get me a dupe of your video recording," Detective Brownley said. "I'll give you a receipt for any items you remove. You'll need to sign a statement saying that they'll stay under lock and key unless you're working with them, and if they're out of the safe, they're under your direct supervision. Okay?"

"As long as you can include Sasha and Fred in that, we're fine. They're both bonded, so there shouldn't be a problem. Eric also has access to the safe, and he's bonded, too, but he won't be working on them."

She agreed that would be acceptable.

Holding the video recorder steady, I described what I saw, starting with the six fruit plates. With Detective Brownley looking on, I packed them up, wrapping each plate individually in several layers of bubble wrap.

"Do you have an ID on the victim yet?" I asked, wondering if she'd answer.

She didn't reply right away, maybe deciding whether to respond at all. I kept my eyes on my work. I didn't want her to think I was challenging her in any way.

"No," she said finally.

I looked up. "I'm surprised."

She shrugged. "Sometimes it takes time. Don't read anything into it. No news is no news."

I nodded, picked up the camera, and walked over to the pedestal. The thin coating of dust surrounding the circle measured eight inches, a common base size for a variety of bowls and vases. "Mandy told me that Gretchen kept a vase here. A blue-patterned Asian-style vase about eighteen inches high."

Detective Brownley jotted a note. After I recorded the pedestal, I did a slow survey of the room.

"What are you looking for?" Detective Brownley asked.

"Nothing in particular. I just want to be sure I'm not missing something. So far I haven't seen anything else that stands out."

She followed my gaze. "That looks good," she said, pointing to a Picasso print framed in black metal.

"Picasso's great," I acknowledged, "but it's a reproduction, so for our purposes, there's nothing to appraise." I nodded toward three other contemporary art prints that adorned the walls. "Those are repros, too. The furniture is pretty standard fare. The fireplace screen looks new."

I stared at the fireplace tool set. My heart leapt into my throat as I pictured the angry red mark on the dead man's head. Suddenly I was parched. I coughed as I tried to speak, finally managing to say, "The poker's missing."

Detective Brownley nodded. "We have it. It's at the lab."

I was willing to bet that the poker had been used as a weapon. Someone had slashed at the murder victim, and an off-center or off-balance blow had struck his skull. I shivered, then forced myself to continue my inspection. I walked into the bedroom. The mattress rested on a metal frame. There was no headboard. The bedside tables were wicker. The only object on the particleboard desk was a mouse pad.

"Did you take her computer?" I asked.

"Yes. For forensic examination."

Framed botanical prints, the kind we sold for twenty dollars each, were the only art in the room. Her clothes were neatly organized in the double-wide closet. I pulled a hatbox off the top shelf. It contained a jumble of belts.

In the kitchen, I opened drawers and cupboards and saw no antiques or collectibles. She owned no silver, fine porcelain, or crystal, nor were there empty shelves implying that a theft had occurred. There was nothing remarkable in the linen closet or bathroom. When I was done, I said, "I don't see any photographs. Did you find any—maybe in an album or a scrapbook, anything like that?"

"Why do you ask?"

"Some photos have value, and they might be traceable." I shrugged. "If nothing else, we might see pictures of the vase."

Detective Brownley nodded. "We haven't found any photographs."

"How about on her computer? Lots of people have gone digital."

She shook her head.

I thought about that for a moment. "Isn't it unusual for someone to have *no* photographs?"

She weighed her words. "People are different. I get the impression that Ms. Brock is pretty private."

I nodded. "But one man's 'private' is another man's 'secretive,' right? It's all in the perception."

She looked around. "What do you call a design style like this? It's pretty simple, right?"

"Minimalist."

She nodded. "So it looks like Gretchen isn't the kind of person who leaves a lot of personal things around."

I considered her comment. "At work she has a couple of photos taped to the side of her computer. Trolls on top, too."

"Right. One photo is of the beach and the other is of Halloween decorations. She has no photos of people."

"That's true," I said, nodding, thinking about what that might imply. "Was there anything of interest on her home computer?"

"We're still looking into it," she said, her tone cool and neutral, and I understood her unspoken message—she wasn't going to discuss that aspect of the investigation with me.

"Have you found anything on the computer or in her files that might help me with the appraisal? A past appraisal, a bill of sale, a handwritten note from somebody giving Gretchen one of the plates as a gift, that sort of thing?"

Detective Brownley shook her head. "No paperwork or online records."

"I mean her paid bills. Some people tuck receipts and appraisals into a 'Miscellaneous' file, for instance."

"I knew what you meant. Gretchen kept no paperwork. She paid her bills online but kept no receipts."

I thought about it for several seconds. "How about charge card records? Maybe she used a credit card to buy the object that's missing from here."

"We'll check. We've ordered copies of the charges from her bank."

"A safety deposit box?"

"If she has one, it's not in New Hampshire," Detective Brownley replied.

Another question for Wes, I thought. In the past, he'd used his sources to ferret out financial information that the police couldn't access without a warrant and private citizens couldn't access at all. Thinking of Wes got me wondering what he was up to and what he'd written in today's *Seacoast Star.* I had so many questions and so few answers. Only one question really mattered, though. Where was Gretchen?

We were about to leave the apartment when I stopped short, struck by a sudden realization. Maybe the object that had sat on the pedestal would provide a clue to Gretchen's whereabouts, maybe not, but there had to be a reason it was, apparently, the only item in the entire apartment that was missing.

CHAPTER ELEVEN

D etective Brownley followed me back to Prescott's so I could give her a copy of the recording I'd made and a receipt for the items I'd taken. After she left and I had explained to Sasha and Fred the need to keep the plates in the safe unless they were being worked on, we discussed the next steps.

"My guess is that the basic valuation will be pretty straight ahead," I said, "but it would be great if we could figure out where the plates came from. For instance, if we can learn that Gretchen bought one of them at a shop in, say, Bangor, we can check whether anyone in the shop recognizes her. Maybe she's from Bangor, and when she found a dead man in her apartment, she ran home. Do you see what I mean?"

Sahsa nodded. Fred pushed his glasses up and asked, "Any records?"

"No, not so far. The police are looking into it. So, what will you do first?"

Fred shrugged and said, "Complete a basic assessment of each one."

"Given the urgency," Sasha said, "I think we should try to trace each purchase first, then determine its value."

"Which will be easier," Fred argued, "the more we know about the plates themselves."

"Actually, the first thing we should do is to identify specific marks or numbers. If any of the plates come from a limited edition, that'll be a shortcut," Sasha stated.

"To valuation, maybe, but it won't help us trace Gretchen's acquisition at all—you can tell by looking that none of them is unique."

"I can't believe you're saying that!" Sasha exclaimed. "You should know that superficial examinations are merely a starting place, not an educated judgment. At this point, we know nothing."

As they continued their good-natured squabble, I realized that I had additional—and more important—questions to ask Lina. I surreptitiously glanced at the wall clock.

"Well," I said, "I'll leave you two to it. One thing, though. It looks like the object that sat on the pedestal in Gretchen's living room was a vase." I described it. "Does either of you know anything about it?"

They both said no.

I turned to Cara. "How are you doing?"

"Pretty well. I'm trying to follow the Hippocratic oath—first, do no harm!"

"That's a pretty good approach. I approve! I have an errand. I'll be back in an hour or so. Any questions before I go?"

"No, I think I'm okay . . . oh, wait . . . I forgot to give you a message." She extracted a white slip of paper, torn from our WHILE YOU WERE OUT call log.

"Thanks," I said. The note read: JACK STENE CALLED FOR GRETCHEN. I had no idea who Jack Stene was. *Maybe he works for one of our vendors,* I thought. His callback number started with the 207 area code. Maine. "Did he say what he wanted?"

"No. He just asked for her, and when I said she wasn't here, he thanked me and hung up."

I shrugged and smiled. "A mystery!" I said.

As I approached the Bow Street Emporium, I observed Lina waiting on a customer, but she didn't see me. I entered, setting the sleigh bells ringing. A young woman with strawberry blond hair and big brown eyes approached me with a pleasant smile.

"May I help you?" she asked.

"Thanks, no. I'll just look around," I replied.

I edged my way toward the display of hand-dipped candles, where Lina stood talking to a man. As I approached, she thanked him and pointed to the cashier. He walked away holding a box of beeswax candles.

"Hi, Lina."

"Oh," she said, recognizing me. "Hi."

"May I ask you something? I don't mean to interrupt you at work, but it's important."

She glanced at the sparsely populated store. "I'm the manager on duty, so I guess it's okay."

"Thanks," I said, following her to a corner. She positioned us out of earshot and stood with her back to the wall so she could observe the store. "I'll be as brief as I can. First, when did you last speak to Gretchen?"

"On her way back from the airport."

"You picked her up?"

"Yeah. At the Circle."

"Then you took her to get her car."

"Right."

"How did she seem?" I asked.

"Excited. She said she had a great time in Hawaii. She met a guy from somewhere outside of Portland—a chemist working for a small biotech firm. She was psyched." The door opened, and three women entered. One of them waved to Lina, who waved back. She turned to me. "Sorry," she said. "I've got to get back to work."

I told her I'd love to stay in touch, and she agreed, hastily giving me her cell phone number.

I left the shop, frustrated because I hadn't had a chance to ask about Gretchen's plants or the missing vase. Unsure of what to do next, I walked across the street and stood under the Blue Dolphin's copper overhang. Even from this distance, I could tell that Lina had a friendly manner, smiling and maintaining good eye contact. I bet she was a terrific saleswoman.

Vince drove by and stopped in front of the store. He glanced around and spotted me. I nodded and sort of smiled, acknowledging that I recognized him. He nodded back, but he didn't smile.

Mandy stepped out from somewhere in the back of the showroom, smiling, an oversized purse on her shoulder. She was taller and bigger-boned than Lina. She said something to Lina, and they both laughed. Mandy's eyes crinkled engagingly. I suspected that she was a terrific saleswoman, too. She hurried outside and stepped into Vince's Jeep. He drove away without looking at me again.

I stopped at a deli to pick up a sandwich for lunch and spotted a stack of this morning's *Seacoast Star* under a display of candy bars and gossip magazines.

One glance, and I felt my pulse speed up. I wiggled the issue from the rack. Wes's headline read:

MURDER IN NORTH MILL POND CONDO
PAST MURDER SUSPECT JOSIE PRESCOTT QUESTIONED BY POLICE

Annoyed at Wes, I placed the paper on the counter headline down, paid for everything, and ran to my car. As I read the article, my initial anger subsided. I had, in fact, been questioned by the police. I did discover the body. No charges had been filed. Everyone who worked at Prescott's had been interviewed.

I even learned some new things: According to the medical examiner's preliminary report, the man had been struck in the head, but it was a non-life-threatening blow. *I was right,* I thought; *he was hit with Gretchen's poker.* The cause of death was a gunshot wound to the chest, and the probable time of death was Wednesday between 11:00 A.M. and 1:00 P.M. I thought about that timing, then continued reading. The rest of the article was classic Wes—bloodthirsty innuendo implying that Gretchen was the killer.

My finger hovered over the button to call and chastise him both for putting my name in the headline and for his treatment of Gretchen, but I didn't.

I took the long way to give myself time to assimilate everything I'd discovered. I got occasional glimpses of gentle waves as I drove along Ocean Avenue. Golden flecks glinted on the smooth surface of the ocean, and the soft rolling motion of the water quieted my lingering agitation.

Back at Prescott's, I saw Eric on his knees doing something under a big round pedestal display table in the tag sale shack.

One of the part-timers was working on a display of gardening implements, while another arranged sterling silver serving pieces in a display case. A third was organizing plastic-encased copies of *Life* magazine by date.

Eric reached his hand up and moved the table a little bit. It shimmied.

"Hi, Eric," I said, squatting next to him. "What's up? Wiggly table syndrome?"

"Yeah," he answered, his voice muffled. "I think I've got it." He touched the table again and nodded, satisfied. "I used a shim." He stood up. "Any news about Gretchen?"

I shook my head. "I don't think so." I glanced around, then added, "Things look like they're coming along."

He nodded. "Yeah, except that I still think we're a little light in quality items."

"I'll pick out a couple of super-dupers."

I left him to his work and walked across the warehouse to the front office. Cara was on the phone, giving directions. Fred was on the phone, too, asking someone named Mr. Wragge whether the map had any rips or tears. I didn't know what map he was referring to. Sasha had one of Gretchen's fruit plates in her hand and was frowning at it.

"I don't think we're going to learn anything from these," she said. "Without documentation, there's nothing to trace. They're really wonderful examples, though. Gretchen has excellent taste and a good eye."

I nodded. "Any news on Phil's locks?"

"Yes. Fred says there's nothing special, but we got them for a song. Phil wasn't there, but Johnny said Phil just wanted them gone."

"Well, at least we got a bargain."

"Detective Brownley dropped off the belt buckle. It's in the safe, bottom left, number four."

"Great!" I glanced at the clock. It was almost two. I walked across the warehouse to the far corner, where a walk-in vault the size of a room was positioned against a wall. I spun the dial, heard the clicks as the tumblers fell into place, and opened the door. Separate lockboxes, ranging in size from two to twelve feet square, were positioned around the perimeter—safes within a safe, extra security and an easy way to keep everything organized. An index card slid into a slot on the front of each lockbox and served as a sign-in/sign-out log. Unit four, on the bottom left-hand shelf, was labeled BELT BUCKLE. The first entry noted when Sasha had placed it in the box. I slid the card from the slot, annotated it with my name and the date and time I was removing the box, and replaced the card. I used the master key that hung on the ring at my waist to open the box.

The belt buckle was in a see-through plastic evidence bag. I held it up to the light. The old Native American man was looking left, his features in repose. He was wearing a lavishly feathered headdress and what appeared to be war paint, but he didn't look warlike. I turned it over. There was a seam, a raised ridge, which meant it had been produced from a mold. There were several marks, but no signature visible to the naked eye. The primary mark was a large *H* in a double-edged circle. Below it, in a smaller font, were the characters "SFC 79" and "3."

I spun the wheel on the vault door to lock it and returned to the front office.

Sasha had her headset on. She was typing while asking someone about the hard paste porcelain that had been used at the Richard Ginori factory in Milan.

Fred was reading something on his monitor. He looked up as I approached his desk, and I handed him the plastic bag. "Did you see this, Fred?"

"No," he replied, removing it from the bag and looking at it with laserlike focus. "What do we know besides that it's not custom?"

"Nothing. The man killed at Gretchen's was wearing it. What's your take on it?"

"It's well designed, but my guess would be that it's not particularly valuable—it's molded. Most likely brass, modern era. We can probably trace the marks—and maybe the mold."

The phone rang, and Cara answered with a pleasant "Prescott's. How may I help you?"

I nodded to Fred. "That's what I thought, too. I don't know about the value, though. It looks like a limited run, and the mold has great detailing, very high quality."

"Hold on, please," Cara said. "Josie, it's Wes Smith for you."

I felt my irritation return. "Tell him I don't want to talk to him."

Cara hesitated, her mouth opening.

"Go ahead. Tell him that. He'll know why."

She repeated my words, then listened for a moment. She pushed the hold button again. "He said to tell you he understands, but it's urgent."

"Tell him ha. Just that. Say, 'Josie says ha.'"

I was aware that Fred was watching our exchange as if it were a tennis match, but I didn't care. I was too angry.

Cara followed my instructions, listened for several seconds, then said, "Oh, my. All right." She placed Wes on hold again. "He said to tell you that he has urgent, crucial information about Gretchen."

I pursed my lips and grabbed the spare phone that sat near the photocopier and punched the button to take him off hold. "What is it, Wes?"

"I'm sorry, Josie. I didn't write the headline. My editor did. I didn't even see it until this morning. It was a last-minute thing."

I felt my resentment drain away. It wouldn't be the first time his editor revised his headline. I sighed deeply. "Fair enough. What's the information about Gretchen?"

"Not on the phone. It's too sensitive," he said, dropping his voice conspiratorially. "Can you meet now?"

I was about to tell him to forget it when I thought about the many times Wes had fleshed out facts and given me information I couldn't have gotten in any other way—far more often than he'd failed. He never bragged or engaged in hyperbole, either. If he said he knew something significant about Gretchen, he did, and if he had news about Gretchen, I wanted it. "All right," I agreed. "Where?"

"Our dune?"

"Fifteen minutes," I said. I hung up and turned to Cara. "Sorry about that, Cara."

"No problem. Do you think he really has information about Gretchen?" she asked.

"Maybe," I replied. "He's got his teeth into something." I turned to Fred. "Will you take a crack at the circle-*H* mark?"

"You bet," he said, swiveling to face his computer.

I grabbed my sandwich and headed to the beach.

CHAPTER TWELVE

I spread out the old wool blanket that I kept in my trunk. From where I sat at the top of the dune overlooking Rocky Point beach, I had a clear view of the ocean.

Wes and I had met at this dune frequently over the years. It was private and convenient to get to, and we could see people approaching from any direction long before they reached us. I nibbled my sandwich and waited for him to arrive.

I heard his car sputter to a stop at the sandy edge of the road and watched as he stepped over wild rose bushes and sidestepped up the dune. He wore a leather jacket I'd never seen before. He handed me a cup of coffee, milk, no sugar; a peace offering.

"I am sorry," he said. "As soon as I saw the headline, I knew you'd hate it. The one I submitted read 'Murder in North Mill Pond Condo: Apartment Owner Missing.' "

"That's better writing," I said, accepting the coffee, a little touched that he'd bought it for me—and that he'd remembered how I took it.

"Thanks. So . . . about Gretchen. I've got a real shockeroonie. It's about her background." He lowered his voice. "Her Social Security number."

"What about it?"

"It's only seven years old," he revealed.

"So what?" I asked.

"It was *issued* seven years ago," he stressed. "Don't you see what that means? What happened seven years ago that made her get a new Social Security number?"

"I don't know. Seven years ago, she would have been twenty-two."

"Why does someone get a new Social Security number at age twenty-two?"

I paused, considering his question. "Maybe the social security card isn't *new,* per se. If she never had one before, she'd have to get one when she started working. Isn't it possible that she didn't apply for a job until she was twenty-two? Maybe she went to college and didn't work until after she graduated."

"You don't know if she went to college?" he asked, sounding surprised.

"No."

He shook his head, his eyes fiery alive. "She'd have a Social Security number whether she had a job or not. Everyone does . . . just like you have to file tax forms whether you owe money or not. You need it for health insurance, too, right?"

I nodded. "I guess, but isn't it possible that she lost her original card and just signed up for a new one? That must happen all the time," I remarked.

"This one wasn't issued as a replacement—it's *new.* Why?"

I looked into his eyes, trying to understand why he seemed so excited. *Is he saying she's engaged in some sort of scam?* I asked myself, shocked that he could even think such a thing about Gretchen. *Don't waste time on pointless indignation,* I warned myself. *Think objectively. How could it work?*

Wes watched me think, his expressive eyes alerting me that he thought he had the answer.

How could I use a new Social Security card to get money? Credit card fraud, I thought all at once. *With a fake Social Security number, I could build a new credit history, get lots of credit lines and personal loans—and use it all. I'd run up huge tabs, then ditch the identity, running out on the bills.*

Although my idea fit the facts, I just didn't believe it. *Gretchen's not a crook.*

"Have you checked her finances?" I asked, knowing that if he'd done so, a fraud like the one I'd imagined might have surfaced.

"Always. It's mind-blowing how often money—or the lack of it—figures into crimes. In this case, there's nothing there. She pays her bills on time, has no debt except for her mortgage, and has decent savings."

"Any unusual purchasing patterns?" I asked, enormously relieved to hear that my instinct about Gretchen was right on.

"You're thinking credit card fraud, am I right?" Wes asked.

I shrugged, unwilling to acknowledge that I'd had such a thought.

" 'Cause there's no sign of it. No unsecured loans, no credit lines, no multiple credit cards with huge amounts of cash available. Nada. Plus, she doesn't charge a lot—a few dinners out a month, some clothes, gas, groceries—and she pays in full every month."

I nodded, not surprised. "What do you think it means?" I asked, not wanting to hear his thoughts but wanting to know.

"She's on the run," he said. "I figure she jumped bail. I'm checking with bounty hunters now."

"That's crazy!" I protested, shaking my head. "Gretchen is no criminal."

"Maybe you just don't know her as well as you think you do."

I stared at him, stunned. *No way!* I thought, reacting emotionally, then felt vindicated as I realized that his miserable speculation couldn't be true—objectively. "It's not possible, Wes. My insurance company conducts background checks on all employees. If Gretchen had a criminal record, she wouldn't have passed."

"There's got to be a catch," he said, sounding displeased that she might have a stellar record after all.

"Oh, my God!" I exclaimed, suddenly realizing the flaw in my reasoning. My heart plummeted. "She passed with her *new* number. The insurance company wasn't checking how long the Social Security number had been in force, just that there were no wants or warrants associated with it."

"Got ya!" Wes responded, energized again. "If she's on the run, no way would she have been okayed under her *original* Social Security number. Which is why she had to get a *new* one."

I stared out over the ocean and considered Wes's idea on its merits. Gray-white clouds streaked from west to east, propelled by a fast-moving wind. To the south, clouds were static and thickening.

Could Gretchen really have a criminal past? I wondered. Then

I remembered one additional fact, and the depression that had begun to weigh on me began to lift. I looked up and met his eyes.

"They do a fingerprint check, too," I told him. "If her prints were on file, they would have found the record. A new Social Security number wouldn't have protected her."

Wes looked disappointed, which was logical, since I knew he'd much rather discover dirt about people than learn they were clean. It wasn't that he was mean-spirited. Wes was a diligent reporter seeking the truth. To him, dirt was a means to an end: Dirt often led to secrets, and secrets often led to news.

"So why is she on the lam?" he asked.

"We don't know that she is."

"Give me another reason to explain her getting a new Social Security number."

"I don't know," I said, then had a startling thought. I looked at him, stricken.

"What is it?" he asked, his eyes boring into mine.

"Witness protection," I whispered.

He leaned back, bracing himself on the palms of his hands, and gave a low whistle. "You know, you may have hit on something."

"How can we find out?"

He shook his head. "No contact of mine would even discuss it." He paused. "If I can find her picture in some news report describing a past crime in which she was a key witness . . ." he mused, his voice trailing off.

"You won't find anything," I stated, discouraged and upset. "How can you possibly survey all the newspapers in the country for a photo of a person whose name you don't know?"

"Maybe I can; maybe I can't. For sure I won't find it if I don't even try."

My worry-meter ratcheted up. If Gretchen was in witness protection, it was because she'd seen something or she knew something that put her at immediate and grave risk. What had she seen? A mob hit? A corrupt government official moving beyond white-collar crime into some deadly enterprise? A terrorist making a bomb? Had she run back to the U.S. Marshals? Or had she just run?

"According to my police source, eight calls came into Prescott's and three to Gretchen's apartment from disposable cell phones," Wes said, and I turned in his direction.

"So they can't be traced," I said.

"Right. There's more. Gretchen's apartment was wiped clean—except for one fingerprint."

"Wiped clean?" I repeated, forcing myself to put aside my apprehension and listen to Wes's words. "So what? Maybe Gretchen's a good housekeeper."

"That's not what I'm talking about. Somebody wiped surfaces people naturally touch—doorknobs, light switches, that sort of thing—but not all of them. There are fingerprints, yours and Meryl's, and presumably Gretchen's, on her bedroom closet door pull, as you'd expect, but not on the front door's inside knob. They're on the bedroom light switch but not the living room or kitchen switches. See what I mean?"

I gaped.

"Guess where the print is?" Wes asked, his eyes shining with intelligence.

I shook my head.

"On a carton of milk in the refrigerator."

I continued to stare at him for a long moment, trying to take in the significance of his revelation. "Gretchen left milk in the fridge for two weeks?"

"Nope! There's only one store nearby that carries that brand—a convenience store. From the codes, they can tell that this carton was part of a lot delivered Wednesday morning—the day of the murder. Which means that someone bought the milk *that very day*."

"Can they identify the buyer?"

"No. The clerks say they're so busy they don't remember anyone, and there's no security camera."

I nodded. "And the fingerprint doesn't match anyone in the system, am I right?"

"Right. So . . . my source tells me you have information about a friend who was going over to Gretchen's place to water plants. It's possible that she picked up the milk en route."

Who's Wes's source? I wondered for the thousandth time. At first, I'd been shocked at Wes's ability to learn almost anything about almost anyone from his mysterious "sources." Then I realized that, almost by definition, experts in every field have access to an array of sources within their universe. I could pick up the phone, for instance, and reach the most influential and knowledgeable leaders in most aspects of art and antiques from Elizabethan decorative arts to Native American textiles to pre-Columbian pottery and everything in between. Wes's universe included police and accountants and bounty hunters—and me.

"It would be a friendly gesture to bring in milk for a friend returning home after a two-week vacation." I thought for a moment. "Maybe Gretchen stopped at a grocery store on her way back to her apartment after picking up her car. Is the print on the milk carton the same as the one on the closet door or bedroom light switch—presumably Gretchen's?"

"The police are checking with your insurance company to get a sample of Gretchen's prints, but it doesn't seem likely that it's hers. It's a different print—*and* it's the only one in the whole place that's different."

I nodded.

"But you just raised a good point. How did she get home from Logan? Do you know?"

"Yes—she took the bus to Portsmouth Circle, and her friend Lina drove her to get her car."

"She picked up her car? Why didn't you tell me?" he asked, sounding a little hurt.

"I assumed you knew."

"I didn't. Fill me in."

I repeated what Fern Adams, Gretchen's neighbor, had told the police in my hearing about Gretchen's car and described my morning visit to the Heron dealer. Wes took a single sheet of lined paper from an inside pocket and wrote as I spoke.

When he finished, I asked, "Why do you think it's taking so long to ID the victim?"

"According to my source, the victim's fingers are scarred, and while that doesn't *change* his prints, it makes ID'ing him tougher."

"What do scars have to do with anything?" I asked, confused. "Wouldn't a scar show up when they print someone?"

Wes shook his head. "Sure, but if you're constantly getting scars, the prints won't match. I mean, they will, but it's a tougher job to match them because some of the injuries are older and healed, but others are new. Based on the condition of his fingers, they've concluded that he works with his hands. So maybe they can trace him through his occupation."

"Oh, I see. Like if he's a carpenter, they could survey general contractors to see if anyone knows him."

"Exactly."

"What about his DNA?"

"The FBI databank is as close as we come to a national registry, but not all criminals' DNA is sent in. Unless the crime involved is a federal offense, every state follows its own rules about both the collection of data—DNA and fingerprints—and its submission to the FBI. Some states require DNA samples from all people convicted of a felony, but others require it only if the felony conviction results in jail time. If the guy gets probation—guess what? In *that* state, no DNA is collected." Wes shook his head. "According to the FBI and the state of Tennessee, neither the victim's prints nor his DNA is in the system, and Sal Briscoe, the guy from Tennessee who owns the Chevy parked outside of Gretchen's place, has no criminal record under that name. Of course, that may be a red herring, since they don't know if the victim *is* Sal Briscoe. Maybe he's just some schlub who stole Sal Briscoe's car, you know? Or maybe his presence in Gretchen's apartment is completely unrelated to Sal's car. The police have asked a judge to impound it so they can investigate."

I'd wondered about that possibility, I recalled. Surely the car would provide meaningful information to help find Gretchen.

"Since neither the victim's prints nor his DNA is in the FBI's databank," Wes added, ticking off points on his fingers as he made them, "they know he's never been convicted of a federal crime or a felony in a state that submits fingerprints and/or DNA samples, that he's never applied for a federal job or a license that requires fingerprinting, and that he wasn't in the military."

"All negatives," I remarked, thinking that in some way, police investigatory procedures mimicked the process of appraising antiques. In both circumstances, when you got rid of all the false leads and dead ends, you either knew the truth or you knew you'd probably never discover it.

"Goes with the territory," he said, flipping his hands palms up. "Anything else you can tell me?"

"Nothing," I said. "I wish I had news to share."

He nodded. "Talk soon," he said and slid down the dune.

After Wes left, I sat for a while longer. That Gretchen was in the witness protection program was possible, I supposed, but it seemed so darned implausible. Still, I was aware of a niggling fear that something larger and more dangerous than I could even imagine was happening just out of my range of vision.

There was too much I didn't know. For instance, if Gretchen *was* in the witness protection program—why? What unseen and unknown factors were at work? Had someone she'd testified against hunted her down? Had the killer found her there with the man and shot him, on purpose or by mistake? Or had the murderer brought him there to die—perhaps as a warning to Gretchen?

"Gretchen is no criminal," I whispered aloud, but even as I spoke the words, I knew that my avowal expressed more prayer than conviction. *Someone,* I thought, *must have answers.* Then I thought again of Lina.

As I began the drive back to my office, I realized that I didn't even know her last name. Deciding not to waste another minute, I pulled off to the side of the road next to a tangle of spiky grasses and called the Bow Street Emporium.

"Lina," I said, when I reached her, "this is Josie Prescott. I was thinking—may I buy you a drink or a cup of coffee after work?"

There was a pause, and I wondered what she was debating.

"Sure," she said. "I get off at six today."

As soon as I walked into Prescott's, Cara asked about my meeting with Wes.

I chose my words carefully, wanting to tell the truth while protecting Gretchen's privacy. "Wes did a background check and reported what I already knew from our insurance company's security review—Gretchen has no criminal record." I flipped up my hand. "Much ado about nothing. Where's Fred?"

"In the tag sale room," Cara said. "He wanted to look at some of the half-dolls to make sure they shouldn't be saved for the auction."

"Good deal. I'll be in the warehouse. Eric needs some high-end items."

I didn't want to break up a collection just to seed the tag sale, which eliminated snow globes, American Arts and Crafts pottery, tinplate toys, beaded silk dresses, Mission furniture, writing implements, and eighteenth-century fine bindings.

Nothing grabbed me except two stoppered perfume bottles, a Bischoff yellow and a Viking purple, both from about 1960. The three-tiered, rounded Bischoff was worth somewhere around three hundred dollars; the bell-shaped one from Viking, formerly known as the New Martinsville Glass Company, would sell at auction for about six hundred dollars. If I priced them 20 percent lower than their auction estimates, they'd be real finds for a collector or a fan. They'd be perfect, except they were too fragile and rare to be good candidates for the tag sale.

I stepped into the walk-in vault to scan the shelves where miscellaneous valuable objects were stored.

Almost immediately, my eye lit on two high-quality, expertly framed bird prints from John James Audubon's *Birds of America*, a whooping crane and a rose-breasted grosbeak. We'd been hopeful they were originals, which is why they were in the safe, but they weren't. They were first-rate copies, though; the color reproduction was extraordinarily detailed and exact, and their condition was excellent.

I nodded and reached for them. At auction, I knew each would sell for about four hundred dollars. I'd have Eric price them at $319 each. With any luck, the buyers wouldn't be able to stop talking about the great finds they discovered at Prescott's tag sale.

As I was swinging the door closed, I saw a small padded envelope that I'd never noticed before. There was only one word on it, written in block letters: GRETCHEN. The envelope rested on its side between a Plexiglas display case housing some fine jewelry that was scheduled to be appraised by a visiting gemologist and a box of ephemera that had come from the estate of a former Miss Vermont who went on to place third in the Miss America pageant.

Gretchen must have put it in here before she went on vacation, I thought. *How could I have missed it? Since she's been gone, I've popped in and out a gazillion times.* Apparently I'd been so preoccupied I hadn't noticed.

I reached for it, then stopped. I knew better. I backed out and spun the wheel to lock the safe, carried the bird prints into the front office, and called Detective Brownley on her cell phone.

"I found something," I told her. "An envelope with Gretchen's name on it, in our safe."

"Don't touch it. I'm on my way."

"I won't. I haven't," I assured her, but she'd already hung up.

I paced, too keyed up to do anything else. I could barely stop myself from running back to the vault and ripping into the envelope to discover the secrets it contained.

CHAPTER THIRTEEN

etective Brownley stepped into the office ten minutes later. The concrete warehouse was cold, and sounds echoed.

"Do you know anything about the envelope?" she asked, her voice reverberating. How it got there? Or who might have touched it?"

"I called you as soon as I saw it, and I haven't asked anyone anything about it. As for me, I have never seen it before, and I didn't touch it."

Detective Brownley stood off to the side as I unlocked the steel door and swung it wide.

"There," I said, pointing.

She snapped on plastic gloves, took a pencil from her pocket, and used the eraser end to ease the envelope out. When it was an inch or so beyond the shelf's edge, she toppled it into a plastic evidence bag. She probed with the eraser, fussing the unglued top flap open. She aimed the opening toward the light and looked inside. "There are some papers, but it's too dim to see well. Let's go to the office, where the light's better."

We stepped into the front office. Fred was back at his computer. Eric was pouring himself a cup of coffee. Sasha was reading.

I greeted them and told Eric about the bird prints.

Detective Brownley held the bag up and asked, "Have any of you seen this envelope?" Fred, Sasha, and Eric shook their heads. The detective nodded, then went to the round table by the windows.

She squeezed the plastic bag, forcing open the envelope, and tried to see inside, then turned it upside down and shook it. Nothing fell out. Whatever was in there was stuck. Using her pencil eraser, she gentled out the contents, one piece at a time. There was a typed note, a greeting card, and two Polaroid photos.

The typed note read:

```
A Meissen baluster vase of Chinese design.
-- crossed sword mark, left blade off center
and thin at tip
-- "AR" in underglaze blue
I inherited the vase from my mother, Lynne
White. My mother said she bought it in 1949 at
Faring Auctions in Cheyenne for $1,685, but
there's no receipt.
```

The greeting card was a beauty. The illustration on the outside showed a lush garden scene. Inside, the preprinted message read:

For a Special Young Woman
a Special Birthday Wish

Just below that, someone had added a handwritten message:

M,
Never forget this vase's history. You're that strong, too. I just know you are!
A.

I turned my attention to the Polaroids. One photo showed a vase of traditional Chinese design—a bird and garden scene—in shades of ethereal blue. The other showed the marks that the writer described in the typed note. Both the ornate, interwoven "AR" and the rapier-thin crossed swords appeared hand-drawn and stylized. Above the swords were three letters: "JGH."

Detective Brownley looked up. "Do you know where it is?"

"No." I stared at the photo of the vase. "It's a beauty, isn't it?"

"Is it old?"

"Probably."

"How old?"

"I don't know. From the marks, assuming *these* marks are on *this* vase, it's likely that we can date it." I looked up. "Remember the pedestal in Gretchen's apartment? I'll bet this vase is what used to sit on it. Do you want us to see what we can find out about it?"

Detective Brownley looked at me, down at the photo, the card, and the receipt, then back at me. "These have to go to the lab."

"How about if I record them? We can work from the video. If it ever comes to authenticating the documents themselves, we can figure that out then."

"Great. Thank you, Josie."

I got one of our video recorders and carefully shot the note, the card, and both photos, front and back, having her flip each one over with her pencil. All the reverse sides were empty, except the greeting card, and the only text there identified the artist and production company.

As soon as she packed up the documents and left, I turned to Sasha. "Did you follow that? Here," I said, handing her the camera. "You take a look. Fred, you, too."

Fred leaned over her shoulder, absorbing the details. He pushed his glasses up as he stood and returned to his seat.

Sasha's brown eyes were steady and focused. "It's a lovely piece," she said, looking up.

"The marks are Meissen, right?" I asked.

"Right," she said, "but you know how many replicas there are out there. Just by looking, I don't know if this is original or not. Do you?"

"No. How about you, Fred?"

"No, I'm not familiar enough with the marks. Listening to you, my first thought was to go back to Faring Auctions in Cheyenne. If they're still running, they might have records. Sixteen hundred eighty-five dollars back then . . ." He paused to tap something into his computer, then finished his thought. "It's more than fourteen thousand in today's dollars. Lots of places would have a record of something in that price range—even after all these years."

"Have either of you heard of Faring?" I asked. "I haven't, but that doesn't mean anything. As we know, there are scores of small auction houses around the country."

They shook their heads; then Sasha said, "The auction house is definitely worth checking, but we should educate ourselves about the marks first."

"Calling Faring is almost sure to be a shortcut," Fred countered. "They'll either know something useful or they won't, which will help us set the appraisal parameters right off the bat."

"Well, I'll leave you two to figure it out," I interjected, "but keep in mind that it's your top priority. One thing, though, Fred, before you get going. Did you learn anything about the mark on the buckle?"

"Yup. Good news."

He reported that the belt buckle's primary mark, the large *H* enclosed in a double-edged circle, had been used by the Indianapolis-based Harrison Metal Works since 1894 and was still in use today.

"That's great!" I said. "Fast work. I'll try calling them."

I took the buckle upstairs to my office. I easily located Harrison Metal Works' phone number and followed the automated instructions to finally reach a human being. "Hi. My name is Josie Prescott, and I have a question about a belt buckle."

Three transfers later, I reached April, an account executive in the custom promotions department. April understood what I wanted before I finished my explanation.

"Gotcha," she chimed in. "You're in luck, I think. We've just finished computerizing the seventies, and I'm betting the number '79' refers to the year. You can't imagine the nightmare this job has been—but we're making progress! Okey dokey, let's see what we've got here. Tell me the marks again?"

" 'SFC 79' and the number three," I repeated.

"Okay. 'SFC' is probably shorthand for the client, or maybe the artist. Is the design signed? In the mold, I mean? Can you see an artist's signature on the design side?"

"No, not even with a loupe."

"If it was there, you probably wouldn't need a loupe. I mean, whoever heard of an artist signing his name so small you need a magnifying glass to see it!"

"Good point," I agreed, enjoying April's dry humor.

"Darn! 'SFC' isn't there . . . hmmm . . . hold on . . . okay . . . *uh, oh* . . . Houston," she said, lowering her voice a notch, "it looks like we've got another problem . . . okay . . . one sec . . . *oh, brother!* We have no search field for marks or abbreviations—can you believe it? Only for the company's name. If you'd called and asked for a listing of the promotions ordered by XYZ Company, I could have told you in a snap, but we don't have the capacity to search by the mark. *Duh!* I'll alert the IT department. Meanwhile, let me think. How can we find the company you're looking for?"

Her question was rhetorical, but I ventured to suggest an idea. "How about searching through the companies whose names begin with *S*?"

"Yeah, maybe, except that we have over seven hundred customers whose names begin with *S*."

"Okay, then—that calls for plan B!"

"We're up to plan C, I think. Let's try this—let me search two parameters, the year and the first letter, *S,* and see if we can narrow it down."

"That's a good idea."

"Keep your fingers crossed! Here goes nothing!"

While I waited, I swiveled to look out the window. The sky was densely gray. It looked as if the rain would start any minute. *Gretchen,* I wondered, *are you nearby? Can you see the clouds?*

"It worked!" April said seconds later, sounding as excited as I felt. "Okay . . . there are four companies that ordered custom belt buckles in 1979 whose names start with *S*. But there's only one with the initials 'SFC.' Got a pen?"

I wrote the name as she spoke it aloud: Sidlawn Fencing Company. "April, you totally rock. What about the number three? Does your database tell us how many buckles were produced?"

"Ten total. This one must be the third in the series."

"Great. Do you know who got it?"

"Sorry. That's something only Sidlawn would know."

"Can you tell me anything else about the company?"

According to April's records, the Sidlawn Fencing Company was headquartered in Springfield, Illinois, and Harrison Metal Works' contact at the time the order was placed was the Sidlawn Fencing Company CEO's secretary, Laverne Matthews.

I thanked her profusely and took her direct phone number in case I had additional questions.

Springfield, I thought. Located more than a thousand miles from Rocky Point, far enough away to relocate a witness in danger.

Sidlawn Fencing Company wasn't listed in any phone directory I consulted. Googling the company's name got only two hits, both for old information from a defunct Springfield newspaper. According to the archived snippets, Sidlawn Fencing Company won a government contract for chain-link fencing in 1984, and the company's founder and CEO died suddenly of a heart attack in the late 1980s. Apparently the company was out of business. *Now what?* I asked myself.

A soft pattering on the roof told me that it had started to rain, and I glanced outside. The sky had darkened to iron gray.

I turned back to my computer and considered avenues to research, finally settling on contacting the Springfield Chamber of Commerce. Three minutes later I learned that the Sidlawn Fencing Company had changed hands in 1989 when the founder's widow sold it to Belcher Wire, a German conglomerate.

One phone call later, I learned that Belcher Wire still maintained a small manufacturing facility in Springfield. Then I hit a dead end. Neither the receptionist nor the current CEO's assistant, Serena Carson, had ever heard of Laverne Matthews, belt buckle promotions, or Harrison Metal Works.

I bit my lip, thinking for a moment. "Any chance that I could talk to someone who worked for the company in 1979?" I asked Serena.

"Gee, I don't know anyone who's worked for the company that long."

I knew that a question from the CEO's assistant to someone in human resources was far more likely to be answered than one from an outsider with no official standing, if I could convince Serena to make the call. When in doubt, I'd learned over the years, tell the truth. There's nothing as persuasive as the truth, simply told.

"I hate to bother you with this, but it's so important. May I explain a little bit about why I'm asking?"

"Okay," Serena replied, sounding wary.

"I work for a company that appraises and sells antiques and collectibles, and sometimes we help the police. That's what I'm doing now—helping the police try to track a collectible, the belt buckle. I'm wondering—do you think you could call human resources and ask if anyone has worked for the company since the late seventies?"

"What kind of police investigation?" she asked, breathless with curiosity.

"We're trying to identify someone. He was wearing the belt buckle." I took a deep breath. "What do you think, Serena?"

I could almost hear the wheels in her head turning. "I guess I could do that," she said. "I don't see how it could hurt anything."

I expressed my enthusiastic gratitude and prepared to do one of my least favorite things: wait.

CHAPTER FOURTEEN

T he time display on my computer said it was almost time to leave for my appointment with Lina. I called down to Sasha and learned that her quick-and-dirty search for information about Faring Auctions in Cheyenne, Wyoming, had borne no fruit.

"As near as I can tell, it's gone. That's just from phone books and antiques association directories. I'll try business associations and the chamber of commerce next."

"All right. Meanwhile, I'll get started on researching the mark."

A Google search revealed what we'd suspected: The "AR" mark had originated with the Meissen factory, as had the crossed swords, but both marks had been fraudulently used by competitors for hundreds of years. The AR stood for Augustus Rex and indicated that the vase—if it was real—had been made for royalty. This particular style of crossed swords was first adopted in 1723. The initials above the swords, "JGH," probably referred to the painter, Johann Gregor Höroldt.

Höroldt had been named chief painter for the factory in 1720 and was known for his use of bold, bright colors and gilt. Gretchen's vase, if it had in fact been painted by him, was an anomaly. *Why,* I wondered, would he have painted a scene in delicate blues when his expertise and reputation revolved around his use of innovative colors?

I pursed my lips, intrigued. I needed to discover if another artisan who worked for Meissen during the time those marks were used shared Höroldt's initials, or if any records indicated that Höroldt had used blue paint on Asian-themed designs.

According to a reference book on our library shelves, no one but Johann Gregor Höroldt had used those initials, but the book might be wrong. Maybe a fellow named Josef Gustav Heinlein had only worked for Meissen for a week or two. If so, the researcher could easily have missed him. I knew that details fell between the cracks all the time.

I read that Höroldt had started his career as a wallpaper painter and tapestry designer and learned to paint porcelain at the Du Paquier porcelain manufactory in Vienna. In 1720, Meissen announced expansion plans and decided to hire an additional porcelain painter. Höroldt got the job. He flourished on many levels—innovator, designer, and businessman.

After countless experiments, Höroldt developed sixteen new enamel colors, including a violet luster made from gold that created a continent-wide stir and won him instant acclaim. These sixteen colors still comprise the spectrum most commonly used in porcelain decoration.

I glanced out into the rain. *Incredible,* I thought and read on.

Höroldt was also one heck of a good manager. He created the lexicon to describe his painting style and work products, trained dozens of painters, and established a workshop system—an early assembly line—so other painters could copy his designs.

Höroldt also designed chinoiserie scenes. "Chinoiserie," I knew, referred to fanciful, idealized Chinese motifs.

Bingo, I told myself.

Höroldt painted Asian-style vases. *Okay then,* I thought. If the vase was original and not a repro, it might well have been painted by one of the finest artisans of the day. If only I had the vase in front of me.

I stretched and spun toward the window, seeking answers in the sky, but I saw nothing but a rain-streaked reflection of myself.

Downstairs, I went into the tag sale venue. It looked good: well stocked with both unusual and expected objects. In addition to the displays of gardening tools, silver, samplers, and glassware that I'd already admired, and our usual assortment of art prints, porcelain, sewing items, and miscellaneous household objects, there was a collection of ornate picture frames that I was sure would sell quickly. Most were in gilt, priced from fifteen to seventy-five dollars, depending on the frame's size and condition, but some were pewter, and a wrought-iron one featured clusters of wisteria. At fifty dollars, I was willing to bet that it would be gone within an hour.

"Great job," I told Eric.

He smiled a little. "Thanks," he said.

I decided to head out to the Blue Dolphin and get myself situated for my meeting with Lina. On the way, I stepped into the front office to say good night to my staff. Seeing photographs of the Cissy doll on Fred's desk, I asked if he had any news.

He shrugged, leaned back, and pushed up his glasses. "Seven hundred. Maybe eight."

"Including the wardrobe?" I asked, surprised at what seemed like a low price for a popular vintage doll with a nearly complete wardrobe—in its original case.

"Yeah. I expected higher, too. Turns out, there's a lot of Cissys knocking about."

"Some collector's going to be thrilled."

I told everyone good-bye and ran through pelting rain to my car. *April showers bring May flowers,* I thought. The temperature had dropped, and I knew there was a good chance that the rain would turn to snow overnight.

Once I was settled in my car, a wave of sadness hit me, and I leaned my head on the steering wheel and waited for it to pass.

It didn't.

The rain was steady, drumming a staccato beat on the roof. Finally, I took a deep breath and prepared to carry on. As I latched my seat belt, I realized that I felt like talking to Ty. Hearing the deep timbre of his voice would, I knew, bolster my mood.

He was in the middle of a training exercise and couldn't talk for more than a few seconds, but it was long enough for him to deliver good news—he expected to be home by seven thirty, relatively early on a day he commuted to Vermont.

The Blue Dolphin took up the entire ground floor of an oddly shaped eighteenth-century fieldstone building. The structure had served as a public house since it was built. Roughly triangular in shape, the restaurant was positioned at the Bow Street end of a row of four-story brick buildings that ran along Market Street. The back sides of the buildings faced the river. The ground-floor units housed a real estate agent, an expensive clothing store, a jeweler, a specialty crafts store, a high-ceilinged elegant coffee shop that featured small jazz trios in the evenings, a children's book and toy store, and a day spa. There were recently gentrified apartments above each one. The Blue Dolphin's entrance, shielded by the shell-shaped overhang, was directly across from the Bow Street Emporium.

Safely underneath the hammered metal overhang, I shook out my umbrella, then pushed through the heavy wooden door and greeted Frieda, the hostess.

"Oh, look at you, Josie! You're as wet as a dish rag!"

"But better looking, right?"

"*Much* better looking. I'm so tired of bad weather."

"You know what they say about April showers . . . they're good for the flowers!"

Frieda shook her head ruefully and smiled. "I'm so ready for flowers! You don't have a reservation, do you?"

"No. Not tonight, Frieda. I'm aiming for a warm something-or-other in the lounge. I'm expecting a guest. Her name is Lina."

"I'll send her in!" Frieda said and turned to greet a just-arriving couple.

A man sitting at the bar with a beer looked up expectantly as I entered. When he saw that I wasn't the person he was waiting for, he looked away, then glanced at his watch. Two women stood near three tables and discussed pushing them together. One woman said she thought ten people were coming.

Jimmy, the bartender, waved hello. "Hey, Josie," he called. "How's it going?"

"Good, Jimmy. You?"

"It's going!"

My favorite table was tucked in a corner overlooking the Piscataqua River. It was available, and I nabbed it. After I got settled, I cupped my hands over my eyes and pressed my forehead against the bay window, trying to see the lighthouse on the far bank. I knew it was there, but in the darkness and rain, all I could make out was its light. A wide sweep of gold arced rhythmically side to side, over and over again, alerting ships that they were approaching land. It was hypnotic.

"What'll it be?" Jimmy asked, flipping a cocktail napkin onto the table as if he were skimming a rock over water.

I turned away from the window. "On this dreary day, I think I'm in the mood for a Cocoretto," I said. The drink always reminded me of a lovely afternoon I'd spent with my friend Jo-Ann, the drink's inventor. I'd taken the train out from New York City to Connecticut on a bitterly cold winter day to meet her for lunch. She wanted a warming drink, and the next thing I knew, we were drinking Cocorettos.

"You got it," Jimmy said, interrupting my thoughts. "Hot chocolate and amaretto, coming right up!"

Lina arrived just after six, saw me, and threaded her way through the now bustling room to reach me. She looked worried.

She didn't want anything to eat. "Just tea, please," she told Jimmy, then asked me, "Do you have news about Gretchen?"

"No. I wish I did. What I mostly have is questions."

She nodded. "It's just awful."

"It occurs to me—I don't even know your last name."

"Nadlein. Lina Nadlein—quite a mouthful. Don't try to say it three times fast."

I smiled. "How did you and Gretchen meet?"

"At the Laundromat. Gretchen started chatting with me." She smiled a little, somewhere between wan and fearful. "She's so friendly and outgoing. We hit it off right away."

"Have you spoken to the police again?"

She nodded. "This afternoon. They said they may have even more questions for me."

"Would you mind telling me what they asked?"

"Everything, it seemed like, and mostly they were the same

questions they'd asked before. What plans we made, when I last spoke to her, who her other friends are, that sort of thing."

Before I could respond, Jimmy delivered her tea. It was served in an elegant porcelain pot, a match to the one containing my Cocoretto.

"Were you able to give them a lot of names?"

"Sure. Gretchen has a lot of friends."

She poured a little milk into her tea. With her face in repose, she looked like Ginevra Benci as Leonardo da Vinci had painted her, with pale, flawless skin, wide cheekbones, and intelligent eyes that stared at something offstage.

In college, I'd looked at the painting for a long time. I'd been working on a paper discussing what da Vinci's subjects' expressions implied about the artist, and I'd been unable to articulate the emotions showing in Ginevra's demeanor. Instead, I'd listed what the young woman wasn't expressing: surprise, joy, pain, fear, anger, sorrow, love, amusement, or anxiety. Yet her expression wasn't neutral. I could tell that her mind was busy. She was attentive, but I couldn't see to what—it was off the canvas. That's how Lina looked as she stirred her tea: alert and watchful, with an important but elusive emotion in play.

"Are she and Mandy close?" I asked.

"Sure. They're friends."

"How close?"

She shrugged. "I don't know. A bunch of us hang out. You know, we'll all meet up at some restaurant or bar over the weekend. Or we go to the beach or have a barbecue. Or someone will have a party. That sort of thing."

"What about Vince?"

Lina's eyes fell to her teacup, then rose again to meet mine. "Have you met him?"

"No. I've just seen him from a distance. Even so, he seemed kind of intense, you know? Do you know anything about him?"

She bit her lip and looked down again. "No," she said.

From the uneasy look on her face, I didn't believe her, but I couldn't think of what to ask to get her to open up. "Can you tell me about any of Gretchen's other friends?"

"Well, there's the Eagler sisters and Buddy and Roberta and Brenda and Morley and Preston and Alexis and—I don't know, a bunch of others, too. Why?"

I shook my head. "No reason in particular. I'm just trying to figure out what's going on. I'm so worried." I looked at her but saw nothing but mildly friendly interest. I changed the subject. "Do you know anything about Gretchen's background?"

"Why are you asking me that?" She looked startled and uncomfortable all at once.

I circled my cup with my hands to absorb some warmth and took a deep breath. Suddenly I felt exhausted. "I just want to help her if I can."

Lina nodded. "Me, too."

I reached over and patted her hand. "So, do you know anything about where she comes from? If I know where to look, I can check. Maybe she went back there."

"Down south. That's all she ever said—that it was freezing here in Portsmouth compared to where she was from, down south."

"Did she ever mention family or friends from before she moved here?"

"Only once. She said that it was easier being alone than dealing with her family. I thought it was kind of sad."

"Where down south?"

"She never said."

"Not even a state—Georgia or South Carolina, maybe?"

"No," Lina replied, shaking her head.

I didn't want to bully her, yet I had to try to find a kernel of information she might not remember but possessed nonetheless. I couldn't just sit around and do nothing while Gretchen might be desperate, wounded, or terrified—or all three. She might need help, help I could provide.

"Did Gretchen ever say something about her life growing up or an activity that she did as a kid—like her dad was a shrimper or she lived near a museum, or she learned to water ski on the lake before she could walk, something like that?"

"I'm sorry."

"Isn't there *anything* else you can tell me? *Please?*"

She looked at me and shook her head again, a sad-sweet smile on her face. "I've wracked my brain—but I don't know anything else."

I tried hard to think of another question to ask, and then I gave up. There was no magic bullet that I could use to get information Lina didn't have. I smiled. "Thank you for meeting with me."

She zipped up her coat. "One thing I can tell you for sure. Gretchen loves her job. She thinks you're the smartest business-woman she's ever known."

"Thank you," I said, surprised at the accolade. "Wow. You've completely made my day."

After she left, I thought about what I'd learned. Not much. Gretchen hung out with a large group of friends, and the police had their names. She came from somewhere down south. And Lina seemed afraid of Mandy's boyfriend, Vince.

CHAPTER FIFTEEN

 got to Ty's house just after seven thirty. "Hello!" I called, entering with my key through the front door. "Anyone home!"

"In the kitchen!"

His place was bigger than mine, a contemporary with two fireplaces, one in the master bedroom, and huge picture windows that framed sweeping vistas of maple, oak, apple, elm, chestnut, poplar, and birch. Last autumn, when the leaves had turned the colors of fire, molten red melding into iridescent orange and flame-hot yellow, I'd sat staring into the woods, thinking that I was in the presence of God.

Tonight, Ty had a fire going in the living room. As I walked past, I heard a soft hissing sound, then crackling. I found him in the kitchen, making pizza from a box.

"We're having pizza, I see."

"And salad."

I sat in a club chair he kept in a corner of the kitchen, my legs curled under me, and watched as he chopped vegetables, his motions confident and quick. I filled him in about my call to the Sidlawn Fencing Company about the belt buckle, our find in my vault about Gretchen's vase, and my conversation with Lina.

"Your lip curls when you mention Vince. How come?" Ty asked.

"When I think of him, I just feel . . . I don't know . . . yuk."

"Yuk," Ty repeated. "That's a technical term, is it?"

"Yes."

He nodded. "Can you be more specific?"

"Well, Gretchen set the scene by telling me that in her view, Vince wasn't good for Mandy. Keeping in mind I've never even met the guy, I have the impression that Grtechen was right, that he seems to influence Mandy in ways that are bad for her—but subtly bad. I mean, it's not like he hits her or tells her to obey him or anything. It's not overt like that." I floundered, trying to find a way to explain. "Here's an example: Mandy told me that Vince said that painting flowers in her kitchen was stupid. It's not that he's merely *not* supportive—it's worse than that—he's denigrating." I shrugged. "In other words—yuk."

Ty looked up from his chopping. "How do you know he hasn't hit her?"

"I don't know. I mean, it never occurred to me."

"Have you seen any marks or bruises on her? Maybe she said she'd fallen down or tripped or something, so you didn't think anything of it at the time."

"No." I looked out into the night. It was still raining and, I knew, cold.

"Did you mention him to Detective Brownley?"

"No. I had no reason to."

"You should. It can't do any harm." He placed a stalk of celery on the cutting board.

I nodded. "Is it important enough for me to call her now?"

"Yes."

"Really?"

"Yes. It isn't like you're gossiping with a girlfriend, Josie. It's a murder investigation. The more she knows, the better."

"Okay."

I went into the living room, where I'd left my tote bag. The half-burned apple log spit sparks toward the screen, then popped as sap ignited. I selected a medium-sized log and laid it crosswise on the smoldering cinders.

"So Ty thought I ought to mention that I have a negative reaction to Mandy's boyfriend, Vince Collins," I said after exchanging greetings with Detective Brownley. "Even though I've never met him. I have no reason to think Vince is involved or a particular threat, but he thought I ought to call, so I did."

"Thank you, Josie," she said. "You did the right thing."

I reported my observations, recounting what Gretchen and Mandy said to me. She thanked me again and hung up. I had an idea, and as I considered its merits, I watched the pepper-red flames turn gold, then white, then red again, and then I called Wes.

I got his voice mail and left a brief message. "Can you check out a man named Vince Collins?" I asked. "I have no evidence, but my gut tells me that there's a teeny tiny chance he's involved in whatever is going on."

Knowing Wes as I did, I was confident that I'd get a full report by morning.

"Good tip, Josie. This Vince Collins guy—he's got a record," Wes said when he called at ten the next morning.

I took the call on the tag sale room phone. "What kind of record?" I asked, turning my back to the crowd and lowering my voice.

"Assault. Two counts. He did jail time."

I gulped. "Tell me about the assaults."

"One was a bar fight the night of his twenty-first birthday. He broke a beer bottle over some guy's head, put him in the hospital. He pleaded out and served thirty days. Three years ago, when he was twenty-nine, he beat another guy pretty much to a pulp. They said it was a road rage thing. He wasn't drunk, which when you think about it makes the whole thing worse, you know what I mean?"

"Yes," I said, and I began to breathe again. Vince was, it seemed, a man for whom violence came easily. "Did he go to jail that time?"

"Yup. He refused to plead to a lesser charge, insisting that the other guy attacked him and it was self-defense. No one believed him, including the jury, and he served more than two years of a three-year sentence for assault. He was found not guilty on the other charge—attempted murder. He's been out for about eight months."

"What does he do?"

"He's in construction."

"How long have he and Mandy been dating?"

"About six months. According to my source, they're pretty serious."

"What else does your source say?" I asked.

"Pretty strong stuff, actually." Wes paused to maximize the effect of his next words. "One person I talked to said he thought he was a ticking time bomb ready to explode."

"What sets him off?"

"By all reports, he's jealous and controlling—and arrogant."

Had Gretchen warned Mandy to get away from him? I wondered. "Is there any connection between Vince and the dead guy?" I asked.

"Who knows? We still don't know who the dead guy is. But there's more," he said enticingly.

I braced myself. "What?" I asked.

"An APB has been issued for Gretchen—and her car. Which means they think she's involved," he said, sounding thrilled at the prospect.

Wes's enthusiasm shocked me. "Wes, it's not an action movie, for goodness sake! Something horrible is going on, but Gretchen's not the criminal here. If anything, she's a victim."

"What do you know?" he asked, pouncing on my innocent remark.

"I don't know anything about where she is or why she's missing," I said sternly, "nor, may I add, do you."

Disappointed that I had no secrets or speculation to share, but resilient as ever, he ended the call with an energetic "Talk later!"

I pressed the phone into my ribs and stared unseeingly into the tag sale crowd, seriously shaken by both of Wes's revelations. I took deep breaths as I tried to think what I should do—or what I could do.

Ideas came to me, only to be immediately dismissed. I couldn't do anything about the belt buckle until I heard from Serena, hopefully on Monday. I couldn't do anything about Vince at all. I could continue trying to find Faring Auctions; maybe they were bought out like Sidlawn Fencing Company. I wished I could locate the vase itself. All at once, my mouth fell open.

I was willing to bet that I knew exactly where to find Gretchen's vase.

CHAPTER SIXTEEN

I spun the heavy vault lock and stepped inside. The largest boxes were positioned on the bottom two shelves. I squatted and reviewed each box's index card, one by one, starting in the near left corner.

The first box contained rare books—a twelve-volume set of gold-tooled, burled-leather-bound Shakespeare, dating from 1784, in beautiful condition, last examined by Fred a month ago. The second box was empty. The third box contained carefully packaged early Baccarat glassware, last viewed by Sasha last week. The fourth box's index card read GRETCHEN. PERSONAL.

I fell back on my heels and stared at the index card for a long time. Then I scampered up and called Detective Brownley.

"I don't know why I didn't think to look before," I said after I explained my find. "I didn't open the box, but I'm willing to bet money the vase is inside."

"You don't maintain an inventory of what's in your safe?" she asked.

"We will, starting now," I replied.

She told me she'd be there in ten minutes.

The vase was magnificent. The imagery was evocative of natural beauty and simple pleasures, and while the painting appeared effortless, a closer examination revealed complex layering and delicate, softly shaded brush strokes. I hated to see the vase disappear into the trunk of Detective Brownley's vehicle, but I accepted her assurance that I'd get to examine it as soon as the lab completed its work.

The intercom buzzed.

It was Cara, and she sounded agitated. "Come to the tag sale," she whispered. "Hurry."

"What's going on?" I asked.

"A man is looking for Gretchen. Hurry!" she repeated and hung up.

I ran across the warehouse, then stopped short at the door that opened into the rear of the tag sale to peer through the peephole. He was easy to spot. He was tall, maybe six feet, with a barrel chest and skinny legs, somewhere around thirty. His hair was an unnatural shade of yellow, cut short, and curly. I could see a faint hint of black near the roots. He wore a long-sleeved, collared black T-shirt, jeans, hiking boots, and a beige anorak.

Cara was standing near the cash register, her back to the wall. She held an auction catalogue opened wide, high enough up to block her face. She was doing a pretty good job, I thought, of pretending she wasn't watching a man by the entryway. If I hadn't received her frantic phone call, I might have fallen for the subterfuge myself.

He stood off to the side, scanning the room in a grid pattern. His eyes were moving from sector to sector on a three-second swing. Nine sectors, I counted, like a sniper hunting quarry or a private pilot on the lookout for other aircraft. It was as if he were looking at nine slices of half a pie, one at a time. His focus was absolute.

I entered the room and walked slowly toward the front, watching him. When I got closer I could see that he'd pinned a tiny silver airplane to his lapel. I planted a welcoming smile on my face as I approached him.

"Hi," I said. "I'm Josie Prescott. Can I help you find something?"

"Hi," he said, smiling back. "I'm Chip Davidson, a friend of Gretchen Brock's."

When he smiled, his whole demeanor shifted from intense to warm.

"She'll be sorry she missed you—but she's not here."

"No wonder I can't find her!" he kidded. "Darn! When do you expect her?"

Maybe this was the fellow Gretchen met in Hawaii, the chemist from Maine. "Sorry," I said, "but we never talk about employee schedules. I can have her call you, if you'd like."

"No way! Don't you dare tell her I was here!" he said, laughing. "I want to see her face when she spots me. Can you at least give me a rough idea of when I could hook up with her? Will she be here later today? Monday?"

I shook my head and smiled. "Sorry. Company policy."

"Rules are made to be broken," he said, his eyes glittering with fun and promise and trustworthiness.

"I haven't heard that since high school!"

"I'm betting it didn't work then, either, am I right?"

I laughed. "You are! I've got to get back to work, Chip. Are you sure you don't want to leave a message?"

"No—thanks, though."

He extended his hand, and we shook.

"I hope to see you again," I said.

"You will!" he assured me, and with a last quick, charming grin and a cheery wave, he was gone.

As soon as he was out the door, Cara came up to me, her eyes big with curiosity.

"A friend of Gretchen's," I reported, smiling. "He seemed nice, actually."

"What a relief!" Cara said.

"You did the right thing to call me."

"Thanks," she said, smiling a little.

As I made my way back to my office, I thought about Chip. I had no reason to think he represented any threat or possessed any relevant knowledge, but I decided to call Detective Brownley on Ty's principle that the more information she had, the better.

I couldn't reach her, but left a detailed message on her cell phone describing Chip's appearance and behavior.

Curious, I Googled "Chip Davidson" and got too many hits to be useful. I added "chemist" and got one hit—a university professor working in Dubai who appeared closer to eighty than seventy, obviously not the right man. Knowing that Chip is often a nickname for Charles, I tried "Charles Davidson" and got tens of thousands of hits. Adding "chemist" and "Maine" still left me with too many options to pursue.

Now what? I asked myself. Suddenly I had another thought.

Vince was in construction, and when Wes told me that the police were checking whether the murder victim had a job that might result in his hands getting cut a lot, I'd thought of a carpenter. Could they know one another? Could Sal Briscoe have worked with Vince?

The New England Regional Council of Carpenters stated that they represented twenty-four thousand carpenters, pile drivers, shop- and millmen, and floor coverers. I found the union membership directory but then was stymied. Neither Vince Collins nor Sal Briscoe was listed. There were no photos. It would be an overwhelmingly laborious process, I thought, to seek out each worker listed, one by one, and vet him. To say nothing of all the nonunion laborers. *Leave it to the police,* I thought, and wondered if they were making any progress.

I stood up, frustrated, then almost immediately sat down. *The vase,* I admonished myself. *I can do more with the vase.* The vase was a direct link to Gretchen. If we learned where Gretchen got it, we might be able to learn enough about her to find her.

In a traditional appraisal, the challenge would be to verify ownership from the time the vase left the Meissen factory to the present. I could either trace the vase backward from the Wyoming auction house to the factory or forward from the factory to the auction house. Backward is sometimes easier—but not when the last known transaction occurred sixty years earlier from a seller who'd gone out of business.

With the "AR" mark in mind, I decided to search for textual references to royal purchases of Meissen vases starting in 1723, the first year the mark was used. There was no one definitive source to consult; according to the Meissen company, which was still in existence, there are no sales records that go back that far. By following linked references from an auction catalogue to a scholarly article, I found a reference to a Ph.D. candidate's inventory of decorative items at St. James's Palace, the royal residence.

The inventory wasn't posted online.

The student's name was Percy Oliver Johns. He'd been a student at the University of Southern California back in 1969. I couldn't find any current record of him at all, and couldn't think of anything else to look up.

Instead, I returned to the tag sale room to take my turn in the Prescott's Instant Appraisal booth. Every Saturday, Sasha, Fred, and I each did hour-long stints. Anyone could walk into the tag sale with an object or a photo and get an on-the-spot, quick-and-dirty assessment. It was good fun, and it was good business. Between the three of us, we appraised between thirty and forty objects each week, first come, first served.

Fred left the booth as I arrived, and I turned to greet the first woman waiting in line. As I introduced myself, she shook my hand and smiled, and I felt myself relax a bit. She reminded me of Mrs. Horne, my junior year high school English teacher. Mrs. Horne introduced me to Jane Austen, Virginia Woolf, and Helen MacInnes and taught me about gerunds, ellipses, and the power of selecting the correct noun. She was one of my favorite teachers.

"I'm Kathy Franzino."

"Welcome! What did you bring me to look at today?"

"A music cabinet." She laughed. "Don't get worried! I didn't bring the whole cabinet, just some snapshots. I hope they're good enough for you to see."

She handed me four photos, and I laid them side by side.

The music cabinet stood on Chippendale-style legs. The doors opened to reveal six drawers. The hardware was brass throughout. The cabinet appeared to be constructed of mahogany and rosewood, and there was ornate decorative detailing at the bottom and top. On the front, there were flowers painted in gilt and accented with tiny mother-of-pearl inlays. It appeared to be in excellent condition. One photo showed a small bronze plaque reading PATENTED OCTOBER 1892.

"It's lovely," I said. "What do you know about it?"

"It's been in my family for as long as anyone can remember, but no one knows where it came from. I've always loved it. My daughter, Elizabeth, thinks it might have come from Greece."

"Why Greece?"

Kathy laughed again. "No reason except that my mother is of Greek origin. My boys, Frank the third and Joe, they thought the style was likely to be Italian."

"And your father's Italian, am I right?"

"How'd you guess?" she asked, laughing so hard that her pretty eyes crinkled nearly shut.

I joined in laughing, then turned my attention back to the photos. "I think we'll find it's American made. Give me a minute to do a little research."

Using one of the specialized Web sites we subscribed to, I was able to confirm my suspicion easily—the music cabinet was, in fact, made in the U.S.A.

I turned to Kathy and said, "This is a good example of an American-made late Victorian music cabinet. The detailing to the doors gives it charm, and it's in wonderful condition. Before recorded music became widely available, many families owned musical instruments, and thus there was a demand for furniture designed to store sheet music. The fact that the company had bronze plaques cast to indicate it was a patented design tells me that these examples were made in fairly large numbers."

"So selling it won't let me take my family on an around-the-world cruise, is that what you're telling me?"

I laughed again. "I'm afraid not. If you wanted to sell it, I would expect it to fetch between six and eight hundred dollars."

"Well, I wouldn't sell it for the world anyway, so it doesn't really matter. I was just curious."

"When you look at it, you think of your grandmother, right?"

"And my mother, and all the wonderful times I had as a child."

I gathered up the photos and handed them to her. "That's price-less."

Next in line was a woman named Eleanor Glass Moe. She had short gray hair and a huge smile and was holding a doll.

"Here's Shannon," she said.

"I'm not familiar with that brand," I replied. "What can you tell me about it?"

She laughed. "No, no. That's the name I've given her. Irish proud, that's me!"

"Got it! Let's see what Shannon can tell me about herself."

The doll was close to life-size, with movable joints and eyes that blinked. She had short blond hair and wore a white dress detailed with lace and a blue and white beaded necklace. She was missing a finger, and there was visible wear on her arms. The back of her head, under her hair, was marked with the numeral "99" and the word "Handwerk," probably indicating the year of manufacture and the company—1899 and Heinrich Handwerck.

Since Fred was the lead appraiser for our upcoming doll auction, I wanted to hear his views. I IM'd him, "Heinrich Handwerck—99—finger missing, wear on arms, original lace dress w/necklace in fine cond. Price?"

While waiting for his reply, I asked, "Does Shannon have other clothes?"

"No," Eleanor said. "The poor girl owns only one dress."

Fred's IM arrived. "Clothes+, condition−, prob $400–$500."

I told her our assessment and explained our thinking and watched her easy smile reappear. We shook hands, and Eleanor thanked me again. I watched her weave her way out of the tag sale, cradling Shannon in the crook of her left arm like a baby.

Four appraisals later, my shift was over.

Sasha approached for her second turn in the instant appraisal booth. I stood and stretched and was walking toward the front just as Mandy stepped inside and spotted me. She looked petrified, as if she were losing ground in a race against the devil.

CHAPTER SEVENTEEN

D o you have a minute to talk?" Mandy whispered.

"Sure," I said.

We entered the warehouse through the inside door. I led the way to the nearest corner, and we stood behind a stack of crates taller than me. I touched her arm, just for a moment, and waited for her to speak.

She stood stiffly, her hands clenched into fists. Even in the dim light, I could see moisture glistening on her eyelashes. She seemed unable to begin.

"What's happened?" I asked.

She took a deep breath and then another and then she said, "A reporter from the *Seacoast Star* has been asking people about Vince and me. Wes Smith. He even came into the store and talked to my manager."

"That's what reporters do, Mandy. They ask questions."

"Vince is so angry at the thought that our names will be in the paper." Mandy crossed her arms across her chest. "I know you know him. I see you quoted in his articles all the time."

I took a deep breath, bracing myself to be the bearer of bad news. "If what you're hoping is that I can get Wes to stop, I can't. Nothing and no one can. If you give Wes an interview, you'll be quoted by name. If you don't, he'll write that you're refusing to talk to reporters." I shrugged. "Pretty much, it's a given that your name will be in the paper."

She looked down and was quiet for a long time, then looked up at me. "Why would *anyone* talk to a reporter?"

I shrugged. "To vent. To make your point to the world. To expose

corruption or wrongdoing. To have the right to ask questions in return to someone in the know."

She didn't comment.

"Does Vince have something to hide, Mandy?" I asked softly.
"Do you?" She still didn't speak. I shrugged. Without knowing the
specifics of why Vince was so upset about seeing their names in
the paper, I could only offer her general guidance. "If you do decide to talk to Wes, or any member of the press, make sure you
know whether you're on the record or not."

Her brow was lined with worry. She looked very young. God
knew that I'd done my share of ranting against the press over the
years, but I sensed that something else, something deeper than
mere irritation or annoyance, was in play. The only explanation I
could think of for her anxiety was fear. The question I couldn't
even begin to answer was what she was afraid of.

"Thanks, Josie," she said finally—and left.

Ty called just after six to tell me that he was running late. "There's
a guy I've got to talk to. He's just not getting it."

"What's he doing wrong?" I asked.

Ty laughed, not a ha-ha sound of enjoyment but a derisive chor-
tle. "He was positive that all of his equipment was in his car the
first time we ran the drill, so he didn't check. The second time he
brought only the equipment he figured he'd need, not the equipment on his checklist. He said he was experienced enough to
know what he needs, so why not save time."

"And you're a by-the-book sorta fella who doesn't really see his
perspective."

"Well, he is, after all, a first responder, not a strategy planner,
you know?"

"So you need to have a little talk with him."

"Exactly. I think it's time for him to decide if this position is a
good fit with his interests and expectations about the job. He might
be happier behind a desk somewhere in a planning capacity."

"You're kind to put it that way," I observed.

"Nah, it's true. He's a good guy—he's just thinking too much for this job."

"Sounds like an unpleasant conversation."

"It has that potential," Ty acknowledged. "And it's going to make me late. Do you want to go to my place?"

"Why don't I go home? I have a lot to do. You can decide whether to come over once you're en route."

"Sounds good," he said.

By the time I shut down my computer and walked downstairs, it was almost six thirty, and everyone was gone. I left right after confirming that Eric had walked the cash drawers into the safe and locked all the doors and windows.

At home, I showered and ate and curled up in my living room with Rex Stout's *Plot It Yourself.* Ty called just after eight to say he was about an hour away and would come over if it was okay. "Yeah," I said, grinning from ear to ear, "it's okay."

When he got there, he sat at the kitchen table, his long legs stretched out in front of him, his ankles crossed, listening. He drank Smuttynose from the bottle. I stood at the counter, transferring leftovers from plastic containers to a plate for reheating in the microwave as I filled him in on my day.

Ty was a great listener. He never interrupted, nodded when he understood a point, and asked smart questions. He paid attention. I told him everything that had happened and ended by asking his opinion. "Do you think Mandy or Vince has a specific secret? Or is it just general angst?"

"I don't know, Josie. What's your sense?"

I wrinkled my nose, thinking. The microwave clicked off. "Mandy's hypersensitive when it comes to all things Vince, but I don't know why. I don't know if she's protecting him or if she's afraid of him," I said as I carried Ty's dinner to the table.

Ty nodded. "To further complicate the issue, sometimes people react as you expect, and a lot of the time, they don't. Probably she's acting scared for one or both of the reasons you suggest, but maybe not. There's a possibility that's just her way of handling stress."

"Plus which," I added, nodding, "with Vince, there's probably an element of control going on. What's that old saying? Just because you're paranoid doesn't mean they're *not* out to get you. Just because Vince is a control freak doesn't mean he *doesn't* have secrets he's determined to keep private."

"True, and sometimes a cigar is just a cigar. Maybe Mandy knows something that would implicate one of them in some way—because they *are* involved."

Ty finished his Smuttynose and walked to the fridge for another bottle. "Want me to ask around, see what I can find out?"

I smiled and slid my hand across the table, stopping near his plate. "Thank you, Ty."

He covered my hand with his and gave a little squeeze. "You're welcome. Now, get out of my way, woman. You're keeping me from food."

Sunday morning, Ty and I went to his house and spent the day relaxing. Anxiety about Gretchen was never far from my mind, but for the first time since entering her apartment and discovering the corpse, I felt a bit encouraged that I was getting closer to finding her. Between my research on the belt buckle and the vase, and questions I might be able to ask Mandy to draw her out, I was hopeful that we might finally begin to get answers soon.

First thing, I brought in the newspaper the delivery person had tossed on the front stoop. Wes's headline blared with innuendo, as usual:

APB Issued for Murder Apt Owner:
Have You Seen This Woman—Gretchen Brock?

The article's overall tone was more restrained than most of his work, and my name only appeared twice, first in paragraph three, mentioning that I was Gretchen's boss, and once in paragraph eight, referring to me as an antiques expert. Somehow Wes had acquired a photo of Gretchen's vase. The caption stated that the police planned on asking me to examine it after their lab had finished its forensic work.

Later, I made my mother's fancy Raspberry Chicken Roll and we watched *Sea of Love,* one of my favorite old movies.

While I was setting the table for dinner, the phone rang, and Ty went into his den to answer it. When he came back, he reported, "Vince Collins is, by all accounts, a bad guy."

I met his gaze and waited for the details.

"Here's what I've learned: Collins works for a residential real estate development company that's doing well. He's a project manager. From all reports, he's a real hard-ass to work for. He believes in management by choking. No, really," he said, reacting to my startled look of inquiry. "No charges were filed because the guy he choked quit. In fact, he's left the state." He shrugged. "Moving along, it seems that the police are keeping close tabs on Vince, and he knows it. There have been a couple of altercations— shouting only—in which he's challenged the officers tailing him to justify their actions."

I laughed. "I love your diction," I said.

He smiled. "Vince is on probation, so I'm betting he won't do anything beyond shouting, if you get my drift."

I found his common sense persuasive, but I was still worried about Mandy. I had an edgy, amorphous feeling that she knew something about Gretchen and was afraid to tell—something we needed to know.

CHAPTER EIGHTEEN

Monday morning, I woke up more worried than when I'd fallen asleep and more convinced than ever that Mandy was key. She knew something. It was like having an itch I couldn't scratch—frustrating, all-consuming, and irritating.

I drove straight to her apartment to try to persuade her to confide in me.

It was sunny and cool, with a hint of hoarfrost shimmering on the lawn and a chill in the air, but I could tell it would warm up by afternoon.

Vince's Jeep wasn't there, but a silver Honda was. I parked under the willow tree, ran up the front steps, and rang the bell. I heard it chime, but no one came to the door. I rang again. Still no answer. Sounds of water running came from somewhere to the left. I stepped around the corner of the building.

Mandy stood with her back to me, watering flowers. I called to her, and she whip-turned, startled.

"Oh, hi, Josie," she said. "Did you ring the bell? Sorry, I didn't hear it."

"I'm sorry to bug you. Can I talk to you for a minute?"

She laid down the hose and led the way across the small patch of lawn and tiny garden into the mudroom. Mandy wiped her feet on the rough coir mat, then sat on the built-in storage box to exchange her bright yellow rubber boots for slippers.

As I waited, I glanced up, saw the light fixture, and nearly fainted. The light fixture I was staring at was a match for the one in Gretchen's hall—a hand-painted Dutch scene with tulips and a windmill.

I'd noticed Gretchen's light fixture the first time I was in her apartment—when Meryl and I discovered the corpse. Yet when I'd returned with Detective Brownley specifically to collect any object that might be traceable, I'd missed it. I could have kicked myself, I felt so stupid.

Mandy stood up, ready to enter the kitchen.

"That's beautiful," I said, pointing to the fixture.

"Thanks. Vince got it for me last month. I love it."

"Is it an antique?" I asked.

"I think so."

I waited until Mandy served us coffee and we were settled at the kitchen table to speak.

"I'm worried about you." I aimed for a soothing tone. "I think you know something about Gretchen or the dead man, and I think you're afraid to tell. I want to help you manage the situation."

Mandy looked away and tucked her hair behind her ear. I couldn't read her expression at all. "Thank you, Josie, but you're wrong."

"I promise you that I will do everything I can to protect you from whatever danger you might be in."

She shook her head. "I was just upset about that reporter. Vince and I talked about it. He's going to call him, so I don't have to." She tried to smile, but it was a pretty feeble effort. "Vince will take care of it."

"It wasn't just the reporter. There's something else."

She shook her head.

"If you change your mind about telling, you can always come to me," I added.

"You're wrong," she repeated. She stood up. "I'm sorry, but I have to get ready for work."

Outside, a soft breeze had kicked up, and shadows from the willow tree danced on the hood of my car. I called Detective Brownley. As soon as I got to the part about the light fixture that matched the one in Gretchen's hallway, she interrupted me.

"Couldn't it be a coincidence?" she asked.

"No way are they stock items. They're hand-painted and probably antiques. I feel so stupid for having missed it before."

She thanked me, told me she'd check into it, and hung up before I could ask her to let me know what she'd learned.

As I drove toward my building, I had a thought. If I wanted to buy an antique light fixture, I knew where I would go—Phil's Barn, known for carrying high-quality architectural artifacts.

Phil's Barn was accessed from a small dirt road about half a mile off of Oak Street in Exeter, a pretty drive through a traditional New England town. As I crossed over the Squamscott River on High Street, then turned onto Oak, the forest closed in on either side. It felt like a movie set. I could have been a million miles away from civilization. I turned into Phil's gravel-strewn yard and saw Phil standing with his hands on his hips, his head tilted back, gesturing as he talked to someone on the roof.

I parked off to the side. A young man with a cigarette dangling from the corner of his mouth hoisted a section of wrought-iron fencing into the back of a brown pickup. Another man, this one middle-aged and fat, rolled an old carriage wheel toward his SUV. At Phil's Barn, commerce started early and continued steady all day.

"Did you check the valley flashing?" Phil called, pointing to the metal gully that ran from the peak to the gutter.

"Doing it now," the voice shouted back.

"Hey, Josie," Phil said as I walked up to join him. "I got a leak. Damn thing. Can't find it."

"I hate leaks."

"Damn straight." He shrugged. "Glad you stopped by. I was going to be calling you. I've got a dozen glass doorknobs on brass shanks. Five pair are green glass, one's lavender, four are clear, and two are black. I set aside the chipped ones. All these are in excellent condition."

Glass doorknobs were popular items, hard to find in unchipped and nonrusty condition. At the tag sale, we'd always price them at fifty dollars or more a set.

"You are a source of wonder and awe, Phil! You must have quite a supply chain going. First the locks and now the knobs."

"Thanks. I do okay. Sorry about not getting you the knobs last week. I've been out sick for a couple of days." He exploded into a coughing fit that lasted several seconds. "Damn cough—my wife has been pestering me to stay home to try and shake it off."

"Maybe she's right—you sound bad. You feel all right?"

"'Bout the same. You know that old adage about it taking a week to get over a cold if you stay in bed, but if you go into work, it takes seven days? Seems true in my case."

I laughed. "You're on what, day five?"

"Exactly right. The doorknobs came in last Wednesday, just after I went home for lunch and my wife chained me to the bed."

I laughed again; then we talked price. At a guess, Phil had paid no more than thirteen or fourteen dollars a set, so my offer of seventeen dollars per pair represented a nifty profit for him for his few minutes' work examining their condition. We shook on it, and the deal was done.

"They're inside." He lifted his head and called to the man on the roof, still crab-walking along the flashing. "Don't come down 'til you find that damn leak."

I followed him across the old barn to a worktable on the left. As we walked, I asked, "You expecting more salvage pieces?"

"Wouldn't surprise me. There's a lot of construction going on hereabouts."

"You have any light fixtures? Something hand-painted, maybe?"

"Nope, nothing like you might have in mind. Just eighties trash."

"You get anything, you call me, okay?"

"You bet."

The doorknobs were layered with generations of grime, but they were in good condition.

"As described," I acknowledged. "I'll pack them up."

Another customer called to Phil.

"See ya, Josie," Phil said and started off toward the front.

Using supplies I kept in the trunk of my car, I individually wrapped each knob in bubble wrap and placed them in a sturdy cardboard box. As I worked, I looked around. Phil's inventory was basically unchanged from my last visit. He had almost no small items, but he had plenty of large objects. I spotted a windmill, in pieces; two weather vanes; shelves of broken appliances, mostly sold for parts; layers of Oriental rugs, some rare and in extraordinary condition; and miscellaneous used furniture stacked partway up the back wall.

I drove to the ocean, crossed the sandy scrub brush onto the beach, and approached the surf. The ocean was calm. White froth licked at my boots as the tide washed in.

I wanted to try to come up with new tactics to find Gretchen. I had no new information. There were only three options that I could see to account for her disappearance: She was voluntarily absent; she was being held somewhere under duress; or she'd been whisked away by the U.S. Marshals. I stared out over the water.

Close to shore, the ocean was cobalt blue. Farther out, it turned bottle green. Farther still, the water appeared black.

Wes said she got a new Social Security number seven years ago. *How?* I wondered. Of course, if she was in the witness protection program, everything was provided for her, but what if she wasn't under government oversight, if she was, as Wes suggested, on the run for some reason? In this age of terrorism and ID theft, surely it couldn't be easy to sign up for a new Social Security card.

Then I thought of a way Gretchen might have gotten her new ID. I ran across the beach to my car and was on my way to work in nothing flat.

I arrived about ten thirty and greeted everyone in a hurry. As soon as my computer booted up, I Googled "City Clerk" and "Welton, Massachusetts," my hometown. The first listing gave me the phone number.

"Welton City Clerk's office, may I help you?"

"I lost my birth certificate," I said. "How can I get a replacement?"

"Easy as pie! Send us a letter listing your date of birth, your parents' names, and a check or money order for ten dollars."

"That's it?" I asked, astonished.

"That's it," the woman confirmed.

It's frighteningly simple, I realized. *Anyone can do it for any reason.* All you'd have to do is canvass graveyards until you find someone born about the same time as you who died in infancy and do a little research to discover his or her parents' names. Even if a child had been issued a Social Security number before he or she died, the plan would work—you'd get either a new number or a replacement card for a number that hadn't been used in years.

I tried a search for "Gretchen Brock" and "obituaries" and got a few hits, all recent. If the Gretchen Brock whose identity she adopted had died before newspapers archived their issues online, finding the obit would require as much luck as science.

Another idea, another dead end.

I glanced at the clock and wondered when I could expect to hear from Serena about the Sidlawn Fencing Company belt buckle. I decided to wait until late afternoon. Instead, I picked up the photograph showing Gretchen's vase's marks.

I'd reached a stumbling block when I hadn't been able to locate Percy Oliver Johns's inventory of decorative items in St. James's Palace. I wondered whether I should keep trying or continue Sasha's efforts to discover whether Faring Auctions was still in business.

If the note we found in Gretchen's envelope was accurate, sixty years had passed since the vase had been purchased, and finding someone who remembered selling a certain vase back in the 1940s—even a special one like the Meissen—was unlikely in the extreme. My best hope lay in finding archived notes. While most professionals are loath to include details that can't be proven in a written appraisal, they're equally unlikely to throw their research notes away. In fact, many organizations keep original or computerized records of appraisal notes archived forever. It was a long shot, for sure, but I'd discovered over the years that sometimes long shots paid off.

I visited the Web sites of the Cheyenne Chamber of Commerce, the Wyoming Better Business Bureau, and the Wyoming State Historical

Society. At each site, I looked up the Faring auction house. I'd follow up with phone calls just to be sure, but from the online evidence, it seemed that Faring Auctions wasn't a member of the chamber of commerce and no complaints had been filed against it with the Better Business Bureau. On the Wyoming State Historical Society site, despite learning that the society hadn't been established until 1953, I found my first evidence that Faring Auctions had existed.

When I entered "Faring Auctions" in the Web site's search bar, I got two hits, both from scholarly articles. One of them, from a Washington, D.C.–based university journal dated 1939, referred to Faring's track record as a purveyor of Native American crafts, and the second, from an art magazine in the 1940s, described a specific item that had been sold in 1942, a folk art painting by a little-known artist.

I jotted down the three organizations' contact information and got ready to work the phone. From the Cheyenne yellow pages, under the category "Antiques, Dealers," I selected three businesses to query. It's hard to gauge substance from ads, but all three appeared to be well-established firms.

At noon, 9:00 A.M. on the West Coast, I began making my phone calls. I struck out at the Better Business Bureau. The historical society also had no record of the auction house, but unless it had been located in a landmark building or owned by a founding family or something of that nature, the absence of information about it didn't indicate anything one way or the other. At the chamber of commerce, I finally got some information—but it wasn't easy.

The friendly woman who answered the phone had trouble understanding why I was calling but was game to figure it out. From her perspective, if I didn't want to join the chamber, reach a current member, attend a function, buy a raffle ticket, sell something, or contact an employee—why was I calling? Finally she gave up and connected me to Wilma, the member services representative.

"I'm trying to locate information about a company that operated in Cheyenne in the 1940s called Faring Auctions," I explained. "I don't think they're still in business, but—"

"And you want to know if they've ever been a member, right?" Wilma asked, reading my mind and breaking in.

"Yes, and if so, when they dropped out."

"I've never heard of Faring Auctions," Wilma said, "and I've been here almost six years. Let me check a directory from before then. Hold on a sec." Less than a minute later she was back. "I checked the 1999, 2000, and 2001 directories—no Faring. How far back do you want to go?"

"Could we go back to 1949?" I asked, thinking that it would be great to get a benchmark. According to the note, that was the year the Meissen vase had been purchased. Surely Faring Auctions existed then, and most likely it had been a member of the chamber.

"For that I need to go to the executive director's office. She has a complete set of membership directories on her shelves. Do you want to hold or do you want me to call you back?"

I asked to hold, clicked over to the speakerphone function so I could have my hands free while I waited, and turned my attention back to ways to research the vase's provenance.

"Faring Auctions is listed in the 1949 directory," Wilma told me, sounding as pleased as if she'd found a twenty-dollar bill on the sidewalk. She chuckled. "I deputized the executive director's assistant to help. She started with the recent directories and I started with the old ones, and we had a race. I won. Their last mention was in 1969."

"Wilma, you are sharp as a tack and bright as a star," I said, quoting one of my mother's favorite compliments. To merit that accolade you had to both show initiative and do well. "When is the directory published?" I asked. "How far in advance?"

Again Wilma read my mind. "They would have had to renew their membership by the end of July 1968. Back then, that was the closing date for the next year's directory." She laughed. "I remember because we only changed it to October a couple of years ago when our printer went completely digital, and as you might imagine, a change that major created quite a stir. In any event, to be fair, I ought to mention that Faring Auctions might *still* be in business," she said with another chuckle. "Hard to believe, but some companies do drop their memberships."

Wilma agreed to photocopy the 1969 directory entry and fax it to me. We ended our conversation by comparing weather notes. When I told her I'd seen crocuses, she was amazed, reporting that she wouldn't expect to see them for a month or more. I added her to my online address book. If I ever went to Cheyenne, I'd definitely look her up.

I was back to dead ends with my calls to the antiques dealers. Not one person had heard of Faring Auctions.

I tried to approach the lack of information philosophically. Negatives are an integral part of an appraisal. Knowing what something *isn't* helps narrow the field and guides you in identifying next steps.

I was ready to move to the next stage of my research: I had to find that darn St. James's Palace inventory. All at once, I thought again about how the murder victim's fingerprints were difficult to match because he had so many scars crisscrossing his fingers. The kind of markings that might come from a job in construction—like building houses for Vince's company—but I'd already looked for Sal Briscoe's name in the union directory, and he wasn't listed.

He wasn't listed under *that* name, I corrected myself, and nothing said he wasn't a contract worker, one of the thousands of casual day laborers who worked off the books and, sometimes, lived off the radar.

I called Wes and left him a voice mail asking if he knew whether the police had made any progress in identifying the murdered man, and specifically, if anyone had reviewed the personnel rolls at Vince Collins's company.

This is it, I told myself, thrilled at my thought. *Now we're onto something!*

After lunch, I had another thought: Universities keep copies of their students' dissertations. I went to the University of Southern

California's Web site, clicked through to the library's section, and located the links to Ph.D. candidates' dissertations. It was password protected.

I reached a librarian who explained that the site was only available to current students, faculty, and authorized users.

"How can I qualify as an authorized user?" I asked.

She detailed the rules: You had to have a scholarly reason to access the dissertations and guarantee to respect all copyright and intellectual property regulations. I described my need to know, and she took down pertinent details, including Detective Brownley's contact information, and said she'd get back to me. Another unwanted delay.

Wes called around two.

"I got your message," he said. "We need to meet."

I didn't question the urgency I heard in his voice. I felt pretty darn urgent myself. "Okay. Our dune?"

"Hurry," he replied. "I have news about Gretchen."

CHAPTER NINETEEN

T he police checked Vince's employees first thing," Wes said. "There's nothing there."

We stood together facing the ocean. Yellow-white sparks glinted on the smooth midnight blue water. To the north, near the Rocky Point jetty, a young man tossed driftwood for a golden retriever.

I felt disappointment, but not surprise. My idea about checking Vince's employees had been a sensible theory to pursue, but more guess than conclusion.

"The police are all over him because of his record," Wes continued, "but he has a tight alibi. You know he's a project manager for a company that builds residential developments, right? Well, he's in the middle of tearing down a mess of old houses to build a new subdivision in Rocky Point over by Winton Farm, and he was at the site or his company's office all day. But you know that tip you gave the police about the light fixtures?"

"How on God's earth did you learn about that? I just told the police about them this morning."

"Thanks," he said as if I'd complimented him. "Hold on to your hat. The police went right to Gretchen's place—and guess what? Vince's prints were all over the light fixture."

"I knew it. I just knew it. So that places him *in* her apartment," I said. *Maybe* that's *the secret Mandy wouldn't reveal,* I thought.

"He's at police headquarters now, refusing to talk."

I watched the frothy waves rolling in to shore for a moment, then turned to face him. "You said that you had news about Gretchen."

"I do—a real info-bomb. Let's finish this first, though. Tell me how you found out about the light fixtures. I want a quote—a quote I can use. I need something fresh." Wes pulled a ratty piece of paper from his pocket.

I shook my head, resigned. I knew what Wes wanted—scandal or raw emotion. "The light fixture in Gretchen Brock's hallway appeared to be a custom-designed, one-of-a-kind, hand-painted antique. Without examining it, I can't give a more exact assessment."

"It's okay," Wes acknowledged grudgingly, "but it's pretty white-bread, you know? It doesn't make you sound very interesting. Why don't you add a sentence about Vince's fingerprints—or that there's another fixture at Mandy's?"

"No," I replied. "I'm not going to speculate."

Wes sighed in eloquent testimony to his disappointment. He finished writing and stuffed his paper into an inside pocket, then asked, "Do you remember how the police were looking into that red mark on the dead guy's head?"

I nodded. I could picture, with sickening clarity, the long, blood red gash that ran vertically from the man's temple to his ear.

"They've conclusively identified the weapon—it was definitely the fireplace poker. They can tell by the ridge patterns. The markings on the wound line up exactly."

"What kind of markings?" I asked.

"The poker has indentations and burrs from the manufacturing process, plus there are nicks and dings from normal wear and tear, but here's the clincher—they can ID the poker but not the attacker. There was nothing on the poker. No hairs or fibers, no fingerprints, no DNA, nothing that points to anyone."

"It sounds like it was cleaned with bleach."

"Scoured is more like it," Wes agreed.

I nodded and turned back to face the diamond-flecked ocean.

"Nothing yet on the gun," Wes said. "No permit was issued to anyone involved in the case in Tennessee or any of the New England states. They're checking the rest of the country now."

"What kind of bullet is it?"

"The ballistics report says it's a nine millimeter."

"So that takes us nowhere."

"Right. About Gretchen—I've got a real sit-ya-downer. Someone who was in the Chevy with the Tennessee plates, maybe the guy it's registered to, Sal Briscoe, was after Gretchen in particular."

"You're kidding!" I said, shocked at the thought.

"Nope. They could tell from the car. The police got shot down on their first attempt to get a court order to impound it. That was Friday, after it had been sitting there for two days. Even with the fact that the car had just been purchased in Tennessee for cash—it didn't impress the judge at all. He accused them of going on a fishing expedition, which, of course, they were. Then, over the weekend, Detective Brownley took her time looking inside the car—and guess what she spotted?" Wes asked. "The top banner of December's *Antiques Insights* magazine was poking out from under a pile of empty fast-food bags."

My mouth fell open. That was the issue I'd just had framed—the one with Gretchen's picture on the cover.

Wes nodded, pleased at my reaction. "Pretty amazing, huh? According to the documents the police filed with the court this morning, Detective Brownley was able to recognize it because she saw it hanging in your office. So today, based on the fact that the issue was in plain sight, she was able to get an emergency court order. The car's in police custody already."

I was right, I thought. *Sal Briscoe is the murder victim—he must be.* "Sal Briscoe must have been stalking her," I managed, my mind roiling. "Gretchen must know him."

"Not necessarily. Some stalkers pick their victims because of physical attributes or other random factors. I mean, maybe this guy's a little whacked and decided he and Gretchen were soul mates simply from the cover photo. It's possible."

I nodded. There was so much I wanted to know, yet my brain was moving too fast to frame follow-up questions.

"I figure she walked in on him and killed him—and that," Wes concluded, his voice fired with unbridled excitement, "is why she's on the run."

"No," I replied, my mind snapping into focus at his words. "If it happened that way, Gretchen would have called the police. That would be a clear case of self-defense."

"You're forgetting Gretchen's new ID. She couldn't turn herself in. Whether she's in witness protection or whether she's a criminal—all she could do was get away."

The picture Wes was painting was horrible and vivid and had the ring of truth. From the start, I'd intuitively believed in Gretchen's innocence, and I still did, but it was getting harder to stay resolute in the face of Wes's logic.

Detective Brownley called as I was driving back to Prescott's to report that the lab was almost done with its rush analysis of the vase. It would be delivered to me between four and five. As I pulled off to the side of the road so I could focus on our conversation, my heart lurched in anticipation of getting my first hands-on look at Gretchen's vase. I told her I'd be there to receive it and then, without pausing for breath, snuck in an unrelated question.

"Were you able to get any information about the light fixtures?" I asked.

She was quiet for a two-count. "It was a valuable tip, Josie. Thank you again for bringing them to our attention."

I took the hint and didn't ask any more questions.

Before continuing my drive, I called Serena, only to get her voice mail. I decided there would be no harm in leaving a cheery follow-up message about my belt buckle research. I crossed my fingers that she'd call me back right away.

When I entered the front office, Cara was on the phone with the University of Southern California. I'd been approved, and my user name and password had been e-mailed to me. I rushed upstairs, found the e-mail, and just like that, I was in.

Percy Oliver Johns's dissertation was online and searchable. I entered "vase" and "Meissen" in the search engine, beginning the search in 1723.

Several Meissen objects were listed, but time after time, it was clear that none of the decorative pieces could possibly be Gretchen's vase. There was a ewer, a bowl, two open, thin-necked vases, and a pair of opulently decorated women carrying baskets of flowers. Then, on May 3, 1730, the palace steward recorded that a Meissen vase had been purchased by King George II.

According to the steward's notes, the vase passed by the king's hand to a long-term servant to the queen, H. Howard, in August of that year. Still searching within the document, I looked for references to "H. Howard" and "King George II" and "gift," and much to my amazement, I hit pay dirt.

Henrietta Howard, in addition to serving as a woman of the queen's bedchamber, was the longtime mistress of the king. According to a footnote, the king's steward reported that Henrietta Howard admired the vase in the king's presence, and he gave it to her on the spot. The footnote went on to detail that the author's source for the explanation of the transfer was a letter written to her by Lord Chesterfield in which he congratulated her on having acquired such a wonderful object. I sat back, amazed, then turned to the photographs of the vase. *I would have been over the moon,* I thought, *if someone gave it to me, let alone my lover, let alone the king.*

I was considering how to learn more about Henrietta Howard when Cara buzzed me. Detective Brownley was downstairs with the vase.

CHAPTER TWENTY

I signed the forms accepting responsibility for the vase.

"Call as soon as you know something, okay?" Detective Brownley asked.

"Absolutely," I promised, hoping I had something to call about soon.

She touched the porcelain with her fingertips as if for luck, then left. I watched as she strode to her car. The sky had darkened, and suddenly it began to shower. Detective Brownley ran the last couple of steps to her car.

Back inside, I carried the vase to the cushioned worktable in the warehouse. It was spectacular, and goose-bumpy chills ran up my arms and spine and down again and made me shiver, just thinking that a king might have bestowed this very object on a woman he loved nearly three hundred years ago. I positioned it on its side. As I began my examination, Sasha stepped into the warehouse.

"Cara's gone for the day. Is it all right if Fred and I head home, too?"

"Absolutely. I'm going to get started on the vase."

She approached the worktable. "Fred," she called over her shoulder, "come and look at this."

"What?" he asked from the threshold, shrugging into his coat.

"Gretchen's vase." Sasha pointed at the marks on the bottom. "Look at the underglaze."

"It's hard to know where to take a scraping from," Fred said, joining us at the table, assuming we'd want to confirm that the object had been created with period-appropriate materials.

"Inside, I think," Sasha said.

"Because there's a better chance of getting an unadulterated sample?"

"That, and because we wouldn't risk damaging the visible surface."

I didn't anticipate trying to date the vase through a materials analysis, since we didn't care whether it was real or not. Our only concern was finding Gretchen. I was going to examine the vase for clues—additional marks, for instance, integrated into the design, that might have been overlooked and that might lead us to a seller or previous owner.

"Höroldt was very talented," Sasha noted. "Look at those swirls—they're freehand and incredibly even. Like calligraphy, almost."

We admired the vase awhile longer, then I told them both good night and asked that they set the phone to the night message and lock up.

"Will do," Sasha called.

Through the cracked door, I heard their leaving noises. The front door clicked closed, and then I was alone.

What, I asked myself, looking at the vase, *besides extra marks could help me find Gretchen?* Maybe she tucked the tag into the vase's cavity, saving it for future reference. If so, there was a chance that the tag would be imprinted with a store's name. I aimed a high-wattage work light into the vase's hollow center and peered inside. It was empty.

Using a grease pencil, I marked a start point on the vase's lip. I examined the vase, millimeter by millimeter, in concentric circles, each about an inch high, staring through a loupe. It was precision work, with no room for error.

The blue hues were luscious and subtly varied. I'd reached the third circle when suddenly the image blurred. I removed the loupe, stretched, and turned to the wall clock. It was just after seven. I pressed the heels of my hands against my eyes for a moment, then considered pushing on. I couldn't. If I tried, I risked missing something. I marked my stopping point and gently lowered the vase into its protective box, annotating the index card in keeping with our current protocol.

I hoisted the box and started off toward the vault. The only illumination in the windowless warehouse came from the low-wattage overhead bulbs and the work light, its beam stretching along the wall to the ceiling. Long, thin shadows shifted as I moved. It was spooky.

The doorbell rang, momentarily startling me. *A customer,* I thought.

The bell chimed again, this time followed by a series of fist-pounding knocks. *A persistent customer,* I joked to myself and walked on.

I heard someone jiggling the doorknob, and I paused, uneasy.

The phone rang, and the machine clicked on, then off when the caller hung up. Almost immediately, it rang again. I frowned, uncertain what, if anything, to do. Several seconds passed. *They left,* I thought. I told myself I was just a scaredy cat. I started off again, relieved. The tag sale room buzzer sounded.

"Oh, my God!" I exclaimed in a whisper, startled.

Someone had decided to try another door. I wanted to see who was out there. I carefully lowered the box to the floor and slid it into the passageway against a shelf, out of the center aisle, and sprinted to the tag sale room door. I placed my eye against the peephole and surveyed the room. The last vestiges of dusk filtering in through the windows provided a measure of comfort and allowed me to see outside. Nothing alarming was visible.

Into the silence came a sharp crack, then the sound of glass shattering, followed by the tinkling pings of glass on glass. *Someone's breaking in,* I realized, picturing a gloved hand sweeping shards off the windowsill. My heart was beating so ferociously I couldn't swallow. My lips were suddenly dry. I darted into the closest row of shelving. I was five rows back.

A thump sounded, then the harsh, loud scraping of metal against metal. I tried to picture what was happening. Besides a few appliances like the microwave, the only metal object in the front office was a four-drawer file cabinet. It sounded like someone was using a metal tool to jimmy it open. *Why?* I asked myself.

I looked up. Red lights told me that the cameras were recording, but no amber lights were illuminated, which meant the alarm wasn't set—no surprise, since we only activate the system when we leave for the day. No one was coming to my rescue. I had to save myself.

If I could reach my office on the mezzanine level, I could lock myself in and call for help. To get upstairs, I'd have to traverse the fifty-foot-wide open area—and part of the time, I'd be visible from the front office through the door, still slightly ajar. Worse, once upstairs, I'd be trapped. There was no alternate way out.

Or I could hit one of the panic buttons placed strategically throughout the building. The nearest one was twenty unshielded feet away. I'd be vulnerable, but less so.

I nodded, my decision made. The panic button it was. I listened for a moment, preparing to run. I heard confusing noises—papers rustling, a small crashing sound, footsteps. *Footsteps!* I thought, my heart leaping into my throat.

I calculated distance and time and realized that if the intruder was heading into the warehouse, the panic button was too far away—I'd be an easy target.

Still, I had to do something, and I had to act now. Of the two flawed options, this one was marginally less risky than the other.

I sidestepped toward the tag sale room, slowly, ever so slowly, walking as if the floor were made of eggshells. Every step on the concrete floor reverberated in the high-ceilinged, cavernous space. I reached the end of the shelving unit and took a deep breath. My palms were moist and my heart was throbbing. I felt sick.

The door from the front swung wide. I swallowed a scream and froze, then sank to the ground, making myself as small as possible. I stood up and found a slit that provided a clear sight line through the mechanical toys and children's books stacked on the shelves around me to where he stood just inside the doorway. He was about six feet tall, with an average build. He wore jeans and work boots, a shapeless black trench coat with the collar up, black leather gloves, and a black knit ski mask that covered his head and face. I couldn't describe his hair or eye color or skin tone—not one inch of him showed.

He scanned the entire warehouse, then started moving toward

the spiral staircase that led to my office. I felt light-headed at the realization that he was heading where I'd almost gone. I'd need only a few seconds to reach the panic button, but from his position on the steps, he'd be sure to spot me. I decided to wait until he reached the top and disappeared into my office. I readied myself to run, and as I did so, I touched a toy near my elbow, a monkey playing a drum set, and the cymbal sounded.

Shocked, I gasped and stepped back instinctively, smashing into the shelving unit in back of me with a dull thwack, sending a pair of heavy bronze bookends crashing to the ground.

Damn, I silently cursed, and tiptoed to the end of the row, to distance myself as best I could from the noise. I held my breath. I couldn't see him clearly, but it felt like he was staring right at me. He plunged down the steps and ran in my direction.

I scooted into the far aisle, dashed toward the rear, then dove into the back row, desperate for a plan. *He'll track me by my footsteps,* I thought, on the edge of suffocating panic, uncertain what to do or how to escape. The vault came into view in front of me. *Safe haven,* I thought.

I swiped my sweating palms on my jeans so my fingers wouldn't slip on the slick steel keypad of the combination lock. I punched in the code, but the wheel wouldn't spin. I'd gotten the numbers wrong. I looked over my shoulder. He'd found me. He was at the far end of the row, running full speed straight at me.

Forcing myself to concentrate, I entered the numbers again and got them right.

I wrenched open the door, shot into the safe, and dragged the door closed, throwing the bolt and spinning the wheel only seconds before he reached me. I slapped the panic button positioned by the combination pad, and only then did I breathe. Unless the intruder had brought a bomb, he wasn't going to reach me—the safe was that secure.

I leaned against the back wall, waiting for my tumultuous pulse to begin to quiet. Time passed, then seemed to stop. I leaned for a while longer, then sat down. I couldn't hear sirens, phones, or people, but I wasn't worried. I had enough oxygen for six hours, but the security service should be there within minutes. Still, it was terrifying. It felt as if I were alone in the world. I decided to have a telephone jack installed first thing in the morning.

Finally, after what felt like hours but was probably only fifteen minutes at the most, a muffled voice called out, "Ms. Prescott?"

"In here!" I called as loudly as I could. "I'm locked in the safe!" I thumped the door and shouted my position again.

I heard more than one voice as people approached, but I couldn't make out any words until someone asked me to identify myself. I could have wept, I was so relieved. We exchanged our preset code words. If I called "cat," I was informing them that I was being held hostage. If I called "dog," they'd know I was safe. If they spoke the word "machine," I'd know it was really someone from the security company, not a bad guy up to no good.

"Dog," I yelled. "It's Josie. Dog. And you?"

"Machine," someone said, sounding close.

With trembling fingers, I released the bolt.

Two uniformed security men stood in a half-circle facing me, their expressions grave. "Are you injured?" one asked. His name tag read JAYSON.

"No," I replied, and I realized that I was shaking. "A man in a mask was inside, chasing me. I heard glass break." I looked around the vast warehouse. Nothing looked disturbed. "I heard noises in the front office."

"That seems to be the entry point. We called the police as soon as we arrived and saw the broken window."

Shrieking sirens announced their arrival.

The front office was a mess. One of the windows stood open. I stared at it as Detective Brownley instructed a technician to gather up the glass pieces and try them for prints.

Evidently, the intruder had demolished a single pane of glass and reached in to unlock the window. *Easy as pie,* I thought, anger replacing fear. *Damn him.*

"Aren't you surprised that he'd risk entering through a front window?" I asked. "Anyone driving by would see him. Plus, didn't he think someone might be here? I mean, my car is in the parking lot!"

She shrugged. "There's almost no traffic out here that time of day, and you said he rang the bell and knocked and called, right? Obviously, he thought no one was here and it seemed like a reasonable risk to him."

"What about those calls? Can't you trace the number?"

"I'm betting it will turn out to be a disposable cell phone. What I want to know is what he was after."

I surveyed the damage. An African violet that sat on the table had been knocked over, the pot broken, and its delicate purple blossoms scattered in the dirt. Gretchen would be heartbroken. She'd rescued the nearly dead plant from the trash room at her condo, then spent weeks nurturing it back to health.

Locked file drawers had been pried open, probably, according to the crime scene tech guy, with a crowbar. File folders were strewn across the floor. Papers were heaped in chaotic piles. Desk drawers stood open.

"Gretchen's personnel file," I said. "Maybe he wanted to find her emergency contact, thinking he could look for her at that person's house."

"Is her file there?" Detective Brownley asked the technician. "Gretchen Brock. Do you see it?" To me, she added, "She didn't list anyone, so it's moot anyhow."

He extracted a thin manila file from the mishmash. No papers were missing.

The night manager at my security firm called to let me know that they'd e-mailed the digital camera output to the police as I'd requested, but that they agreed with my assessment—the man was unrecognizable.

I called Ty and reported what had happened. "I need to nail up some wood," I explained, "so I don't know exactly when I'll get home."

"I'm almost back—look for me in about fifteen minutes."

"You don't need to come."

"Yes, I do. Fifteen minutes."

"Thanks," I said, my eyes welling. A little of my anger faded away.

As I stood near the broken window, watching Detective Brownley huddle with Griff, I flexed my back and shoulders, trying to relax. It felt like a steel rod was embedded in my neck. Although the parking lot was brightly lit, Griff lifted heavy-duty handheld spotlights from his vehicle's trunk. Starting in opposite corners, they walked the parking lot seeking evidence on the still-damp pavement. *Of what?* I wondered. *Tire marks. A discarded cigarette butt. A candy wrapper.*

Griff squatted, aimed his lamp at something, then called to Detective Brownley. She joined him, examined whatever he'd found, and nodded. She photographed it, then continued snapping as she walked away from the building. *She's recording footsteps,* I realized. Footsteps that led straight like a shot into the woods. Detective Brownley and Griff stepped behind a chestnut tree, and for a moment they were lost in the darkness. Then their spotlights came on, and I could follow their progress as they wended their way toward the church parking lot.

When Detective Brownley returned to the office, she confirmed that they had identified footprints they suspected belonged to the intruder and would be casting molds right away in case it rained again overnight.

Ty arrived, and without even taking off his coat, he hugged me. I buried my face in his chest, and for one long glorious moment my world was comprised solely of the earthy aroma of leather, the beating of his heart, and the security of his embrace.

Half an hour later, when Detective Brownley announced they were done with their inside crime scene work, Ty nailed a plank of wood into the window frame while I tested the doors in the auction venue and tag sale room to be certain everything was secure. I spun the wheel on the safe, and only then did I remember that I hadn't returned Gretchen's vase to the vault.

I rushed over to the spot where I'd left the box. It was gone. I'd left it in this exact spot, I was certain of it, and now it was gone. I couldn't move. I couldn't think. I was hyperventilating. Ty called my name, but I couldn't reply. I couldn't speak at all. I stood, immobile, until he found me.

"It's gone," I whispered, pointing to where it had been. "Gretchen's vase. The man stole it, and now it's gone."

Ty guided me back to the office and told me to sit down. "You're in shock, Josie," he said. "Do as I say."

Within minutes, Detective Brownley was back with the team of technicians in tow. It was surreal, a nightmare. I felt overwhelmed and helpless. I couldn't find Gretchen, and now I'd lost her vase.

CHAPTER TWENTY-ONE

I didn't even try to sleep. At Ty's suggestion, I took a hot shower, had a cup of tea and then a glass of brandy—but nothing helped. I was beside myself. I couldn't read, watch a movie or TV, or listen to music. All I could do was fret.

About two thirty, I decided to use my wakefulness in the only productive way I could think of—doing research. As I viewed the images of Gretchen's vase I'd downloaded onto my laptop, I began to tear up. I stopped myself from crying.

I'd left off at the discovery that the vase might have been a present from King George II to his mistress, Henrietta Howard. Deepening my investigation, I found several articles that revealed additional details about Henrietta's struggles and tenacity.

Henrietta Howard, a gentle-born woman, survived an abusive marriage, reinvented herself as a member of Queen Charlotte's staff, and, after spending years as the mistress of King George II, went on to become one of the most sought-after women of her generation, friends with the greatest poets and intellectuals of her day. Alexander Pope wrote of her:

> *I knew a thing that's most uncommon*
> *(Envy be silent and attend)*
> *I knew a reasonable woman,*
> *Handsome and witty, yet a friend.*

Pope's attitude toward women reflected his era, I thought, highlighting the magnitude of Henrietta Howard's accomplishment. In an age when women had few rights, she'd rescued herself from battery and penury.

I spent the next two hours trying to locate the full text of Lord Chesterfield's letter, the one that Percy Oliver Johns had referenced in his dissertation, without luck. A wave of fatigue swept over me. I e-mailed Sasha, describing where I'd searched and asking her to give it a try.

As I clicked SEND, I thought that finally I might be able to rest.

I slept fitfully for a few hours and woke up feeling unrested and fretful.

Ty had left a pot of coffee on the burner and a note taped to the refrigerator: "I'll be home early. You're doing everything you can. Detective Brownley is very, very good at her job. Love, Ty." I held his note against my heart for a moment, grateful for the concern and care that resonated from his words.

Wes called at eight, just as I was preparing to leave for work. "We need to talk," he said, his tone grave.

We agreed to meet at the Portsmouth Diner.

I got there first, selected a booth near the back, and ordered coffee.

Wes came in a few minutes later. Sliding onto the bench, he said, "Are you okay? You don't look so good."

I looked out the window at scores of tiny yellow and white crocuses blooming along a grassy knoll. I didn't want to discuss how I felt. "I'm holding up as best I can."

"Yeah . . . well . . . I hear the police are making progress."

I felt myself perk up, just a little. "Tell me."

"First, about last night—fill me in. I got the news on my police scanner, but I was too far away to get to your place in time."

"That doesn't sound like you, Wes," I replied, forcing myself to adopt a light tone.

He looked embarrassed. "I was kind of tied up."

"What kind of tied up?" I asked warily, prepared to hear something offensive or insensitive.

"If you must know, I was with my mother in Hampton. I took her to dinner. It was her birthday."

I smiled. "Good going, Wes!"

His cheeks reddened. "So what happened?" he asked.

I paused, then said, "Someone broke into Prescott's and stole a valuable vase."

"How? Come on, Josie, I need details."

I met his eyes. "I can't talk about it yet, Wes. I'm too upset." I pushed my coffee mug away and prepared to leave. "If you have something to tell me, great. Otherwise, I've got to go."

"Don't go. If you can't talk about the details, list the things you want to know. Maybe I can help."

I paused. That was a good offer, and it was kind of him not to challenge my refusal to talk—in addition to being expedient, of course. If he got me describing what I wanted to know, he'd be that much ahead of the game.

"Thank you. I'd like to know who broke in, of course, and why. The intruder was completely covered up—all I could see was that he was about six feet tall. What was he after? Information about Gretchen? He went through papers in the office before stealing a vase packed in a box. With all the inventory available, why did he take that one object? The police found footprints. I want to know if they got good imprints and what they were able to learn from them." I shrugged, thinking whether there was anything else. "That's what I'd want to know."

Wes wrote furiously on his lined paper, then nodded and looked up. "Thanks, Josie."

"Do you have any news, Wes?" I asked.

"Not yet," Wes said, "but I will."

I left him sitting in the booth and drove straight to work.

I filled out several online forms, reporting Gretchen's vase to the various national and international stolen art and antiques registries that Prescott's, like all reputable auction houses, subscribed to. If the vase were offered for sale, we might catch the seller and, from that information, find Gretchen, or at least, the thief. I was attaching photographs when Cara called up to say that someone named Jack was downstairs asking to see me.

"Jack who?" I asked.

"Jack Stene. He's a friend of Gretchen's," she added, lowering her voice as if she were revealing a secret. "You remember—he called last Friday."

"I'll be right down."

Jack Stene was in his early thirties. He wore khakis and a button-down blue shirt. At a guess, he was about five-eleven and well built. His hair was sandy brown and long enough for him to have gathered it into a ponytail. He had brown-black eyes and an affable smile.

"You must be Josie," he said as I walked into the office.

"I am." I extended a hand and smiled back.

He took my hand in his and shook it—a good one, strong, but not too strong, and lasting just the right amount of time—as he introduced himself. "Is there somewhere we can talk?" he asked.

I led the way into the warehouse and paused by the stacked crates.

"I met Gretchen." He looked away as if he were embarrassed.

Gretchen's chemist, I thought.

"I got back last Monday. Since then . . . well . . . I've heard the news . . . about the murder and everything . . . I just don't understand . . . I mean, the police have asked me—"

"The police?" I broke in, surprised.

He nodded. "They got my name from her cell phone call log and my e-mails to her. I mean, that was bad, but then it was on the news that an APB had been issued . . . and this morning I heard that there was a break-in here last night . . . I was hoping you could tell me what's going on."

"What did you tell the police?"

"Nothing. I don't know anything. Do you?"

Jack was waiting for my reply, his eyes conveying sincerity and concern and nothing else, except determination. I had to say something, and from the set of his jaw and his unwavering gaze, I could tell he wasn't going to be put off by a politely worded general statement.

"Only that it's crazy to think that Gretchen did anything wrong," I said. Without warning, my voice cracked, and I looked away. I took several deep breaths to compose myself.

"She talked about you a lot, about what a smart businesswoman you are and how much she trusts you. I can't help thinking . . . if anyone knows where she is, it would be you."

I took another deep breath. "I wish," I said.

He looked past the rows of shelving, toward the back wall. Then he met my eyes and held them. "Are you sure you don't know how to reach her? Even to deliver a message?"

Even if I had a way of contacting her, I wouldn't have told him so. I had no reason to trust him. None. He might be just what he purported to be—a new fella in Gretchen's life, confused and worried and eager to know she was all right. Maybe he wasn't, though; it was possible that he was just a good actor.

"No," I said. "Do you?"

"Me?" He seemed nonplussed at my question. "No. That's why I'm here."

I nodded. Probably it was true. He gave me his business card, jotting his cell phone number on the back. We promised to let one another know if and when we heard from her.

I fingered Jack's card as I watched him walk to his car. I didn't just need information—I needed answers. *When in doubt,* I thought, *call Wes.*

His phone went directly to voice mail. "I'm hoping you can check out someone for me—a friend of Gretchen's named Jack Stene," I said in my message. "He works at Dobson Corporation." I read off Jack's contact information, but I didn't articulate the obvious point: Within days of meeting him, Gretchen disappeared.

Cara buzzed up about ten minutes later. Serena Carson was on line two. I nearly toppled off my chair diving to punch the button marked 2.

"I found someone for you to talk to," Serena said. "His name is Jed McGinty, and he started working at Sidlawn fencing in 1978. According to what I've been told, he knows *everything*." She giggled, and I wondered what juicy nugget she'd been given as an example of Jed's long memory.

"You're the best!" I exclaimed.

"Thanks! Jed is expecting your call. He's kind of excited to think he's assisting in a police investigation."

Jed answered with the easy manner of a man who had all day to chat, and lucky for me, he recalled the belt buckle well.

"It was incredible," Jed said, "the best prize ever—a dude ranch. Back then, every year, the CEO took the company's top sales reps and executives somewhere. You know the kind of thing—a resort in Puerto Rico, Disney World in Orlando, Broadway shows in New York. They were *all* sweet, but a dude ranch in Montana? Man, that created some buzz in the company, let me tell you."

"I can imagine. Did you go?"

He laughed, a deep, rolling chuckle. "Are you kidding me? I'd been with the company less than a year at that point. I was an associate accountant, about five levels too low to even qualify to be invited." He chuckled again, and I wondered what struck him as funny. "The CFO, Barry Rackham his name was, he was lucky enough to go, and when he got back, he showed us all the swag. That belt buckle you're asking about, it was part of his haul. It was in the gift bag." He laughed again. "I asked my boss what it would take to get one of those puppies for myself. He told me that given my age and experience, my best bet was marrying the boss's daughter!"

I laughed politely. "What can you tell me about the buckle?"

"It was custom made, a great design—an Indian in full war paint. There were only a few of them produced, so getting one was, like, up there with getting a bonus." Another huge laugh. "Didn't happen, you know?"

"So, Jed, tell me," I said, crossing my fingers for luck, "is there a list of recipients?"

"Now that I *don't* know."

"Darn. Who might?" I asked, disappointed but not surprised.

"Hmmm," Jed murmured. "I think you'd better talk to Serena about that."

"Will do." I thanked him, and he transferred me back.

"Serena," I said when she was on the line, "I have another question. Jed was very helpful. He was able to describe the belt buckle, which is great, but he didn't know if there's a list of recipients. How about it? Can you think of any way I could track it down?"

"Oh, my," Serena commented. "Jed didn't have any ideas?"

"Yes, he did. His idea was to ask you." I laughed a little, and she joined in. "I'm pretty sure that there were only ten produced. Doesn't it make sense that the company would have kept track of that sort of information? I hate to ask you to go back to HR."

"No problem. To tell you the truth, it's fun! I feel like a real detective."

"You're good at it."

"Thank you, Josie. I'll call you back as soon as I can," she said.

I resigned myself to another agonizing wait.

CHAPTER TWENTY-TWO

G ood news," Serena told me when she called back. "I found out who knows about the recipient list. I've conferenced you in to Grady. Grady, are you with us? He knows where the belt buckle records are. I'll let him explain."

"Josie, no one here has thought about those end-of-year celebrations since the owner died. I mean, we're talking a lot of years ago already! We used to have framed lists of the top performers hanging in the cafeteria, one per year, but we moved locations, and those lists got put into storage."

"Oh, no! The dreaded storage nightmare."

"Exactly, except that I am the company-wide document manager, so I know where they're located. We're talkin' warehouse, though, so you've got to give me a little time."

"The only problem is that I have no time. How long are you thinking?" As soon as I asked the question I could sense a mood shift. I bit my lip and held my breath.

"I don't know," he said, sounding defensive. "A while."

I paused to find the right words. "I know it sounds weird to suggest urgency when we're talking about a 1979 belt buckle, but"—I laughed, embarrassed at what I was about to say—"we're actually talking life and death."

"Run that by me again?" Grady said.

I could hear Serena breathing in the background, listening. "I'm helping the police in a criminal investigation. I'm not at liberty to discuss particulars, but I can tell you that the belt buckle was worn by a victim of a crime. There's no implication that your company is involved in any way. This is all about tracking the buckle—learning who received it from Sidlawn Fencing in 1979 and tracing it from there. If you need more information, I'll ask the police to get in touch with you."

If Grady was like most people, I figured, he'd rather have a root canal than invite the police into his home or office to snoop.

"Of course, we're glad to cooperate with any police investigation," he said. "Let me just think for a second."

Serena stayed quiet. After almost a minute, I concluded that I'd muffed it. *You should have told him about Gretchen,* I berated myself, *about how it was possible that his efforts might save her life.*

"Okay then," Grady said. "I'll get cracking."

"Do you need help? I mean, if we're talking about digging through boxes, I could arrange for some guys to help."

"Nah, we got workers on site. It's all priorities, you know?"

"How long do you figure it will take?" I asked.

"No idea. I know the plaques are stored in boxes, and I know which warehouse the boxes are in, but not their exact location. But trust me—your request has made it to the top of the heap. I'll get you your answer just as soon as I can."

Despite my urge to be up and doing, I thanked him, and then I thanked Serena, too.

"I have news about Henrietta Howard," Sasha told me. "There are hundreds of her letters extant, most of them in private hands, including Lord Chesterfield's, but no one source that tracks everything. I'm afraid it would be like looking for a needle in a haystack to find a reference to that particular vase."

"Darn. At least we have other irons in the fire," I said. "See if you can track down Dr. Johns. Percy Oliver Johns—the author of that inventory. He referenced the letter, so he must know where it is. In fact, he might have additional information that didn't make it into his dissertation."

Gretchen's chimes sounded. Mandy and Lina stepped inside.

"We wanted to stop by," Mandy said. "We heard the news about the break-in." Her eyes went to the plywood. "Are you okay?"

I smiled a little. "Thanks. That's really nice of you both. I'm fine." I gestured toward Fred, Sasha, and Cara. "We're all fine."

"Did you see who broke in?" Mandy asked, sounding apprehensive.

My mouth went desert-dry. *Vince,* I thought. *She's wondering if Vince is involved—and if so, whether I can identify him. Is he?* "Yes," I said, leaving it open whether I recognized the intruder or not. "It was pretty frightening."

"Was anything taken?" Lina asked.

"Just one item," I replied, avoiding revealing that Gretchen's vase was stolen. "No one was hurt, and that's the main thing." I shook my head. "It sounds trite to say so, but it's true. Can either of you think of anything that might help the police?"

They couldn't. After a few more minutes of expressing our shocked dismay, Mandy said, "Well, we better get going or we'll be late to work."

I thanked them again for stopping by and watched as Lina got behind the wheel of an old Ford Focus and drove off. As they pulled out of the lot, a gold Taurus pulled in. The blond man who'd wanted to find Gretchen at the tag sale, Chip, parked and sat for a minute, then stepped out, saw me standing at the door, and waved, smiling like he meant it. In the sunlight, his yellow hair looked totally fake.

"Hello again, Josie Prescott." He extended his hand as he approached, and we shook. "What happened here?" he asked, nodding toward the wood-covered window.

"A broken window. The glazier's en route. Chip, right?"

I shut the door, and he nodded around, silently greeting the staff. "Good memory. I don't see Gretchen. Don't tell me I'm out of luck again."

"Sorry. Maybe next time."

"Are you sure she really works here?" he asked in a teasing tone, semismiling.

My something's-wrong-here-meter switched on. He sounded more annoyed than jovial. I found myself wondering what his story really was—and then I had an idea. I smiled again, warmly this time.

"Can I get you something?" I asked. "A cup of coffee? Maybe you want to sit a little and talk."

He met and held my eyes. "I'd love a cup of coffee."

I placed cups and spoons and napkins on a tray, added a plate of macaroons, and carried it upstairs. Chip sat on the wing chair, seemingly at ease. I skewed sideways on the love seat to face him.

"So, you said you've known Gretchen for quite a while, is that right?" I asked.

"Yes, but we lost touch. It was great to find out where she worked."

"How did that happen?" I asked, avoiding his eyes, selecting a macaroon instead. When I was a junior in college, I took an acting course. In the parlance of the field, what I was doing was giving myself "business."

"One of those happenstances." He chuckled appealingly. "You know how it works. A mutual friend told me he saw her working at the tag sale a few weeks ago. He didn't speak to her 'cause she was busy. Apparently you do a very good business."

I smiled modestly. "We've been very fortunate. So you decided to surprise her. That's so fun!"

He laughed again and leaned forward. "A picture came to me of what would happen when Gretchen first saw me. As soon as she spotted me, she'd call my name, leap up, and hug me. Can't you just see it?"

He was right. Gretchen would bound across the room, shrieking with pleasure, and the thought of it tore my heart out. I met Chip's eyes but didn't see him. Through a veil of anguish, I pictured Gretchen being dragged away by unknown hands. Now, nearly a week later, I imagined her trapped in some makeshift prison, terrified and hopeless.

I pushed the horrific vision aside, took a deep breath, and said, in the most animated tone I could muster, "Surprising her sounds like a great idea! I want to be there when you two finally connect. Where do you know her from?"

He waved it away and winked. "A gentleman never tells."

I smiled, pretending to succumb to the allure of his flirtatious manner, while thinking that on the face of it, he was pretty darn cagey.

"How about you? Did you know her before she started working here?"

"No," I said. "She applied for a job and got it, and she's been here ever since!"

"How long ago was that?"

He's playing me, I thought. *He's trying as hard to get information from me as I am to get some from him.* "I'd have to look it up," I said, fluttering my fingers. "I have no head for dates. Not at all." I smiled again. "How's your coffee?"

"Hits the spot. Thank you." He downed his cup, placed it on the butler's table, and stood up. "Duty calls. I've got to go."

"I'm glad we had this chance to chat," I said. "Are you off to work?"

"Late for work is more like it." When he saw that I intended to follow him, he added, "You don't need to bother. I can find my own way out."

I shrugged. "No bother. Plus it's another one of those pesky rules. No civilians are allowed to wander around unescorted."

He laughed and started down the spiral stairs. "A civilian, huh? I've been called worse."

I waved a final good-bye at the front door, watching as he crossed the lot to his Taurus. It had Massachusetts plates. I memorized the number, then jotted it down on a scrap of paper. Upstairs, I decided to solicit Wes's assistance again.

He picked up the phone on the first ring. "I was just going to call you. I've got nothing on Stene. He's been with Dobson Corp. a little over three years. No wants, no warrants, no debt to speak of. Nothing. Did you get a something's-fishy smell, or were you just asking on spec?"

"I don't know that I'd say on spec, exactly," I replied. "It just seemed prudent to me. There's something else, though. A man who says his name is Chip Davidson has been in to see Gretchen twice. Which tells me he doesn't know where she is now—but wants to."

"So?"

"So Chip was on edge and too familiar. He wouldn't leave a message, and he avoided answering my friendly questions. I got his plate number. He drives a Taurus. It wouldn't surprise me if it's a rental. Lots of car rental places have Tauruses." I gave him the number. "There's more. I've got his fingerprints—and his DNA—on a coffee cup."

Wes paused, and I could picture his thoughtful expression. "Tell me again why you're suspicious of him."

"I felt immediately comfortable with him. He's charming, but I starting sensing that he's not charming-nice; he's charming-glib, if you know what I mean. Also, he doesn't look like the type to dye his hair, but I'm pretty sure he does. I mean, he's polished, but he's not a pretty boy, and he's not punky or goth or anything. I know none of what I'm saying is conclusive—but taken together, it adds up to trouble. I'll tell you what I think. I think he's a con man."

"Worth a look, I guess," Wes agreed without enthusiasm. "When can I get the cup?"

"Now. I have to go to the bank," I said, thinking that I needed to make a deposit. I told him the location. "Can you meet me there in fifteen minutes?"

He could.

I slipped a stubby pencil through the handle of Chip's cup and picked it up. It tilted and wobbled. Using the eraser end of another pencil, I leveled the cup and carried it gingerly to the sink, slowly tipped it sideways to drain the last few drops of coffee, and gently lowered it into a plastic bag, the kind we keep in stock by the thousands for packaging purchases at the tag sale. I twisted the plastic tie into a screw and held up my prize.

Gotcha, I thought.

Wes seemed underwhelmed as he dangled the plastic bag and stared at the pretty cup.

"I'm still not sure I get the significance," he said. "You're asking me to call in a favor to check prints and DNA on this coffee cup because some guy came into your place twice to ask about Gretchen, have I got that right?"

"Well, yes, but it's not just that. It's the way he asked. Besides which, what harm can it do to check?"

Wes shrugged. "I only get so many favors, you know?"

I nodded, understanding his point. "Obviously, there's a lot that we don't have a handle on. While it's possible that Gretchen has some kind of guilty knowledge of the murder, I just don't believe it." I held up a hand. "I know, I know. Whenever a polite young man is arrested for a crime, everyone says how quiet he was and how surprised they are. I get it, Wes, but that's not this. I'm talking about *Gretchen*. Think about it—she's not some stranger. She's someone I've worked with for four years."

"I think you're off track, Josie. I know you like her and everything, but you're sounding pretty starry-eyed, you know?"

I turned away from his penetrating gaze, not wanting him to see how his words dashed my hopes. "What do you think?" I asked, my eyes still averted.

"Gretchen *is* a stranger. Her identity is only four years old. She's likable, warmhearted, and a good employee, but you don't know anything about her, not really. Think about it objectively, Josie. She comes back from vacation but doesn't show up at work. You don't know why. You're just making it up to suit the picture you hope is true."

If he was right and this was just wishful thinking, I was engaged in one of the most dangerous of indulgences—self-deception. I couldn't think of what to say.

"The police have verified that the victim's fingerprints match prints found in the Chevy," Wes said.

I looked up. That was new information.

Wes nodded, then continued. "From what we can tell, the dead guy is Sal Briscoe—unless, like we talked about before, he stole the car from Sal Briscoe and that's why his prints are inside the car, or he was in the car because he's Sal Briscoe's buddy or something." Wes shrugged. "Regardless, no one seems to know who Sal Briscoe is. He's not in the federal databank, and he doesn't have a record in Tennessee. The police are still checking other states." Wes shrugged again. "Gretchen's friends are no help. No one knows anything."

I shook my head, saddened and frustrated: "Do you think Chip is worth checking out?" I asked.

Wes opened his car door and placed the cup on the passenger seat. "Yes."

"What about last night's break-in? Any news?"

"Vince has an alibi for that, too. He was with Mandy all evening."

"She'd lie to protect him."

"I know. The police think so, too."

"Do you mean the police think he's involved?" I asked.

"Yes, but not for publication. They're looking into *both* his alibis."

"What about his motive? Why would he break into my place?"

"He's a crook. You've got valuable antiques."

I shook my head. "That doesn't make sense. Everything really valuable is in the vault. Besides which, breaking into a business just after business hours with a car in the parking lot is crazy—it's too risky."

"Probably he thought that the car's owner had gone out to dinner with a friend or something and would be back in an hour or two. Which meant that the alarm wouldn't yet be set for the night." Wes shrugged. "What the heck—he was right about the risk factor, you know? He got away with it."

I sighed. "You make sense. Anything else?"

"Nope. Catch ya later," he replied, and waved as he drove away.

CHAPTER TWENTY-THREE

W hen I got back to the office, Cara handed me a message. Grady had called about the belt buckle. "Hi, Grady. It's Josie. I got your message," I said when I called him back.

"We found the plaque, and I transcribed the list, but I don't know if it's in numbered order. I can't find anything indicating which person got which number buckle. Nothing's easy, right?"

"Isn't that the truth? Regardless, having the names is great. You really went above and beyond. Can you e-mail me the list?"

I gave him my e-mail address and heard the muted tap-tap as he typed it in. I felt excited enough to do a jig. I was certain that a clue to Gretchen's disappearance was at hand. I stared at my in-box until the e-mail appeared, then downloaded the listing and printed it out. The names on the list read:

1. Alvin Smith
2. Bernie Winslow
3. Orrie Cather
4. David Mackaw
5. Robert Boulanger
6. Barry Rackham
7. Victor Norris
8. Louis Steinberg
9. Mortimer Brazenford
10. Roland Sisto

I read the list, carefully considering each name, one at a time. *Surely,* I thought, *Gretchen has or had a relationship with one of these men.* To me, though, the only familiar name was Barry Rackham, the CFO who showed Jed the belt buckle in 1979. I felt deflated. I'd been so hopeful.

The owner of the belt buckle might have given or sold it to someone Gretchen knew, I reasoned. Or the original recipient might have pawned, sold, or consigned the buckle to some dealer somewhere. If so, tracing it to its current wearer—the dead man now tentatively identified as Sal Briscoe—might be irrelevant or even impossible.

I called Detective Brownley and said I'd e-mail her the list.

"Thank you, Josie. Great job. We'll check out all ten names," she responded.

Me, too, I thought, sending the e-mail.

I started with Orrie Cather on the off-chance that the third name on the list had actually received the buckle stamped number three. Googling his name brought up dozens of hits, and I scanned the first several references. Nothing leapt out at me as germane. I repeated the process for each name, with the same disappointing result. Until I got to the fifth name on the list—Robert Boulanger.

When I typed in his name, there were more than a hundred hits. The first was a short newspaper article that had appeared in the *Denver Globe* on October 2, 2002, the day after a woman named Amelia Bartlett had been beaten to death in her Denver antiques store. According to the article, Robert Boulanger's son, Morgan Boulanger, was a suspect in the murder. He'd been twenty-two when the murder had occurred.

The newspaper report from the next day provided the details of Amelia's death. It was ghastly. Two days after her sixty-third birthday, she'd been bludgeoned to death. Morgan Boulanger's fingerprints had been found on the murder weapon, a leg that had been snapped off a balloon-back chair. Morgan's prints were in the system because in the two years before the murder, he'd been arrested three times for domestic abuse. The last time, he'd pushed his wife, Marie, down a flight of stairs. He'd pled down to assault and had spent less than eight months in prison—and Colorado hadn't submitted his prints to the federal databank.

Accompanying the article was Morgan Boulanger's mug shot. I was staring into the soulless eyes of the man on Gretchen's sofa. He'd fled the scene of the crime, and according to the article, a nationwide manhunt was under way. Apparently he'd taken the name Sal Briscoe to avoid capture.

I read on. Two of Amelia's employees had been in the store when the murder occurred, Iris Gibbons and Marie Boulanger. That explained why Morgan was in the store, I realized. He went to see his wife.

I wondered what had caused Morgan to explode. Had someone done or said something that set him off, or had he entered the store angry enough to kill? I couldn't imagine the rage that must have consumed him. Fury powerful enough to drive him to break off a chair leg and batter his wife's employer—a woman old enough to be his grandmother, for heaven's sake.

The article reported that Marie and Iris were missing, too, and quoted an anonymous source who said that Marie went with her husband voluntarily and that the pair might have kidnapped Iris because she was a witness to his—or their—crime, maybe forcing her to handle some of the logistics of their escape.

Amelia's cousin, a man named Sam, had been interviewed for the story. Sam stated that Amelia kept large quantities of cash in a store safe, since many of the antiques were purchased from walk-ins. Sam said that if the cash was a factor in the murder, the police needed to look at the only person who had access to it besides Amelia—her trusted employee, Marie. The police refused to discuss whether the safe had been cleaned out.

The next day there was more information about Morgan. He was a line cook at the upscale Gold Mine restaurant in Denver's Jeffrey Hotel. According to the restaurant's executive chef, Morgan picked up his paycheck the day of the murder but never showed up for work again. The apartment he'd shared with Marie had been ransacked, as if someone were searching for something or had packed in a hurry.

A line cook—a man who worked with a knife every day. That would account for the scars that crisscrossed the dead man's fingers.

Three days later, with less fresh news available, the *Globe*'s article about the murder was relegated to page four. Mostly it recycled previously reported information and quoted predictable comments stating the police were aggressively pursuing several valuable leads. It also included a photograph from happier days.

The photograph showed Mrs. Bartlett handing a check to the director of a literacy society, an employee smiling in the background. Another person's hands were visible on the left, applauding. The caption read "Rosebud Antiques Shoppe owner Amelia Bartlett handing a $500 check to Marcus Linden, executive director of Denver Reads! as staffer Marie Boulanger looks on."

I stared at the photo, transfixed.

My heart stopped, then began to thump so hard I had trouble breathing.

I closed my eyes, then opened them, disbelieving, shocked.

"Oh, my God," I whispered, unable to take my eyes off the photo.

I was staring at a younger version of Gretchen.

CHAPTER TWENTY-FOUR

I f Gretchen was the woman called Marie Boulanger, that meant that the dead man in her living room wasn't a random stalker—he was her husband.

In the photograph, her hair was the same dark red mixed with amber as now, but shorter and spikey and moussed into peaks. Her makeup was darker and more dramatic. Now her look was more mature and subtle, her cosmetics softer in hue and smokier in shading. Her fashion style appeared to be the same. Gretchen always wore heels and skirts and trendy accessories, and in the photo she was wearing a black leather pencil skirt, a cheetah-print blouse, and a wide gold-toned metallic belt, fashion-forward at the time.

I pushed away from my desk and stood. I felt incapable of looking at the image for one second longer, and equally incapable of processing what I'd just seen.

Without being aware of moving, I found myself on the far side of my office, my chest heaving, and then I was back at the computer, braced for the worst, girded to learn that there was evidence suggesting or proving that Gretchen had been the killer.

I needed to call Detective Brownley. Probably she had already discovered Gretchen's involvement in the Amelia Bartlett murder and gotten in touch with the Denver authorities, but if she hadn't, I needed to alert her.

My first call, though, was to Ty. I needed to talk to someone who would understand the conflicting emotions ricocheting through my brain. I got his voice mail and tapped the desk in frustration as I listened to his outgoing message. I wanted to talk to him *now*.

"Ty, if you can give me five minutes, I'd really love to talk to you. It's about Gretchen," I said. My voice broke as I spoke her name.

He called back ten minutes later. "Is Gretchen all right?" he asked first thing.

"I don't know . . . I mean, it's not news about her *now*. It's what I discovered. Oh, Ty, it's just horrible." I began to cry. *Stop, breathe, think,* I reminded myself. I took a deep breath.

"It's okay, Josie. Take your time."

I closed my eyes and managed to continue. "I don't know what to think. I've identified the murder victim from an old mug shot. There's no doubt about it—the dead man isn't Sal Briscoe. His name is Morgan Boulanger. Ty, I can barely say it—but I found an old newspaper photo of Morgan's wife, Marie Boulanger. It's Gretchen. Gretchen is Morgan's wife—his widow. The news reports said that they think Marie—Gretchen—vanished with her husband after he killed her employer, a woman named Amelia Bartlett, the poor soul."

My voice disappeared, and I dissolved into a fit of coughing. I drank from the bottle of water I kept on my desk.

"Read me the article, okay?"

"There's more than one. I'll start at the beginning."

When I finished, he said, "Well, no matter what that reporter Wes Smith would say to the contrary, newspapers don't always get it right. Sometimes they report conjecture as fact, and sometimes they quote people who deliberately mislead the journalist."

"Why would anyone do that?"

"To encourage her to come forward to clear her name."

"But she didn't."

"That doesn't change the fact that the police might have tried the tactic. The bottom line is that from what I can tell, the article is about sixty percent innuendo and surmise. For all we know, the reporter made the whole damn thing up. You don't *know* anything, Josie. You're doing as much speculation as any of them."

I leaned over, supporting my forehead on my fingers, and allowed tears to stream down my cheeks unabated. Ty didn't speak, but his support came through loud and clear nonetheless. The tension in my neck eased. After a while, my crying slowed, then stopped.

"I need to call Detective Brownley," I said.

"Yes," he concurred. "Why don't you e-mail her the link to the article?"

I took a deep, long breath, wiped wetness away, and said, "I'll do that now. Thank you, Ty. You just made a bad situation easier to bear."

"I love you, Josie."

"Me, too," I replied, smiling at his words.

I e-mailed Detective Brownley. The subject line read "Colorado report re: Gretchen." In the body of the e-mail, I wrote, "I found this link, which seems to be relevant. You'll note that the fifth name on the Sidlawn Fencing belt buckle list is Robert Boulanger." Then I added the URL and "Best, Josie," and clicked SEND.

I felt increasingly anxious and decided to turn my attention back to the Meissen vase, even though there was only a bluebird's chance of tracing it to Gretchen. I had no better ideas, and I needed to stay busy.

As I stood by my window, ready to jump back into researching the vase, I found myself wondering how Chip Davidson knew Gretchen.

I Googled "Chip Davidson" and "Gretchen Brock" and got no hits.

I tried "Chip Davidson" and "Marie Boulanger," and again I came up empty.

I shrugged and decided to see if any of the men who seemed to be involved in either murder, or with Gretchen, shared a public history. I Googled all combinations of the three men's names and pseudonyms, in tandem. Since Sal is often a nickname for Salvatore, I added it, too. I netted eleven possible matches.

- Vince Collins and Sal Briscoe
- Vince Collins and Salvatore Briscoe
- Vince Collins and Morgan Boulanger
- Vince Collins and Chip Davidson
- Vince Collins and Charles Davidson
- Sal Briscoe and Chip Davidson
- Salvatore Briscoe and Chip Davidson
- Sal Briscoe and Charles Davidson
- Salvatore Briscoe and Charles Davidson
- Morgan Boulanger and Chip Davidson
- Morgan Boulanger and Charles Davidson

Methodically I searched for each pair of names, and I was rewarded by a smattering of irrelevant connections. For example, in 1972, in Indiana, someone named Vincent Mark Collins played in a garage band with Charles (Chuck) Davidson.

Nothing, I thought. I tried adding in the women's names: Gretchen Brock, Marie Boulanger, Mandy Tollerson, and Lina Nadlein. *Still nothing.* I added Jack Stene, and in case Jack was a nickname, I added John Stene into the mix, too, methodically comparing pairs of names. *Nothing.*

I closed my eyes, and the picture of Gretchen, so full of life, so young and pretty, standing beside Amelia Bartlett, came to me. *Marie,* I corrected myself. *Gretchen's name is Marie.*

She'd appeared proud and pleased to be helping with the literacy cause. I began to speculate on the current status of the Amelia Bartlett murder investigation, dismissing the idea that Gretchen/Marie had been involved in any way, then stopped myself. I didn't know enough to have an opinion. *Time for more research,* I thought.

I Googled "Amelia Bartlett" and "murder" and "2009," hoping to learn the current status of the case. The first listing sent me to a personal blog written by Mrs. Bartlett's cousin, Sam.

The entry was dated October 2, 2008. "After six years," he wrote, "I continue to miss my cousin Amelia so much that it hurts like a painful scrape. We were reared as brother and sister. Her mother, my aunt, Lynne White, was like a second mother to me."

Lynne White! I thought, remembering the name from the note in Gretchen's envelope. Amelia Bartlett's mother, Lynne White, had evidently been the winning bidder for the vase at the now defunct Faring auction house—and Gretchen had worked for Mrs. Bartlett. I read on.

"We were more than cousins. We were best friends. I counted on her intelligence, and I trusted her judgment. Amelia helped me choose my college major, introduced me to my wife, was god-mother to my first child, and was there for me at every step." Sam went on to beg for assistance. "My entire family misses Amelia every day. Please help us find her killer. Someone reading this must know *something*. The police still want to talk to Morgan Boulanger." Sam linked to Morgan's photo, the same mug shot I'd seen earlier. "Do you know where he is? If so, please get in touch with Detective Parker of the Denver police." He gave the phone number and a link to Detective Parker's official e-mail, then added, "Please. Help us."

Agonies of loss overwhelmed me. I understood Sam's pain only too well. My father had been murdered, too, leaving me pummeled by misery, as if someone had used me for a punching bag. When he'd died, I'd wanted to die, too, but I didn't have the strength to kill myself. I'd felt doomed to live, to suffer alone.

I shook off the memory, grateful that I didn't hurt that way anymore.

My eyes scanned my office. *You've come a long way,* I thought, *since the forlorn days.* I picked up Ty's photo and smiled.

I'd taken the photograph one day last October. Ty had been splitting logs in back of his house. The halcyon day had been as warm as summer. Golden sunlight caused orange and pink maple leaves to glow with an iridescent sheen. He took my breath away. He looked so gorgeous, I thought I might faint. I grabbed my camera, stepped outside, and called to him. He turned as soon as he heard his name, and I pressed the button, capturing an unposed image of the sexiest man I'd ever known.

I sighed, remembering the moment, then replaced the framed image on the corner of my desk and turned my attention back to the computer. I found the photo of Amelia Bartlett handing the check to Marcus at the literacy organization.

Amelia looked younger than sixty-three, with shoulder-length brown hair and an hourglass figure and a big smile. Gretchen—Marie—looked tickled pink to be associated with the check-giving event. I touched the monitor, touching Gretchen's guileless, open expression. It was a singular moment in a young woman's life. Her expression showed a flicker of promise, of her potential to help others, frozen in time.

Back at Google's search results, I found another reference to the ongoing investigation—an end-of-the-year roundup. The December 31, 2008, *Denver Globe* had a sidebar on cold cases. According to the report, the Amelia Bartlett case was still open.

Whether Gretchen's vase had once been owned by Henrietta Howard or not, it had definitely crossed the Atlantic at some point, because in 1949, Lynne White bought it from Farings in Cheyenne. When she died, it had apparently passed to her daughter, Amelia Bartlett. Gretchen, then known as Marie, worked for Amelia Bartlett's antiques store.

I didn't believe that Gretchen had stolen the vase—she wasn't a thief. She could have purchased it, but not on a salesgirl's salary, even if she combined it with her line cook husband's pay. Which meant that in all probability Mrs. Bartlett had given it to her. Which suggested they were close. If Sam Bartlett felt like a brother, not a cousin, to Amelia, it was possible that Gretchen felt like a niece, not an acquaintance, to Sam. If she had run away from Rocky Point, maybe she'd run to him. Years ago, she wouldn't have wanted to put him at risk, but now that Morgan was dead, Sam might have been her first call.

I located Sam Bartlett's phone number and was tempted to dial it, but I didn't. If Gretchen was there, my call might terrorize her and make her run again, this time deeper into hiding. Instead, I called Detective Brownley. After I explained my thinking and gave her the phone number, she paused, then said, "This is a very interesting idea, Josie." She promised to let me know as soon as she learned anything relevant.

Wes called with an urgent request to see me. We agreed to meet near the salt pile in downtown Portsmouth.

I got there first and watched as he parked with a jerk in front of me and hustled into my car.

"I only have a few minutes," he said, "but I've got a real-deal bombshell."

"What?"

"In a sec. First, your insurance company came through with Gretchen's fingerprints. The print on the milk carton isn't hers."

"Whose is it—do they know?"

"No. It's not in any national databank or known to the New Hampshire police."

I shook my head, disappointed. "So it's not Vince's."

"Right. Nor is it the dead man's—Sal Briscoe, now known to be Morgan Boulanger."

Another negative. "What about tracing the gun?"

"Nope. Not so far."

I shook my head. "Now what?"

Wes shrugged. "I have news about Chip Davidson. Examining his fingerprints got us nowhere—he doesn't have a record—but I got some info from the plate number you gave me. The Taurus is a rental. He picked it up in Massachusetts from Siva International on Friday."

"Where in Massachusetts?"

"Burlington."

A suburb north of Boston. "Why there of all places?" I asked.

"I have no idea. Do you?"

"No, but if you got his rental record, you have his credit card info."

"Right, and from that, I got everything we need. He has a Virginia address. Are you ready for the bombshell? His driver's license was issued for the first time seven years ago."

I gaped.

"So was his credit card," Wes said with relish.

"That's unbelievable. Astounding."

"It's a heck of a coincidence."

"It can't be a coincidence."

"Probably not."

"What does it mean? Who is he for real?"

"You tell me."

The salt, used to treat the icy roads in winter, was at its springtime low. I stared past the mound and over the sun-specked Piscataqua, the river that separated New Hampshire from Maine, to a private dock on the Maine side as I considered Wes's question. Chip Davidson must somehow be involved in the Amelia Bartlett killing, but for the life of me, I couldn't think how. I glanced at Wes. He was watching me, eager for news.

"All we can say for sure is that he doesn't know where Gretchen is now. Otherwise he wouldn't keep showing up where she works and asking for her. There's some connection among the three of them—Chip, Gretchen, and the dead man, Morgan," I said, deciding to use his real name, not his alias of Sal. I took a deep breath and turned to face him. "Something happened seven years ago that resulted in them all getting new IDs. I think I know what it is, but I don't know how Chip is involved. You know how you were going to search for a photo of Gretchen involved in some past crime as a way of seeing if she might be in the witness protection program?"

"Sure. I've dug around a little, but I haven't had any luck so far."

"I have." I turned away again and kept my eyes on the distant shore as I described what I'd discovered about the Amelia Bartlett murder. Soon after I started my explanation, Wes began taking notes on the dirty scrap of paper he kept in his pocket.

"Why didn't you tell me this right away?" he grumbled.

"I just learned about it today. I am telling you right away." I turned again to face him. "Did you ask if Chip's fingerprints match the one on the milk carton?"

His eyes lit up. "Good question, Josie. I'll check." He tucked the paper away and headed for his car.

After he left, I sat for a long time, listening to an old Duke Ellington recording and thinking about Chip Davidson. I reached no conclusions. I didn't even know what questions to pose.

CHAPTER TWENTY-FIVE

D riving home after work, I tuned in the local news station. "The police report that they've identified the dead man found in a North Mill Pond condo last week," the announcer stated. "According to a high-ranking police official, the man is Morgan Boulanger, a suspect in a 2002 Colorado murder. In another story, Lina Nadlein can thank her dog for stopping a break-in. Her neighbor Andrew Yorne called nine-one-one to report the incident after the dog's nonstop barking alerted him to the situation. The suspect got away before he could be apprehended. And now to the weather."

I punched the OFF button and pulled over to call Lina. My hand shook a little as I dialed.

She wasn't at the Bow Street Emporium. Her cell phone went straight to voice mail. An answering machine picked up after four rings at her home number, but I didn't leave a message. Instead, I drove to her house.

The shades were drawn. Her car wasn't there. I ran up to the porch and rang the bell, thinking that she might have put her car in the garage. I heard the tinny buzz from inside and a dog barking, but no one came to the door. I cupped my eyes to see into the garage through the small side window, but the glass was tinted and I couldn't see a thing. I walked to the rear and climbed the steps to the small back porch. Curtains blocked my view. There was no bell. I knocked gently on the glass, then hard on the door frame.

"Lina?" I called and knocked again. "Lina?"

A dog barked, then bayed, then growled a little. He sounded

close, right on the other side of the door. No one shushed him. The apartment felt empty.

I drove to a side street and parked facing the house, deciding to wait for a while. I wanted to hear what Lina thought was going on. It grew dark, and still she didn't come.

Ty called to tell me he was stuck in Bangor for the night. "This training is like ten pounds of sugar in a five-pound bag. These guys aren't as far along as I'd expected—or as they need to be. I've got to stick here until they get it right."

I expressed disappointment and understanding in equal measures. After we were done, I tried Lina's cell phone again and got her.

"I've been worried," I said. "Are you okay?"

"It's pretty freaky," she replied. "Thank goodness for Blitzie. If he hadn't barked, who knows what might have happened."

"Did anyone get a description?"

"Not much. A white guy wearing a baseball cap pulled down over his face and a coat with the collar turned up."

It could be anyone, I thought. "Are you going back there to-night?" I asked.

"No way. I'm staying with Mandy. She kept me company while I walked Blitzi and got him squared away for the night. I'm having an alarm system installed tomorrow. Then I'll go home again."

"Do you have any idea why someone would try to break in?"

"No," she said, and from her tone, I believed her. All I heard was fear.

"Call me if I can do anything, okay?" I said. "Anytime."

She thanked me, and we agreed to talk soon.

With a final glance at her house, I drove home, glad to see the golden glow from the lamp that greeted me. I hated coming into a dark house. Inside, I walked from room to room turning on lights.

I cooked to the soothing sounds of Vivaldi's *Four Seasons,* and at just after ten I decided to go to bed. I felt worn to a nub, emotionally exhausted. I was certain I'd toss and turn all night, yet I slept deeply, my rest untroubled and uninterrupted, the sleep of the innocent.

The next morning, I cooked myself scrambled eggs and bacon and sat for a long time at my kitchen table eating and sipping tea. I had no fresh ideas for finding Gretchen but still felt a solid gut-deep confidence that once all the facts were known, her blamelessness would be proven.

As I was loading the dishwasher, the local news hit the airwaves.

"According to a highly placed police official, Gretchen Brock, wanted for questioning in the death of the man found murdered in her North Mill Pond condo, who has been identified as Morgan Boulanger, her husband, is also a suspect in an earlier murder," the announcer said, sounding exhilarated as he recounted the appalling details of the Amelia Bartlett case.

I turned off the radio and hurried to my car. It was a raw, cloudy day. It looked like rain.

I stopped at a convenience store to pick up a copy of the *Seacoast Star* and winced as I read Wes's headline:

DID GRETCHEN BROCK KILL HER HUSBAND?
HAS SHE KILLED BEFORE?

I hated the overtones of the headline: Asking if Gretchen had killed *before*, implied that she'd killed *now*.

As I stood in the middle of the store and read the article, I had to acknowledge that Wes's recap of the 2002 murder was clear and to the point. There was no mention of Chip Davidson, nor, I noted, much to my surprise and relief, of me. Wes didn't even mention that Gretchen worked for Prescott's. A sidebar titled "Crime Wave?" mentioned the break-in at Prescott's and the attempted break-in at Lina's, questioning whether all these crimes that involved people who were known to one another typified the kind of coincidences to be found in a small city or were a matter of cause and effect.

The main article focused on Gretchen's alleged role in both murders. Wes even quoted a retired Denver police officer who predicted there was a better-than-even chance that Gretchen— i.e., Marie Boulanger—had instigated the entire crime and that her hapless husband was merely a pawn in a chess game of her making. His theory was that Amelia's murder resulted from a robbery gone wrong, and since Marie knew better than Morgan what objects to steal and where the cash was stashed, she had to be the brains behind his brawn.

Despite my protestations to the contrary, my Gretchen-as-criminal guilt-meter was inching up. At first, I'd denied the possibility that Gretchen could be involved in any way, thinking it was more likely that she was a victim of a kidnapping than the perpetrator of a crime. Then I'd found myself acknowledging the merit of Wes's argument that no one gets a new Social Security number without cause and wondering if she was in the witness protection program. Now I was questioning whether I'd been wrong about Gretchen's innocence from the start.

Is it possible that Gretchen has been playing me for all these years? I wondered. In my heart, I didn't believe she was guilty of anything, but neither could I deny the facts. I felt trapped between what I felt and what I knew, a prisoner of dissonant truths. Maintaining optimism was grueling. I felt the weight of the effort as I trudged to my car.

Once settled inside, with the heat on, I called Wes to ask if he had any news about the fingerprint on the milk carton. I wanted to know if it was Chip's. His cell phone went directly to voice mail, and I left a message.

Feeling restless, I decided to stop at Phil's Barn instead of going straight into work. I'd just turned onto Oak Street when, out of nowhere, a black Jeep bore down from the other direction.

Vince Collins was at the wheel. He saw me, too. He slowed as we passed and eyed me with stony dislike. My heart thudded against my chest, and I kept glancing into the rearview mirror and held my breath until he rounded the corner and disappeared from sight. *What did I ever do to him?* I wondered.

My cell phone rang, and I jumped a little, startled.

I recognized the number—it was Wes. I pulled over to take the call.

"Wes," I said, relieved to talk to someone I knew.

"Whatcha got?" he asked.

"Nothing. I was wondering about Chip's fingerprint. Was it a match for the milk carton?"

"Nope. I was gonna call you later. I'm still checking, but so far it's as if he's a phantom or something, you know? He obviously exists, but he's not real."

"Wes, you make him sound like a spy!"

"A spook, yeah, maybe. I was thinking that. Except that I can't find any international connection or anything. Maybe he's in witness protection like we thought Gretchen might be. What do you think?"

"I have no idea," I said. "Wes, I'm just beside myself with worry. Do you have any news at all?"

"No, but I got like twenty feelers out. We're on the brink—I can smell it. Catch ya later," Wes said. He hung up.

He can smell it? I questioned silently. *What can he smell?*

I was glad not to see Vince's Jeep again on the road to Phil's. When I arrived, I parked as close to the big barn door as I could.

"I was just fixing to call you," Phil said as soon as I entered. "I got in a beauty of a window. Stained glass."

"Victorian?" That was a safe bet, since most stained glass in our region originated from the late nineteenth century.

"Yup, but it's something I've never seen before."

The window was magnificent. Shaped to fit a custom-designed transom over double-wide entrance doors, it was fifty-seven inches long and twenty-seven inches tall at the top of the arch. Clusters of flowers in varying hues of pink, from deep rose to soft salmon to pale seashell, were framed by leaves in undulating shades of dark green as they draped over rich brown branches. The background was a clear azure blue formed of irregular rounded shapes joined together in a patchwork leaded design. A one-inch amber border ran in six-inch lengths along the outer edge. It took my breath away.

"It's something, huh?" Phil said, his eyes on me, his customer, not the window.

"Is it signed?" I asked.

"Nope."

I nodded. Tiffany wasn't the only well-respected stained glass artist. Several lesser-known but highly regarded studios had produced scores of gorgeous pieces. This window wasn't one of them. Still, it was a unique object, with an unusual yet classic design flawlessly executed in popular colors. I didn't need to research it. We'd already acquired half a dozen similar but smaller examples for the auction, so I knew its value. Properly marketed, I would expect the window to sell for thirty-five hundred dollars, maybe as much as four thousand.

"Do you know where it came from?"

"It's local. Someone's tearing down an old house to build some McMansion. At least they had enough sense to salvage the good stuff."

I readied myself for the negotiation I knew was about to begin. Phil and I might not haggle much over the price of glass doorknobs or locks, but this was a different ball of wax. Because we were preparing for an auction, I wouldn't have to market this piece individually, which gave me a little wiggle room. I could go as high as seventeen hundred, about half of what I expected the window to sell for. With luck, I thought, Phil wouldn't start any higher than two thousand.

"Without a maker's mark . . ." I let my voice drift off and shrugged, feigning indifference. "How much?"

He started at twenty-five hundred. *Darn,* I thought.

After several rounds of back-and-forth, he said, "Wish I could come down further, Josie, but I can't. Two thousand. Final offer."

It was more than I wanted to pay, but the window was worth it. "Sold. You drive a hard bargain, my friend."

"Jeez, Josie, I'm a pussycat. I let you beat me up nohow."

I laughed as we shook on the deal. "Right. In your dreams, Phil!"

He smiled knowingly.

I called Eric to come and get it, bringing blankets, cardboard filler, a crate, and a helper.

On the drive back, I turned on the radio to hear the morning news. The report was a repeat of what I'd heard earlier, fleshed out with details from Wes's article.

"According to *Seacoast Star* reporter Wes Smith, there's still uncertainty as to how the two murders relate and whether a recent break-in and another attempted break-in also figure into whatever's going on," the reporter intoned. Wes's voice came on the air. "Gretchen Brock, a.k.a. Marie Boulanger, seems to be involved in both killings—but the word 'involved' has many meanings. Just because she was in a certain place at a certain time doesn't make her guilty. It could be cause and effect. It could be coincidence. Until more facts are known, we in the media need to be careful how we use words."

Wes sounded reasonable and smart, not as if he were trying to stir things up. *Way to go, Wes,* I thought.

CHAPTER TWENTY-SIX

I greeted Fred and Cara as I hung up my coat.

"Eric left for Phil's already," Cara reported.

"Great! Wait 'til you guys see the stained glass window I just bought. It's stunning."

Fred pushed his glasses up and asked, "Marked?"

"No. It's a no-name dazzler."

He nodded and looked back at his computer, no longer particularly interested in my find. Fred was an antiques elitist: If an object wasn't signed, stamped, or marked, it held less allure for him.

The phone rang. Cara answered with her friendly greeting, listened for a moment, then put the call on hold. "It's Lina Nadlein for you."

"Tell her I'll be with her in a minute," I said, then, wanting privacy, added, "I'll take it upstairs."

I ran to the steps.

"Hi, Lina," I said, grabbing the phone and punching the flashing button. "Sorry to keep you waiting."

"Hi," she said in a tiny voice, and from her tone, I could tell she was upset.

"Are you okay?"

"Not really. I'm so—" she started, then broke off. She sounded baffled. She cleared her throat. "I just heard the news about Gretchen having another identity . . . and on top of yesterday . . . I'm feeling pretty rocky. Is it true?"

"I think so," I said softly.

"And about her being involved in a murder?"

"I don't know, Lina. It looks that way."

"How can it be? It's impossible!"

I wanted to talk openly to her, Gretchen's oldest friend, but didn't know if I could trust her not to blab to Mandy or someone else. I needed to see her in person to gauge her attitude and her integrity. I looked out the window, past my maple tree. A misty drizzle had settled in. The whitewashed church appeared gray.

"I know. I agree. It seems incredible," I said.

"Gretchen can't be a killer!"

Listening to her was like reliving my own doubts and disbelief. "Lina, by any chance, are you free for a cup of coffee?"

"Sure. The alarm system is in, and I don't have to go to work until eleven thirty."

It was just after ten. "How about meeting at the Sunshine Café in half an hour? That's near your store."

Another moment's silence. "I can get there by then. Thank you, Josie."

Downstairs, I told Cara and Fred that I was going to run an errand and would be back by noon. I drove through thick fog, praying Lina had news.

Lina was sitting at the counter, her hands circling a steaming mug as if she were absorbing its warmth. Her shoulders were bowed.

"Hi, Lina," I said as I approached. "Shall we grab a booth?"

She jerked up, startled. "Oh, hi. I didn't hear you come up."

Once we were sitting across from one another, I was able to see that her Ginevra Benci face was lined with—what? Worry, maybe. Or perhaps she was merely distracted. The waitress came and took our order and was back almost immediately with my coffee and more hot water for her tea.

"I'm so frightened," she whispered as she gave the tea bag a dunk. "It's Mandy."

I waited for her to continue, but she didn't.

"What about her?" I asked.

"I think she knows something. I don't know what. It's about something I overheard last night. She was talking to Vince."

I wondered why Lina was making me drag the story out of her, sentence by sentence.

"And?" I asked.

She took a sip of tea, then said, "She and I were at her house, just hanging out, listening to music, you know? Vince called and asked to come over. He brought Mandy a framed stained glass window for the hall. He said it was an antique. Anyway, while he's hanging it from the top of the window, Mandy asks him in a kind of whisper if he still thinks she shouldn't tell. She didn't know that I could hear her—I'd gone into the kitchen to refill my wineglass, but I could hear every word. Don't you think that she must know something that relates to either Gretchen or the murder or the break-in at your place?"

"She could have been referring to anything. Maybe she and Vince are planning on eloping." I shrugged. "Did you speak to her after Vince left?"

She shook her head. "I went to bed before he did." She sighed and gazed out the window. "I don't know if I should tell the police or just mind my own business. Mandy's a good friend of mine. If she knows something that might help find Gretchen . . ." Her voice trailed off. She turned freshly moist eyes in my direction. "But if Gretchen will get in trouble, maybe I should leave well enough alone. Except that it's not well enough, and I know it. I just don't know what to do."

"We need to find Gretchen no matter what. She might be in real trouble, Lina. If you know anything that might help, you've just got to tell. You've just got to."

"If I tell, the police will talk to Mandy, and it'll come out that I told on her, and Vince will go ballistic."

I nodded. She was right. "The police are aware of his volatility," I said, selecting my words carefully. "They'll be discreet."

Her lips came together, and for a moment she looked defiant. "I was the only other person there. There's no way the police can hide where they got the information." She shook her head. "I'm seeing Mandy in about half an hour at work, and I feel guilty and sad and bad already." Her voice caught, and she angrily wiped away tears. "I'm scared, Josie. I'm scared for Gretchen, and I'm scared for me."

"Would you like me to call Detective Brownley for you?"

She wiped away tears with the back of her hand. "It doesn't seem fair for me to get you involved, too."

"I'm glad to do anything I can to help. If I talk to Detective Brownley before you do, she'll be prepared when you talk to her."

Lina looked unconvinced and didn't respond.

"She's smart, Lina, and she's cautious. She'll investigate fully, but in a nonconfrontational manner."

"She may think her manner is nonconfrontational, but Vince won't. He thinks *everything* is confrontational."

"He's on probation, Lina. He'd have to be crazy to turn nothing into something. Even if he finds out—which I don't think he will—it's a classic 'he said, she said' situation. Detective Brownley will investigate around the edges, seeking out what Mandy might have been referring to without letting her know that she's looking into anything at all. What she *won't* do is say to Mandy, 'Lina said you said.' I mean, why would she? Mandy would respond, 'Lina misunderstood. Or she misheard. Sorry, but I didn't say anything even remotely like that.' Then Vince will back her up and it's two against one. I'm telling you, Lina, it just won't happen that way."

She was listening hard, wanting to believe me, wanting to help Gretchen.

"I'll talk to Detective Brownley and explain everything," I said. I felt confident that the rapport Detective Brownley and I shared was substantial enough for me to offer her word with confidence. "She'll understand your concern. I guarantee it."

"Okay." Lina sighed again. She looked as if she bore the weight of the world on her shoulders. "I hope I'm doing the right thing."

"You're doing the *only* thing."

She glanced at her watch. "I have to go," she said, sliding out of the booth. "Thank you, Josie."

I smiled a little. "It will be okay. You can trust Detective Brownley."

She nodded and left. I watched her thread her way through

parked cars, cross Bow Street, and enter the store. I paid the bill, left the tip, and stepped outside. The temperature was dropping, and the drizzle had thickened into something close to freezing rain. It was bone-chillingly raw. The sky was solidly gray. The storm wasn't passing. I was glad I'd found a parking space close by, and once I was inside my car, I turned the heat up high.

Vince's black Jeep passed me and double-parked about a hundred feet from where I sat. After a minute, Mandy stepped out of the car, holding her coat closed tight to her throat. She jogged into the Bow Street Emporium, and Vince turned into Islington.

I followed him, not on purpose but because I was going the same way.

I was driving to my office and had planned to take the back roads. I didn't know where he was going. We turned right onto Greenland.

He didn't get on the highway. Neither did I. We both stayed on Greenland.

Even though my being behind him was happenstance, I stayed in the right-hand lane, out of his direct line of vision, and at least two cars back. I didn't want to get on his radar. He wouldn't believe that I wasn't tailing him, and I could only imagine his reaction if he spotted me.

He was heading inland, so he wasn't going to his Rocky Point job site. I could have peeled off, but instead I decided to stay with him. He turned onto Route 33 heading south, then merged with 108, and then we were in Exeter. He turned onto Oak Street, and I sailed on past, glad to be away from him. I turned around and wove my way back to my office.

I was almost there when I slowed to a near stop, then pulled onto the shoulder and set my blinkers. Disparate facts clicked into place like a jigsaw puzzle: the hand-painted light fixtures and the stained glass window Vince gave Mandy, the glass doorknobs, Phil's wife, and Oak Street, and then I realized that there was a better-than-even chance I'd just discovered who'd killed Morgan Boulanger—and how to prove it.

CHAPTER TWENTY-SEVEN

I called Detective Brownley.

"What's up, Josie?" she asked.

"I need to tell you—" After so many dead ends, false starts, and failures, I finally sensed that I was onto something—and that, with any luck, my realization would lead us to Gretchen. "I think I know who the killer is. There's too much to tell you on the phone, and it's too important to delay. I'm about half an hour away. Can we meet?"

After a short pause, she said, "Why don't you come here? I'll set up the video so we can talk."

Her words brought back more than one uncomfortable memory of other interviews with the police. "Of course," I said, my voice sounding surprisingly unruffled. "I'll call Max Bixby, my lawyer, and see if he's available."

Another pause. "Good. I'll expect you here in half an hour."

Max was leaning against the Rocky Point police station door, protected from the rain by the portico, gazing into the eastern sky. Just seeing him boosted my confidence and made me smile. Max was kind and gracious, and I trusted his judgment completely.

I parked as close to the building as I could and dashed through the now steady freezing rain to join him. He stepped forward to greet me.

Max was tall, probably an inch or two taller than Ty, and thin, lean like a runner. Under the leather duster he wore with flair, I saw a brown nubby tweed jacket and a green bow tie. He wore dark brown slacks and cowboy boots. His leather cowboy hat sported a green feather.

"Hey, Max. Thanks for coming on such short notice."

"Glad I was available." He smiled and pulled open the door. "Ready?"

I nodded without enthusiasm and walked into the station house. Words Emily Dickinson wrote came to mind:

> *If in that Room a Friend await*
> *Felicity or Doom . . .*

"Thanks for coming in," Detective Brownley said, extending her hand to me, then to Max. "Good to see you again, Max."

"You, too, Claire."

"Shall we head to the back? I got us set up in Room One."

She turned left and headed down the corridor. "I see it's still raining," she said as we walked.

"Cats and dogs," Max said. "Have you heard the forecast?"

"Yeah. It's supposed to stop overnight, but we're getting a bucket-load before then."

Detective Brownley opened the door to the depressingly familiar interrogation room. I sat with my back to the cage, a nasty-looking, single-person-sized, wire mesh cell. Ty had told me years ago that it was used to control unruly guests. The room was unchanged since my last visit. The table was wooden and scarred. The chairs were cold metal and uncomfortable.

Now that I understood that this was a formal police interview, I knew what I was supposed to do. It was my job to wait until I was asked a specific question and then answer it without embellishment.

Max, relaxed as ever, sat next to me, opened his briefcase, and pulled out a lined legal-sized pad and two small bottles of water. He unscrewed the cap on one and slid it over to me. "Talkin's thirsty work, little lady," he said in an undertone. "Thought you might want to wet your whistle now and agin."

"Thank you, Max," I whispered, touched beyond reason.

He winked at me.

Detective Brownley pushed the RECORD button and spoke into the microphone. She gave our names and the date and time, then said, "Thanks for coming in, Josie. You called me this morning and said you had information about the murder that occurred in Gretchen Brock's apartment, is that correct?"

"Yes . . . well, sort of . . . I mean, I don't know that . . . what you said . . . that it's related to the murder." I paused to gather my thoughts and choose my words. "I called because I had information that, to my mind, cast doubt on Vince Collins's alibi. I don't think he was where he says he was at the time that man, Morgan Boulanger, was killed."

I glanced at Max's profile, worried that I was overexplaining. Max once told me that one-word answers to official police questions were good. He sensed that my eyes were on him and turned his head to look at me. He nodded reassuringly. *Whew,* I thought.

"Why don't you tell me about it," Detective Brownley said, leaning back in her chair, at ease and ready to listen.

I took a deep breath. "It was the stained glass that got me thinking. I had a cup of coffee with Gretchen's friend Lina this morning. She mentioned that Vince had brought an antique stained glass window over to Mandy's last night." I looked from Detective Brownley to Max and back again. "Where did he get it?" I asked rhetorically. "From the project he's managing. The company he works for tears down old houses to put up new ones. Vince doesn't own them. He's an employee. Don't you see? If he's taking architectural remnants, well, that's stealing."

Detective Brownley looked thoughtful for a moment, then asked, "Besides the stained glass, what items has he allegedly stolen?"

"Another stained glass window I bought this morning, the two light fixtures in Mandy's mudroom and Gretchen's hallway, glass doorknobs, and antique locks. Probably more."

"So I can understand the context of what we're discussing, how much are these things worth, would you estimate?"

"The stained glass window I bought would sell at auction for about four thousand. I don't know about the one Lina mentioned—

I haven't seen it. The two light fixtures, probably about three hundred dollars each. The other items are worth less than fifty dollars each, but there are scores of them, so it really adds up. I should specify, that's retail. He probably got a quarter of that amount, maybe less."

"I'm a little confused. What makes you think he stole these items?"

I nodded. "It's circumstantial. Let me explain. I was driving to Phil's Barn in Exeter when Vince's Jeep passed me, coming from that direction."

Detective Brownley started to speak, and I held a hand up to stop her.

"I know, I know, there's nothing illegal about driving in Exeter. It's not that. It's the timing. Phil said they acquired the doorknobs on Wednesday—after he went home sick at lunchtime. He apologized for making me take another trip. I'd already had the antique locks picked up, and he said if his wife hadn't made him stay home with his cold, he could have saved us a trip." I shrugged. "Look at the time line. If what I've been hearing on the radio and reading in the paper is right, Vince's alibi just got busted. He was at Phil's on Wednesday, sometime after Phil left for the day."

Detective Brownley asked, "What time did he get to Phil's?"

"I have no idea," I replied.

"Seems like asking Phil a few questions is in order," Max said.

"Thank you, Josie, for reporting this. What else did Lina tell you?"

I glanced at Max, and he nodded. "Before I answer that, I need to communicate her very real, and I think completely reasonable, concern. She overheard a conversation between Mandy and Vince, and she's scared to death that he'll find out that she's the one who told you about it, and he'll explode the way he does sometimes. Since only the three of them were present, if they get wind of it, they'll know who told you."

She nodded. "We're pretty deft at investigating so no one knows our sources."

"I know you are, and that's what I told her."

"Okay then. Point taken. So, what did she overhear?"

"Mandy asked Vince if she should tell."

"Tell what?"

"Lina didn't hear, and she says she doesn't know. We talked about how it could be anything. Maybe Mandy's pregnant and was asking Vince if he thought she should tell. Maybe Mandy's got a new job. There's no way to know, but I thought Lina ought to report it, in case it does, in fact, relate to the murder or Gretchen or my break-in."

Detective Brownley tapped her pen for a four-beat, then said, "Okay, then. We'll check it out."

"Anything else we can tell you while we're here?" Max asked, slipping his pad into his briefcase.

She turned off the recorder. "Nope, that about covers it."

"Anything you can tell us?"

She shook her head. "Thanks for coming in, Josie."

She walked us out, and at the front door she shook my hand and said, "You hear anything more, you let me know, okay?"

"Sure."

Outside, under the overhang, I said, "I think it was smart to have you join me."

Max nodded. "It can't ever hurt to have your lawyer present." He stared out over the dunes toward the rain-shrouded ocean. "I get the sense that there are many layers to this investigation."

There are many layers, I kept thinking as I drove back to work: two murders, a missing woman, and a break-in; too many people with fake IDs; a thief and, maybe, a liar. *There are many layers of deception.*

CHAPTER TWENTY-EIGHT

C hip Davidson called as I was walking into my upstairs office with the bag containing my deli lunch.

"Josie," Chip said, and I could picture his smiling eyes and appealing grin and neon-blond hair. "I'm glad I got you. How ya doing?"

"I'm good, Chip. You?" I replied, glancing at the phone, ready to jot down his number. The display told me it was private.

"Fine, thanks. Listen, Josie, I just heard about Gretchen. I'm completely shocked. Do you know anything about it? Is it for real that she's a suspect in two murders?"

"I've heard the same thing," I replied. "Unbelievable, isn't it?"

"One thing, Josie. I'm her friend, not the cops, so if she needs some help, well, you can tell me, you know?"

He was openly suggesting to me, a relative stranger, that we conspire to hide a fugitive. He was willing to lie. My father had warned me about people like him: "Once a liar, always a liar." I chased the memory away. Chip was waiting for my response to his offer to help Gretchen.

"Sorry, Chip," I said firmly. "I don't know anything. Is there any way I can reach you in case I hear from her?"

"I'm afraid not. I'm still moving around a lot."

"How about your cell phone?"

"I don't own one," he replied, chuckling. "Can't believe it, right? I'm a Luddite at heart. I'll call you every once in a while to check in, if that's all right. I'm pretty darned worried about her."

My eye gravitated to Jack Stene's business card, the one on

which he'd scrawled his cell phone number. Jack's openness contrasted positively with Chip's reticence.

"Anytime," I said, wondering once again how Chip fit in and what he wanted with or from Gretchen.

I spent the rest of the afternoon on edge, struggling to come up with ways to stay abreast of Detective Brownley's investigation. I was jump-out-of-my-skin curious, but I couldn't think of any approach that wouldn't get me in trouble.

I thought of calling Wes, but since I hadn't alerted him before or after I met with the police, I could only imagine how he'd react. Worse, the news was relevant and significant, so probably I'd end up as his lead in the next issue of the *Seacoast Star*.

I had no choice but to wait. I checked e-mail, then sent a howdy message to my pal Shelley in New York, a short-lived distraction. I was trying to decide what to do next when Fred buzzed up and asked me to come downstairs. In response to one of our ads soliciting dolls for our upcoming auction, a woman had arrived with an old Barbie.

"Sure. I'll be right down."

Barbie, the first-ever mass-produced teenage doll, was launched in 1959 at the American Toy Fair in New York City. She was an immediate hit and remains one of the nation's most recognized brands.

As I entered the office, Cara was reciting the tag sale hours to a caller, then reading from the cheat sheet to explain how our instant appraisals worked. Fred was leaning against his desk, his tie loosened, chatting with a woman he introduced as Dana.

"I think it'll turn to snow overnight," Dana said as I joined them. "It's getting bitter out there."

She was about fifty-five, with brown hair that hung to her shoulders in soft waves. She wore jeans, a beige to-the-knee down coat, and work boots.

I introduced myself. "Thanks for coming in," I said.

"Fred here tells me you might be interested in making an offer for my Barbie."

Fred handed me a sheet from his notepad and stepped away from his desk so I could see the doll. I glanced down at the paper. Fred had written, "$2,000 max, okay?"

Barbie stood on a black circular pedestal and wore a gold brocade dress with a matching coat and hat. There were mink cuffs on the coat. She wore white gloves and pumps and carried a pale blue evening bag. She was a brunette. Standing beside her was a mint-condition orange-topped box decorated with silver and black silhouettes of Barbie.

"Is this your doll?" I asked.

"Yeah. It was a birthday present for my seventh birthday in 1959."

I nodded. Laid out beside the box were two additional sets of clothes: a winter holiday set, complete with tartan plaid tote bag, and an Easter outfit including a patterned sheath dress, coat, shoes, and a gold-tone necklace.

"Everything looks to be in great shape." I smiled. "It would seem you played with her very gently."

Dana chuckled. "To tell you the truth, I never played with her at all. Sacrilege, right?" She chuckled again and shrugged. "I was a tomboy."

"That accounts for the condition. Are the sets complete?" I asked Fred.

"Yes."

I picked up the doll and looked at her bottom. The patent stamp was there—the doll had been manufactured during the first year of production. Since we were deep into planning for our upcoming auction, I was up-to-date with doll data, and I knew that this Barbie would sell at auction for about six thousand dollars, maybe even more. I turned to Fred and nodded. His price point was right on.

"Dana, do you have any thoughts about how much you're looking for?" he asked.

She chuckled again. "Lots."

When I'd first opened Prescott's, I'd set a policy for taking the high road in our dealings. We never tried to deceive people. We were transparent in our pricing strategy: If a seller asked how we priced things, we told the truth, but people rarely asked. We never deceived anyone, but we also tried to never pay more than we had to.

Fred pursed his lips, thinking. He glanced at the doll. "We'd love to include it in the doll auction we're planning. Based on its condition and scarcity, we can offer you fifteen hundred."

"You're kidding!" Dana responded, looking impressed, then cagey, as the thought that maybe she'd struck gold occurred to her. That happened sometimes when people had no idea what an object was worth or how the antiques business worked. "How about four thousand?" she countered.

Fred shook his head. "We don't have a lot of room to negotiate. I can up the offer a little—say, seventeen hundred—but that's as high as I can go," he said, sounding disappointed, as if he expected the deal to fall through.

Looking at Dana's ardent countenance, I thought Fred might be right.

Dana looked at me. "What do you think?" she asked me. "Don't you think it's worth more?"

"To a private buyer, maybe." I shrugged.

"Maybe I should sell it on eBay or something."

"That's certainly an option," I acknowledged.

"If I could get more for it on eBay, why should I sell it to you?" she asked, glancing from me to Fred, then back again.

I stayed quiet and let Fred handle it.

"A lot of people are happy selling on eBay or other auction sites, but, like most everything, it's not as easy as it seems. You have to write a description and take photos and upload them. You have to be prepared to answer dozens of questions. Serious collectors may demand a written appraisal before bidding for an item likely to sell in this price range. You have to decide if you want to set a reserve price, and if so, how much that should be. If it sells, you have to pack it carefully and ship it, and most common carriers won't insure antiques and collectibles over a certain age—like twenty years. Plus, don't forget the costs; you're charged whether the object sells or not. Then, after all is said and done, you may not get more for it.

People expect bargains when they buy at an online auction." Fred pushed up his glasses. "We pay cash."

"That all makes sense," Dana said, sounding disconcerted. She nodded. "Can we call it two thousand and be done with it?"

Fred paused, then said, "Yes."

We completed the paperwork, and Dana left, thrilled to have cash in hand.

As we wrapped Barbie's clothes in acid-free tissue paper and placed everything in the warehouse for further screening, I said, "That was masterful, Fred. Really well done."

He grinned, left side up, giving him a debonair air. "Thanks," he said.

Back in the main office, I glanced around, looking for something to capture my interest. The phone rang.

"It's Wes," Cara told me.

I nodded and took it at Sasha's desk.

"I'm pretty upset, Josie." His tone was so severe my heart flip-flopped.

"What's wrong?" I asked.

"You know what's wrong—you didn't call me. I was tempted to not call you either."

I couldn't speak openly, not with Fred and Cara in the room. "I can't explain right now," I said, my tone neutral.

"We need to meet."

I looked through the rain-streaked window. "How about at Shaw's?" I asked.

"Now?"

I glanced at the computer monitor. It was already three o'clock. "How about at five thirty?"

"It's too important to wait. There's been a new development—it's about Gretchen."

His somber tone frightened me. "Okay," I said. "Now's good."

CHAPTER TWENTY-NINE

W es and I stood in a corner near the front of the grocery store, next to the rows of shopping carts. People glanced at us as they dislodged each cart from its fellows, but no one questioned why we were huddling in the corner.

Wes stood with his arms crossed, looking as angry as he'd sounded. "Why didn't you tell me what you found out about Vince?"

"I didn't want my name in the paper."

Wes shook his head. "Josie, fair's fair. I tell you things. I tell you *everything*."

He was right, and I felt a little guilty. "Did you learn about it from your police source?" I asked, avoiding a direct response by posing another question.

"My sources are confidential, but they're reliable."

I stared at his frigid countenance. "I was frightened, Wes," I confessed quietly. "I still am. Vince scares me."

"That's good," he said, reaching for the sheet of lined paper he used for notes. "Why?"

"That's not a quote, Wes. That was my attempt to explain my reticence."

"But it's news."

"Gimme a break, Wes! *Everyone* is scared of Vince. That I'm scared of Vince is not only not news—it's *old* not news." I sighed. "Listen, change of subject. You were terrific on the radio. Smart and competent."

Wes smiled. "Thanks."

"So," I asked, "what do you know about Gretchen?"

"You first," he said stubbornly. "Give me something."

It occurred to me that negotiating with Wes was similar to negotiating in business. "What do you want?" I asked.

"An on-the-record report of how you figured out that Vince was lying about his alibi."

I shook my head. "I can't do that. I have sources that must be protected, too."

"A quote, then. A *substantive* quote." Wes pursed his lips and tempted me to talk with a nugget of what he had to offer. "The police have already interviewed Phil and Johnny at Phil's Barn."

"Did Phil confirm that Vince was lying?"

"I say nothing until I get my quote."

"What about what you said—that you have news about Gretchen?"

Wes shook his head. "You first."

"Okay. Here goes: From what I can see, there are many layers to this investigation," I stated, paraphrasing Max's comment. "A lot of deception seems to be at work."

"That's good, Josie," he said eagerly, writing quickly, "but flesh it out. I need more."

"That's enough, Wes. You can summarize some of the areas of confusion—Gretchen's role in Amelia Bartlett's murder, why she might have got a new identity, and where she is now—and then close with my quote. Good stuff."

"Maybe. Link up the break-in at your place and the attempted one at Lina's for me."

"I can't imagine how they're connected. Maybe the motive is buried under one of those layers."

He nodded, making a note. "Yeah, that'll work." He finished writing and looked up. "Vince's alibi might not be so airtight after all. Phil and Johnny confirmed what you hypothesized to the police. Vince is Phil's supplier for the bulk of those building things—" He broke off and read from his notepaper. "Architectural artifacts. He went to Phil's twice on Wednesday to sell stuff, once early in the morning, and once in the afternoon, after Phil had gone home sick. Since Phil wasn't there, Vince did business with Johnny."

"Vince can't be the murderer," I said, thinking aloud, "if he was all the way in Exeter when Morgan was killed."

"Probably that's right. There are two issues: Who was covering for Vince at his job site and why, and did he have time to both sell the artifacts and kill Briscoe—Boulanger? A carpenter named Lenny gave him the alibi. I think I mentioned before that the police did a minute-by-minute time line for Vince, and he was covered the whole time. Except Lenny lied. He said that Vince was with him for more than an hour discussing how to take down a double-wide staircase without destroying the railing and balusters. Now he says they discussed the staircase the day before and he covered for Vince because he's his boss and he told him what to say." Wes shrugged. "Apparently that happens a lot. Vince didn't make an explicit threat, but since he has the ability to fire him, he didn't need to."

"The police believe him?"

"Yeah, because it fits. Apparently Vince ran the architectural artifact trade like a cartel. From Phil's sales records and the building owner's revenue reports, it looks like the owner got sixty percent of the take, Vince got thirty percent, and the guys on the job split the remaining ten percent. Except the owner thought he was getting it all. He's already fired Vince and stopped all work on all his projects until the police can sort it out."

"Has Vince been arrested?" I asked, awed at the speed with which the police got results.

"Yes. For trafficking in stolen property."

Vince is going to be out for bear, I thought. *Poor Mandy.* "What about the time issue you mentioned?" I asked.

Wes shook his head. "It's tight. He was on a routine call with his parole officer from eleven that morning until about eleven fifteen. The police can tell his general location by which cell phone tower transmitted the call, so they know he was either at his job site or close by the entire time. It takes an hour and a half to drive from the job site to Phil's, then to Gretchen's, then back to his company's Rocky Point office, where he attended a one o'clock meeting. He was with Johnny for about fifteen minutes." Wes shrugged. "It looks like he's not the killer."

I nodded. My information had helped uncover a crime, but it was a different crime from the one I'd taken aim at. I made a mental note to ask Max whether we would need to return the architectural remnants. I looked at Wes. "So we're nowhere."

"Not hardly," he said. "The owner's agreed to let the police search all the houses Vince had access to. Guess what they're looking for."

"More stolen goods?"

"Nope—Gretchen."

My mouth fell open. "I thought we just proved that Vince couldn't be involved."

"We demonstrated that he *probably* couldn't be involved. The police are taking no chances."

I didn't buy anything at the store. I jogged to my car and drove straight to Vince's Rocky Point job site. As I drove south, the freezing rain turned into snow and visibility plummeted.

I turned onto Ocean Avenue. *Avenue! Ocean Lane would be more apt,* I thought, wondering how the narrow two-lane road had ever received such a grandiose label. I passed a dozen of the small weathered-wood bungalows and contemporary stilt houses that gave Rocky Point its eclectic feel.

When I reached the job site, I slowed to a crawl. The cluster of run-down old houses stood in vivid contrast to the well-maintained, upscale residences I'd just passed. These Victorian white elephants stood like silent behemoths, relics from an earlier time.

Up until the last quarter of the twentieth century, the 120-acre family-run Winton Farm had been a major producer of apples and blueberries. In 1870, young Josiah Winton, the scion of the family, built six houses on the eastern edge of the property for his relatives. The land abutted Ocean Avenue, and each house enjoyed an unobstructed view of the ocean. When the last Winton died in 1947, the entire kit and kaboodle passed to Hitchens College. Over the years, the college sold everything piecemeal to raise cash.

It took the company Vince worked for five years to buy up all six houses and twenty-seven acres of surrounding land. The acquisition included a hundred yards of beachfront property, with only Ocean Avenue separating the land from the dunes. It took them another two years to obtain the permits they needed to build a luxury condo development complete with a man-made lagoon and a private nine-hole golf course. They'd begun demolition only a month or so ago. One house was completely gone. The others were partially stripped, almost ready for the wrecking ball.

As I approached, I saw that yellow and black police tape had been stretched from tree to tree, circling the houses, marking the border. I counted four marked police cars parked in driveways. Lights shone in all the houses.

The snow wasn't sticking, but it was coming down thickly, and I was having trouble seeing through the white haze. There was nowhere to park, or even to pull over. Heading south, with the ocean on the left, there was no curb. Where the asphalt stopped, tall grasses, brambles, and wild roses grew in jumbled abandon. On the other side, the street led directly to crabgrass-covered private property.

I turned around and inched back past the work site at near-idling speed. I looked into each house, seeking out signs of life, but I saw nothing. *Is Gretchen inside, a prisoner in a hidden basement?* I wondered, horrified at the thought.

Wherever the police were working, it wasn't near the windows. I made two more passes, and both times I failed to see any signs of life. Knowing I had no way to convince the police to let me join in on the search, I gave up and drove back to work.

Ty called. I set aside the catalogue copy I was proofreading. Sasha had done a great job—the cobalt glassware really came to life.

"Hey, Ty," I said.

"I can tell by your voice, something's wrong."

"From two words?"

"Sometimes I can tell from one."

I smiled from my toes. "How are you doing?"

"Better. I'm en route home."

"That's great! I was braced to hear about another delay."

"Nope. I'll be there in an hour or so, depending on the snow. Lots of black ice around. Want me to stop at the store?" he asked.

"Yes. I have almost nothing in the house. I'll cook whatever you get."

"You sure know how to woo a guy."

I laughed. "Should you be talking on the phone while you're driving? Is it safe?"

"Yeah, I'm fine. I'm hands-free, and pretty much, mine is the only car on the road. So fill me in. What's wrong?"

I recounted the events of the day, sticking to the facts and not venturing into the murky arenas of opinion or speculation. "What do you think it all means?" I asked Ty when I was done.

"If they find Gretchen, you'll hear about it soon enough," he said. "As for Vince's alibi—alibis are funny things. Johnny might be convinced that Vince was there for fifteen minutes, but the truth might be that it only *felt* like fifteen minutes. It's possible Vince was only there for five minutes. About the police timing how long it takes to drive that circuit, well, maybe, for whatever reason, there was no traffic the day Boulanger was killed, and Vince hit every light just right. So now the trip that they say takes no less than an hour and a half actually took Vince an hour and twenty-five minutes. So add the ten minutes Johnny was off to the five minutes the police were off and you have fifteen minutes, plenty of time to shoot someone and clean up the scene of the crime if you put your mind to it."

"That makes a lot of sense." I paused. "You know what I'm going to do, Ty?"

"What?"

"Go home and make soup." I glanced out the window at what was shaping up to be a major snowstorm. The tree branches were covered with crusty snow, and the parking lot was totally white. "I'll stop at the store, so you don't need to."

I'd said good-bye to everyone and had my coat on and my umbrella in hand when the phone rang. Cara told me it was Sam Bartlett. I stared at her for a moment, trying to place the name, then ran upstairs to take the call. With my coat half off, I snatched up the receiver and said, "This is Josie. Mr. Bartlett?"

"Yes. I'm calling to thank you. I just got back from the police station. I understand you're the person who connected the dots between Amelia's murder and your missing employee, Marie—I mean, Gretchen. That's what she's calling herself now, right? That's quite a job you did."

"Thank you." I looked out toward the woods. It was still snowing, but the flakes were fluffy now. It was warming up. "Am I right in thinking that Gretchen—Marie—and Amelia were close?"

"Like mother and daughter."

"And you and Amelia were like brother and sister. It occurs to me that maybe Gretchen—I mean Marie—might consider you an uncle. If I was in trouble and had an uncle I loved and trusted, I'd call him."

He paused so long I thought I'd offended him. Finally he said, "I wish she had."

"Then you don't think she had anything to do with Amelia's death?"

"Hell, no. Never did. Forget the fact that Marie really did love Amelia like a mother, and never in a million years would have killed her, did you know that Amelia kept nearly five thousand dollars cash in her safe?"

"I knew she kept cash—but not how much."

"Not one dime was taken. This crime shouted Morgan. No one ever thought Marie was involved. It was his fingerprints on that chair leg, and it was, as the police say, a crime of passion. Whoever killed Amelia was out-of-his-head angry. Marie didn't have a temper, not that kind of temper—but Morgan did."

I thought of Morgan, and then I thought of Vince. He had that kind of temper, too. Gretchen escaped Morgan while Mandy made excuses for Vince. How far would Mandy go to protect him?

"Poor Marie," I said.

We exchanged contact information and agreed to stay in touch.

"If you hear from her," Sam said, "tell her she's welcome anytime."

CHAPTER THIRTY

Z oë invited us for dessert. "I made a peach pie, so you have to come over."

I laughed. "Why does your making a peach pie mean we have to come over?"

"Because if you don't, I'll eat it all."

"Well, only because we love you so much, we'll throw ourselves on the sword of your peach pie."

We jogged to Zoë's through steadily falling snow. The weatherman on the local news station was predicting that we'd have a foot by morning. April snowstorms weren't unusual, but I'd gotten myself mentally ready for spring—I was tired of winter.

Zoë told us that the kids were asleep upstairs and to get ourselves settled in the living room. She had a fire burning. I took the club chair nearest the fire. Ty sat on a leather chair next to the couch. Toys, dolls, and games leaned against the outside wall, stretching the entire length of the room.

"Creative storage," I said to Zoë as she walked in carrying a tray containing half a pie and the fixings for coffee.

"I call it the poor man's baseboard."

"Very avant-garde."

"Thanks." She placed the tray near me. "Go ahead and cut the pie, will you, Josie?"

I reached for the knife as Zoë got situated on the sofa. She put her feet up on the coffee table and crossed her ankles. "Any news about Gretchen?" she asked.

I served pie as I filled her in.

Zoë sipped coffee. "What do you know about Morgan Boulanger?" she asked.

"He was Gretchen's husband. He was a jerk."

"He beat her, right?"

"Several times, apparently, according to the Denver police."

"And killed that store owner—the woman Gretchen worked for?"

"Right."

"And the police think Gretchen was an accomplice in the murder?" she asked.

"They think *maybe* she was an accomplice," I corrected. "There's an APB out for her."

"Do the police know whether Gretchen left her apartment voluntarily?"

"I don't think so—no, well, maybe . . . I mean, her purse and suitcase are gone, too. That sounds kind of voluntary, I guess."

"Maybe she left them in her car because she was just running up to her apartment for a second."

"Why would she do that?" I asked. "She'd already been gone for two weeks."

Zoë tilted her head, her eyes serious, even somber, her mouth twisted into a wry grin. "Jeez, Josie, I can't imagine. Whatever would keep a young woman from going home?"

A man! I thought. *Maybe the man she met in Hawaii—Jack Stene.* I shook my head. "She would have surfaced by now. The man she met, Jack, was checked out and came out clean."

"Maybe. Maybe not. Let's say that Gretchen goes off with Mr. Right on Wednesday as soon as she picks up her car, hears the news that Morgan is dead on Thursday morning while she's getting ready for work, and something about it flips her out—I mean, more than the normal flip-out one would expect on hearing there's a dead guy in your living room. Maybe she knew who killed him." She paused. "Maybe she's convinced that the killer is coming after her next. What would she do? She'd run, or she'd go into deep hiding somewhere she felt safe."

I thought for almost a minute, considering this new slant. "What about the luggage tag I saw in Gretchen's entry way?"

Zoë shrugged. "Beats me."

I sighed. "There's so much about Gretchen I don't know."

Zoë nodded. "I think that's right. I think you haven't given full consideration to her mental condition. Beaten women act differently," she said. "When someone abuses you, it changes how you feel, and it changes how you act. You're guarded and worried about offending your attacker. You're wary."

"Gretchen's not like that."

"No, because she got free." Zoë watched for a moment as I tried to process what she was saying, then continued. "Apparently this Morgan asshole—excuse my French—kept his ego in his fist. Which means Gretchen had no alternative but to escape as quickly and as quietly as she could. His murder of her boss gave her the cover she needed to get out. The dirtbag was so busy worrying about saving his own skin, he took his eye off of her long enough for her to get away. From where I sit, Gretchen isn't guilty of anything but terrible taste in men."

"Gretchen once said that there wasn't a loser within a hundred miles who hadn't found her and who she didn't think was kind of cute and for sure worth saving," I suddenly remembered. "Then she'd roll her eyes the way she did and say, 'What a judge of men am I.'" I shook my head. "I thought she was being funny."

Zoë leaned back with a quirky-sad smile. "Isn't that something? She was aware that she had that—what should we call it? A proclivity? A weakness? A bad habit? Whatever. She was aware that, for whatever reason, she attracted the wrong sort of men—and, obviously, she wanted to change but couldn't. The same kind of guys kept coming around. It was like she was wired wrong or something."

"When I was with the police, I heard variations on this story all the time," Ty remarked. "Any expert will tell you that most battered women think, on some level at least, that they deserve what they get. There's another point, too, that lends credence to Zoë's hypothesis. The last stats I saw on stalkers were pretty disheartening. Something like twenty-five percent of battered women are stalked by their abuser *after* they leave."

"It's like you hear about all the time—a woman gets a restraining order and the guy comes around anyway." *Poor Gretchen,* I thought.

"Exactly," Ty said. "Boulanger might be one of those guys who wouldn't take no for an answer. Gretchen got away once and thought she was safe, but in reality, he never stopped trying to find her. He knew she liked working in an antiques store and would probably gravitate to a similar job, so he regularly read that magazine—what's it called, Josie?"

"*Antiques Insights.*"

"And if Morgan showed up again after all those years," Zoë said, "with Gretchen thinking she'd finally got rid of him—*bam,* she'd flip." She snapped her fingers as she spoke. "I know I would. Luckily, my ex is just a bum, not a stalker."

"Did he beat you?" I asked, shaken at the thought.

"Beat? No, he never beat me exactly. He slapped me once, and once was enough. He's one of those guys who can't hold a job, but, mind you, it's never his fault. He had more bad bosses in a year than most of us have in a lifetime. What really got under my skin was that he was lazy around the house. He didn't work, but he wouldn't wash a dish." She shrugged. "I'd thought about leaving him for years, but I had kids, you know? I thought it was marginally better for the kids to be in a two-parent household even though one of the parents was an idiot." She paused. "Then he slapped me. If you've never been there, you don't know how easy it is to think that maybe you did something so bad, you earned the slap." She shook her head. "I packed up and was outta there in about two hours, but I gotta tell you, I almost stayed—even after he hit me, shame on me. I bet most women would have. I got out because I got lucky and because I'm me. My uncle died and left me a house and a rental property and a little money—and I'm filled with piss and vinegar. No one hits me. *No one.*"

"I'm so lucky you're my friend," I said, tears moistening my eyes as she spoke. I took a deep breath. "Do you think Gretchen was in a similar situation?"

"Sounds like it—except a lot worse. If she got away from Morgan the way I'm picturing, on impulse and fast, can you imagine how she must have felt when she realized that she hadn't escaped after all? She wouldn't just be terrified—she'd be heartbroken. Maybe she went crazy, killed him, and took off. Or she saw him already dead in her apartment, knew that whoever had killed him was gunning for her next, and took off." She shrugged. "I would have done the same thing."

"Which brings us full circle," I objected. "If what you say is true, why wouldn't she contact me? Or Sam Bartlett? She *has* to know that we'd help her."

"I think you're missing part of the complexity, Josie. Probably she's ashamed that she ever married such a snake in the first place. Meanwhile, she's been living a lie for years. Now she's spending most of her energy keeping herself alive—just coping. If I'm right, she has no idea that she has friends who would stand up for her. Plus, she might be scared to go back to Denver. As far as she knows, Morgan's family and friends still live there, and she might expect them to blame her for his death just like they blamed her for everything else when she lived with him. So that lets out Sam Bartlett. As for you—she knows that you'd never lie. She'd figure that if she asked you for help, you'd tell her to turn herself in and you'd get her a good lawyer. My guess is that she doesn't trust the system. If she's like many battered women, reporting Morgan to the cops only got her a worse beating. All she knows now is that her life is in danger and she has to be very, very careful or she'll get caught and killed."

It was one thing to hear that Gretchen had been a battered wife—but it was another thing altogether to listen to Zoë's emotionally charged description of what being a battered wife *felt* like.

Zoë looked at me. "You've got to reach out to her with unconditional support."

"How? I don't know where she is."

"*Somehow,*" Zoë insisted.

"You know how to reach her," Ty told me.

"I do? How?"

"Think about it," he said, then turned to Zoë. "Good pie. I wouldn't mind another slice."

He met my gaze but didn't speak. It took me about ten seconds to catch up. *Got it,* I thought, and I wondered why it hadn't occurred to me long before now. *Of course* I knew how to find her.

"Excuse me," I said. "I need to make a phone call."

CHAPTER THIRTY-ONE

◄

T he next morning, just before seven, I ran downstairs and turned on my computer. I went to the *Seacoast Star*'s Web site. Wes's article was the lead story. The headline screamed:

GRETCHEN BROCK INNOCENT!
JOSIE PRESCOTT SAYS "I'LL PROVE IT!"

I thought I might faint. I reached for the phone and dialed Wes. Before the call connected, call waiting clicked in. I looked at the display. It was the Rocky Point police station number—I'd called it a million times when Ty had worked there.

I answered with as much pep as I could marshal. "This is Josie."

"It's Detective Brownley," she stated, her tone icy. "I got in early today to do some paperwork. Imagine my surprise at seeing this morning's *Seacoast Star*."

"I can explain."

"Good. Because if the article is accurate, if you can prove Gretchen's innocence, it would seem that you're withholding evidence in a criminal investigation."

"No, no," I gasped. "It's not like that at all. I just saw the article myself. Wes misquoted me. What I said was 'I believe Gretchen is innocent of all charges, and if she can get in touch with me, I'll help her prove it.' That's different from what he wrote."

"What's happened to convince you of her innocence?"

"Nothing. I did it because I know in my heart she's innocent. Don't laugh. I know it sounds lame, but I *know*."

"Why now? What's happened?"

"Nothing." I paused, thinking how to explain. "I want her to trust me, is all. I want her to believe that no matter what, I can help her. If she's frightened, I could hire a bodyguard. If she needs a lawyer, Max will represent her. I hadn't realized the impact of her past abuse—now I do. Don't you see? She's traumatized, and she doesn't know I'll support her."

I listened to silence for several seconds. Then Detective Brownley said, "If you hear from her, you've got to call me right away. Do you understand? She'll be opposed to your doing so, but you *must*. I'm not her enemy, Josie. No one hopes she's innocent more than I do. If you don't call me right away, though, *you'll* be guilty of obstructing justice, and I'll see that you're charged."

I promised to do as she said. After she hung up, I sat and stared at the computer monitor for a long time, then walked slowly into the kitchen to get coffee started.

"Detective Brownley called," I said as Ty entered the kitchen around seven thirty.

He was dressed in a suit and tie, meeting attire. Today he was scheduled to attend a high-level strategy session in Boston.

"She saw the *Seacoast Star* headline," I continued, describing the article's contents. "I don't think she's very impressed with my tactics."

"I'm not so sure she's right. Let's assume Gretchen is able to read the article. The story will get her thinking. She may be ready, or close to ready, to surrender—being on the run isn't for the faint of heart—and if she believes what you say, it could tip the balance. Maybe not today, but soon."

I reached out and touched his cheek. "Thank you," I said.

The storm had passed overnight, leaving fourteen inches of fluffy snow in its wake. The sky was cloudless, the sun strong. The snow had already begun to melt.

I drove by the Winton Farm job site. The police were still there. I saw flashes of uniforms through one of the front windows.

As soon as I arrived at Prescott's, Cara told me that reporters from the Manchester Daily, the Boston Inquirer, and *Maine Record* had called. Also, a producer from the local New Hampshire TV station wanted to schedule me for an on-air interview.

"Someone from the *Denver Globe*, too," Cara said. "Think about that: They're on Mountain Time! It wasn't even seven in the morning there when they called."

"From now on, tell them I have no further comment, okay? No matter what they ask or how they rephrase their questions, just keep saying that I have no further comment. Of course, it goes without saying that you have no comment, either."

"I don't know anything to comment about!"

"That won't stop them from asking."

"Good point. I'll be careful."

"Thank you. This is the voice of painfully earned experience speaking—the best way to be careful is to be mindful of what you're saying every time you open your mouth."

"Got it. Chip Davidson called, too."

"Really? It's been a busy morning. What did he say?"

"It was a very quick call. He asked for Gretchen, and when I said she wasn't here, he thanked me and hung up."

"How did he sound?"

"Friendly."

"Thanks, Cara. By the way, when I said that I don't want to talk to any reporters, that includes Wes."

Cara nodded her understanding, her eyes alert and attentive.

Chip sure is persistent, I noted. I thought back to last Saturday—Chip standing by the door methodically scanning the tag sale room, wholly absorbed in his efforts. His fierce concentration had reminded me of something. *What?* It was on the edge of my memory, elusive, indistinct, yet there.

Then, all at once, I remembered: He'd reminded me of a pilot seeking motion—or rather, in this case, recognition—and he wore a small airplane pin on his lapel. What if he wasn't just acting like a pilot? What if he was a pilot?

I Googled "Siva International" and called the 800 number that popped up.

"I'm looking to rent a car in Burlington, Massachusetts. Can you tell me where your rental counters are located?"

"We only have one location in Burlington, at the Galleria. Would you like to make a reservation?"

"No, thank you," I said.

Like dominoes falling in perfect alignment, an idea came to me fully developed. The narrowed cast of Chip's eyes, squinting as if he were staring into the sun. A barely noticeable lapel pin. My insurance company's security requirements. A rental car from a suburb north of Boston.

I turned to my computer, but before I could open my online address book, Cara buzzed up. It was Mandy, and she said it was urgent.

ince has been arrested," Mandy said, sounding as if she might burst into tears.

"What's the charge?"

"Grand larceny. They say he's been stealing artifacts from where he works, but I know that's not true. He sold them on his boss's orders."

"Maybe he didn't tell the truth about how much they sold for."

"Lie to his boss? Vince would never do that!"

I shook my head. People create their own mythology. "If that's true, then there's no problem. His boss will confirm their arrangements, and that will be that."

I could hear her breathing on the phone. "Do you think he's guilty?" she asked quietly.

I hesitated, then said, "It looks that way."

"I don't know what to do. I really love him."

"Grand larceny is a pretty serious charge."

"Are you saying that you think I should leave him?"

"What do you think?"

"How can I even consider it when he's in trouble? That's so not right."

I thought about how to reply. I didn't want to pour salt on her wounded heart, but neither did I want to sugarcoat the situation. *Everyone's different,* I thought. *What might send me running for the door might be a minor inconvenience to Mandy. Who am I to judge?* "Only you can decide that, Mandy. I'm not you, and it's such a personal decision." I took a deep breath. "To be fair, though, an arrest is not a conviction."

"That's a good point. I'll wait until after the trial. I'm sure he'll be found not guilty."

I couldn't think of how to respond. *Denial,* I thought, *your name is Mandy.*

We ended the call with an exchange of good wishes and an agreement to talk soon.

Time was of the essence if I was going to check out my idea about Chip. I suspected that Vince would be out of jail soon. His bail might be high, but he would pay it and be out.

I found the security company's phone number, and called my contact, Dobby. "Can I take a look at last Saturday's tag sale security video?" I asked.

"Sure. Any particular time of day, or do you want it all?"

"Morning. From nine to ten. All three cameras."

"Sure thing. Hold a sec." I heard tapping as he entered my search criteria into his system. "The files are too big for e-mail, so I'll post them to our FTP site and e-mail you the retrieval instructions."

Cranston Security, following my insurance company's directions to record all activities involving the public, had hung three cameras in the tag sale room. One was placed high up on the rear wall aimed directly at the front entrance; the second was perched over a side window and faced the cash registers; and the third rested on a ledge over the main door and photographed anyone who entered or departed through the warehouse entryway. Each camera took high-resolution black-and-white still photographs every three seconds.

I thanked Dobby, and within minutes I'd downloaded all three files.

Chip Davidson had been standing by the front door scanning the room when I'd entered from the inside door, so I started with the camera mounted on the back wall. One at a time, I clicked through the still shots. I watched as a mother and daughter pushed through the door, early birds eager to find bargains. They were frequent customers, and I smiled as I watched their progress in the sequential shots. Next came three older women, laughing and chatting as they shopped. I continued to click through the photos until Chip David-son appeared. I viewed them all, then selected one that showed him full face.

I right-clicked to save the image to my desktop, cropped it tight around his head and shoulders, then printed it out on glossy paper.

I slipped the photograph into a clear plastic sleeve, then cropped and printed a shot of Gretchen from our December holiday party, her eyes alive with joy, and eased it into the sleeve so the two im-ages were back to back.

Time for a road trip, I thought.

Harrison Air Field in Burlington, Massachusetts, had grown up.

When I was a girl, it had been an airstrip with a sometimes-open coffee shop called Olson's that served stale doughnuts and burnt coffee. I'd always figured the two Olson brothers who ran the joint bought the day-old stuff at the grocery store, so the doughnuts really were stale and the coffee really was burnt. No one cared. Back then, it was all about flying. My dad had fre-quently taken a chartered four-seater from Harrison to his meet-ings in New York City, and my mom and I had often seen him off. Thinking of those two young men who'd worked so hard at the food stand to help pay for their flying addiction made me feel old. I missed seeing them.

Now Harrison was a busy regional airport, and the coffee shop was a professionally run concession called Amstead's. According to a sign on the door, it was open regular hours, and from what I could see as I walked past, it served cooked-on-the-spot standard fare.

Just before security, I spotted a door labeled OFFICE. A woman about my age sat at a big desk doing something with a topograph-ical map. There was a brass tent-shaped sign on her desk that read JENNY MARSH.

She looked up and smiled. "Hi, there," she said.

"Hi. I'm Josie Prescott. I have a few questions about a flight last Friday. Are you the right person to ask?"

"What kind of questions?"

"What time it landed, who was the pilot, where it came from, that sort of thing."

"Scheduled or private?"

"Private," I said.

"You want to talk to Brice. Brice Trumbull."

She directed me to a metal hangar at the back of the airfield. A twelve-foot-high chain-link fence with barbed wire on top was bolted to both sides. A wind sock mounted to the roof fluttered toward the south. A weathered sign over a glossy red door read TRUMBULL'S AVIATION.

A tall, thin man, about fifty, opened the door to my knock and stepped back with a jaunty flair to let me enter. "Hello, there," he said.

His skin was the color of honey. He was bald. He had a scar on his cheek, a puckered circle, like maybe he'd been struck by a pebble kicked up from a plane taking off back when Harrison was still a flyboy airfield. I didn't know him, but I knew his type. He was a devil-may-care flying nut, you could just tell.

BRICE was embroidered on the pocket of his green jumpsuit.

"I'm betting you're Brice," I said, smiling.

"How'd you know?" he asked, smiling back.

"I'm Josie Prescott. Brice, I have my fingers crossed that you'll help me by answering a few questions."

"Come on in and tell me about it." He led the way across the cold concrete floor to a ripped leather sofa positioned kitty-corner to the field entrance. "Want a cup of coffee? It tastes bad, but it's fresh-made."

"With a recommendation like that, who could resist?"

"Have a seat," he said with an easy grin. He reached over to a Mr. Coffee machine that looked older than me and poured steaming black liquid into a foam cup.

"Do you remember the Olson brothers?" I asked.

"Hell, yes. You know them?"

"From when I was a kid. My dad always said their coffee was the worst in the world."

Brice laughed. "Your dad had the right of it, all right. That's why I got myself a Mr. Coffee."

"What are they doing now, do you know?"

"Last I heard they moved to Florida. That was about ten years ago. They were smart boys. I'm sure they're doing well." He put the pot down. "I only have that powder stuff—what is it? Coffee-mate. Want some?"

"No, thanks," I said, hoping the coffee wasn't too awful.

"Sugar?"

"Nope. Black is fine."

He pulled up a wooden chair and straddled it backward, his arms resting on the back rung, facing me. "So, what can I tell you?"

"When did this man arrive on Friday?" I replied, showing Chip's photo.

He stared at it, then rubbed his nose and looked up at me. "Why do you want to know?"

"Because I think he's involved in the disappearance of my friend." I flipped the sleeve to show Gretchen's picture.

"Fine-looking woman," he remarked.

"She's a wonderful woman—and she's missing."

He nodded. "He arrived around two in the afternoon."

I smiled in relief. "What's his name?"

"He was flying a Dragon 850A, a beauty. I never forget a plane."

"Can you look up his name?" I asked.

"Don't need to. Don't forget names, neither. His is Chip David-son."

"Where did he fly from?"

"Harrisburg."

"Pennsylvania?" I asked, mystified.

"Yup, but that don't mean nothing. He might have come from anywhere, and Harrisburg was his last stop."

I nodded, understanding. "When's he planning on leaving?"

"He didn't say. He paid for a week, a little extra, too, 'cause he

asked me if I could have his plane ready to go on an hour's notice."

About how long it would take to drive from Rocky Point, I thought.
"Can I see the plane?"

"Sure, but I can't let you in it."

"I understand."

We walked out to the field. I carried my coffee with me. To my
surprise, it tasted pretty good. About twenty planes ranged over a
quarter mile of concrete, separated from the active runway by a
locked gate. Mounds of melting snow dotted the perimeter.

"There it is," he said, pointing to the fourth plane in.

"It has markings on it," I observed, "and numbers."

"Right. That's how the pilot identifies himself to the tower."

"Can I look it up somewhere?"

"Sure. Easy."

"Can we do it now?"

Brice took me to his work area, a small enclosure configured using shelving units. He sat at an old wooden desk. I sat on a wooden
chair next to him. He tapped a few instructions into the computer,
brought up an official registry site, and entered the plane's call numbers into the search window, and within seconds I had my answer.
The plane was registered to Peter Boulanger of Evergreen, Colorado.

Boulanger, I thought. He and Morgan must be related somehow,
brothers or cousins, probably. I considered the time line. Chip—
whose real name might be Peter—probably knew that Morgan had
fled Denver after Amelia Bartlett's murder and was in Tennessee
using the name Sal Briscoe. If he also knew that Morgan was tracking his wife, Marie, and that he'd discovered her in Rocky Point using the name Gretchen Brock, well, then . . . when he heard the
news that a man had been found dead in Gretchen's apartment, he
would have immediately headed for Rocky Point to see what was
what. My logic was sound, I thought, but the conclusion it led me
to was grim: The only reason I could think of for Peter to use an
alias was that he intended to avenge Morgan's murder.

"Did he have anyone with him when he landed?" I asked.

"Nope."

"How about a hotel contact? Did he tell you where he'd be staying?"

He shook his head. "He didn't say nothing about that. As soon as the paperwork was straight, he had me call him a taxi. I heard him tell the driver to take him to Siva's, in the Galleria. Maybe they can tell you more."

I stared into space, trying to come up with another question. I couldn't think of anything else to ask. "I guess that's that, then."

"Sorry I can't help more," Brice said.

I patted his shoulder and smiled. "Are you kidding me? Brice, you're the answer to a prayer. I can't thank you enough."

"You think he got that pretty girl?"

"No, but I think he's trying to get her."

Brice nodded. "You gonna find her first?"

"I'm going to try like hell."

"Well, you need a quick getaway, you give me a call. I'll fly you anywhere you want to go. Don't need no hour's notice neither."

"Thanks," I responded, touched.

I got a business card from my case and wrote my cell phone number on it. "If you hear from him, you call me, okay?"

He tucked the card into his pocket. "You bet I will. Here," he said, taking one of his cards from a little stand on the desk. "You need me, you holler."

The card was yellowed with age.

"Thanks for the information, Brice—and the coffee. It's pretty good."

"No, it's not. It's just better than I told you it was. I've learned the trick of managing expectations."

I smiled at Brice's application of a well-respected business principle, paused for a moment, then said, "I'm going to need to tell the police, Brice."

"I got no problem with the police."

"Once the police get into it, reporters are sure to follow."

"Free publicity."

I smiled again and extended my hand. "You're something spe-cial, Brice," I said.

"Nah. I just try and do the right thing."

He walked me to the door and watched as I got settled in my car. He smiled and waved as I pulled out of the lot, heading north. *Something* way *special,* I repeated silently.

CHAPTER THIRTY-THREE

I pulled over and set my blinkers before calling Detective Brownley.

"I have information about the man calling himself Chip Davidson," I told her. After recounting my conversation with Brice, I added, "It looks like his real name is Peter Boulanger. I'm guessing that he's the dead man's brother, out for revenge. Since he's been calling or coming by my business every other minute asking for Gretchen, I bet he thinks she killed him and wants her blood."

"What's Brice's full name and number?" she asked coldly.

I fingered the yellowed card and read off the information.

"So let me get this straight. You went down there because he scanned your tag sale room like a pilot scans the sky? Do I have that right?"

"Also because he wore an airplane lapel pin and because his Taurus was rented in Burlington, Massachusetts."

"Just how do you know about the Taurus?" she demanded, sending my heart plunging.

I couldn't tell her the truth—that Wes had filled me in—and I wasn't willing to lie. "Does it matter?" I asked.

"Yes."

"Sorry, I can't say."

"Can't or won't?"

I could hear Max telling me to be quiet. "I have nothing else to add, Detective. Except that Brice was really helpful."

"Tell me this—did you get the information from someone in this department?"

That I could answer. "No."

There was a long pause, then she said, "You should have called me before you went down there."

"If I'd called and said that a man named Chip had stood in my building looking around like a pilot so I wanted to check out an airport in a different state, you would have laughed me out of town."

"No, I wouldn't," she said quietly, her anger replaced by solemnity. "I would have gone with you."

"Really?" I asked, pleasantly surprised. "I figured you would have told me to butt out."

"Next time, call me first."

I didn't respond. I wasn't sure I believed her.

"And tell your buddy Wes Smith that if he learned about the Taurus from someone on my team, heads are going to roll."

My stomach tightened. I was on precarious ground, and I knew it. "You tell him yourself, Detective. It's none of my business. You have no reason to think that Wes told me anything."

"Are you saying Wes *didn't* tell you?"

"I'm saying nothing."

Another pause. "Next time, call me before you do anything on your own."

I was glad to get off the phone. I could sense her disapproval. I could understand her concern.

I didn't call Wes until I was back in New Hampshire. I owed him an exclusive, but I wanted Detective Brownley to have a head start.

As soon as I stepped into the office, Cara handed me a sheaf of message slips.

"More reporters," she said. "I told them you had no comment."

I flipped through the messages. "I'll be upstairs," I told her.

Sasha was on the phone but held up a finger to arrest my progress. I nodded and listened to her end of the conversation.

"Thank you again, Dr. Johns," she said. "Yes, certainly . . . we'd love it. Absolutely. Josie may call you herself if she has additional questions . . . you, too . . . bye-bye." She looked up at me, smiled, and tucked her hair behind her ear. "That was Dr. Johns. He wrote that dissertation you found. He's an associate professor at Maxwell State University outside of Chicago, and he was pretty darn excited to hear about the vase."

"He hasn't heard any rumors of it being offered for sale?"

She shook her head. "No, but he said he'd be on the next plane once we had it back in hand."

"From his mouth to God's ears," I said. "Was he helpful?"

"Yes. Very—if our goal was to authenticate it."

"Does it help us find Gretchen?"

"I don't see how." She glanced at her notes. "He has documentation that the vase King George II gave Henrietta Howard was acquired by a small museum outside of London in 1767—that's the year she died—then deacquired for unknown reasons in 1883. The museum sent it to auction, where it was acquired by an American woman named Shirley Bosley. Mrs. Bosley was from Cheyenne, Wyoming." Sasha smiled shyly. "That's where Dr. Johns lost track of it. He didn't get a whiff of Faring Auctions."

"Wow," I said. "So provenance is almost set. Good job, Sasha."

She blushed a little. "Thanks, but it was your idea to call him."

"Good job to both of us, then." *Sasha is right, though,* I thought. *It doesn't bring us any closer to finding Gretchen.*

Eric called from the warehouse. "I wanted to show you a mark on the stained glass window we got from Phil's Barn. I think it's just dirt, but I'm not sure how to clean it."

"I'm glad you asked," I said, thinking how lucky I was to have such a conscientious worker, "but you know what? We need to hold off on doing anything with it—in fact, we need to hold off on all the architectural artifacts we got from Phil's. There's some question about whether everything has clear title."

"Okay. I'll crate up the window to keep it safe."

"Good idea. Pack up the doorknobs and locks, too, okay?"

"Will do."

When I hung up, I saw that Cara was frowning at the computer. "Is something wrong?" I asked.

She looked up, surprised. "No, everything's fine. It's this formatting." She smiled a bit. "I'm getting a little frustrated. I want a page number at the top of each page, but then when I edit the document—this is the sales summary report you asked for—the page numbers no longer line up properly."

"Believe it or not, I know how to do that! Let me show you." I selected "Page Number" from the "Insert" pull-down menu, checked the correct box, and closed the window. "That's it!"

"I can't believe it's that easy!" she said, her pleasure at learning apparent—a fair measure of the potential of a new employee, I thought.

"Whenever you have a question, please ask. Sasha and Fred know a lot about the software we use, too. Don't wait until you're frustrated, okay?"

"I will. Thanks, Josie."

Her frown was gone. *Maybe Cara would consider staying on permanently,* I thought. *That would free up Gretchen to take on more responsibility with our outsourced vendors. Instead of just coordinating the details, she could supervise the relationships. That would free me up to do more outreach to grow the business. When Gretchen gets back, we can talk about it. When Gretchen gets back,* I repeated. *When she gets back.*

"I'll be upstairs," I said and headed toward the warehouse entrance.

As I approached the door, I glanced at the framed *Antiques Insights* cover art and smiled. *What a great milestone,* I thought. *For all of us. We all look pretty good, too.* It was a tribute to the photographer the magazine sent to take the shot.

Then I noticed something that had never registered with me before—Eric's elbow had been cropped out of the photo. I'd thought that he'd felt so embarrassed at being in the limelight, he'd tried to remove himself from the photo, but I'd been wrong. From his demeanor I could tell that he was, in fact, embarrassed, but that wasn't the only reason why the photo conveyed the impression that he was hiding off to the side—it was a function of the way the photo had been cropped.

I pushed through the door into the cavernous space. Inside, it was cold and echoey and dim. I waved to Eric, carefully wrapping the stained glass window in protective plastic. Suddenly I was struck by a memory and stopped short.

In the *Denver Globe* photo I'd found, Gretchen was standing with the fellow from the Denver Reads! program and Amelia Bartlett. On the right, there was a pair of clapping hands, but the person doing the applauding stood out of range. I hadn't thought about that missing person before. Who was it? Another employee? Someone shy like Eric who positioned himself as far away as possible from the central figures?

During my first year at Frisco's, as part of my training, I'd observed a photographer as he struggled to capture the detail in a glistening nineteenth-century cut crystal decanter set. No matter what lighting or backdrop he tried, shadows striped the glass, rendering the images unusable. Finally, satisfied that he'd tried everything he could, he turned the best of the photographs over to an artist who'd meticulously, dot by dot, retouched the image to eliminate the shadows while preserving the integrity of the rendition. When we got it back, I was dazzled by the accurate representation the artist had achieved.

Then, all at once, I'd exclaimed, "Look!"

In a corner of the photograph, glistening in a highly polished silver mug, was a tiny, shimmering image of myself. Our attention had been so completely riveted on the distracting shadow, we hadn't noticed the out-of-place reflection. I called the photographer to share the bad news.

"No problem," he said. "I'll crop it out."

I'd known what cropping was, of course, but I hadn't known how frequently it was used. As I watched him eliminate the mug, I realized that any part of any photograph could be removed and no one would ever know what wasn't being shown.

I charged up the spiral stairs, so excited I could hardly breathe.

Upstairs, I brought up the *Denver Globe* article and stared at the clapping hands. They were smooth and soft-looking. They belonged to a young woman who wore no rings and had manicured nails. Who was she?

According to the credit, someone named Helen Mishenko had taken the photograph.

I Googled "Helen Mishenko" and "Denver Reads!" and easily found the nonprofit organization's Web site. From its home page, I visited the "picture album" page. Twenty-odd photos in, I came to the one I sought, uncropped.

"Oh, my God," I whispered, incredulous. I held on to the edge of my desk. I blinked, then I blinked again. "Oh, my God," I repeated.

Then I got mad.

I felt snookered, the way I'd felt when, as a green freshman, I'd eagerly accepted a beauty school's free makeover offer. When I'd showed up and discovered that my "free makeover" was nothing more than a haircut and blow-dry based on the lesson of the week, I'd walked out. I'd been eighteen at the time, and I'd learned that when something was offered for free, usually you'd be lucky to get your money's worth.

Now, staring at the photograph, I realized that I'd been played. There, off to the right, applauding enthusiastically, stood Lina.

CHAPTER THIRTY-FOUR

The Denver Reads! caption read "Amelia Bartlett, owner of Denver's Rosebud Antiques Shoppe, presenting Executive Director Marcus Linden with a generous donation as store employees Marie Boulanger and Iris Gibbons look on."

I shut my eyes for a long moment to gather my thoughts, then turned to the window and watched the weak April sun flicker on the branches of the pine trees that ringed the parking lot. *Lina,* I thought, shaking my head. Things would have been so much easier if she'd trusted me.

Seeing her photograph explained so many mysteries. Clearly she and Gretchen were friends; they'd left Denver together and stayed together. In just a few minutes, I had the outline of a plan. The first step was getting Lina out of the way.

The woman who answered the Bow Street Emporium's phone had an appealing English accent. When I asked for Lina, she said, "Just a sec, luv," and placed the receiver on the counter. While I waited I heard her tell someone, presumably a customer, "Thanks ever so much."

"Hello?" Lina said, turning the word into a question.

"Hi, Lina. It's Josie. I'm just checking in. How are you doing?"

"Okay," she replied, but she sounded tense and worried.

"You can't talk, right?" I asked.

"Right."

"Okay. I just wanted to know if you had any news."

"No."

"In case I need to reach you later—do you get off at six today?"

"Yes."

"Thanks, Lina. I'll be in touch."

Okay then, I told myself. I told Cara I had to go out for a while and ran to my car.

Driving into Portsmouth, I had to concentrate to keep from speeding. I parked in the central garage, then hurried toward Market Street. The street and sidewalk were wet with liquefying snow. At the corner of Bow Street, I whipped into the alley that ran between the Blue Dolphin and the river, nearly slipping on the slick pavement. The restaurant had positioned a huge copper tub filled with tall plantings at the mouth of the alley. I stepped behind it and leaned against the mellowed brick wall. I had a clear view of the Bow Street Emporium.

I looked over my shoulder. No one else was in the alley. I nodded, satisfied.

Keeping my eyes on the store, I dialed Detective Brownley at the Rocky Point police station.

"I have news," I said. "Pretty astounding news, actually. You know the woman who disappeared at the same time as Gretchen, right after Amelia Bartlett's murder, Iris Gibbons?"

"What about her?"

"She's Lina."

I heard a sharp intake of breath. "What makes you think so?" she asked after a long pause.

I explained. "There's no question about it—it's Lina."

She didn't speak. Through the shop window, I could see Mandy talking to a customer.

"I'm pretty sure Lina's at work," I added.

"I spoke to Brice," she said, unexpectedly shifting gears.

"Great guy, isn't he?"

"Very. Are you sure you don't know how to reach Chip Davidson?"

"No. I mean yes, I'm sure. I've asked him for his phone number more than once, but he always says he's hard to reach, doesn't have a cell phone, and will be in touch with me."

Another pause. "Thanks, Josie," she said and ended the call.

I settled in to wait. The sun shone past me, dappling the snow-tipped cobblestones. I was glad I was wearing a sweater under my coat.

I was sure Detective Brownley would reach the same conclusions I had. The difference was that she'd need a court order. I was going to rely on persuasion.

Eight minutes after we hung up, Detective Brownley pulled up in an unmarked car and parked illegally in front of the shop. Griff parked his patrol car right behind her. They entered the shop.

I held my breath, then reminded myself to breathe, then found I was holding my breath again. After five agonizingly long minutes, Detective Brownley stepped outside just ahead of Lina. Griff comprised the rear guard. Lina, sickly pale, was placed in the back of the patrol car. Mandy's face appeared at the window, her nose pressed against the glass. She looked dazed.

I hurried back to my car and drove to Lina's apartment, parked on a side street with the building in my direct line of vision, and dug my cell phone out of my tote bag. Before I could make my call, it rang. It was Wes.

"I picked up a report from my police scanner that Lina's been taken in for questioning," he said. "Do you know anything about it?"

"Yes. I was going to call you, but I can't talk now."

"Why not?"

"I'll call you as soon as I can, Wes. I promise."

"Josie!" he whined.

I flipped the phone closed to end the call, then opened it again and was midway through dialing Lina's home phone number when Wes drove up.

I froze.

He parked directly in front of Lina's house and jumped out of his car. He ran onto the porch and pushed the bottom buzzer. I counted twenty before he pushed it again, then, after a ten-count, he pushed both of the other units' buzzers. Thirty seconds and two pushes later, he walked to the house next door, another triple-decker, and tried his luck there. Everyone was at work, it seemed.

Wes walked to the next unit, a duplex, apparently determined to get a quote about Lina from a neighbor.

I didn't have the time to allow it. The Rocky Point police might show up at any moment, search warrant in hand. I couldn't proceed with him here, and I couldn't wait for him to finish his canvass of the neighborhood.

I called him and watched as he eagerly checked the number on the display and answered.

"Hi, Wes. It's Josie. Sorry about that. Listen, I do have information, and if you can meet me at my office, I'll fill you in."

"What's it about?"

"I can't talk on the phone, but we can be private in the parking lot. Can you come now?"

He glanced at his watch, then surveyed the dwellings on his left, the direction he'd been headed when I'd called him, then turned to assess the ones to his right. Suddenly I realized that if I could see him, he could see me, too. I scrunched down, crossing my fingers that he wouldn't look in my direction, and if he did, that he wouldn't recognize my car.

"It's important, Wes."

"I'll be there in ten," he said decisively.

I stole a look over the dashboard in time to see him trot to his car. I held my breath until he was out of sight. I felt a pang of guilt at sending Wes on a wild goose chase, but I needed Lina's neighborhood to myself. I'd make it up to him later—in spades.

I called Cara. "If Wes Smith comes into the office asking for me, tell him something came up and I'll call him later, okay?"

Now, I told myself. *Now I rescue Gretchen.*

As soon as he was out of sight, I dialed Lina's number.

After six rings, a machine picked up and Lina's voice invited me to leave a message. I shut my eyes for a moment and took a deep breath. It was important to sound calm.

"Gretchen," I said after the beep, "it's me, Josie. I think you're there, at Lina's. Are you? If so, let me in, or come out. I'm right outside in my car. Please . . . no matter what you did in Denver, no matter what you did here, let me help you."

I kept talking until the machine cut me off, my time up.

I kept my eyes on the front door. Nothing. I felt overwrought with dashed expectations, my eyes welling with tears, but kept on watching the door. I was unwilling to give up hope.

My concentration was so focused on the front, Gretchen was halfway down the driveway before I spotted her. She'd come from the back, carrying her purse and nothing else. I opened my car door and stepped into the street. I stood still, directly in front of her, fifty feet away. I smiled and used the back of my hand to whisk my tears away.

Gretchen looked shell-shocked.

I gestured that she should hurry, and she needed no additional urging. She sprinted toward me.

I wanted to hug her but didn't. I had pictured our reunion—she'd screech and embrace me, and we'd rock back and forth, and I'd jump up and down, unable to contain my joy. We didn't have time for such luxury. I kept expecting to see a battery of police cars race onto the block.

"Get in!" I called. "Hurry, get in!"

I leaped into the car and shoved the passenger door open. She dove in. Before she could speak, I directed, "Squash down! You've got to stay out of sight."

Without hesitation, she tucked tight, so no part of her was visible above the dash board.

Every inch of me wanted to floor it, but I didn't. I drove like a little old lady, well below the speed limit and pausing for an extra-long time at stop signs.

I didn't speak until we were on the interstate. "I'm so glad you're okay, Gretchen. I've been sick with worry."

"Thank you," she said, her words indistinct. "Where are we going?"

"Ty's. We can hole up there while we figure out what to do next. He's at work in Boston. He won't be back 'til much later." I snuck a look at her. Her position looked painful. "That looks really uncomfortable. It won't be long."

"I'm okay."

Five minutes later, I used the spare remote to open Ty's garage door. When I lowered the door behind us, I realized that my heart was beating so hard and fast it felt as if my ribs might break.

"You can sit up," I said. "We're in Ty's garage."

She unfurled herself slowly and turned to me, wide-eyed.

I touched her arm. "Let's go."

I led the way through Ty's mudroom into the kitchen. I punched the codes into the alarm box to signal I was an authorized visitor, then reactivated the system.

"Stand here for a sec while I lower the blinds and shut the curtains," I told her, leaving her in a short corridor that connected the kitchen to the study. Starting in the kitchen, I went from room to room, turning on lights and closing out the outside world. "All clear," I called as I reentered the kitchen.

Gretchen walked slowly toward me, looking petrified. I'd never seen her in any other mood but buoyant, and it was harrowing to witness.

"First things first. Are you okay?" I asked. "Physically, I mean. You're not wounded or anything, are you?"

"No. I'm fine."

"Second, are you hungry?" As soon as I asked, I realized that it was a singularly anticlimactic question, a probably futile attempt to return to normalcy.

She shook her head.

"How about some tea?"

"That would be good."

She sat at the table while I started water boiling. For the first time I noticed she was wearing jeans with a tropical-patterned, short-sleeved bright red blouse. Exotic birds flew among jungle plants. It was pretty jazzy.

"You only had the clothes you brought with you on vacation," I observed.

She nodded. "Now all I have is this outfit. I didn't even take my toothbrush. When I heard your message, I just grabbed my purse and left."

"Are you cold? Do you want a sweatshirt? We have plenty of spares."

"Thanks," she said, nodding.

I ran upstairs and dug through one of Ty's drawers. The sweatshirt would be huge on her, but there was no way that any of my petite-sized tops would fit.

"Did you hear that Lina's in custody?" I asked as she slipped on the sweatshirt.

"No. My God. No. Why? What charge?"

"All I know is that she's been identified as Iris Gibbons."

Gretchen accepted the cup of tea I handed her. "Thank you." She looked up at me. "I can't believe any of this is happening." Her eyes moistened, and she looked down. "It's just a nightmare."

"I can only imagine," I said softly. "Do you feel up to telling me what happened?"

She shivered. Her luminescent green eyes darkened. "Where should I start?"

I shook my head. "Actually, you shouldn't talk to me—or anyone—until you've received legal advice. I shouldn't have asked you anything about it. We need to get you a lawyer."

Her eyes grew wide with fear. "I don't know any lawyers."

"Sure you do. Max. I'll take care of his fee. If you're comfortable having Max as your attorney, I'll give him a call."

"Oh, Josie. Thank you so much."

She covered her face with her hands and her shoulders shook, but she made no sound. Silent tears, the loneliest kind. I touched her shoulder so she'd know she wasn't alone. She leaned into me, just a little, enough to signal that my touch was welcome, and we sat that way for a long, long time.

CHAPTER THIRTY-FIVE

ax was in a meeting and couldn't be disturbed. I left an urgent message for him to call me the instant he was available.

While we waited, Gretchen asked me how I'd located her. She didn't talk much, but it seemed to do her good to listen. Then she asked about her vase. "I heard on the news that it was stolen," she said, wiping away fresh tears.

"I still can't believe it. I'm so sorry, Gretchen. It was in my care and it was taken. I'm so upset."

She shrugged. "It's only a thing, you know?"

"That's just like you to say so, but we both know it's more than just a thing." I shook my head. "Did you hear that Vince has been arrested?"

She nodded. "For stealing artifacts."

"I think there's a chance he's the one who broke into my place. If so, I'm hoping that when the police search his apartment and car, they'll find your vase."

She didn't comment, and to change the subject, I asked, "Did Amelia give you the vase?"

"Yes. For my birthday."

Before she could describe the occasion, Max called, and I heard her exhale loudly. She'd been on pins and needles waiting for his call, and it showed.

"Max," I said, after thanking him for getting back to me so quickly, "I need you to make a house call."

"Sure. Where and when?"

I smiled. Max was a rock. "Now. Ty's house." I gave him the directions. "Call when you're turning into the driveway, okay?"

"Why?"

"I want your car out of sight, so when you arrive, I'll open the garage door. And one more thing—don't tell anyone where you're going or why."

His tone changed from friendly to businesslike. "Maybe you'd better tell me what's going on first."

"No. It's better this way."

"Better for whom?"

I glanced at Gretchen, watching me with fierce attention. "For all of us," I replied. "Trust me on this one, Max."

"Okay. I'm on my way."

I smiled as I hung up. "He's on his way," I repeated to Gretchen.

Gretchen reached out her hand and grasped mine. "Thank you," she whispered.

My throat closed, and I swallowed hard. "You're welcome."

She wanted a refill on the tea, and I was glad for something to do. Everything was on hold until we spoke to Max.

Max had Gretchen give him a dollar as a retainer.

"That means you can talk openly to me," he told her. "It's a privileged communication. No one can compel me to repeat it. If you speak in front of Josie, though, that changes everything. If you talk with her in the room, it will be assumed that you've waived privilege, and she can be compelled to repeat what you say."

Gretchen recoiled at his words and shot a frightened glance in my direction. "She has to leave?" she asked Max, tears springing to her eyes.

We sat in Ty's living room. Yellow stripes of late-day sunshine penetrated the outer edges of the shade. I arranged the drapes to better block out the light.

"No," Max replied, "but as your lawyer, I think she needs to. You need to be able to tell me the truth without editing yourself."

"But I haven't done anything wrong!" Gretchen objected. "I can tell you the truth and she can hear it and so can anyone else!"

"Josie, would you excuse us, please?" Max asked.

I looked at him, but he didn't see me. He was looking at her.

I walked into the huge master bedroom upstairs and stood for a moment in the doorway. I heard nothing from downstairs. I was tempted to sit on the steps and try to eavesdrop, but I didn't. I closed the door and settled on the window seat to wait, feeling miserable.

Half an hour or so later, Max called, "Josie? You can come down now!"

Gretchen sat on the front half of a club chair, making a game effort to smile.

"You okay?" I asked.

She nodded.

"Gretchen and I are leaving," Max said. "She's decided, wisely, I think, to let me arrange for her immediate surrender. I've spoken to Detective Brownley, and we're all set. Gretchen understands that she may have to spend the night in jail. Regardless of when she gets out—it will be today or tomorrow depending on the charges they decide to file, if any, and how quickly I can arrange bail—she doesn't want to go back to her apartment just yet."

Gretchen shuddered, and I didn't blame her.

"She can stay with me."

"That may be a good solution," Max said.

I wondered what her other options might be. Go back to Lina's? Stay with another friend?

"You'll let me know about bail?" I asked him.

"Yes. If and when."

"Thank you," Gretchen whispered, her tone so low I could barely make out her words. Her eyes remained fixed on the floor.

I burned with curiosity and couldn't do a thing about it.

I called Ty as I retraced my steps, lifting shades and opening curtains. I got his voice mail and left a long message telling him everything that had happened.

I paused at the oversized picture window in the living room.

Who killed Morgan Boulanger? I asked myself. *Why?* Was it an accident—a struggle for a weapon, perhaps? Was he killed because he attacked someone and that person defended him- or herself? Or was it murder, plain and simple?

A yellow bird with a black crown caught my eye, and I watched it fly from tree to tree.

Mandy was devoted to Vince—I was convinced she'd lie for him if she thought he was being wrongly accused of something—but would she kill for him? *I pass,* I thought, knowing that when it comes to matters of the heart, all bets are off.

I forced myself to be objective. Gretchen had plenty of motive, too. What if she entered her apartment and found her abusive ex-husband inside? What if he'd pointed a gun at her, saying that he'd told her he'd never stop trying to find her, that he'd never let her go?

Before Max had stopped her from talking, Gretchen said that she hadn't done anything wrong. If she'd killed him, her wording would have been different. She would have said, "I couldn't help it" or "I had no choice" or "It wasn't my fault." Not, "But I haven't done anything wrong."

The bird flew away, soaring over the treetops to the west.

I contrasted what I knew about Morgan with what I knew about Jack. Thinking about Jack made me remember my promise to call him; if I were Gretchen, I'd want him to know I was okay. I called his work number.

"Jack Stene," he said crisply.

"Jack, it's Josie Prescott. I have news about Gretchen. She's safe. She seems pretty traumatized, but physically I think she's fine. She's surrendered to the police."

"What happened? Did she say?"

"No, and now she has a lawyer who's told her not to talk to anyone, me included. There's nothing we can do at this point except wait for the police to sort everything out."

"If you see her before I do, will you pass on a message? Please?"

"Sure."

"Tell her that I want a rain check. We had plans to go to dinner

Saturday night, and she missed our date. I want her to know that I want a do-over."

I smiled. "I'll be sure she gets the message."

I decided not to go back to the office. I was in-my-bones upset. I couldn't imagine the tumultuous emotions that must be churning in Gretchen's heart. She'd been a fugitive for nearly a week, and now she would be interrogated by two separate sets of police detectives—Denver and Rocky Point—about two separate murders that had occurred more than seven years apart.

Every time my phone rang, I grabbed it, hoping it was Max calling with information about Gretchen or Ty telling me he was en route home.

Ty called first, saying how glad he was that Gretchen was safe and telling me he'd be home by seven thirty.

Wes reached me as I was preparing to leave for my place. "Josie," he said, "talk to me. I'm writing my next article now."

I ran my discoveries through a quick assessment: Arrests were public information, and describing my role in facilitating them wouldn't hurt the police investigation. The ongoing search for Chip, a.k.a. Peter Boulanger, was different; revealing his alias and his relationship to Morgan and Gretchen might well scare him off before the police could locate him.

"I'll tell you what I can." I detailed how I came to identify Lina as Iris and how I located Gretchen.

"So that's why they're under arrest as material witnesses."

"Are they? That's horrible! It seems so unfair after what they've been through."

"You said you figured out that Gretchen was at Lina's—I'd just arrived when you called. Is that why you sent me to your office, to get me away from Lina's house?"

"Yes," I admitted.

He sighed loudly, Wes-speak for profound disappointment. When I didn't comment, he asked, "So what did Gretchen say?"

"On the advice of her attorney, Gretchen isn't talking to anyone but her lawyer and the police. She barely said hello to me before she surrendered."

"She has to have said *something*, Josie," Wes insisted. "Did she say hello? Did she say whether she was injured? Did she say what it felt like being a fugitive? I'm not asking for state secrets here. Just some color I can use in the article."

"I won't repeat anything she said, Wes."

"Why not?"

"Because it's Gretchen. I've got to go. I'll call you if there's anything I can talk more about."

I heard the beginnings of his sputtered objection as I slapped the phone closed.

I called Max's cell phone. It went to voice mail. "Max," I said. "I just heard that Gretchen's been arrested as a material witness. What about bail?"

Max called back about an hour later. I was sitting doing nothing, every nerve on edge.

"I'm so glad you called," I said. "I've been worried."

"It's a complicated situation."

He sounded tired.

"Has she been charged?" I asked, not wanting to receive confirmation of Wes's news.

"Yes," he answered. "No bail."

"No bail?" I repeated, shocked. "Isn't that extraordinary?"

"It's unusual, but not unique. Gretchen is deemed a flight risk, for obvious reasons, since she ran away before."

"Can't you have her released into my custody?" I asked. "She could give up her passport, and I could guarantee her presence or something."

"That's the point of bail—it guarantees her presence by risking forfeiture of the money or other assets. I'm not representing you in this, Josie, but I can advise you that it wouldn't be smart on your part to get involved. There are other issues in play." He paused. "I can talk to you openly because Gretchen has given me permission to do so, for reasons I'll explain in a moment. First, though, you need this background: I think the Rocky Point police have been quick to charge her, and to resist my application for bail, because they are anticipating a move by the Denver police to try and extradite her to Colorado." He paused. "There's more. It involves Lina, who has also been charged and denied bail, and is also likely to be the subject of an extradition filing. Gretchen is hoping you'll do something for her. She wants to see you and explain in person. I've arranged with the police to make an exception to standard visiting hours. Can you come now?"

I didn't hesitate. "Yes."

I called Ty and left a quick message, then ran to my car. Visiting Gretchen in jail was a prospect as alarming as it was comforting.

CHAPTER THIRTY-SIX

Detective Brownley looked as tired as Max had sounded. Her normally porcelain-white complexion was tinged with gray, and there were dark shadows etched under her eyes. Max appeared serious but not somber, which I took to be good news.

"This way," the detective said.

Max and I followed her down a corridor past the fingerprint station and the door to Interrogation Room Two. We stopped at an unmarked door. She opened it and waved us in.

The room seemed to be half office and half interview space. There was a metal desk pushed to the side, blocking access to a tall file cabinet. An oak table and six chairs sat in the center of the room. The walls were painted celery green, and ivory-colored cotton curtains were drawn across a window that looked out on the back parking lot.

Max sat at the head of the table, facing the door. He got his legal pad ready. I sat to his right. I heard footsteps and looked toward the door. Gretchen entered the room.

"Thank you," she said to someone behind her, out of sight.

She looked sick, as if she were about to collapse. My heart lurched, then sank.

"Thank you for coming," she told me politely.

"Of course."

She sat across from me, on Max's left.

"You look like you're having a terrible time of it," I said.

She shook her head helplessly, unwilling or unable to accept comfort. "I'm okay. It's Lina."

"What about her?" I asked.

Gretchen looked straight at me, then glanced at Max, then back to me. She took a deep breath. "I need to ask you for a huge favor. *Huge*. I'll pay you back," she said earnestly, adding, "*We* will." She paused, maybe to harness the energy she needed to continue. "Lina only has a court-appointed attorney. I hate to ask, but the truth is that there's no one else I *can* ask. Neither of us has any family." She paused for a moment, then continued. "You know that my real name is Marie Boulanger. I was born Marie Holbert. In Texas. I was an only child. My dad was in construction, and he was killed in a work accident—he fell off some scaffolding when was I was nine. My mom moved us up to Denver for a fresh start. She died in a car accident when I was eighteen. It was a drunk driver. I married Morgan a month later." She swept her hair back, her eyes fixed on mine. "Lina—Iris—is my oldest friend. We went to middle school together. And high school. We got jobs at Mrs. Bartlett's antiques store together. When Morgan killed Mrs. Bartlett, we—" She broke off and closed her eyes as tears ran down her cheeks. "Sorry," she said, after a moment. She opened her eyes and continued. "We got away from Denver together. After everything she's done for me—including hiding me and protecting me when it would have been smarter and safer for her to tell the police the truth—I can't let her go through this without proper legal representation." She swallowed heavily to quell another flood of tears, then forced herself to continue. "*I just can't.*"

Her conviction echoed silently throughout the room. She leaned toward me. Her urgency became an imperative.

"Lina has no one besides me to help her," she said. "She never even knew her father, and her mom ran out on her when she was six. Lina was reared by her grandmother. She died a few months after we left Colorado. Lina couldn't go to the funeral. She has no one but me—and I have no one but you." She took a deep breath as she began to cry again. "Please, Josie. Will you get her a lawyer? We'll pay you back."

Gretchen's appeal touched my heart. I turned to Max. "What's your assessment of Lina's legal situation? Does she need a better lawyer than the public defender she's been assigned?"

"Her public defender is a very capable young man. He's a recent law school graduate."

"You didn't answer my question—does Lina need a more experienced lawyer?"

Max tapped his notepad, then looked at me. "Yes."

I nodded. "Okay then." To Gretchen, I said, "You don't need to worry about the money. Consider it a gift." I moved my chair closer to her and rubbed her back. "Can you take it on, Max?" I asked.

"No. It wouldn't be wise. Lina should have her own attorney. I'd recommend Shirl Sheriden."

"Isn't she an assistant district attorney?" I asked, remembering an article Wes had written a few months ago about a case she was prosecuting.

"Not anymore. She was with the DA's office for years, but she just went private. She's good."

"Okay." I glanced at Max. "May I ask about what happened?"

"If Gretchen feels like telling you, that would be all right. She's given the police a signed statement, so she's free to speak." He turned to face her. "As long as her story doesn't vary—even a millimeter—from her statement."

I turned to Gretchen. "Could you tell me about it?"

She shrugged. "Talking seems so pointless, but I don't mind." She took a deep breath. "On Wednesday, I took the bus from Logan Airport, and Lina picked me up at Portsmouth Circle. She drove me to the Heron dealer. We got there about one. My car was ready. I paid for it, and I drove home. As soon as I stepped into my apartment, I saw Morgan on the couch. Dead." She shivered and hugged herself. "I couldn't believe it! I thought I'd escaped from him, and then after all these years—he found me. Except now he was dead." She sighed. "I grabbed my suitcase, drove to Lina's, and hid my car in her garage. I let myself in with my key. I've been there ever since." She blinked. "That's all I know."

"What about the luggage tag I found in your hallway?"

She looked blank for a moment, then said, "Oh. I'd taken that off at the airport while I was waiting for the bus. There wasn't a trash can nearby, and I hate to litter, so I just tossed it in my tote bag." She shrugged. "When I got back, I had it in my hand, ready to throw away. I must have dropped it."

"Do you know where Lina was that morning, before she picked you up?"

"I wouldn't allow Gretchen to speculate on Lina's whereabouts to the police, and I won't allow her to do so to you," Max informed me.

A ghost of a smile crossed Gretchen's face. "It's okay, Max. She got a manicure. She had a hot date that night."

I nodded, thinking. "Did they ask you about the milk?"

"Yes," Max said. "We don't know anything about milk. What do you know?"

I shrugged. "Not much. From what I hear, someone placed a carton of milk in your refrigerator," I told Gretchen, glancing at Max. "From the date stamp and lot number, they know it was purchased nearby on Wednesday, the day you returned—the day Morgan was killed."

Max rubbed his nose, thinking, and didn't speak.

"It must have been Mandy," Gretchen said. "That was awfully nice of her, wasn't it?"

"Completely," I agreed, "but why do you think it was her?"

"Well, it wasn't Lina, because she would have mentioned it to me, and there's no one else it could be. They're the only two people who have keys. Besides the property manager, I mean. Mandy and Lina split up the plant-watering duty. Mandy must have stopped by on her way into work that day."

As far as I knew, no one had checked whether Mandy's fingerprints matched the one on the milk carton.

"Do they both have keys or did they share?" I asked.

"They each had one. I made a copy for Mandy just before I left. Lina's always had one."

I nodded as a germ of an idea took hold. I put the thought aside and asked, "Were you inside Lina's when that attempted break-in happened?"

"Oh, God, it was terrifying. I didn't know what was going on, just that Blitzie was going nuts. I hid in the bathroom. Thank goodness the neighbors called the police."

I extracted the plastic sleeve containing Peter Boulanger's picture from my bag and showed it to her. She looked at his image, then at me.

"That's Peter, Morgan's brother," she said, taken aback. "Why do you have his picture?"

"He's here using the name Chip Davidson. He's been asking for you."

Her eyes opened wide, but she didn't speak.

"I think he's the one who tried to break into Lina's apartment. He guessed you were there."

"How?" she asked. "How could he possibly have guessed?"

"The other day, Lina and Mandy drove into Prescott's just as Peter was leaving. He must have recognized Lina as Iris and tracked her down."

Gretchen stared at me, then slowly nodded. "That explains it. I didn't know if the attempted break-in was related to Morgan's murder or not." She sighed, closed the folder, and slid it back to me. "Lina thought maybe we should just take off again, but we were so scared—scared to stay and scared to leave." She laughed a little, an ironic sound, simultaneously self-mocking and resigned. "Having worked at Prescott's, learning so much about computers and databases, and having had my fingerprints taken for the security clearance, I knew enough to know that getting ourselves established a second time wouldn't be as easy as it was last time around." She sat up straight. "Plus, it felt so unfair. Neither Lina nor I had done anything wrong, and we love our lives. We love New Hampshire. We wanted to stay." She shook her head. "I kept thinking something would happen and it would all come out all right."

"It will," I said. "I'm convinced of it." I shot Max a look. He didn't comment. I cleared my throat and changed the subject. "I spoke to Jack Stene." I repeated what Jack said about wanting a rain check.

"Just my luck, right?" she said softly. "I finally meet a great guy, and look at me. I'm a mess and I'm in jail."

"He knew all that, and he didn't seem to care," I said, smiling. "Is it okay for me to tell him you say yes to a rain check?"

She sat up straight. "Absolutely," she said. "Please tell him yes."

There was a knock on the door, and a uniformed guard poked his head in and said that our time was up. Gretchen hugged me, thanked me again, and was even able to smile a little as she left.

Max walked me to my car.

"I'm hoping to work out an arrangement with the Denver police tomorrow morning providing for Gretchen's cooperation," Max told me. "If I do so, and if the Rocky Point police feel that Gretchen has been open and honest with them, I'll go back to court to ask that the question of bail be revisited. There's no guarantee, of course, but if all goes as planned, Gretchen could be out as early as tomorrow afternoon."

"Max, you're a wonder man. Thank you."

As I drove to Ty's, I thought more about who might have killed Morgan. *Mandy,* I thought—*or Vince.* There was no one else.

I was convinced that both Mandy and Vince had been in Gretchen's condo the day Morgan died—Vince to install the light fixture, Mandy to water plants and drop off the milk. Either they entered and found a pugnacious Morgan inside, or they unlocked the door and Morgan forced his way in. Both men, Vince and Morgan, were violent by nature. Their first instinct, not their last, would be to fire up and attack.

CHAPTER THIRTY-SEVEN

he next morning, first thing, I checked out the online edition of the *Seacoast Star*. The headline wasn't too bad.

BROCK & NADLEIN ARRESTED
BAIL DENIED, EXTRADITION POSSIBLE

At least it doesn't imply they were killers, I thought.

Wes's article summarized the current status of the investigation and bullet-pointed the facts about Amelia Bartlett's murder in a side-bar. Another sidebar posed the question: "How Did Josie Prescott Know?" and described how my research led me to the original photo showing Lina and how I discovered Gretchen's whereabouts.

He quoted me as saying, "I can't imagine that either Lina— Iris Gibbons—or Gretchen—Marie Boulanger—possesses criminal knowledge of *anything*. Back in Denver, they were young and afraid and they ran for their lives."

I looked out over the meadow. It was a sparkling sunny day, great for my spirits but bad for business at the tag sale. According to the thermometer Ty had mounted outside the kitchen window it was already 58 degrees. *Nice,* I thought. We might approach 70 by afternoon if we were lucky. The woods gleamed with a faint red glow, a sure sign of spring—red buds illuminated by morning sun.

I walked Ty to the door. He was off for another long day of mock emergency training, this time in Augusta, Maine, the need urgent enough to justify working on a Saturday.

"See you tonight," he said, touching my cheek.

I listened until the sound of his SUV faded away.

I poured coffee into my thermos and headed to my own house before going into work. I didn't feel like wearing my usual attire—jeans and a work shirt. This fine spring day demanded khakis.

As I drove home, an idea occurred to me. *It worked once,* I thought. I dashed upstairs to change, then stepped into the kitchen to check the time. According to the mahogany and rosewood clock mounted above the refrigerator, it was eight thirty. I smiled every time I looked at that clock. It had been one of my first "grown-up" purchases, a genuine Dan Chessman original, and it was one of my favorite possessions.

Eight thirty. Early, I thought, *but not too early.* I called Mandy, who agreed to meet me for coffee.

I retrieved the see-through sleeve containing Gretchen's and Peter Boulanger's pictures, the one I'd shown to Brice. I slid Gretchen's photo out and set it aside. Using a soft cloth, I carefully rubbed the plastic until it was smudge-free, then slipped the sleeve into a folder for safekeeping.

Mandy sat sipping from a heavy white mug. She looked just about done in.

"I'm so glad you suggested meeting," she said as I slid into the banquette. "I'm hoping you can fill me in." Her hands trembled as she placed the mug on the table.

"And I'm glad you were able to meet me," I replied. Her eyes were rimmed in red. "I'll tell you everything I can—but first, how are you doing? You look like you haven't slept much."

She looked down for a moment, then said, "I'm pretty upset. Have you—" She stopped speaking as the waitress approached to take my order, then finished her thought. "Have you spoken to Gretchen or Lina?"

"Gretchen, briefly. You know that they've both been arrested and that bail's been denied?"

"I heard that on the news, but why?"

I explained their connection with the ongoing Denver investigation and said, "Gretchen's lawyer thinks they'll be able to get bail soon—maybe even today. What about Vince?"

The waitress placed a mug in front of me. The coffee smelled good, rich and strong.

"His lawyer thinks he'll be released today, too. I'm expecting a call anytime."

She was frowning as if she were fighting a bad headache. "How are you feeling about him and the situation?" I asked, concerned for her. "Have you done any more thinking?"

She shrugged. "All I do is think, but that doesn't seem to get me any closer to knowing what's best to do."

I nodded. "I hate that feeling—you don't even know what to think about, am I right?"

"Or how to weigh things. I want to make decisions with my heart, but then I think that's stupid and I should use my head and ignore my heart. Then I decide I want to follow my heart, to be a trusting person. Then I end up exhausted and all mixed up."

Poor Mandy, I thought. "Have you spoken to the police again?"

She nodded, looking as if she might cry. "They asked me about Wednesday all over again. Whether Vince went to Gretchen's to put in the light fixture. Whether I was there, too. They wanted to fingerprint me." She paused. "It was a nightmare. They asked about the break-in at your place, too, and the attempted one at Lina's."

"What did you tell them?"

"Nothing. Vince told me to refuse to answer questions and not to let them take my fingerprints."

"That must have been hard—to not answer, I mean. I know you want to help with the investigation."

She nodded. "Everything is hard—but Vince said that facts can be twisted, so I shouldn't talk to them at all."

"Would you tell me one thing?" I asked, knowing that I was treading on dangerous ground. Neither the police nor Vince would approve of my questioning Mandy, but I was revealing no secrets since Wes had already published that Vince's fingerprints were on the light fixture. "I'm curious about something. The police know that Vince installed the light fixture. His fingerprints are all over it. I'm wondering why—why did you give it to her?"

She shrugged. "I only had room for one of them, and Gretchen loved the design, so we decided to give the other one to her."

"That was really nice of you—of both of you," I said softly.

"Thanks."

Her eyes were guileless. It was almost as if she were under Vince's spell. She seemed able to think independently, yet when push came to shove, she did as she was told.

I placed the folder on the table next to her mug and opened it up so Peter's photograph was visible. "Do you know this man?"

She picked up the sleeve and held it out in front of her. "No," she said. "Who is he?"

"His name is Peter Boulanger, but he's been using the name Chip Davidson. He's the dead man's brother. Does either of those names ring a bell?"

She shook her head. "No. Should they?"

I finished my coffee and signaled the waitress for the check. "He's involved somehow. I'm not sure how," I said. "I'm not sure about a lot of things."

"I know that feeling," she said with mordant humor, then added, "If you see Gretchen or Lina again, will you tell them I asked after them?"

Mandy was such a sweet girl, spiraling down instead of rising up. Part of me wanted to shake her and ask if she couldn't see how bad Vince was for her. The rest of me just wanted to hug her and wish her luck.

"Sure," I said.

———

From the parking lot I called Cara to tell her I'd be late, then Wes who agreed to meet me at our dune in ten minutes.

I waited in my car, and when he pulled in behind me with a jerk, I got out. We scrambled up the shifting sand. Once at the summit, I surveyed the beach ten feet below, but I saw no one. Spewed-up wet black-green seaweed littered the shore. A few pieces of sun-bleached driftwood were lodged, half hidden, under the tall grass that separated the dunes from the beach. The ocean was calm, the tide gently ebbing.

"I need you to check something out, but it's a tricky situation." I met his eyes. "No joke, Wes. If it gets out in the wrong way, people may run. People may destroy evidence. People may kill. You've got to promise."

"Okay," Wes said.

"It's Mandy."

"What about her?"

I faced the ocean. Far out, I spotted a tanker heading south. "Gretchen told me something. You can't write about it. It was told to me in confidence."

"No prob."

"I'm trusting you, Wes."

"I got it, Josie. Jeez. I heard you the first time."

"Okay. Here's the thing. Except for the property manager, only Mandy and Lina had keys to Gretchen's apartment. Lina was fingerprinted when she was charged as a material witness, so I'm assuming that the police checked whether her prints matched the one on the milk, am I right?"

"Yup. According to my source, there's no match."

I nodded. "So by process of elimination, it has to be Mandy's fingerprint." I handed him the folder containing the plastic sleeve. I'd removed Peter's photograph. "Don't touch the plastic. Mandy's prints are all over it."

"Tell me," Wes said.

I explained my alternate theories of the crime, then said, "We can worry about the details of their alibis later." I pointed to the plastic sleeve. "First we need to know if it's Mandy's fingerprint."

Wes nodded, his brain running full-tilt. "Gotcha. Good stuff, Josie." He started off, then looked back at me. "You know my word is good, Josie—but if the print matches, it's out of my hands."

"The police will pick her up."

"So quick your head'll spin."

"Fair enough." I paused, then asked, "Do you think it will match?"

He grinned. "Oh, yeah."

My next stop was Shirl Sheriden's office to drop off a check for Lina's retainer. Her receptionist, a short, white-haired woman, offered me a cappuccino.

I accepted and sat down to wait. The cappuccino was good.

Ms. Sheriden was a tall, voluptuous brunette, and she was a sharp dresser. Today she wore a royal blue suit with a pale peach blouse.

"Come on in," she said, smiling broadly, inviting me into her office. It was vast and modern. She favored blond wood and contemporary art. "Max called me," she said, pointing to a chair, indicating that I should sit, "so I'm up to date."

"Then you know that I'm paying for Lina—I mean Iris's—defense."

"Assuming she wants to retain me, yes."

"Have you seen her?"

"No. I will soon. When I spoke to her, she asked me to call her Lina, by the way."

"So many different names—it's confusing. Here," I said, handing her the retainer check. "Max told me that he hopes to arrange bail for Gretchen today. Do you think you'll be able to get bail for Lina, too?"

She tapped the check on her desk, then looked at me and said, "This is awkward. You're paying me, but you're not my client, so I can't comment on any aspect of either my strategic thinking or my tactical plans."

I nodded, disconcerted. "Right. Sorry." I stood up. "I should go. 'Bye."

"Sit, sit. Just because I can't talk to you doesn't mean you can't talk to me."

She smiled again, and I found myself smiling back. She radiated warmth and sincerity. I bet she was a superb litigator.

"Assuming I take on Lina as a client, what can you tell me that will help me represent her well?'

I sipped the frothy drink as I considered her question. "She's loyal to Gretchen. She's a great actress."

She wiggled her fingers. "Engaging opening," she said, grinning. "Flesh it out."

"Loyalty—that one's easy. Lina hid Gretchen for a week despite obvious personal risk to herself. The actress one—that's more complicated and more disturbing. She's maintained a fictional identity in perfect harmony with Gretchen for years, but it was all a fabrication, and I never suspected it. As an antiques appraiser, I'm trained to recognize liars. It's not a perfect science, but I'm pretty good at it, and I had no clue."

Shirl shrugged. "Couldn't the same be said about Gretchen?"

"Yes, sort of, but with Gretchen, it was obvious she was hiding something. To be fair, I know Gretchen way better than Lina. Still, with Lina, I never suspected a thing. Lina even created a back story about how they met in a Laundromat, for example, and I never doubted it for a minute. Gretchen, on the other hand, wouldn't talk about her past at all—you just hit a stone wall." I took a deep breath. "I admire Lina's performance, and from where I sit, she did nothing wrong. Her motive was all about self-preservation—she wasn't trying to put one over on people for some nefarious reason." I paused, trying to find a way to clarify my point. "If you hate mushrooms but eat all of your mushroom omelet because you don't want to offend or upset your hostess, is that a lie? If Lina pretended to know nothing about Gretchen in order to save her life, is that a lie?"

"Ah, semantics!" Shirl said with a big smile. "A lawyer's favorite playground." She stood up. "I'm sure I'll have more questions later, but you've been enormously helpful. To answer your question, yes to the omelet, no to the saving a life."

"You wouldn't eat the omelet to avoid hurting your hostess's feelings?"

"Hell, no. Why would it hurt *her* feelings to learn that *I* hate mushrooms?"

I'd never thought of it that way, but immediately, I could see that Shirl was right. "What would you say so that she didn't get upset?"

"I'd tell her the truth. I'd say, 'I can't believe how gorgeous this omelet looks, but I've got to confess that I hate mushrooms. Isn't that appalling in a guest? You go ahead and don't think anything about it. I'm perfectly fine with bread and butter. In fact, pass that puppy over here. I *love* your bread.'" She shrugged again and smiled wide enough to wow a crowd. "Telling the truth is an undervalued tactic." She winked. "I use it all the time."

She reminded me of my mother: strong and kind and as honest as the day is long. *Good for Lina,* I thought. Maybe she couldn't have Max as her lawyer, but she got herself a prize in Shirl Sheriden.

CHAPTER THIRTY-EIGHT

 got to the tag sale to find Sasha working in the instant appraisal booth and Fred manning the phones.

"Everything under control?" I asked.

"Yup," Fred said.

"Great. I'll be upstairs if you need me."

As soon as I was settled behind my desk, I called Gretchen's new flame, Jack, and got his voice mail. "I told Gretchen about the rain check. She said yes."

I forced myself to work. There was nothing I could do until I heard from Max or Wes. I made an impressive dent in the pile of project updates, catalogue drafts, and consignment contracts awaiting attention, and took a stint in the instant appraisal booth. Just after noon, Fred buzzed up.

"It's Wes Smith for you on line one. He says it's urgent."

"I got hot news," he said, breathless with excitement. "We've got to meet. I'm around the corner. Outside your place in three minutes, okay?"

I agreed, told Fred I'd be back in a few, and dashed outside just as Wes was pulling into the lot. He jumped out of his car and ran to meet me. He looked tickled pink.

"I handed over the plastic sleeve before ten, and they ID'd the fingerprint within minutes. Mandy's already in custody."

"Oh, my God, Wes! That's awful. Poor Mandy."

"Poor Mandy? What if she's the killer?"

I nodded, shaken. "You're right, of course. It's just such a shock."

"Yeah, I guess. "Mandy's clammed up again, but before she realized what she was saying, she told the police officer who picked her up—in front of everyone in the store—that she brought the milk over to Gretchen's on her way into work, then lied about it because she thought it didn't have anything to do with anything, and she didn't want to get involved. What do you think? Does that have the ring of truth?"

I shook my head. "Not really. It's more likely she lied because Vince told her to."

Wes nodded. "That's what I think, too. She said the Chevy with the Tennessee plates wasn't there when she got there, that she went into the apartment, put the milk in the refrigerator, and left. She won't confirm or deny that Vince was with her. She insists she knows nothing else."

"Why did she wipe the milk carton down?"

Wes's eyes sparkled. "She says she didn't."

"So either she's lying about that part or someone else wiped it down to protect her—that must be Vince." I nodded. "He'd know how to clean up a crime scene."

"Vince," Wes said, enthused, then shook his head. "It can't be Vince. We already checked him out, remember? You said we'd worry about their alibis later, but the fact remains that Mandy got to her store by a quarter to ten the day Morgan was killed and was with customers or co-workers until she left at six. Vince was at work all day, too—except when he was off selling those architectural remnants, and then the timing was just too tight."

"The timing could have been off," I said, explaining how easily Ty introduced reasonable doubt to Vince's minute-by-minute alibi. "Plus, if his employees lied for him about the architectural remnants, what's to say they wouldn't cover for him about when he actually showed up for that one o'clock meeting?"

"So how do we prove it?"

I thought about it, then shook my head. I was out of ideas. "Have the police finished searching his place?"

"Yes. Also the houses due to be demolished. And his Jeep. Why?"

"I was hoping they might locate Gretchen's vase."

"You think he stole it?"

I shrugged. "I don't know. Sometimes I think it's Peter. Sometimes I think it's Vince. Sometimes I think it's someone else I haven't thought of." I sighed. "You said you had hot news."

Wes grinned again. "Yeah. *Very* hot. According to my police source, they think there's a better than even chance that Peter's fled the country. Along with his entire family."

"What?"

Wes nodded, his eyes feverishly bright. "Can you believe it? The Denver police went to talk to him in his hometown—Evergreen— and his wife and two kids have vamoosed. Gone. One neighbor said she saw them drive off over the weekend, their car loaded down with suitcases. They found the car parked at Denver International Airport and traced the family's movements. Are you ready? They've gone to China!"

"So? Maybe they're on vacation."

"They withdrew their kids from school. They said they were moving overseas."

I stared at him for several seconds. "China," I said. "No extradition."

"Right. The police think Peter's probably already joined them. They can't find any record of his flight, but they know that he carried faked papers once—Chip Davidson, right?—so they figure he might have another set of false documents, too."

"What about his plane?" I asked.

"The police think he's abandoned it. Same with his rental car."

"Did they find his car at the airport?

Wes shook his head. "Nope. Not Logan. Not anywhere that they can find. As of about an hour ago, they issued a nationwide BOLO."

"BOLO? Be on the lookout?" I confirmed. "Wow."

Peter Boulanger is gone, I thought. I nodded. It made sense. As much as he wanted to exact revenge on Gretchen, he didn't want to get caught. He must have learned that his real name was known. How did he learn that?

"If he's after Gretchen, why would he leave town just when she resurfaces?" I asked.

"He knows the police are onto him."

"How?"

Wes whistled. "You think that maybe he didn't leave, that he's just gone to ground?"

"I don't know. What if he got his family out now so he didn't have to worry about them later? Meanwhile, he's just lying low, waiting for his chance to strike."

"So the first time Gretchen steps out in public, boom, you think he'll try to get her?" Wes asked with morbid anticipation.

I looked into the woods, past the first lines of trees, over the thick tangle of Boston ferns, into the shadowy center. *So many of the trees are evergreens,* I thought, *that even in early spring before the leaves are out, anyone could hide there and lie in wait.* "I don't think he's gone," I whispered. "I think he's here." I looked around again and shivered.

Max called as I was talking to Eric about an important auction of nineteenth-century European chairs coming up in two weeks. We were in the early stages of furniture arranging.

"It looks good, Josie," Max told me. "We're on a break now, but the Denver police are almost done questioning Gretchen, and they've expressed gratitude for her cooperation. I'm confident that we'll get bail. We're scheduled to meet with the judge at three."

"That's fantastic!"

I had Eric and Cara come with me to the front office. I wanted us all to share the excitement.

"I have good news," I announced. "Nothing is definite yet, but it looks as if Gretchen may get bailed out—today!"

Sasha leapt up in a completely uncharacteristically demonstrative expression of joy. She clasped her hands against her chest. "Oh, Josie!"

Fred leaned back, his laid-back demeanor undisturbed. "Cool," he said.

Eric smiled and nodded and said, "Good."

"Oh, Josie!" Cara said, her voice cracking.

All in all, it was a moment of elation in the midst of turmoil.

As I was about to return upstairs, Jack called.

"Thanks for your message," he told me. "Any news about bail?"

"Yes. A hearing is scheduled today at three."

"Terrific. I'll be there."

"You will?" I asked, startled.

"Yeah. No time like the present, right? I figure that after being in jail, she'll be ready for a good square meal, so I'm calling in my rain check right away."

Wow, I thought. *Decisive. Masterful.*

I sat next to Jack Stene at the bail hearing. Wes sat on the other side of the room, furiously taking notes. Gretchen was led in by uniformed officers and sat next to Max. She was still wearing Ty's sweatshirt. Her eyes stayed forward, and I couldn't tell whether she was aware we were there. It was over in minutes. The ADA withdrew his objection to bail; Max stated that Gretchen was gainfully employed, with deep roots in the community, and that she would give up her passport.

"What about the passport in her other name, Marie Boulanger?" the judge asked.

"She never had a passport in that name."

The judge turned to the ADA. "She's not a suspect in any violent crime, is that right?"

"That's correct, Your Honor. The charges of material witness relate to her fleeing the scene of a crime—twice, once in Denver and once here in Rocky Point. Both the Denver police and ours are satisfied that her actions resulted from a reasonable fear of reprisal. She's been fully cooperative."

"Give me a number," the judge instructed.

"Twenty thousand."

"Mr. Bixby?" he asked, turning to Max.

"No objection, Your Honor," Max replied.

The judge issued a series of instructions. After he warned Gretchen that she couldn't leave the jurisdiction, I stopped listening.

My attention was on Wes. He slipped out of his seat and scooted out of the room. *A reporter on deadline reacting to breaking news,* I thought. The entire hearing lasted less than half an hour.

I signed a ream of documents guaranteeing that Gretchen wouldn't skip town and stood by an unmarked door to wait. Jack stood next to me. Max had disappeared inside.

Before long he pushed open the door, smiling, and then, finally, Gretchen appeared. She saw me, and her lips quivered.

"Gretchen," I said softly, opening my arms, offering a hug.

She stepped forward and allowed me to hug her. She was rippling with tension. "Thank you so much," she whispered. "Thank you."

"It's okay," I murmured.

She stepped back, her eyes moist, and noticed Jack. "I can't believe you're here!"

"Josie said you'd give me a rain check for dinner. I'm hungry. How about you?"

She burst into tears and melted into his arms. Max and I stood and watched Gretchen's shoulders shake. Jack patted and stroked her back. His head was bowed and curled into her neck. He was whispering something I couldn't hear.

She raised her head and tried to wipe away her tears, but they kept coming. I dug a packet of tissues out of my tote bag and handed it to her.

She thanked me and gulped. "I'm just a mess. How can you stand to look at me?" she said, mopping up her tears, turning her face away.

Gretchen looked gorgeous, as always. Her titian hair fell in stately waves below her shoulders. Her eyes were as dark a green as jade, and flecked with gold. Her skin was a rich ivory, the color of Devonshire cream. The stress and weepiness of her ghastly experience seemed to have taken no toll on her appearance. I opened my mouth to reassure her, but Jack spoke first.

"Now I know to expect you to look a little ragged when you get out of jail. Next time, I'll be prepared."

She chuckled. "There won't be a next time."

"Never say never," he teased.

I grinned, enjoying his lighthearted approach.

Gretchen smiled up at him, then turned to Max. "Now what?" she asked.

"Now you go and do as you choose so long as you don't leave the jurisdiction. There's something else you need to be aware of, though—Peter Boulanger may be nearby."

Her joy shifted to fear immediately. "Is that why the police were asking me about him?" she asked Max.

"Yes."

"What does he want?"

"To talk to you, apparently."

"I don't want to see him," she insisted.

"You don't have to," Max reassured her.

"Who's Peter?" Jack asked.

"Morgan's brother. My brother-in-law." She turned to me and asked, "Have you seen him?"

"He's stopped by Prescott's several times asking for you," I told her. "From what I hear, he may be with his family in China. No one knows."

"I'll take care of you—you'll be safe at my place," Jack said.

"You live in Maine, right?" Max asked.

"Yeah."

"No way. Gretchen can't leave the county, let alone the state."

"You can stay at my house," I offered. "He'll never know you're there."

"I'm running out of ways to say thank you," Gretchen said softly.

I smiled. "I'm glad to help, Gretchen. I'll take you over now and get you situated."

I eased my spare key from its nook in my tote bag and handed it to her.

She smiled and took in a bushel of air. "Any news about Lina?" she asked Max.

Max shook his head. "Josie? Have you heard anything?"

"I met her new lawyer this morning. Shirl Sheriden. As of then, she hadn't decided whether to press for bail, but I think you can relax. I get the sense that Lina's in really good legal hands. I was impressed."

"Thank you," Gretchen whispered.

Max said, "You'll need this." He handed Gretchen a slip of paper listing the police impound unit's address and hours of operation. "The police are releasing your vehicle as we speak. They found nothing incriminating in it."

She half-smiled. "That's a relief."

"I can take you now or in the morning," I volunteered.

Gretchen smiled again. "Thank you. I vote for morning. What I want now is a shower."

Max reminded her to bring ID, and we walked to the parking lot together.

"I'll ride with Jack, if that's right," Gretchen said shyly.

"Sure," I said. Max and I stood watching as they walked to his car. The last thing I heard Gretchen say was, "The only clothes I packed were vacation outfits, and there's no way I'm going back to my place, even if the police would let me. I guess I need to go shopping."

"After your shower, why don't we go to the mall, then grab dinner?" Jack responded.

"He seems like a great guy," I remarked to Max.

"About time she caught a break."

We left Jack in the kitchen pouring himself some ginger ale while Gretchen and I went upstairs. I showed her where everything was, put out fresh sheets and towels, told her to raid the refrigerator and cupboards at will, and asked if there was anything else I could do at this point.

"I have everything I need, and then some." She smiled as she spoke and hugged me again. It felt like she was relaxing in front of my eyes.

"I overheard you guys planning on eating out, but I'll be cooking dinner in case you change your minds. No need to call or anything. Just know that food will be available!"

I heard the shower running as I walked down the stairs. Zoë's car wasn't in the driveway, so I called and left her a message explaining that Gretchen would be staying at my house for a while. I mentioned that Jack might be around as well. With no expectation of actually getting him, I called Ty, planning to leave him a quick good-news update, and was lucky enough to catch him between training exercises. "At least I have some good news on this end—Gretchen's out on bail!"

"That's great! Tell me how it went."

I gave him the details and explained that she'd be staying at my place.

"You're a good friend, Josie," he remarked.

"Thanks," I said, pleased at the compliment.

I said I felt like making Thyme Chicken for dinner, and Ty said that sounded perfect.

After Ty and I finished our conversation, I called work. Fred answered, and I asked him to pass on the good news—Gretchen was safe and out of custody. He reported business at the tag sale was brisk, despite the warm weather.

I was asking Jack about his work while I chopped onions when the doorbell rang. I rinsed my hands quickly and grabbed a dish towel en route to the front door.

One glance through the glass, and muscles contracted in my shoulders and neck and my stomach sank. It was Chip—Peter Boulanger—and beneath his jacket, near his waistband, I saw a bulge.

I dropped to the floor, trying to make myself small. I knew he couldn't see me if I stayed low. The hall was dim and the sight lines from the small window set into the door were limited. My cell phone was in my tote bag in the kitchen. So was the nearest landline phone. I wanted to call to Gretchen and Jack but didn't want Chip to hear me. *He must have followed us from the courthouse,* I realized, *and I didn't even think to check.* Staying close to the ground, I crawled down the hallway.

The bell rang again, then he knocked, hammering the door.

The kitchen seemed miles away. Jack appeared at the arch, saw me crawling, and ran the few yards to join me.

"Who is it?" he asked.

"It's Peter," I whispered. "Chip."

The pounding stopped. I heard Chip tramping across the porch and down the steps.

Jack stepped toward the front, and I grabbed his pant leg. "Don't. Let him go."

Faintly, I heard an engine turn over. I scrabbled forward, clawed my way up the door, and looked outside. I was just in time to see the gold Taurus turn the corner, heading toward Portsmouth.

I ran to the kitchen and dialed 911.

CHAPTER THIRTY-NINE

etective Brownley didn't hesitate. Three police vehicles arrived within minutes, and Gretchen and Jack were whisked away moments later.

"Your car will be at the police station," Detective Brownley told him.

A uniformed officer checked all of my doors and windows to confirm they were locked, drew the drapes everywhere, and announced he'd be outside if I needed him.

"Where are you taking them?" I asked her.

"Do you plan on leaving your house tonight?" Detective Brownley asked me, ignoring my question.

"No."

"Okay. If you change your mind, I'll assign an officer to accompany you."

I fleetingly considered protesting that I didn't need police protection. "Thank you," I said.

Wes called about fifteen minutes later.

"Vince posted bail this afternoon, and now he's going nuts! The police got a search warrant for Mandy's apartment, her car, and her locker at work. They're searching them now, and from what I hear, Vince and the lawyer he got for Mandy are ranting around, but, of course, they can't do anything to stop the search. Pretty funny, huh?"

"A real hoot, Wes," I said, wondering what they'd find and where.

"Lina's out—her lawyer got her ROR'd."

"Really? Released on her own recognizance?"

"Yup. She had to give up her passport and wear an electronic monitoring device." He paused. "So, did you talk to Chip—Peter? I picked up that he came to your house on the scanner."

"No," I said, shivering.

"What happened?"

"I can't talk now," I said. I didn't want to relive it.

"Why not?" Wes grumbled. "It's important, Josie."

"I'll call you later," I said.

"When?"

"I don't know. When I can." I hung up.

Gretchen called around nine. Ty was in the kitchen cleaning up the dinner dishes. She sounded scared.

"They have us in a hotel," she said. "Can you imagine? I'm in protective custody."

"Quite a turnaround from being a fugitive."

She cleared her throat. "Yeah. So, Peter called me."

"He called you?" I asked, flabbergasted. "When?"

"Now. Today. About two hours ago. I called my answering machine from here and got the message. He asked if I was back in the apartment yet. Something in his tone—I couldn't listen. I hung up."

I leaned forward and stared at my knees. Icy tendrils of terror wrapped around my throat, and for a moment I couldn't speak. "My God, Gretchen," I said when I could. "Have you told the police?"

"Yes. I called Detective Brownley right away. She said they'd check it out. I guess she did. I just spoke to her. She'll be calling you, too." Gretchen paused, then added, "She wants me to come in to work on Monday."

"You're kidding me! Why?"

"She has a plan." There was a short pause. "She said Jack shouldn't come with me. She wants everything to appear normal when I show up."

"Sounds reasonable," I said, with more conviction than I felt. What it sounded was terrifying. "What's the plan?"

"She said she'd call you to tell you about it. It's pretty complicated."

I paused and considered trying to dig out details, but I didn't. Instead, I reacted to the emotion I heard in her voice. "Are you okay?" I asked.

"About like you'd expect."

We finished our conversation, and after we hung up, I continued to sit in the living room. I heard the swish-swish of water as Ty finished up in the kitchen.

"Hey," Ty said from the doorway when he was done.

I turned my head, then patted the sofa.

Ty sank onto the couch and held out his arm invitingly. "Hey, cutie, snuggle on up," he said.

I wriggled over and got myself situated. "So, tell me about your day," I requested. "Distract me."

I settled back to listen and found myself engaged in the stories Ty told about the personalities and the team's plans. I was impressed that he could find parts of the process boring, yet still leave work energized. The peaceful interlude was shattered when the phone rang just before ten.

It was Detective Brownley. "I want to talk to you about an idea we think is worth pursuing."

"Gretchen told me that you want her to come into work Monday." A picture came to me of Chip attacking Gretchen, and my heart skipped a beat. "Even keeping the doors locked won't help if Chip shows up with a gun."

"That's true, but it's a complicated situation, Josie. You know that Chip's real name is Peter Boulanger, right? I'm going to keep referring to him as Chip because it's important that *you* do so if and when you talk to him again. Here's the thing—Chip's done nothing wrong, nothing actionable. We have to tempt him a little."

"He's using a fake name. Isn't that a crime?"

"No, not unless you use it in an illegal enterprise. Maybe he adopted the fake name because he wanted to sniff around about his brother's murder without having to deal with the police or the media. Maybe he just wants to talk to Gretchen. Everything he's done could be interpreted innocently."

"You don't think he's innocent," I stated.

"What I think is beside the point."

"If he's using a fake credit card, isn't that illegal?"

"If he acquired it fraudulently, yes. If not, and he has no intent to use it to commit an illegal act, then it's legal."

I shook my head, amazed. "Why don't you just bring him in for questioning?"

"There's no probable cause. Trust me, Josie, if there was another way, we wouldn't be having this conversation."

"What about the gun I saw stuffed in his pants?"

"First of all, you say a bulge, not a gun. Second of all, what's to say he doesn't have a permit to carry a concealed weapon?" I had no response, and in a moment, Detective Brownley continued. "Here's my plan—I hope you'll agree to cooperate. Gretchen will pick up her car on Monday and drive straight to work. I'm betting that Chip, cruising by, will recognize it as her car and come in to see her. I want to station a detective in your office."

"How would Chip know her car?"

"Car registration information is easy to access."

"It is?" I asked, shocked. I shook my head. *That must be how he located Lina's apartment so easily,* I realized. "Assuming you're right, that seeing the car will draw him in, why does Gretchen have to be there? Isn't just the car enough?"

Ty stood up and pointed toward the den. I watched him walk out of the living room.

"No," Detective Brownley stated. "We need him to do something. Entering your office during business hours isn't a crime. We need to see if when he spots her he does something that *is* a crime."

"Surely he wouldn't be so stupid. He has to know the police are onto him. News reports have mentioned that the murder victim had a brother."

"Yeah, but he seems pretty set on finding her—and because he *is* smart, he probably thinks he can spirit her away without alarming anyone."

I took a deep breath. "What does Gretchen think about all this?"

"She thinks that I'm right, that he'll come looking for her." She paused. "She's pretty eager to have this situation finished and put behind her."

"Should I tell everyone else to take the day off? I mean, why risk the rest of the staff?"

"First, I think it's crucial that everything appear normal. If Chip drives by and the parking lot doesn't contain the number and kind of cars he expects, I think he'll drive on by. If he steps inside and doesn't see the right people, I think he'll just turn around and leave. Second, I don't think Chip is crazy or stupid; I think he wants to stay alive and stay out of jail." She cleared her throat. "We have reason to believe that he's sent his family out of the country and plans on joining them there. Whatever he's up to—he's not suicidal. I'm telling you, Josie, I still think there's a good chance that all he intends to do is talk to Gretchen. Third, we're doing everything we can to minimize the risk. In addition to a detective, there'll be uniformed officers inside, out of sight, and specially trained police in the woods."

She means snipers, I realized, and swallowed.

"There'll be additional backup units just down the road, in the church lot. We're not doing this on a whim, Josie."

What she said made sense. "Okay, then. So what do we do? Me and my employees?"

"Your day starts at nine, right? Can you meet me there at eight thirty?"

"Yes."

"At nine, I'll go over the plan with everyone, bringing them up to speed. What I'll tell them is the same as what I just told you—to act normal. If Chip arrives, greet him like you have in the past. No one should betray the police presence by word or deed. My expectation is that if he shows up, he'll spot Gretchen and the rest of us will become invisible. Gretchen will arrive close to ten to give us plenty of time to prepare. I've already coached her that she should act normal, too. She should refuse to accompany him out of the building. She—and you—should trust that we know what we're doing."

I took a huge breath. "I've got to tell you, Detective, this seems hugely dangerous to me. What if he doesn't want to talk to anyone? What if he just walks in, guns blazing?"

"He'll be dead before his weapon's drawn."

Her calm confidence was simultaneously horrifying and reassuring. I didn't like her plan, but I couldn't think of any more arguments against it. Gretchen was Chip's target, and Gretchen had already agreed. *She wants it over,* Detective Brownley had explained. I would, too. All I could do now was support her—and hope for the best.

"You said a detective will be assigned to us," I said. "Who?"

"Me."

I couldn't think of anything else to say or ask. "Okay, then," I said.

Ty was at my computer in the den, scrolling down a Web page. I didn't recognize it.

"Hey," I said. "What are you looking at?"

"That new country place, Denim and Diamonds. I thought maybe we could go dancing tomorrow."

"Oh, that sounds wonderful! Let's go dancing now."

He turned to face me. "You want to?"

"Sort of. Yes. Not really."

"I admire a woman who knows her own mind."

I smiled at his sally, then curled up in the big club chair beside the computer desk to recount my conversation with Detective Brownley. Ty listened with his usual rapt attention.

"Should I have agreed to it?" I asked him.

"It sounds like Detective Brownley put a lot of thinking into the plan."

"That's not an answer."

"I don't know that you have any choice, Josie. Anytime Gretchen steps into the open air, she's vulnerable to attack, so doing nothing isn't an option." He shrugged. "They can't just wait a few days and hope he surfaces, because the issue isn't that he's missing or that they want to bring him in for questioning—the issue is that they have no evidence that he's committed a crime. From a strategic perspective this approach is sensible; it's proactive, which is always better than reactive. From a tactical perspective, it sounds as solid as it can be given the multitude of factors Detective Brownley can't control."

I nodded. His calm good sense grounded me. "Gretchen is pretty brave," I commented.

It was only later, as I was getting ready for bed, that I realized the full magnitude of what I'd agreed to. Detective Brownley planned to use Gretchen as bait, and I was providing the lair.

CHAPTER FORTY

I barely slept. Nightmare after nightmare left me drenched in sweat. Around four, breathing hard from yet another terrifying dream I couldn't recall, I sat up in bed and scanned the room. Streaks of silvery moonlight dappled the floor and walls. There were no bogeymen to be seen. I padded to the front window and peeked outside. A patrol car with its roof light spinning sat near the driveway.

I went downstairs so my restlessness wouldn't disturb Ty, got myself settled on the sofa, and watched reruns of *I Love Lucy* until dawn. Thankfully, with the morning light came a reduction in my anxiety, and I fell asleep, gripping the afghan like a child holds a blankie.

Ty woke me at ten. "I was afraid if I let you sleep any longer, you wouldn't be able to sleep tonight."

"Thanks," I said, yawning. "I smell coffee."

"Shall I bring you a cup here or do you want to come into the kitchen?"

I stretched and sat up. "I think I want to get dressed and get the day going. I'll meet you in the kitchen in a few minutes, okay?"

"Great. You can cook."

I laughed and stood up. "Sold."

I made a fancy breakfast using my mother's Double-dip French Toast recipe, and then we sat in the living room listening to Ella Fitzgerald sing songs I'd grown up with, reading our books, and playing my favorite word game, UPWORDS. Later that afternoon, Ty asked if I felt like going dancing, and I told him no. We didn't leave the house all day.

I didn't sleep well Sunday night either. Over and over again, I'd drift off, then awaken with a jerk, my heart racing, damp with perspiration, until finally, just after three, I gave up trying to rest and went downstairs. I made a pot of tea and sat in my dark kitchen listening to the night sounds, the settling of the house, the cycling of the refrigerator's cooling system, an occasional rustling from the meadow.

At six, I took a shower and tried to prepare myself for the day that loomed ahead.

At eight, I was ready to leave. Ty insisted on escorting me to work. He walked in with me and watched as I turned off the alarm.

"Leave the perimeter alarm on until Detective Brownley gets here, okay? And lock the door after me."

He watched through the window as I locked myself in, then smiled and gave me a thumbs-up before striding to his SUV. I stayed at the window. It wasn't even eight thirty in the morning, yet I felt exhausted. He turned toward the interstate, and then I was alone.

I felt like a sitting duck.

In the fifteen minutes before Detective Brownley arrived, I called Cara and asked her to pick up a dozen doughnuts to celebrate Gretchen's homecoming and unlocked the door for a bleary-eyed Fred.

As Fred got situated at his computer, he told me that some of the half-dolls were fab. He was describing one of them when Wes called.

I took the call at the guest table and kept half an eye on the parking lot. "I still can't talk to you, Wes. Not now."

"Why?"

"I don't have time, but trust me, Wes—it will be worth the wait."

"Josie!" he complained. "Give me a hint at least!"

"Did the police find anything at Mandy's?" I asked, ignoring his request.

"Why should I tell you?" he grumbled.

"Because if you don't, I won't tell you anything."

He sighed. "They found a Marley .38 in a Baggie in the back of Mandy's kitchen cabinet."

"You're kidding! Is it the murder weapon?"

"They don't know yet. It was wiped clean, but the numbers weren't filed off or anything, so they can trace it. They're doing that, and they're doing ballistics testing now. Mandy and Vince deny knowing anything about it. Vince is insisting it's a frame-up job."

"Are they under arrest?"

"Mandy is being held for questioning because the gun was found in her place. They can hold her on an illegal weapons charge, but that's not what they want, obviously. On the advice of counsel, she's standing mute. They're seeing if they can connect the gun to Vince, which would be a parole violation, if nothing else."

I wondered how she was holding up under the pressure, wishing there was something I could do to help.

Detective Brownley drove into the lot in an unmarked vehicle. I glanced at the Mickey Mouse clock on Gretchen's—now Cara's—desk. It was eight thirty on the dot. She was accompanied by three plainclothes police officers, all of whom I knew casually from when Ty had been the police chief.

"I've got to go," I said. "I'll call you as soon as I can." I hung up.

Detective Brownley and two officers got out at the door, and the third drove away.

"I want the officers close by but out of sight," Detective Brownley informed me.

Her cornflower blue eyes were clear and purposeful. As she issued instructions, she was capable and focused without being familiar in any way. She looked ready for anything.

The police officers sat on chairs we positioned just inside the warehouse. With the door open two inches, they had clear views of the front door and most of the office.

Detective Brownley sat behind the bank of storage cabinets in a space we jury-rigged by rearranging some furniture. She had direct sight lines for the entire room, but anyone entering the office from the outside would see only the storage cabinets and would have to walk fifteen paces or more to spot her.

Cara arrived about five minutes later, doughnuts in hand, and immediately began fussing around, brewing a pot of coffee and setting out napkins and plates.

Sasha stepped in. "Hi," she said. She noticed Detective Brownley, then turned to me. "Is Gretchen here?"

"Not yet," I said. "She'll be here at ten."

The chimes sounded. Eric entered the room, took in our group stare, and said, "Sorry I'm late."

"You're not late. You're right on time," I said.

Detective Brownley gathered us around and tersely explained her plan, instructing us to act normally, not to speak unless spoken to, and to follow police directions immediately and to the letter. She reviewed various "what if" scenarios including Chip showing up with an associate or not showing up at all, instead sending someone to fetch Gretchen under some pretense.

I sat at the guest table and tried to read an auction catalogue. I couldn't finish a sentence. Mostly I stared into space.

After what felt like hours, Detective Brownley's radio cackled. She turned it down and raised it toward her ear to listen. "There's a spotter in the woods," she announced to us. "Gretchen's here. Any questions about my instructions? If so, now's the time to ask."

We had none.

The door opened, setting the wind chimes jingling. Gretchen stepped over the threshold, and pandemonium broke out.

Sasha flew to her, reaching her ahead of everyone else. Gretchen shrieked and jumped up and down, hugging Sasha, then Eric, then Fred, then Cara, then Sasha again. Everyone clapped and shouted and patted one another's arms and backs. At first, I stood off to the side, awed by the camaraderie I was witnessing; then I joined in.

Gretchen began to cry. "I can't believe I'm here," she said. "It's so wonderful to be back. I missed you all so much. It's just so great to be back."

After a while, I stepped back to look out the window. As the greetings and celebration continued to bubble around me, I surveyed the parking lot.

I had the same eerie sense of being watched that I'd experienced yesterday when I was standing outside with Wes. Itchy shivers raced up my back.

I couldn't see police in the woods, but I found comfort in knowing the sentries were in position. Still, my anxiety lingered. There was no gold Taurus in sight. Chip wasn't hiding behind a tree or vehicle that I could spot. *I should feel relieved,* I chastised myself. *Gretchen is out and safe.* There was nothing alarming, yet I felt a foreboding so strong that, for a moment, I couldn't breathe.

I joined the chattering group in time to see Cara hand Gretchen a tissue, then swiveled my head to take in Detective Brownley's reaction. She wasn't watching us. She had the radio pressed to her ear, alert for trouble.

After several minutes, the fever pitch of excitement moderated, and people began to sit down.

"So," I said, taking a deep breath, then forcing myself to speak as if it were an ordinary day, "Detective, now what?"

"Go about your regular duties. The only difference is that you shouldn't open a back or side door unless one of us is with you. Other than that, ignore us."

As if, I thought. *Okay, I need to show everyone that I'm calm. Or at least that I'm capable of acting calm. I need to lead by example.*

I turned to Gretchen and smiled. "Did you know we found you through a belt buckle?"

Gretchen blinked several times, thinking. "The Indian in the headdress? Oh, my God! I'd forgotten all about that—Morgan always wore it. You were able to trace it?" She sounded incredulous. "That's staggering, Josie."

"Goes to show what you can do when you're cheerful and persistent. That's me—a friendly gnat. People find it's easier to give me the information I want than to keep swatting me away." She tried to smile, and it was a pretty good effort. "Anyway, back to work.

Gretchen, you and I are going to put our heads together with Cara to discuss job duties. There's a promotion in your future!"

"Me?" she asked. "Doing what?"

"Moving into managing client and vendor relationships."

"Wow! I ought to leave town more often!"

"Not hardly," I said, smiling. "Eric, what's on your agenda?"

"Cleaning those bookends we just got in." He approached Gretchen and touched her shoulder. "It's good to see you," he said, his eyes on his shoes.

"You, too," she said softly.

Eric pushed through the door and disappeared into the warehouse.

"Fred, how about you? Dolls?" I asked.

"Yeah, I'm still on the half-dolls."

I turned to Sasha. "You, Sasha?"

Before my words faded away, Detective Brownley's radio came to life. I watched as she raised it to her ear and listened.

"It's Chip," she reported a moment later, and in that instant the atmosphere changed.

Gretchen stood up. She was suddenly pale, and her eyes were clouded with fear. She didn't speak.

The rest of us sat in apprehensive silence. I tried to think of something to do to maintain the illusion of normalcy. *We'd be talking, wouldn't we?* I thought. *Or reading. Or doing something.* I didn't move. None of us moved.

The chimes starting tinkling.

Chip walked in.

CHAPTER FORTY-ONE

is roots showed more black than before.

"A full house, I see," he said, glancing around. His eyes found Gretchen and stayed there.

Her hands curled into tight fists. She looked terrified.

"Hey, there," he said to her. "Long time no see."

"Peter," she said, using his real name, her voice one notch above a whisper.

"You look great, babe. You got a sec? We've got some catching up to do."

I snuck a glance at Detective Brownley, still hidden from Chip's view. She sat back, apparently relaxed. Her weapon rested in her lap.

No one spoke.

"Come on," he said, waggling his palm. He was grinning, but I didn't relax. His eyes were unforgiving. "For old times' sake."

I looked at his waistline for the telltale bulge. It was easy to spot. It was on the left, covered by his lightweight navy blue jacket. *He's a righty,* I thought. He unzipped his jacket halfway, and at the sound, I sensed Detective Brownley tense up.

"Hi, Chip," I said, stepping forward, because, if I were acting normally, that's what I'd do.

He didn't look at me. His eyes remained fixed on Gretchen. "Hey, Josie," he said. "Come on, Marie. We've got to talk."

She shook her head and stayed mute.

"Surely you'll do me the courtesy of talking to me," he said. "My brother—my *only* brother—ends up dead on your sofa, don't you think you owe me an explanation?"

"I don't know anything," she said softly. "Really. I know *nothing*."

He shook his head, back and forth, back and forth, as if he were sad for her because she just didn't get it. "Come on, give me a break. My baby brother's dead. You've gotta tell me about it, you know? Let's go get a cup of coffee or something."

"I don't *gotta* tell you anything," Gretchen replied, her chin up. "You can't make me talk to you, and I'm not going to. Not now. Not ever."

He took two steps toward her, angling around the desk, continuing to unzip his jacket as he walked slowly in her direction. Another few paces and he'd reach the end of the cabinets and see Detective Brownley.

Gretchen stepped back and found herself against the wall with nowhere to go. Her lips moved but no sounds came.

Fred sat rigidly in his chair, his feet pressed back, ready to bolt out and up, maybe intending to block Chip should he attack. Sasha rolled her chair back against the side wall, clearing the way for Fred's run. Cara's head swiveled to follow Chip's progress. Her eyes were wide and filled with fear. I was even with the back of Cara's desk, in line with Detective Brownley. Chip didn't notice any of us. He only saw Gretchen.

Chip took another step, and Gretchen splayed her hands and pressed herself against the wall as if she were bracing herself. Her already pale skin turned parchment white. Chip finished unzipping his jacket. Gretchen spotted the weapon, a shiny black handgun, and her eyes formed huge emerald circles. Her terror was palpable. I hoped she wouldn't faint.

"No," she said, her voice strong. "No."

In one flowing motion he whipped his gun from his belt and held it up sideways, like a toy, and rushed her, seizing her and holding her fast against his torso.

Detective Brownley leapt forward, yelling something I couldn't understand. The two police officers ripped into the office from the warehouse.

Cara squealed.

Fred pounced, lunging to his left, but he was too late—Chip had already passed by him—and Fred tripped and fell.

Detective Brownley yelled that he was to drop his weapon, but he paid no attention.

Chip kicked at Cara's chair and sent her and it spinning sideways, blocking all three police officers and opening up an exit path—a direct line to the outer door.

Gretchen went rag doll on him. Chip held her to his chest and continued making his way step by slow step to the front door. He waved his gun at us and yelled that we were to get out of his way, get out of his way, get out of his way, or he'd kill her.

Without warning, as he sidestepped past me, he stretched out his right arm and, gun in hand, struck out at me, thrusting me aside effortlessly. I tumbled back and landed in a heap beneath Cara's desk, the wind knocked out of me. I got to all fours and heaved and heaved, trying to catch my breath. I watched impotently from under the desk's modesty panel as he dragged Gretchen toward the door.

The police kept shouting instructions that he ignored. When I was able to speak, I sat back on my haunches and raised my head above the desk. "Please, Chip," I begged as loudly as I could. "Don't do this."

"My name is Peter Boulanger," he stated with icy precision. He met my eyes, and I understood that he despised me.

Detective Brownley said in a tone of calm reason, "You can't leave with her. I'm Detective Brownley." She flashed her badge and raised her weapon toward his head. "You're surrounded."

Chip, with Gretchen still pinned to his chest, raised his gun to her temple and said softly, "Back off or I'll kill her."

He backed away into the parking lot, out of sight.

As Detective Brownley and the officers followed, she hollered, "All of you stay inside and stay down."

I scrabbled to the door and peeked out through the crack.

"Police! Drop your weapon! Do it! Drop your weapon! Let the woman go," Detective Brownley shouted. She repeated it over and over again. "Police. Drop your weapon and let the woman go!"

"Go to hell!" Chip retorted, scuttling across the open lot, carrying

Gretchen, her feet a foot or so off the ground. She was elbowing and kicking him and clawing at his arm, trying to break free. As I watched, someone from deep in the woods to the left fired a shot and hit Chip just above his ankle.

He shrieked in surprise and pain and loosened his grip. His weapon clattered to the ground and skittered away. Gretchen didn't hesitate—she leapt forward and rolled away, and Chip, growling with frustration and rage, fell to the asphalt. He lunged for his good ankle and pulled out another gun, a small revolver.

There were so many gunshots, I couldn't count. I winced with each discharge. When the firing stopped, I pushed myself upright, flung open the door, and ran like my life was on the line to reach Gretchen, lying motionless on the asphalt, curled into a tight ball. I covered her body with mine and got my mouth close to her ear and said, "It's finished. I'm here. You're safe."

I repeated those sentences over and over until finally the sirens stopped, and in the sudden blare of silence, Gretchen began moving. I helped her stand. We stood together, shoulder to shoulder, in the warm sunlight and looked around.

Chip's body was a hundred feet away. Pools of blood surrounded the corpse. A dozen police officials, some in uniform, some in plainclothes, two in camouflage, stood in clusters, talking.

Two ambulances pulled into the lot. Detective Brownley ran over to us and tried to lead Gretchen into one for a precautionary trip to the hospital. She refused. The detective insisted.

Gretchen shook her head. "No," she said, brushing grit off the jeans and sweater she'd somehow acquired since I'd last seen her. "I'm fine. Shaken, but fine. Is he really dead?"

"Yes."

"Good," she said, staring at his bloody body. She looked up and met our eyes. "He once told Morgan that I'd sassed him, and that it was Morgan's fault because he let me get away with everything. That was the first time Morgan punched me. Up 'til then, he'd only slapped."

I didn't know what to say. I rubbed her back a little.

"You really should get checked out," Detective Brownley said.

"No. I really should get back to work. My life has been run by the Boulanger brothers long enough. Thank God, it's over."

"Shock is a funny thing. Let the medical experts give you a once-over."

She smiled. "Thank you for your concern. I'm fine."

The detective shrugged. "Take her inside," she told me.

I led the way. Fred and Sasha stood together just inside the door. Cara sat, her head bowed, covering her face with her hands. She was weeping. Eric stood at the warehouse door.

"Is everyone okay?" I asked.

Fred, Eric, and Sasha nodded. I touched Cara's arm. "Cara," I asked. "Are you okay?"

She nodded but didn't look up.

"Okay, then. We're all okay."

Detective Brownley stepped into the office and announced that she'd need to take statements from all of us.

"Can it wait?" I asked.

"No, but it won't take long. Better to get it over with."

She was right. The police had been on-site, so our reports served only as confirmation of the events, and the process was straightforward and uncomplicated.

Just before noon, Detective Brownley called me out to the parking lot. The gold Taurus's trunk was open. Inside was a black box with an index card label. It read GRETCHEN.

I smiled. "May I open it?"

"I will," Detective Brownley said. "We'll need to check for prints." Her hands encased in plastic, she gently removed the lid, and there lay Gretchen's vase. The protective cover had been disturbed, but the vase itself was intact and appeared to be undamaged.

"He took the box because he saw the word 'Gretchen,'" I said.

"Makes sense," the detective agreed. "I bet we'll find his shoeprints match the imprints we took at the scene."

I called Gretchen over. When she saw her vase, she looked at me, then at the detective, and then she placed her hands over her heart. "I prayed that it would be found," she said. "I prayed hard."

The police finished their work both inside and out by one.

Detective Brownley told me I could have the parking lot hosed down if I wanted.

I didn't know what to do first. I wanted to talk to Ty. I wanted a martini. I wanted to discuss what had just transpired with everyone and compare opinions. I wanted to crawl into bed with a good book and not talk to a soul for a week. I wanted to hose down the parking lot to eliminate any trace of the horror I'd just witnessed. Mostly I wanted lunch. For some reason, I was starving.

"Cara," I said, "set the phone on night service. Let's get out of here. I don't know about the rest of you, but I need a little time to process all this. Tomorrow's another day."

No one hesitated.

Gretchen told me she was going to take a hot bath filled with the orange blossom bath salts that Jack had bought for her yesterday, when, accompanied by a police officer, he'd gone to the mall to get her a change of clothes; then she was going to ask him to take her out to dinner.

Fred said he thought he'd go home and take a nap.

Sasha said she still felt pretty shaky. "I'm thinking that an old Audrey Hepburn–Cary Grant movie is in order."

Cara said she was going to take her dog for a long, long walk on the beach. "I'm so glad Gretchen is back," she said. "Any time you need me to fill in, you call. Okay?"

"I'm hoping you'll continue on, Cara. Full-time. Permanent."

"Really?" she asked, her eyes crinkling with delight. "I'd love to!"

I smiled. "See you in the morning, then."

In moments, everyone had left, and Eric and I were alone in the office.

"I can move things back before I go," Eric said.

"Good idea," I said, "I'll help. It will be good to come in tomorrow and see everything back to normal."

"Yeah. I was thinking I'd clean the parking lot, too."

I didn't reply. I cleared chairs away so Eric could move the furniture without tripping.

"After the parking lot, I want to get started on the bookends."

"You don't want to go home?"

He shrugged.

"Are you sure? Maybe you want to take the afternoon and, I don't know, watch a movie, like Sasha. Or walk your dogs like Cara."

"Thanks, Josie, but I feel better when I work. You know?"

"To tell you the truth, Eric, me, too. Are you hungry? How about if I send out for pizza?"

I was placing the order when Fred walked in.

"I'm not sleepy after all," he said, shrugging, his tie loosened, "and I'm really curious about some of those half-dolls."

I changed the order from one pie to two, which was just as well since Sasha arrived about ten minutes later. "I didn't feel like being alone," she said, her eyes haunted, "so I thought I'd see if anyone came back."

Cara popped her head in. "I was wondering if anyone would be here. I'm close to done with that report and thought I might finish it up."

Gretchen pushed through the door a minute later. "Oh, I didn't know you'd all be here. I don't want a bath! I want to get caught up with everything! I feel as if I've been gone a year."

I called the pizzeria back and ordered a third pie. I didn't know about everyone else, but I was so hungry, I thought I might eat an entire pie on my own.

Lunch was a euphoric celebration, and after we were finished, I went upstairs to call Ty. I left him a message. "It's over," I said and described the events of the morning as succinctly as I could.

I looked out over my maple tree. The church parking lot was empty except for the pastor's car. There were no clouds in the robin's egg blue sky.

Throughout lunch, we'd kept telling ourselves that it was over, but it wasn't. It wasn't over because Morgan's killer was still on the loose.

CHAPTER FORTY-TWO

I sat for several minutes gazing out of my window, seeing nothing, reviewing everything I knew about Morgan's murder.

I went through everyone's motives and came up with no surprise insights.

I considered means. Nothing new about the poker or the gun occurred to me.

When I thought about opportunity, though, I realized that an unchecked alibi was staring me in the face. And as far as I knew, the police were unaware of it.

Wes called as I was turning onto Islington, approaching the center of Portsmouth. I slipped my earpiece in and took the call.

"Were you there for the kill?" he asked hungrily.

"It was grisly, Wes. Really bad."

"Tell me everything."

The worse the situation, the more eager Wes was to hear about it. I pulled off to the side of the road, turned my blinkers on, and steeled myself. On balance, I owed Wes big, and it was time to pay up. I shivered, recalling Peter's corpse awash with blood.

"Weren't you there?" I asked, a safe bet since Wes was always where the action was.

"The police wouldn't let me on the property. So tell me what went down."

I spoke for fifteen minutes, describing Saturday night's call with Detective Brownley and this morning's events at Prescott's, culminating with Chip's death. Wes demanded details, only some of which I could provide. He wanted to know where the police sat in my building, what Chip said to Gretchen in the office, what the police did when he dragged Gretchen outside, how many snipers were in the woods, and who fired the first shot that hit Chip in the leg and the others that killed him.

"Thanks, Josie. This is great stuff. Did you hear about Mandy? She's out already."

"Really? That was quick. How come?"

"Her lawyer raised a ruckus, and they didn't have enough to hold her. The ballistics report gives only a forty percent match to the weapon found in her kitchen. Apparently the bullet was nicked up pretty badly. But guess what? They found the dealer who sold the gun. It was purchased ten days ago at a gun show in Virginia for cash. The name on the receipt was Sal Briscoe."

So Morgan had been killed with his own gun. The only question was who pulled the trigger.

We agreed to talk soon.

I parked in the Portsmouth garage and walked to Market Street.

From where I stood, I could see into the Bow Street Emporium. Mandy was waiting on a customer. She must have gone straight to work from jail. When she turned to pick up a bowl, she saw me and smiled.

I stepped into the shop, and she approached me.

"Oh, Mandy," I whispered. "Are you okay?"

She shook her head. "They found the murder weapon in my house. I can't understand how it got there. I don't know what to do."

"Do you like your lawyer?" I asked.

"Vince says he's the best—very aggressive, which is what you want at a time like this. Vince is right, I guess, when you think about it. They let me go without charging me."

I patted her arm, unsure how to respond. "Let's stay in touch, okay?"

She nodded and tried to smile. I patted her arm again, and left, thinking, *Maybe she* is *the killer. It's possible that Vince is protecting her—not the other way around. With any luck, I'll know soon enough*.

Standing in front of Elgin's Hardware, out of sight of the Bow Street Emporium, I looked down Market Street in each direction. I could see Lavinia's Day Spa. I knew the place. Ty had given me a half-day spa experience for my birthday. The spa was elegant, exclusive, and expensive. I couldn't see a single girl on a budget as a customer. I turned up Bow Street, then Ceres, until finally I came to a shop so narrow that I almost passed it by. A small sign was mounted in the window: PORTSMOUTH SALON.

I'd never noticed it before.

The street-level window was covered by a silvery green curtain. I stood for a moment, rehearsing the part I was about to play, then entered. A menu board listing services and prices was mounted over a chest-high reception desk. *This is more like it,* I thought, noting the reasonable charges.

I smiled broadly and said hello.

A stylishly dressed woman old enough to be my mother standing behind the counter smiled back. Her soft brown hair was cut in a stylish bob. Her tweed blazer had been fitted by an expert.

"May I help you?" she asked with a practiced mix of warmth and diffidence.

"Yes, I'd like to make an appointment."

"Of course. What did you have in mind?"

"Yes, I'd like to make a manicure appointment with whoever did Lina's nails last week. Lina Nadlein? Her nails were so perfect! She was here last Wednesday."

She smiled again as she consulted her computer. "Wonderful! Let's see now . . . yes, here it is. Ms. Nadlein's manicurist was Toby. I'll be sure to pass on the compliment. Toby will be very pleased. When were you thinking of coming in? Toby works every day but Thursday."

I flashed a thousand-watt smile. "I might as well channel Lina! I'll take the same appointment this week that she had last week!"

"That would be four o'clock. Were you interested in a pedicure, too?"

Four! I thought. *Four!* I could hardly believe my ears. Lina had told Gretchen that she got a manicure Wednesday morning because she had a hot date, but it wasn't true. She might have had a hot date, but her manicure wasn't until the afternoon. Or was it?

"Really?" I asked. "Are you sure? For some reason I thought it was in the morning."

She took another look at the computer, shook her head, and smiled. "No, we keep careful records. It was at four. Shall I put you down with Toby at four or would you prefer a morning appointment? She's available at eleven."

"Actually, I just realized that I ran out without my calendar. Can you believe it? I'm completely scatterbrained! Do you have a card? I'll call you later today."

"No problem!" She jotted Toby's name on a business card and handed it to me.

I thanked her and left, thinking that in another life, I must have been a con woman. I walked a few paces down the street and paused to consider my next move. I didn't want to make trouble for Lina or upset Gretchen, but as I thought about it, I realized that I had no choice. I had to report my discovery to the police—I'd unearthed what appeared to be evidence in a murder investigation.

I called Detective Brownley. "Lina told Gretchen that she had a manicure the morning of the murder," I explained. "I figured that Lina must have picked a salon that was within walking distance of her work. I found the salon." I paused. I hated having to tell tales. "Lina was here that day, but she wasn't here in the morning. Her appointment was at four in the afternoon."

There was a long pause as the implications sank in. "Stay where you are. I'll be there in ten minutes."

Detective Brownley pulled up in an unmarked vehicle. She didn't smile as she approached me. She had me recount my conversation with the receptionist, then said, "One of these days you're going to get yourself in a boatload of trouble going off on your own. I'm serious, Josie. You could get hurt."

I couldn't think of anything to say that wouldn't sound defensive or disingenuous, so I stayed quiet. I felt abashed.

She pushed open the salon door and disappeared inside.

I left. There was no point in hanging around. No matter what Detective Brownley learned, there was zero chance that she'd tell me anything. As I retraced my steps toward Market Street, I felt sad and mad and confused all at once. Had Lina lied on purpose? Maybe it was just a misunderstanding. *Right—and maybe pigs can fly.*

CHAPTER FORTY-THREE

I drove toward work, then pulled to the side of the road and put on my blinkers. I called the office. Cara answered and transferred me to Gretchen.

"Can you call Lina and arrange for the three of us to meet? Now?"

Gretchen, sounding a little worried, said, "Sure. She's at home. Do you want to go to her place?"

I needed to talk to Lina before the police picked her up for questioning. They might arrive at any minute. "No, tell her to leave now—right away. You, too. Let's meet at my house. Okay?"

I called Wes, and as I listened to the phone ring, I felt the knifelike tension in my shoulders ease a bit. I could smell it—I was confident that I was close to knowing the truth.

"I just left the Portsmouth Salon," I told him and explained what I'd learned. "I left as soon as the police arrived."

"Why? You should have taken a photo of Detective Brownley interviewing the receptionist. That would have been something!"

I didn't reply. Wes was inexorable.

"Don't get me wrong, Josie. This is good. Really good." With a brisk "Talk later," he hung up.

Lina arrived first, and I led her into the kitchen.

She looked harried. Her hair was stringy. She wore a faded green sweatshirt with jeans. Purple-brown smudges under her eyes made her appear ill. She kept fussing with her ankle monitor.

"Are you okay?" I asked her, concerned.

She met my eyes and shrugged. "It's hard, you know? It's really hard, but I'll be all right. Thank you so much for paying for my lawyer. I'm very grateful."

"You're welcome. I'm glad I can help."

The doorbell rang. It was Gretchen.

"Lina!" Gretchen exclaimed as soon as she saw her, clutching her in a bear hug, dancing around the kitchen. Her smile lit up the room. After they broke apart, she said, "So, Josie, why are we here?"

We sat at the round table. "I have a lot of questions."

Lina looked at Gretchen.

"Josie—is this necessary?" Gretchen asked.

I closed my eyes again. I couldn't get the horror of this morning out of my mind. The blood. The staccato quick-fire shots. The hunted look in Gretchen's eyes. The stone-hardness in Chip's. We needed this to finish.

"Yes. You'll have to trust me," I said to Gretchen.

She met my eyes, nodded, and said, "Okay, then. What do you want to know?"

I took another deep breath. "On October 1, 2002, you, Lina, under your birth name of Iris Gibbons, were a full-time employee of the Rosebud Antiques Shoppe. The owner, and your direct supervisor, was Amelia Bartlett. A co-worker was also there. That's you, Gretchen, except that your name then was Marie Boulanger. Your husband, Morgan Boulanger, came into the shop." I turned to Lina. "What were you doing when he showed up?"

"What does it matter? How can it possibly matter?"

"Please," I said.

Gretchen turned to Lina and said, "Tell her."

Lina covered her eyes with her hands for a moment, then straightened her shoulders and looked at me. "We were polishing silver. Gretchen had just gone into the back room for more paper towels."

"What did he say when he came into the shop?"

She grimaced. "He was furious."

"What was he mad about?"

"I don't know. Morgan was always angry, so that was nothing new, but on this day he was especially horrible."

"Why was he mad, Gretchen?" I asked.

She looked away. "I didn't call the credit card company about a mistaken charge. I was busy and hadn't had a chance. The bill was due—and I hadn't called them. I forgot to tell Morgan, so when he went to pay the bill that morning, he just lost it! He called me irresponsible and said I was a terrible wife, a complete waste. I ran out of the apartment, hoping he'd cool down. He didn't. He just got madder."

I shook my head. "Okay, then. Morgan showed up at the store, and . . . ?" I asked Lina.

"He slammed the door," Lina said, wincing at the memory. "He was barely inside when he yelled, 'Where's Marie? Get that bitch out here!'" She shook her head. "Without waiting for any of us to say anything, he pushed past Mrs. Bartlett to get to me, grabbed my shoulders, and began to shake me. He was so strong," she said, choking a little, lifting her hand to her neck. "He picked me up off the ground like I weighed nothing. I was so shocked I couldn't say a word. Mrs. Bartlett did, though. She punched at his back, screaming, 'Stop it! Leave her alone! Get out of here!' He ignored her completely. After a minute, he tossed me aside. I nearly fell over. I didn't know why he let me go until I looked up. Gretchen was walking toward him, and once he spotted her, we were all irrelevant."

I touched Gretchen's arm and looked at her profile as she sat, gazing at Lina. She seemed oddly unaffected by Lina's words, as if she were hearing a mildly interesting story about someone else, someone she didn't know. She didn't respond to my touch, and I withdrew my hand.

Lina went on with the story of that terrible day.

"'What's the matter with you?' Gretchen asked him. 'Have you gone crazy?' He leaped at her, slapping her face and chest and arms, over and over again. He just wouldn't stop. Gretchen was screaming at him and fighting back, and he punched her and sent her flying into a wall. She managed to stay upright, but you could tell she was kind of woozy. I didn't move. I didn't know what to do. I was so scared. All at once, it was quiet. Quiet enough so Morgan could hear Mrs. Bartlett calling nine-one-one. He spun around, grabbed a chair, and slammed it onto the floor, snapping off a leg. He roared as he attacked Mrs. Bartlett."

Lina looked up and met my eyes.

"He roared," she repeated, and I saw that she was trembling. "He pummeled her. Gretchen and I tried to stop him. Oh, my God, we tried!" She began to cry, then angrily brushed aside her tears. "Gretchen broke a vase over his head, and I kicked and kicked at him. Nothing had any effect. It was horrific! Finally, he just stopped. He turned to Gretchen and said, 'See what you made me do, bitch?'

"Gretchen was screaming and throwing things, and he grabbed her arm, twisting it backward, and said, 'Come on, we've got to get out of here. What the fuck did you expect, bitch? The old lady called the cops.' He began pushing Gretchen toward the door, saw me, and said, 'You, too.' He was still holding the chair leg. Blood dripped from it. He tossed it down and grabbed us and propelled us out of the store." She paused and took a breath. "His car was parked at the curb. He made Gretchen drive to his job, a restaurant. He said he had a paycheck waiting for him. He told us to wait while he ran in, but Gretchen floored it.

"She drove straight to my apartment. She said that he'd look for us there, but we had the car, so we had a few minutes' head start. She said she was scared to go to her place but she'd be damned if she left without her vase. You know about her vase, right?"

"Yes."

"She kept it at my place so Morgan wouldn't destroy it during one of his tantrums." She shook her head again.

"Was it Henrietta Howard's?" I asked Gretchen.

"How can you possibly know that?" Gretchen asked.

"We're pretty good at research," I said, smiling a little.

"That's the understatement of the century!" she said. "Mrs. Bartlett gave it to me for my birthday. She said it was from a remarkable woman named Henrietta Howard who managed to survive an abusive marriage and become the toast of London, and if Henrietta could do it in the eighteenth century, I could damn well do it now." Tears ran down her cheeks as she spoke.

"Mrs. Bartlett was a phenomenal woman," Lina added. "She was like a mother to Gretchen. I had my grandmother, and Gretchen had her—and we lost them both." Lina cleared her throat. "We went to an ATM machine to get money. Gretchen got five hundred dollars, the most the machine would allow. I got three hundred, all I had in the bank." She cleared her throat again. "Gretchen—do you want to take over from here?"

She shook her head. "No. You tell her."

"Gretchen said we had to break all ties with the past, and we did. We drove to Colorado Springs, thinking Morgan wouldn't think to look for us to get on a bus from there. We decided to go to Chicago, a big city, a good place, we figured, to start over. Gretchen knew that Morgan would never stop looking for her, so we didn't just get a bus ticket straight to Chicago, we bought tickets to Omaha, and from there we took a bus to Lincoln, and from there we went to Chicago. Am I giving too much detail?" she asked me.

"No. This is perfect. What happened in Chicago?"

"It was easy to get new IDs. We went to a cemetery and found names of two women who were born about when we were. The public library had microfiche birth records." She shrugged. "It was easy. We stayed at a cheap motel and used that address to get replacement birth certificates. We had new driver's licenses, jobs, and an apartment in ten days."

From my call to the town clerk in my hometown, I knew that was completely realistic. All it took was a request and a rush fee.

"After about three years," she said, "Gretchen decided that she wanted to move. She said she was always looking over her shoulder, that Chicago was the nearest big city to Denver and she couldn't stop thinking that Morgan would come looking for us there. She said that when Morgan was a kid, his parents had sent him to stay with some cousins for the summer. They had a cottage on Lake Winnipesaukee here in New Hampshire. He hated it. He told her about how one of his older cousins used him as a football and drop-kicked him across the dock, into the lake. So she said, 'Let's go there. Let's move to New Hampshire. He'll never in a million years move there, and he'll never think of looking for us there.'"

She looked up at me again and gave a small smile. Gretchen was smiling, too, just a little.

"So we did, and it was great. Everything was fine, until he found us."

"You and Mandy discussed bringing some milk over to Gretchen's on Wednesday, the day she was due back from vacation, right?"

"Right."

"Why?"

"Gretchen's a bear without her morning coffee, and she had to be at work the next day," Lina said, smiling.

"Why didn't you do it?"

"I had a manicure appointment that morning."

"Except you changed it. You went at four that afternoon."

Lina froze.

"At the Portsmouth Salon. Your manicurist is Toby."

Lina didn't speak. I glanced at Gretchen. She was watching me, uncertain of where I was heading.

"You went to Gretchen's that morning, didn't you?" I asked Lina. "You can tell me the truth, Lina. I promise I'll never repeat it."

"No," Lina whispered, shaking her head. "I can't."

"Then I'll tell you," I said. "You'd planned on sneaking in a manicure before picking Gretchen up from the bus, but you changed your mind and made the appointment for four that afternoon, I don't know why. Mandy brought the milk, but at the last minute you decided to go over to Gretchen's just to make sure everything was okay. Am I right?"

Lina's eyes were Ginevra de' Benci big. "How did you know?"

I didn't answer her question. Instead, I continued my story. "When you got there, you noticed the Chevy because it was so out of place. How could you not? I mean, Gretchen lives in a well-tended apartment, and the Chevy was a junker. Probably you were at her door when out of nowhere, Morgan jumped you from behind. I don't know where he hid himself or whether he stormed up the stairs in back of you. Do you?"

Lina took a deep breath, then said, "No."

"He ripped the keys from your hand and said . . . what did he say, Lina?"

She looked at me flat on. "He said, 'Remember me, Iris?'"

Gretchen reached across the table and touched Lina's elbow, but she didn't seem to notice.

"What did you do?" I asked.

"I nearly died. He shoved me into the apartment. 'Where's Marie? Where's Marie?' That's all he said to me. He slapped at me and kept asking where she was. I told him I didn't know, that she was away, that I was only here to water her plants. He didn't believe me. He pulled a gun out of his jacket pocket. It was black. I don't know anything about guns." She gulped. "It was so black." She paused, clenching and unclenching her fists. "I was petrified. I was sure he would kill her. I *knew* it." She stopped talking.

"What happened next?" I asked.

"He pushed me toward the living room, shoving his gun in my face the whole time. As we passed the fireplace, without thinking, I reached down and somehow found the poker. I swung at him and missed." She paused again and looked at me. "He roared. It was the same roar he gave just before he killed Mrs. Bartlett. I didn't hesitate. I swung again. Thank God, I connected—he fell backward onto the couch, but I didn't knock him out." She shook her head, shaking off the memory. "I managed to get across the coffee table and knock the gun to the floor before he sat up. He tried to get it from me, but I shot him before he could. It's the first time I've ever held a gun." She met my eyes. "Can you believe that? The very first time I've ever held a gun."

I shook my head empathetically. "Then what?" I asked.

"Then I cleaned up. I wiped everything down, including the milk carton. Except that I missed a fingerprint."

"What about the gun?" I asked.

"What about it?"

"It was found at Mandy's. Morgan bought it. You used it, and you took it with you. You put it in Mandy's apartment, right? The night Vince hung the stained glass window."

She stared at me, then looked down at her hands. "I couldn't leave it at Gretchen's—I was afraid that it would implicate her somehow. Then when Gretchen came to stay with me, I couldn't risk keeping the gun at my place either. I figured Mandy's place was safe."

"Why didn't you just get rid of it?" I asked.

She looked up at me. She was breathing hard. "I didn't know how."

I glanced at Gretchen. Her eyes were fixed on Lina. "Why didn't you tell the police the truth?" I asked.

She looked at me as if I were crazy. "As soon as I shot Morgan, the very next thought I had was that Peter, his brother, would come after us. I wanted to get away, to leave that day, but Gretchen said no. She said it would be all right, that Peter wouldn't know where we were, that Morgan had come on his own. I thought it was wishful thinking, but I wanted it to be true, too, so I went along with her. But go to the police? I might as well put bull's-eyes on us both. If Peter were still alive, I wouldn't be talking to you now."

I nodded. I had what I needed to help them find closure and move on. "You need to tell the police," I said. "Rocky Point *and* Denver."

Lina looked at me for a long time, then sighed. "I know."

I looked at Gretchen. "I'll call Max and Shirl. They'll know what to do."

Her radiant green eyes were moist. "Then it really will be over."

EPILOGUE

TWO WEEKS LATER

es sipped Coke and scribbled notes as I spoke. He was writing a feature article called "Starting Over: From Murder in the Mountains to Life on the Beach." He planned on pitching it to national women's magazines. We'd been at the Portsmouth Diner for almost an hour.

The waitress came over and refilled my coffee cup. "Here you go, dear," she said.

I glanced out the window. It was another gray day, misty but warm. Window boxes filled with daffodils gave mute promise to an abundant spring.

"So you're saying that Max Bixby, Gretchen's lawyer, and Shirl Sheriden, Lina's lawyer, wrote a joint statement for them," Wes asked, "but it only went up to the day Morgan Boulanger was killed? Then they issued separate statements covering the rest. Why?"

"Because their stories were no longer in alignment. Lina described killing Morgan in self-defense, then covering it up because she was terrified that his brother would do exactly what he did—come after them. All she could think of was staying safe and protecting her friend."

"Gretchen's story lends credence to the idea that Lina's fear was warranted?"

"Does it ever. It isn't just her word, either—remember, there were lots of domestic violence calls to the Denver police. Morgan was charged with assaulting Gretchen a couple of times. When Morgan realized Gretchen and Lina had deserted him after he killed Amelia Bartlett, he went straight to his brother, who helped him get the fake ID in the name of Sal Briscoe. He got himself one, too, as Chip Davidson, just in case. Morgan, as Sal, had settled in Tennessee, and that would have been that except that he happened to see the magazine *Antiques Insights*."

Wes nodded. "Now both girls are getting off?"

"Wes, you have a way of putting the worst possible construction on things!" I protested. "They're not 'getting off!' That implies that they're getting away with something. They didn't do anything they should be indicted for! There's a difference!"

"Yeah, yeah."

"Gretchen and Lina say they're happier in New Hampshire than they've ever been, and they both want to keep using their adopted names. Their lawyers are checking into it." I paused. "Gretchen got a promotion, you know?"

"That'll be great in the article," Wes said, unfolding his paper and jotting another note. "What's her new title?"

"Administrative manager. Cara's going to stay on as receptionist."

"Cool. What else?"

What else? I repeated silently, thinking back over the past two weeks. Gretchen spoke at length to Sam Bartlett, and they agreed to stay in close touch. When I told her that we estimated her vase's value at more than six hundred thousand dollars, she glowed but said it didn't really matter since she'd never in a million years sell it. Sasha was writing the text for an upcoming auction catalogue. Fred was still deep in half-dolls. I had approved a request from Eric for new shelving for the tag sale room. New track lighting had been installed in the auction venue and Gretchen couldn't speak Jack's name without glowing.

"Gretchen put her condo up for sale," I said. "The management company was pretty decent about helping her get into a different complex."

"Life goes on, huh? Did you hear about Vince and Mandy?" he asked, folding up his paper again. "Vince copped a plea. The property owner he worked for didn't want the negative publicity, so he refused to press charges. The deal says that Vince makes restitution and gets an extra three years' probation—and he gets permission to move to Vegas. They left yesterday."

Oh, Mandy, I thought. *Oh, no.* I looked away, focusing on the daffodils, and swallowed hard.

"Thanks, Josie," Wes said, buttoning his coat, preparing to leave. I hoped his article sold.

"What do you think?" I asked Ty, spinning around so he could see the flare of my cotton skirt. I struck a pose and swept a hand toward my green alligator cowboy boots.

"You look great."

"These are my favorite boots. My dancin' boots."

"You're a dancing machine," Ty said.

"Only when line dancing."

"How does a city girl like you become a line-dancing fanatic?"

"Would you call me a fanatic?"

"Yes."

"Maybe I'm not such a city girl."

Ty approached me and used his index finger to raise my chin. He smiled down at me, a smile that radiated from his eyes. He hugged me and whispered, "Just so long as you're my girl."

I hugged him back, and hugged him again, and then I said, "Done."

ACKNOWLEDGMENTS

S pecial thanks go to Leslie Hindman, who, with her team at Leslie Hindman Auctioneers, continues to appraise antiques for me to write about. Thanks also go to Kevin Berean for his answers to legal questions and Julie Pietsch for her information about Henrietta Howard. I'm also grateful to Colum McLoughlin who talked to me about liars in business. Please note that any errors are mine alone.

As the president of the Mystery Writers of America/New York Chapter and the chair of the Wolfe Pack's literary awards, I've been fortunate to meet and work alongside dozens of talented writers and dedicated readers. Thank you all for your support. For my pals in the Wolfe Pack and fans of Rex Stout's Nero Wolfe stories everywhere, I've added my usual allotment of Wolfe trivia to this book.

Thank you to Jo-Ann Maude, Christine de los Reyes, and Carol Novak. Special thanks to Katie Longhurst, my eagle-eyed first reader. Thank you also to Dan and Linda Chessman, Marci and James Gleason, John and Mona Gleason, Linda and Ren Plastina, Rona and Ken Foster, Sandy Baggelaar, Karen Roy, and Liz Weiner.

Independent booksellers have been invaluable in helping me introduce Josie to their customers—thank you all. I want to acknowledge my special friends at these terrific independent bookstores: The Poisoned Pen, Well Red Coyote, Mysteries to Die For, Book'em Mysteries, Mystery Bookstore, Legends, Book Carnival, Mysterious Galaxy, San Francisco Mystery Bookstore, M is for Mystery, Murder by the Book in Houston, Murder by the

Book in Denver, and Murder by the Book in Portland, Remember the Alibi Mystery Bookstore, Centuries & Sleuths, Fox Tale Books, Kate's Mystery Books, Mystery Lovers Bookshop, The Mystery Company, The Mysterious Bookshop, Partners & Crime, Booked for Murder, Aunt Agatha's, Foul Play, Windows a bookshop, Uncle Edgar's Mystery Bookstore, Seattle Mystery Bookstore, Centuries and Sleuths, and Once Upon a Crime. Thanks also to Janet Rudolph and Linda Landigran.

For the acknowledgment page of *Antiques to Die For*, I wrote that Manhattan's Black Orchid Bookstore would be sorely missed; it is. I will always be grateful to Bonnie Claeson and Joe Guglielmelli.

Many chain bookstores have been incredibly supportive as well—thank you to those many booksellers who've gone out of their way to become familiar with Josie. Special thanks go to my friend Dianne Defonce at the Border's in Fairfield, Connecticut.

Special thanks to my librarian friends Doris Ann Norris, Mary Callahan Boone, Kristi Calhoun Belesca, Frances Mendelsohn, Mary Russell, Denise van Zanten, Heidi Fowler, Deborah Hirsch, and Heather Caines.

I am deeply grateful for the unerring guidance and acumen provided by my literary agent emerita, Denise Marcil, and my superb new literary agent, Cristina Concepcion of Don Congdon Associates, Inc. Special thanks go to Michael Congdon, Katie Kotchman, and Katie Grimm.

My editor, St. Martin's executive editor Hope Dellon, provided wise and discerning feedback about the manuscript, helping Josie grow as a character—and me mature as an author. I'm indebted to her, and to the entire St. Martin's team. Thank you to those I work with most often, Andy Martin, Hector DeJean, Talia Ross, and Laura Bourgeois, as well as those behind the scenes, including my production editor, Robert Berkel, copy editor, India Cooper, and cover designer, David Baldeosingh Rotstein.